A DANGEROUS GAME

KIRA SHELL

sourcebooks
casablanca

CENTRO
PER IL LIBRO
E LA LETTURA

This work has been translated with the contribution of the Center for Books and Reading of
the Italian Ministry of Culture.

Originally published as *Kiss Me Like You Love Me Vol. 2: A Dangerous Game* © 2019
Mondadori Libri S.p.A. Published by Mondadori Libri for the imprint Sperling & Kupfer.
Translated from Italian by Nicole M. Taylor.

The characters and events portrayed in this book are fictitious or are used fictitiously. Any
similarity to real persons, living or dead, is purely coincidental and not intended by the
author.

All brand names and product names used in this book are trademarks, registered
trademarks, or trade names of their respective holders. Sourcebooks is not associated with
any product or vendor in this book.

Published by Sourcebooks Casablanca, an imprint of Sourcebooks
1935 Brookdale RD, Naperville, IL 60563-2773
(630) 961-3900
sourcebooks.com

Originally published as *Kiss Me Like You Love Me Vol. 2: A Dangerous Game* in 2019 in Italy
by Sperling & Kupfer, an imprint of Mondadori Libri S.p.A. This edition issued based on the
paperback edition published in 2019 in Italy by Sperling & Kupfer, an imprint of Mondadori
Libri S.p.A.

Cataloging-in-Publication Data is on file with the Library of Congress.

Printed and bound in the United States of America.
LB 10 9 8 7 6 5 4 3 2 1

For all my readers

CONTENT WARNING

This is a dark romance series. It includes some sensitive themes as well as explicit content. It contains scenes of nonconsensual and dubiously consensual sexual activity as well as depictions of violence and child sexual abuse. It is recommended for a mature and aware audience.

Love is a giant mess.
It drives us all mad sometimes.

PROLOGUE

....

Neverland did not exist,
but I still believed that I
could fly between the stars.

NEIL

I sat on the living room sofa and stared at a painting of Jesus.

My mom had told me I needed to thank the Lord every day, say a prayer to him every night, and go to church with her every week. She said there was something wrong with me, that the child-eating witch I talked about so often was a monster who only existed in my head, and that only the church could offer me salvation.

She didn't understand what I was saying.

"I swear she exists," I'd told her over and over again, especially whenever I got home from school to find that the teacher had already called her about my bad behavior.

Like the teacher had that day.

"Stop telling stories!" my mother scolded me. "What you did was unacceptable!" She shouted at me because my teacher had told her I'd groped a classmate, but that wasn't really what happened. All I did was put my hand on her thigh while she was crying about getting a bad grade. The teacher found us and assumed I was touching her in a way that wasn't appropriate for a child. So I tried to explain to Mom that *she* did those bad things to me—the child-eater—but that I would never do them to anyone else. But it felt like she didn't hear me.

"You have to believe me, Mom," I said, soft and defeated.

"This is the second time they've called to tell me about your unmanageable behavior. What the hell is driving you to do these things? Are you trying to get my attention? Huh?" She rubbed her belly with one hand. We were only a few months away from Chloe's birth, and my mother was far from calm.

I didn't want to make her mad the way I did last time. When that happened, she got sick, and Dad punished me.

"Mommy, I—" I didn't get to finish because she stalked over to me and slapped me across the face. It hurt so bad my lip started to tremble. I looked up at her, my eyes full of tears, my cheek aching, but my mother just coldly pointed up the stairs with her index finger.

"Go to your room!" she ordered, and I hung my head and obeyed her. I ran to my bedroom upstairs and shut the door behind me. I didn't want to see anyone. I was feeling alone and misunderstood. I kneeled down at the foot of the bed and put my hands together in prayer just the way Mom always told me to, and then I bent my head as I spoke:

"Please, God, make this torture stop. Why did Kim pick me? Did I do something bad?

"Please tell me, because I can't figure it out. I'm sorry. I'm sorry for asking for too much for Christmas last year. I'm sorry for talking back to my mom sometimes, even on accident. I'm sorry for hiding Logan's after-school snack just to spite him. I'm sorry for being jealous of my little sister, Chloe, who isn't here yet, but I'm just afraid my mom will forget about me. I'm sorry for making Dad angry by getting a juice stain on his new shirt. I'm sorry for accidentally spilling my brother's cereal on the floor this morning.

"I'm sorry for everything, but please…just help me."

Children were afraid of monsters that hid under the bed, behind the curtains, or inside the closet, but that wasn't how monsters really were.

They walked carelessly through our world, their appearances misleading, their smiles enigmatic. They stretched out a hand to you and offered you something sweet before kindly asking you to follow them.

There, in the shadows, in some murky, hidden place, they peeled back your skin, and your screams died a slow death.

One day, one of those monsters descended on me and, without ever even asking, battered down the door to my soul, invaded my heart, and contaminated every inch of my body with poison.

I fought for a long time to protect myself, but the monster had confused—and fused with—me so rapidly, making a mess of everything.

My hope began to fracture into shards like glass each time she touched me, and the fortress that was my innocence slowly began to collapse more and more with each wave of misery.

That was when the enemy had been born inside me. Two souls began to coexist—different, opposed, removed. Thus I learned to control and accept them, becoming, with time…my own worst enemy.

1

....

I was trembling because, for the
second time in my adult life, I was afraid.

NEIL

Having sex, making love, fucking—for me, all of those acts belonged to one broad category: *pleasure*.

My pleasure, though, wasn't like other people's. I didn't have sex for the orgasm, which often didn't even happen for me.

No, for me sex was a way to get a sick thrill, imagining that I had beneath me the person who had so gravely wounded my psyche and my soul: Kimberly. The woman who had visited not just physical abuse on me but verbal, emotional, and psychological abuse. People who experienced that kind of abuse in their childhood often developed strange ways of relating to other people in adulthood. They could become manipulative, antagonistic, perverse, and easily agitated.

Like me, basically.

My personality had been seriously warped, and I knew that the earlier the abuse occurred, the greater the long-term damage would be. Eventually, it resulted in a psychopathological change to my innate tendencies. Dr. Lively had once explained the concept to me in detail during a session. And, he added, the suffering and humiliation that I continued to feel inside would manifest themselves in the sexual and platonic relationships that I had with women, spilling over irreparably onto them. In fact, all I was really doing was forcing myself to reenact my abuse, but this time I played the role of the perpetrator. This was a condition that my doctor referred to as "compulsive ego-dystonic behavior."

All at once, my brain, which had been wandering in its own chaos, pulled me back to the present.

I was in bed, and I was not alone.

"Neil." Jennifer continued to rock back and forth on me, groping my sweaty pecs. She bit her lip as she undulated, which only intensified my goddamned nausea.

I used my fingers to direct her, tightening them on her hips as I stared at the steel ring I wore on the middle finger of my right hand. Anything to avoid looking at the place where her body sucked me in greedily and released. Jennifer didn't want anyone but me, and I didn't want anyone but…Babygirl.

To keep from thinking about Selene, however, I mused on how much I hated the position in which I was currently fucking Jennifer. As usual, I couldn't stand being underneath a woman for more than five minutes, so when that fifth minute ticked over in my brain, I flipped our positions until I could straddle her. My erection, still wet from her fluids, rested on her abdomen.

I pulled off the used condom, and her eyes followed the motion ravenously. She enjoyed my size, like women always did, and I knew it. Jennifer, though, didn't even try to hide her longing to savor it like a delicious lollipop.

She wanted me… Of course she wanted me…

She looked up at me pantingly, her cheeks rosy and eyes filled with an expectation that I was about to satisfy. I got up on my knees and aimed my swollen tip right into her beautiful mouth. I put my hands on the headboard and set the same rhythm once again. In-out, in-out, but this time I watched as I possessed her sinful lips. I watched, and I enjoyed what I saw, but even more, I enjoyed the way she had to work to pleasure me. It was hardly easy, taking all of me, but Jennifer knew how far to go; she knew how to meet my needs.

Suddenly, she sputtered, and I paused for a few moments in the heat of her mouth. I waited for her nod before I started moving again. Her hands squeezed my ass as it contracted with each thrust. I could feel her nails sinking into my flesh as I continued to take what I wanted from her.

When Jen started to gasp and the bobbing of her head slowed down, I realized that Xavier had rejoined us on the bed. This time, he'd stuck his head between her thighs. This whole scene, obscene yet quotidian, had started about an hour earlier, the same way it always did, with him and me sharing a woman.

"You really missed my tongue, didn't you, baby doll?" Xavier's rough, aroused voice significantly slowed my rush toward an orgasm that was feeling increasingly far away. My brain didn't want to cooperate at all that day. I felt so tense and nervous that I couldn't let go in the way I wanted.

"Fuck," I grumbled under my breath, pulling out of Jennifer's mouth so I could move away and get up off the bed. I glanced back at the two of them, continuing to seek their own pleasure, and I took note of how Xavier focused on pushing her over the edge with his mouth.

My friend was certainly more generous than I was. Lately, I'd only been granting that kind of privilege to the girl with the ocean eyes who had just gone away: Selene.

Jennifer gave me a pleading look, begging me to come back to where I was before, buried between her lips. But I shook my head and went to the bathroom instead, shutting the door behind me. I could still hear their moans from behind me as they continued to go at it in earnest.

I rested my hands on the edge of the sink and stared at my reflection: My hair was a riot, my lips were red, the tendons in my neck were too tense, and my muscles were still rigid. I really did have the look of an unsatisfied man. Sexual desire circulated through my body like a poisonous drug. I was still stubbornly erect, my body refusing to give me that moment of abandon, those five seconds of total explosion, the chills that went from the base of my spine straight up to my brain. The same ones I'd felt with only one woman.

With my Babygirl.

I could still remember the way I'd climaxed in that soft, oh-so-tight little body; the way she pulled me inside herself and allowed me through the gates of a cursed paradise. I remembered the delicate way her fingers dug into my back, so afraid of hurting me. I remembered the rough kisses she couldn't completely match because no one had ever kissed her while they fucked her before.

I remembered the way she looked at me as I showed her just how much sex with her pleased me. I couldn't hide it because every orgasm we experienced together was so all-encompassing that it stole my breath. But even when I didn't pant, even when I tried not to lose control, she stole a little piece of me. She took it in tiny doses, creeping in on her tiptoes just like a fairy and leaving a little bit of pixie dust sprinkled on my soul each time.

I had thought about calling her and asking her if she'd gotten to Detroit, if she was doing okay, and if she'd found the little present I'd left in her coat pocket.

I had slipped a glass cube with a pearl inside it into her pocket, using the lame excuse of a forehead kiss to get close enough to her that I could do it undetected.

She'd just left that morning, and it was only ten in the evening at that point, yet it felt like an infinite amount of time had passed since I'd last immersed myself in her ocean. I wanted to wrap my arms around her and kiss her and drag her into my bedroom with me, but I told myself not to fuck it up and to let her go because it was the right thing to do.

The right thing.

I kept repeating it to myself like a crazy person just to keep myself from pulling out my phone and sending a text saying, Come back to me right now, Tinkerbell. Because, even if she did, nothing would have changed. I wouldn't have changed. I would still have been the same disturbed Boy who used his blonds, who took countless showers every day, who refused to return to therapy, who couldn't control his impulses, who talked to himself, and who was incapable of love. A person like me would never, ever have been able to accept love because even the most innocent "I love you" would have brought out the beast within.

It was right to let her go, to let her live her own life, maybe with some normal man who didn't have dissociative identity disorder, intermittent explosive disorder, or obsessive compulsive disorder the way I did. A man who treated her with kindness and touched her gently and didn't sleep with anyone except his woman. A serious, respectful man with whom she could build a family, have children, and get her happy ending.

Selene deserved all of that, but it was something I could never have given her. If I hadn't had the problems I did, I would have tried; I really would have tried to hold on to her. But, unfortunately, that wasn't my reality, and I, being the way that I was, would never have considered trying to initiate a stable relationship with a woman.

Not so long as Kimberly was still in my head.

I stared intently in the mirror at my reflection's gold eyes as everything transformed.

Little by little, like a dream…

The Māori-style tattoo on my right bicep disappeared, my imposing shoulders narrowed, my pectorals shrank, and my body overall grew smaller. My hair became longer and lighter, and my beard scruff vanished, revealing features far more…childlike.

And there he was, my cross to bear.

"You're the one who has the constant need to use all these different women." I spoke first, staring myself down in the mirror before he could go on the attack.

The Boy leaned his head to one side and watched me skeptically. He was once again wearing his blue Oklahoma City basketball jersey and the matching shorts. He would surely want to defend himself and blame everything on me, just like he always did.

"You wanna try to deny it?" I went on, clenching my fingers tighter around the edge of the sink.

I was feeling very unsettled, and the unsatisfied need that continued to pulse between my legs wasn't helping at all.

"You can't keep her; she ran away. Tinkerbell's gone, and you should be pleased." I smiled disdainfully and scrubbed a hand over my face. "You're the one making me act like this. You know that, right?" I threw the accusation at him so he'd stop looking at me like this was solely my fault.

It was all his fault—the things he whispered to my conscience, the crying that sometimes wouldn't stop. And we both knew how hard I tried to soothe him.

"I like her," he answered, folding his arms over his chest. He was pouting, but I didn't give a shit because he was the one who had gotten me into that situation.

"You know you can't have a relationship with a girl like Selene when you're sleeping around, don't you? It's disrespectful, and she'd never accept that kind of thing. She wouldn't share. It was right for her to leave," I chided him, raising my voice.

Damn it, why does this kid get me so fucking angry?

"Take a hike; you're getting on my last nerve," I added threateningly before heading for the toilet, a more urgent physiological need forcing me to interrupt my absurd conversation.

The problem, though, was that pissing with an erection like the one I had was not only difficult but also pretty annoying.

I tried to think about something else, to focus on a topic completely removed from sex, like schoolwork, upcoming exams, or graduation. Finally, I managed to get rid of it.

"Fucking Boy," I grumbled at the moody little shit and immediately got into the shower.

Forty minutes of freezing water were sufficient to soothe my anger, cool my arousal, and banish the smell of Jennifer's saliva and our shared sweat. It was my favorite part of the day: just water, body wash, and artificial scent.

Everyone knew how fixated I was on hygiene, just like they knew how choosy I was about the women I fucked and how I was rarely inclined to give my prey oral. I got pleasure from the act but not with everyone. In fact, with almost none of them, except for Tinkerbell, whose taste was still imprinted on my palate.

She tasted different, an intense, unique flavor, simply...her. I needed to stop thinking about that, though, or my hard-on would come back and, this time, a mere cold shower wouldn't be enough to get rid of it.

I emerged from the bathroom completely naked, my body still dripping water, and went to put on my boxers. Jennifer and Xavier had finished by then and were lying comfortably on the pool house's bed, each smoking a cigarette. I could feel their eyes on me, but I didn't spare them a glance.

"Who were you talking to in there?" Jennifer asked, breaking the silence as I pulled on my jeans.

"I was on the phone." I lied. Shit, I hadn't even realized I'd raised my voice so much that I could be heard out here. Making up a lame excuse was really all I could do.

Jen's face turned skeptical, and Xavier sat up to scrutinize me more closely.

"How long does it take you to shower, man? I hope you at least rubbed one out in there, bro. I don't know how you can hold back after fucking for an hour." He taunted me while I pulled a white sweatshirt over my still-damp chest.

My hair was a mess because I'd only dried it with a towel, so I went to the mirror and ran my fingers through it.

"Xavier, you should have no interest in what I do—or don't do—with my dick," I groused before grabbing my keys, cell phone, and pack of Winstons. I turned to look at them then and caught Jennifer staring at my ass, like usual.

"I'm going out to smoke. Clean up in here and crack a window." I walked out the door, tugging the hood of my sweatshirt over my hair to keep out the cold. I sat on a chaise lounge and lit up a cigarette, exhaling smoke into the air.

I stared at the crystalline water of the swimming pool in front of me and relived the moment when, in our indoor pool up on the third floor, I had seduced Selene and stolen her first kiss. I recalled her small body interlocked with mine, her ocean eyes staring up at me in apprehension, and the sweet taste of her spreading across my tongue. I'd become addicted to her full lips.

How many women had I kissed in my life?

Too many.

But no other kiss had ever had such an effect on me.

I could still feel the heat of that moment, as though it had left an indelible mark on my skin. I tried to push those thoughts away, but the memories kept coming back, like my brain was entertaining itself by torturing me.

I relived the moment I saw her in my room that first morning after, scared and swathed in a sheet from my bed. Her auburn hair was tangled, and her lips were swollen and chapped. She woke me up by referencing Bukowski while panic spread through her body as she gazed at the proof of her lost virginity staining my bed. I had stripped her purity from her while I was off my face, but I'd still managed to make myself feel good, like the bastard that I was. Selene was something novel for me. She had always been odd but adorable at the same time, with her little faces and her shyness, which then gave way to her more stubborn and aggressive side. Still, a sly smile or a dominating kiss was enough to break through her armor.

Maybe that was the exact reason I'd taken such advantage of her good nature while never realizing just how worn down she'd become by my lack of respect for her. She was disillusioned by my constant bad behavior, consumed with managing my notably difficult personality.

I knew very well that Selene had left because I'd finally gone too far.

It had been at a Halloween party. Not only had I made a random blond suck me off right in front of Selene days before, but at the party, I'd also asked Jennifer to play one of our perverse games and dragged Selene into it as well. I knew how deeply they hated each other, which was exactly why I'd selected Jennifer to be the third party. I needed Babygirl to understand who I really was—a deviant who used women as he pleased. I needed her to keep her distance from me.

"Hey, I knew I'd find you out here. What's on your mind?" My brother approached me, balancing on crutches. He lowered himself slowly onto the chaise next to me and sighed. It wasn't easy for him, living with the fallout from his near-fatal accident. Though the bruises had mostly faded, every time I saw the bandages and scars on his face, I remembered how close we came to losing him, and my chest tightened miserably.

"Nothing, really," I answered, not telling him that my "nothing" was actually Selene and that I couldn't stop thinking about her.

"Mmm-hmm…" he murmured thoughtfully. I was pretty sure that Logan knew me well enough to know when I was trying to bullshit him.

"Did you call her yet?" he continued, and I instinctively swung my head to stare at him.

What the hell kind of question was that?

I didn't call women. I wasn't interested in talking to them and I didn't give a shit about their lives.

Sure, I had "stolen" Selene's number from my brother's contacts and yes, I had texted her while I watched her from her balcony, but I didn't have *feelings* for her. Just sexual attraction.

"Why would I call her? I don't do shit like that." I did other, much worse, shit.

"Alyssa and I both asked her to give us a heads-up when she got back to Detroit, but neither of us has heard anything. Not even a text," Logan said softly, with a hint of unease in his voice that suddenly made me feel nervous as well.

But I wasn't going to allow myself to spiral.

My brother was different from me. He was thoughtful and kind and got attached to people so easily.

"Relax. It probably just slipped her mind. She probably needed to talk with her mom, unpack her stuff, tell all her friends she's back..." I continued smoking nonchalantly, imagining those exact things happening. "You know, all that bullshit," I concluded tonelessly.

Logan cocked an eyebrow at me. He seemed skeptical and a bit surprised by my indifference. Annoyed, he sucked in a deep breath before turning toward the pool house as we both heard the door shut with a click.

"Here are the keys." Xavier tossed them at me, and I caught them in one hand. Jennifer stood next to him, wrapped up in her jacket because of the cold and grinning at me. Her makeup was smudged, but her hair was perfect again. It was an appealing look.

"Oh, hey princess," Xavier sneered at Logan, but I stared him down with the obvious intention of putting a stop to whatever shit he was about to say or do.

"See you tomorrow," I cut in firmly. He gave me an arrogant shrug and headed for the gate, followed by a winking Jennifer.

"I can't believe you..." Logan burst out. "When are you going to stop doing this shit?"

Maybe I would have stopped one day, or maybe I would have just continued on forever, because that was how I was built—badly.

"Did you come out here to lecture me?" I asked defensively. I didn't need any reminders that I was in the wrong, that I was a twisted person with a deviant personality.

In the end, that wasn't my fault.

If I'd a more normal childhood, I'd probably be a very different person.

"No, I came out here because ever since this morning—ever since Selene left—you've done nothing but avoid me. Fucking Jennifer isn't going to help you get over her, you know," he answered firmly. I turned to look at him, cigarette clamped between my teeth. *"Get over her."* Fuck, that was a heavy phrase. What the hell was Logan thinking? That I was somehow entangled with that girl? That I was somehow...

"Do you think I'm in love with her?" I asked him derisively. I nearly laughed in his face—it was ridiculous even imagining such a thing. I was done with the little brat.

She was back in Detroit, back to her real life and far away from me. Far away from Player 2511 as well and all the other dangers that surrounded me. And that was exactly how I wanted it.

"No, I don't think that. But I think you like her a lot, more than anyone else," he answered with marked certitude. He was right: I liked Selene, and I liked what we had between the two of us, but none of that meant anything. Romantic love was something different for me than it was for everyone else. It had only negative connotations in my mind and I couldn't associate the feeling with any woman other than Kimberly.

For she was love with a capital L—a diseased, shameless, perverted, filthy, immoral emotion. She had twisted my mind, creating within it an awful, distorted view of a feeling other people said was so pure, and it was a perspective I would have to live with forever.

"It's for the best that she goes on with her life. The girl is nothing to me," I told him bluntly, but my brother seemed determined to keep busting my balls.

"Oh yeah?" he asked archly. "In that case, I really hope she finds a guy who deserves her," he continued in a provoking tone of voice. "A guy who spoils her."

For a moment, I imagined Selene with some other guy. I wanted to say that the idea had no effect on me, but instead, an unfamiliar, corrosive feeling began to spread from the pit of my stomach up through my chest.

"Knock it off," I snapped at him, trying to focus on my cigarette. But nothing was banishing the images he had conjured from my mind.

"Someone to kiss her and touch her and whisper sweet nothings in her ear while making her come so hard she'll forget you ever existed…" He kept going, and that's when I leaped to my feet. I stubbed out my cigarette angrily and locked eyes with him while he looked strangely amused.

"Fucking stop!" I was practically shouting like a lunatic as I stabbed a finger at him.

"Hmm… Okay. So you don't care about her at all. Yes, that's all very clear." He wore a cheeky smile as I ran my hands through my hair, lifting off the hood of my sweatshirt. Logan knew me very well, which meant he knew exactly which buttons to push to make me blow up, to lay me bare, and to get me to talk.

Okay, so admittedly I did maybe care a little bit about the girl. After all, she was still my Tinkerbell, my Neverland, and that wasn't going to change in just a few hours. But that didn't mean I was going to go looking for her.

Selene wanted a fairy tale, and I was definitely not the Prince Charming who could make it happen for her.

"You're just trying to piss me off." I accused my brother as I paced restlessly in front of him. Logan just watched me carefully, reminding me of Dr. Lively's annoying way of analyzing me.

"I care about you, and you know that. I just want you to be honest with yourself," he said. He sounded so serious that I stopped to look at him.

"You were the one who told her that I was unstable and that I was going to use and discard her like I do with all the other women and that she should never get tangled up with someone like me. And now that I've actually let her go, suddenly you don't accept that decision?" I gave him a mocking smile. "At the very least, you should understand where I'm coming from and fucking support me on this!"

I was truly furious, the kind of angry that wasn't going to go away until I'd done a few rounds with the heavy bag.

"I do accept it, but it's obvious that Selene means something to you. Maybe she could have been the right person for you? The person you could give something more to, something other than the physical stuff. She's not like Jennifer or the other ones who go to bed with you just because of your looks." He shook his head, and we both knew that he was telling the truth.

Those women didn't want to know anything about me. They weren't interested in my past, the way that I was, or the things I cared about. They didn't care about anything other than my physical appearance and my sexual capability.

"I just got done fucking someone else; how could you possibly think that Selene could be 'the one' or whatever bullshit you're talking about?" I snapped back, continuing undaunted in my quest to deny the evidence that I had already noticed long ago. Selene had always shown an interest in me, in the person I was and the things I liked—my drawing and reading. She'd even snuck into my room to poke around in my stuff so she might understand me better.

It wasn't enough for her to take me sexually. It wasn't enough for her to use me the way I let everyone else use me. She wanted my soul, and she was determined to tear me open and expose it, despite everything I did to protect myself. I had managed to keep her from doing that, and I had escaped her, but only in part.

Truthfully, I had shared things with Babygirl that I had never wanted to share with a woman. I couldn't explain why I had chosen to give her those little pieces of me, pieces that transcended a merely physical relationship.

"Do you miss her?" Logan said, completely out of nowhere like it was a normal thing to ask. I stared at him for what felt like endless seconds. There was just one answer on the tip of my tongue—a no—but I couldn't get it out because I knew that it would be an enormous lie.

Did I miss her?

It hadn't even been a full day since she left, and, to me, it already felt like an eternity had gone by. Like when she was gone, I was gone too. Ever since she left, I had felt her presence around me like a lingering perfume. But I also felt this void, and it was useless trying to fill it because it could only be made whole by slotting in the one perfect piece, and that piece was her.

I had continually rejected her, but I wanted her just as much as if I'd never had her. Or rather, like we had always been together and now, suddenly, they'd taken her away from me.

We were like two speeding cars, chasing each other and then colliding. We threw off a lot of sparks but left a lot of wreckage behind. We always took the wrong way; we were good at screwing up and getting hurt. But we were also unbeatable. Despite everything, we were the most imperfect, beautiful thing in the world.

"No," I answered steadily and complimented myself internally. I was a very good actor.

Logan gave me an irritated look. Maybe he realized that I was lying, but before he could start lecturing me again, I spotted Matt, who was tugging his coat on in a hurry as he ran anxiously in our direction.

I immediately got to my feet. I could see from the worry and exhaustion on his face that something bad had happened.

"Matt!" I called out, and my brother also turned in his direction, frowning.

My mother's boyfriend, who had for the last four years been nothing but pleasant and ordinary, looked manic with his unkempt hair, shoddily buttoned shirt, and panting breaths.

"Guys, we need to get to the hospital," he said. My mother appeared just then, the same shell-shocked look on her face. I began to get truly concerned, a strange foreboding winding up my body like a deadly serpent.

"What happened, Matt?" Logan grabbed his crutches and slowly got up, staring at a visibly distressed Matt and Mia. Then, in a broken voice, Matt spoke.

"It's Selene. She never made it to the airport. There was an accident; the car went off the road and..." He kept explaining, but I stopped listening to him because the words were just bouncing around inside my head: *accident, car, Selene...*

I stumbled back a few paces, suddenly catapulted into the deepest part of my nightmares. I felt breath scraping at my lungs, my heart pumping faster and faster, and the familiar surge of adrenaline coursing through every inch of my body.

A bomb had just detonated in my brain and blew it into a thousand pieces. I was incensed, and if anything serious had happened to her, I was going to be insane. And I had no doubts about who was behind it all: Player 2511.

"Go. I'll stay here with Chloe. I'd just be in the way right now." Logan gestured to his crutches and pasted on a reassuring smile. I immediately dug the car keys out of my jeans. I followed Matt's Range Rover to the hospital where Selene had been taken.

I drove like a maniac while guilt began to bubble up in my brain. If I hadn't encouraged Babygirl to run away, the accident never would have happened. If I hadn't acted the way I did at that fucking *Halloween* party, she probably would have stayed here with us. With me. And she would still be the Tinkerbell that the Boy liked so much.

I passed a hand over my face and then put it back on the steering wheel. I was trembling because, for the second time in my adult life, I was afraid.

I was truly afraid that the consequences of the accident would be grave. All at once, anxiety had insinuated itself into every part of me, digging a trench where all my other thoughts were firmly buried.

Is she okay?

Is she alive?

Of course she is.

She has to be.

I caught a glimpse of the enormous hospital complex in the distance, and memories of my brother's stay in one of those sterile rooms echoed in my mind.

And now that nightmare seemed set to repeat itself.

I pulled over abruptly, not even bothering to park the car correctly. I grabbed the keys and got out, heading for the entrance. My nerves only increased with each step, and I knew I wouldn't have any peace until I had learned the particulars of Selene's condition.

I hurried through the automatic doors, followed by Matt and my mother. Once inside, I wrinkled my nose at the strong scent of disinfectant and looked around.

Matt gave me a forced smile, and we checked in at the front desk. A few minutes later, we were finally able to head for Selene's room.

I was anxious and on edge; my breath caught in my throat at the idea of something really serious happening to her. The idea that I might never see her again.

Shit, I had never cared so much about another person, other than Logan and Chloe.

I must have really looked like a psycho as I followed Matt and my mother down the hospital corridor. I could feel my skin burning underneath my clothes, my hands were shaking, my forehead was blazing and sheened with sweat, my breathing had gone erratic, and my brain was foggy.

When a stocky and bald nurse stepped in front of us with a stern expression on his face, I just scowled at him. I was pretty sure that before the day was over, I was going to beat the shit out of someone here.

Matt immediately stepped up to explain the situation to him, and the guy showed us to the ICU waiting area. Selene was in room number three.

Number three.

The number three symbolized destiny and the strength to face it. I had learned that years before when I was looking for a tattoo to get on my left hip. Before I chose the pikorua, I'd researched various symbols and their associated meanings.

I clung to the hope that Selene's room number was a good sign, trying to ease the desperation that threatened to swallow me. As I followed behind Matt, I gazed into the rooms that we passed. They were all sterile beds, suffering people, and white walls that made the air around me feel thinner somehow, almost suffocating.

I saw nothing and heard no voices. The only thing in my head was the gleam of her blue eyes and the need I had to see them again...immediately. I had to make sure that she was okay, or I would run the risk of truly going crazy and having a total meltdown. I felt this bizarre sensation inside my body, as though a little bit of my heart had been torn away and the remaining organ felt no need to beat without that small but crucial piece.

It was then that I understand just how right Logan had been earlier: I wanted to see her ocean again. The one I'd been pulled into since that very first day, the one from which I'd stolen much more than just a drop. I'd only meant to play there, unaware that in such a short amount of time, I would have gathered in my hands the most beautiful pearl.

"Judith." Matt's voice brought me back to reality as he wrapped his arms around a beautiful woman who looked exactly like Selene.

The woman, who had been curled up on one of the chairs that lined the bare, white wall, dissolved into tears in her ex-husband's arms. Then she turned her sky-blue eyes first to my mother and then to me.

"Hi, Judith," my mother said softly, in a miserable sort of voice. Matt broke the embrace, and the woman wiped away her tears with the back of her hand before giving us an unhappy smile.

"How is Selene?" Matt asked. I wanted to talk to her as well but instead I was frozen in the middle of the room, unable to utter so much as a syllable. I wanted to know how Selene was, what had happened to her, but at the same time, I was terrified.

I wasn't prepared to hear bad news. What if the accident had caused some kind of irreparable damage? I never would forgive myself.

"Selene is just in there. The doctor is taking a look at her right now," Judith informed us, her voice exhausted and pained.

"What exactly happened?" I asked, drawing her attention to me. Her eyes scrutinized me warily, and I was well aware that I probably wasn't making a great first impression on her, but at that moment, it was far more important that I learn what condition her daughter was in.

"The car went off the road and through the guardrail, and Selene hit her head…badly…"

My heart rose up into my throat before falling back into my chest as though it were on its own personal roller coaster ride.

"She lapsed into a coma. They said there was no active bleeding, but there's a…hematoma?" Judith looked to Matt for confirmation she used the correct word, and he nodded. "They'll need to do more tests, but we don't know when she'll wake up. The doctor said she could have visitors, but only very briefly," she continued.

"Can I see her?" I asked Selene's mother, sounding like a desperate man. Her eyes lingered on my face for a long moment. "Please, I need to see her. Just for a few minutes," I continued to beg, though I hadn't even introduced myself. Pleasantries and proper etiquette weren't part of my makeup even under the best of circumstances.

Who could say what Judith—whose last name I couldn't even remember in that moment, though I knew Selene had told me just before she left—was thinking about me? It occurred to me then just how insane this situation was: I had never in my life begged anyone for anything, and here I was practically supplicating myself in front of some woman I barely knew.

"Fine. But just a few minutes," she answered in a frosty tone.

I didn't waste any more time, pushing the door open and walking inside. The room was spartan, and it would have been entirely dark if it weren't for a small light next to the austere bed. A place I never wanted to see my Tinkerbell.

IV lines were connected to her arms, her head was swaddled in bandages, and her beautiful face was puffy with deep cuts across her cheekbones and her slim nose.

I still couldn't believe this had happened to her.

I took a chair and positioned it next to the bed. I sat down and gently touched her pale hand with my fingertips. It was cold. I looked into her inert face and sucked in a deep breath.

"Hey, Tinkerbell," I whispered, swallowing down the lump in my throat that almost kept me from speaking. What a despicable excuse for a man I was. She was in that bed because of me, and I couldn't even look at her because, when I did, the guilt stabbed into my chest like countless shards of glass.

"I don't even know where to start. But, then, you probably already know I'm not good at talking." I licked my lips and kept slowly rubbing her hand. I was reliving all the pain I'd felt just a few weeks earlier with my brother.

"You always want me to talk, Selene," I began. Her presence was just as intimidating as if her eyes had been open, watching me, waiting to delve inside. "So now I will," I continued, smiling sadly. "I would have kept you with me, even though you were so different from everything that I am, because, from the first moment I saw you, you have been my Neverland. Even though we both know that's a place that doesn't exist…" I brushed her hand again delicately, as though it were made of fragile crystal.

"I… I'm not capable of love. That's why I can't give you what you deserve. You were always braver than me, you know? You've always been willing to understand me, to look inside me, but I haven't been able to do the same with you. And I'm sorry for that." I glanced down at her, rubbing her limp hand with my fingertips. "We were over before we even began, despite the many times you tried to upend my world and make it better…" I gave her a small smile and then chewed on my lip, venting my frustration.

"We fought most recently because of me, but you accepted every part of me, even the worst…" My fingers climbed her arm slowly, caressing the velvet-soft skin. "You tried to appease my demons while I did nothing but make it harder for you. You tried to reassemble the pieces of me, but I wouldn't let you." I lowered my gaze, disappointed in myself and my failure.

"I knew when I met you that I would have to let you go because I'm a head case who scares off all the good hearts, like yours." I sighed and examined the delicate lines of her face.

"It's my fault, all of it. I have too many wounds still open inside for me to be able to love," I confessed, my chest clenching with each word. "I'm still not free. I was hurt too much by the people who were supposed to protect me, and I haven't gotten through that pain yet." I clenched my jaw and squeezed my eyes shut, sucking in the air that suddenly seemed to be in short supply.

"Life has treated me so unfairly, Tinkerbell. I found something special, something that I will never be able to keep because I don't deserve you…" I squeezed her slim hand in mine, which seemed so much larger—as vast as the pain I was feeling in that moment.

"But if things had been different—if I had been different—I would have searched everywhere for you, and once I found you, I wouldn't have let you go for anything in the world. Instead, I'm stuck here between the past and the present, and I'll never live a normal life with this monster on my back." I rested my elbows on the bed to get even closer to her. "The truth is, I used you, and I don't regret it. Do you see now how twisted I am? I am so far from the image of me that you've created." I shook my head, angry at my own inability to know her and treat her the way she should have been treated.

"But I want to thank you for giving me a new experience…" I kissed her hand and a series of shivers ran along my spine, making me tremble. "You followed me into the darkness, Selene. You were the only one who could reach my damned soul." I smiled at her and licked my lips, tasting her skin I had just kissed. "But I can't follow you into the light. I won't be able to get out of this shadow…" I just kept staring at her.

I found her so beautiful.

There was no sparkle in her face just then, but to me she was always a gleaming pearl.

"I'm the reason you're here right now. This is part of my past, something I have to face and destroy…" I stopped and took a deep breath, feeling more than ever the enormous weight I had been shouldering for my entire life.

"Do you remember that time when I asked you how the princess and the dark knight's story ended?" A feeling of melancholy wrapped around me like an invisible veil. "You surely deserve to have a princess ending, Tink. But I…" I paused again, building up my courage to admit the truth to myself. "I need to fight off my own monsters before I can come back to life," I said softly. "And I don't know if I'll win. I don't know if I'll be able to escape the revenge of people who, in all probability, want me dead. I don't know if I can overcome the pain that I still carry with me, but I can promise you this…" I pressed my lips against the back of her hand again and kept them there for a few moments before continuing.

"Even if I can't be with you the way I want and the way you want, I will protect you, even if it costs me my life. I'm not going to let anyone or anything hurt you ever again. I'll be the one to pay for all my mistakes and my vile past—no one else. I'm going to make sure that you're happy, even if it's not with me. Because I know that I can be happy too if I know you're safe." I got up out of the chair and stared again into her face. "I'll protect you, like the shell protects the pearl." I leaned closer to her and touched her cheek, drinking in the vision of her pale skin. I stared at her full lips, closed and chapped. I longed to taste them again and again and again but I couldn't, even though feeling her against my mouth was all that I needed.

"I'll make sure that you have the life you deserve, even if I can't live it alongside you…" I said again, pulling my hand away from her face. I could feel the warmth of our contact disperse in the suddenly freezing air.

I left the room, guilt weighing heavily upon me, and immediately locked eyes with Judith. She was studying me, and definitely not with fondness.

"Sorry, I probably took more than a few minutes," I said immediately, assuming her cold look was due to the time with her daughter I'd stolen from her. The woman nodded with no expression on her face, which was so damnably identical to Selene's. It hurt to look at her because it only conjured up memories I would rather have forgotten. So I turned my gaze away and went over to my mother, who was sitting in one of the nondescript chairs. Before I could even say a word to her, the doctor came in, making Matt leap to his feet.

"Folks..."

I turned to face the woman in the white coat, and I didn't like the tension I saw in her eyes. She paused and regarded us closely, maybe waiting for just the right moment to speak.

"Any news?" Matt asked immediately, moving to stand next to his ex-wife.

Obviously she had news for us, and it clearly wasn't all or perhaps even mostly good.

The doctor began to speak after a deep breath, her tone professional and firm. She told us how the trauma was more serious than she'd initially believed it to be and that there would be long-term effects. How Selene might never be the same again and that we should try to be understanding and support her. That we needed to stay strong and we'd get through everything together. But everything she said sounded vague to me.

What will my Tinkerbell really be facing when she wakes up?

2

....

I smiled and reached out to touch him.

SELENE

I regarded my hands, intertwined with Neil's, and still, I couldn't believe that he was really here.

He, who had always been so hostile to the concept of love and of opening up his heart. He, who was so spiky and so far out of reach, so explosive and stubborn, was now here with me. He was holding my body to his, merging our skin, our spirits, and our breath.

"What are you thinking about?" he asked me. I heard his deep baritone, and I couldn't help but stare at his gleaming eyes, his lips swollen from my kisses.

"About how much you hated to talk to me until recently," I answered, cracking a wry smile. I could smell his familiar musky scent. It was intense and all-encompassing.

"How callous I was, you mean," he answered, sighing heavily. "I didn't realize how important you were to me. Or maybe I didn't want to admit it to myself. You didn't just come into my life, Selene. You got in my soul. You wiped out all the evil inside me. I would have just kept wallowing in my own personal hell if I hadn't met you."

I smiled and reached out to touch him. My fingertips immediately met the formidable musculature of his chest. I traced the sculpted lines of his pecs with my index finger, delighting in the smoothness of his skin as I sighed.

"The important thing is that you did realize it." I laid my head on his chest as he put one powerful arm around me.

I felt his heart beating in time with mine, and I tried to commit the lovely harmony to memory.

"Is it normal to want you all the time?" He stared fixedly at my bare breasts in that absolutely unashamed way of his that I loved.

"Don't start this all over again." I was too embarrassed to admit I wanted him just as much.

"You know I'm a demanding boyfriend, don't you?" His voice turned authoritative and dominating.

I considered his question, and my answer—that he was an exceptional partner—was on the tip of my tongue, but I didn't want to overinflate his ego.

"I know it, but I do need to go to class. We'll just have to take a rain check." I brushed his neck lightly with the tip of my nose. He smelled so good, and I never got tired of breathing him in: man, sex, and musk.

Incredible.

Though he had learned how to work with his demons, he hadn't become a different person. He never would, and I liked him just the way he was. It still didn't take much to rile him up, but by the same token, a single touch from me was all that was required to bring out his better side—docile and kind.

I realized that he was giving me a fixed, thoughtful stare and that, every time he looked at me that way, I became a little bit less my own and a little bit more his.

"I love you and your imperfections, Mr. Disaster." I drew closer to him and put my lips to his in a sweet kiss. It was a kiss that tasted like us, like this chaotic world of ours and the love that had saved us, had united our souls and tied us together forever.

Neil, though, had never said those three little words back to me.

And there was no way he was going to, not out loud.

He might have barely whispered them while I was sleeping or distracted or when he was otherwise sure I wouldn't hear him. He had always been a man like none other and that was why no one could ever take his place for me.

Together, we were a perfect disaster.

"Remember, I will always protect you, like the shell protects the pearl." As I listened to his intense voice, a thousand butterflies took flight, fluttering through the air. And then he smiled at me and squeezed me tighter in his arms, the only place I ever wanted to be, the only place I thought of as…home.

································

I lifted my eyelids slowly, taking note of how my lashes clung to one another. Colorful walls gave way to a dull, achromatic white. The scent of Neil faded, as did his lovely voice. The heat of his body was replaced by the biting cold of an empty space.

I glanced around in search of whatever device was emitting that strange beeping noise in time with my heartbeat and spotted a machine right next to me.

My head hurt, as did my abdomen and shoulder. I tried to move, but I just couldn't.

What is going on?

"Don't crowd her; she's still going to be a bit out of it," came an unfamiliar woman's voice. I did feel fuzzy-headed and weak.

"She's waking up…" murmured a voice I easily recognized. "Sweetheart," she added. I shifted my gaze to my mother, who was speaking in her usual gentle tones.

I looked into her face, which seemed drawn and weary, and forced myself to give her a wavering smile.

I was already feeling tired, my eyelids straining to stay open. There was a tube in my nose that kept me from moving the way I wanted to, and my body felt weak and sluggish.

"How are you feeling, little one?" My mother rubbed my arm and gazed at me with misty eyes. "You're in the hospital. You were in an accident, and you hit your head pretty hard, but you're going to be fine," she reassured me quickly.

I shifted my gaze from her face to the rest of the room, and suddenly, I recalled everything.

I had been in a car accident.

I was supposed to be heading back to Detroit to take back my life. Instead, I had almost lost it. It was a miracle that I'd survived. I remembered the lancing pain I'd felt on impact, the blood all over my clothes. I remembered the driver slumped lifelessly in the front seat, his face unrecognizable, gazing dully off into another world.

It hadn't been a nightmare after all. It was all real.

I felt disconnected from everything around me, and bursts of pain in my head made me squeeze my eyes shut before slowly reopening them.

"My head hurts," I rasped. My mother, alarmed, looked immediately to another woman, who must have been my doctor, to judge by her scrubs and white coat.

"That's absolutely normal," she reassured my mom. "The headaches will be more frequent in the beginning." She spoke in a calm, polite tone. She was a young woman with an aura of dependability and a sweet smile.

"How long..." I licked my lower lip, which felt dry and chapped, before continuing. "How long have I been here?" I asked.

The doctor gave a sigh before replying, "About ten days. You've been in a medically induced coma."

I stared at her in shock.

Ten days?

I tried to wrinkle my forehead, but my skin there felt like it was on fire. I lifted an arm to touch my head and felt the rough texture of gauze meet my fingertips.

"That's nothing, sweetheart, just an injury you got in the crash."

Mom gathered my hand in hers and sat down beside my bed, probably trying to calm me down. But it all felt like a dream to me. A very surreal dream.

Meanwhile, the doctor continued her explanation as she patted my arm.

"We chose to keep you in a medically induced coma as a precaution, Selene. This is standard treatment for patients who have sustained traumatic brain injuries. In your case, your CT scan revealed an intracranial hemorrhage—bleeding in your brain—that had resulted in a hematoma, basically a blood clot. We needed to give your body and brain time to rest and heal so the hematoma could be reabsorbed. Fortunately, it was a smaller hematoma, and the impact on your brain was not severe."

I only processed a few of her words, my one consolation being her statement that there hadn't been serious consequences.

"Is it a bad headache?" she asked thoughtfully, and I nodded, unable to do anything else. "Then I'll give you something for the pain." She moved away but turned to address my mother before leaving the room.

"Selene won't be able to have visitors today because we're going to need to run some tests."

After that, I couldn't track anything that was happening. It felt like the world was moving on around me while my life had stopped.

About a half hour later, the doctor came back to free me from the IV and the nasal tube that had fed me for those ten long days. Then, she sat down next to me with a stack of papers ready to be filled out.

She asked me a battery of questions designed to rule out any post-traumatic amnesia. The accident I had experienced could have caused memory loss, but it hadn't. My memories were all right there, completely intact and crystal clear.

She confirmed this when she put me through a normal questionnaire, starting with biographical data like my name and age. Then she asked me to count, compile a list of words, and track an object as she moved it around. When we were finished, she told me that I'd have to get an MRI and some more specific neurological tests. She also said she'd prescribe me some painkillers. I stayed quiet and tried to listen to her, though I was still bleary.

I was so confused and increasingly angry as I realized that my accident had been no accident at all but was instead caused by that masked bastard. The burden of all those emotions only made my headache worse.

While the doctor informed me that I could experience problems focusing, insomnia, and flashbacks to the traumatic event that would only fade with time, my mind was elsewhere. I half-listened in a state of rising turmoil as the doctor continued giving us the technical details, mostly addressing my mother in a composed, knowledgeable tone.

She said around sixty percent of people in my situation recovered on their own in the months following their injuries, though some did require further physical or psychiatric treatment. If I experienced symptoms of post-traumatic stress disorder, she could refer me to a specialist.

Finally, she said that I was generally in good condition and would soon be able to go back to my regular life. But even that wasn't enough to soothe me.

"Thank goodness." My mother pressed a hand to her chest, relieved to hear that I was fundamentally okay. I tried to rub my temples, but the discomfort I felt in my head made me give up immediately.

I wanted to be alone so I could process all that I was going through because no one understood the enormous secret I was concealing inside. My "accident" had been intentional, premeditated, designed by a strategic thinker who likely wanted me dead, just as he had wanted Logan dead.

Why did he target me?

I wasn't really part of the Miller family, but I was connected to Neil, and anyone who was with or around Neil automatically became a potential target. I'd spent more than a month with Neil, which probably made his nemesis suspicious that I mattered more than one of Mr. Disaster's usual flings.

All at once, I was afraid. Afraid of the reality that I now had to face. I was afraid that I wouldn't be able to confront it all, that I would find myself back in his crosshairs, that I wouldn't be able to figure out who he really was, and that he might go after Logan again or Chloe or Neil directly. I was afraid of diving deep into this dangerous, diabolical game and coming out a loser.

When the doctor left the room, a tear rolled down my cheek, and I shifted to look out the window in front of me.

I felt like a boat trapped in a frozen lagoon. I looked out on a frosty landscape that perfectly matched my chilly insides.

I was icebound. A worn-out body. A terrified soul caught up in a reality too large to face. I didn't want to talk to anyone, but at the same time, I really wanted to see the people I cared about again.

Especially him. Neil.

I hated him for what he'd done—hated him for forcing me to run away, for showing me the worst parts of him when he took me into that bedroom where Jennifer waited for us. I hated him for letting me down and wounding me like that, but still, my heart seemed to beat only for him and no one else.

Goddamned feelings, I thought.

My face tightened as I felt another stab of pain, and I decided that this wasn't the best time for thinking too hard. I needed to recover and hopefully get back to normal as soon as possible.

A sudden melancholy mingled with fear squeezed my chest tight, making tears drip down my chin.

"Sweetheart, why are you crying?" My mother touched my face, wiping a tear from my cheek with her thumb.

"Everything is going to be okay. I'm right here with you," she reassured me, but I knew what awaited me. This was only the beginning. Player wasn't going to stop. Not once he'd already started the game. My mother's words of comfort were not enough to cancel out the mental image of that black Jeep, that mask, and that hand lifted in a wave, signaling that he was there to kill me.

"Mom, you don't understand…" She didn't know anything; she was completely ignorant of the macabre packages, the letters, the indecipherable riddles, and the mysterious figure behind Logan's accident—and now mine as well.

All of it was crazy.

"Sweetheart…"

"Mom, please."

The following hour was a succession of nurses and doctors who told me everything I'd have to do that day: examinations, check-ins, and neurological tests. My life had truly taken a turn, and I had no idea what to expect when I left the hospital.

The doctor told me repeatedly that it was "a miracle" I had survived, but it was still impossible to predict exactly what the real fallout of the accident would be. I was sure, though, that I would be staying in the hospital for a while and that getting back to normal life wouldn't be easy at all.

The doctor told me not to skip any meals and to drink lots of water because I had lost weight and needed to hydrate. My body was weak and worn down by everything that had happened.

My mother stayed by my side the whole time. She spent the night next to me, sleeping in a very uncomfortable recliner that someone brought for her.

When I awoke the next day, I was finally cleared to see my first visitors. My mother left the room for a minute, and I took advantage of the time to briefly assess the damage. I touched my left eyebrow because it hurt every time I wrinkled my forehead and felt an enormous bandage, likely covering stitches. If I had had a mirror, I could have surveyed my awful state for certain, but even without one, I was pretty sure that I was going to be left with a scar on my face forever.

I sighed and rested my hands on the cool sheet that covered half my body. I was wearing a hospital gown, and I wondered where my clothes were.

"Selene? May I come in?" Two raps drew my attention to the door, where I saw my father looking exhausted and miserable.

I didn't answer and continued to stare expressionlessly at him. He moved slowly toward me. I could see from his clenched jaw and stiff shoulders just how on edge he was.

"How are you doing?" He asked cautiously. An absolutely useless question, as far as I was concerned.

Matt shuffled uncomfortably, even bit his lower lip before sitting down next to me on the bed and taking my hand in his. It was an unexpected move. He'd never been touchy-feely like that with me.

How long had he been waiting out there to see me?

I examined him: He looked disheveled, and his shirt was buttoned improperly, like he'd thrown it on in a hurry.

"I've felt better," I answered; my tongue was sluggish and my lips dry.

"You have no idea what I've been going through these days. I was terrified I was going to lose you." He stroked the back of my hand with his thumb, and I looked down to watch the gesture, which seemed sincere and unprompted.

My father really was worried about me; his eyes were full of mixed emotions.

"I'm safe and sound, as you can see," I whispered in a small voice. His face took on a happier cast.

"Logan and Alyssa are outside. Would you like to say hello?" He gave me a weak smile, and I nodded without really thinking about it.

I did want to talk to them. I considered them the best friends I'd made during my time in New York.

"Good, I'll go get them." Matt got to his feet, but before he did, I pulled my hand out of his and rested it on my abdomen.

Sorrow flashed across his face.

He had always been such a reserved man, resistant to expressing any emotion. In that moment, though, he looked as fragile and transparent as a sheet of glass. I appreciated his presence, but I still wasn't about to fall into his arms and forgive him for everything he'd done four years earlier.

"Matt, the doctor told her to rest a lot today. Tell the kids they won't be able to stay very long," my mother cut in, approaching the two of us. She smiled indulgently at me and rested a hand on the shoulder of the man she'd once loved. I wondered, once again, how she had been able to forgive him; how she could even look him in the eyes without rancor.

I admired her. I admired her so much for her strength and her tenacity. She'd always been a woman of a thousand virtues, sensible and wise. She had a kind of inner light that could not be seen but only felt in the soul. She was the kind of person whose goodness couldn't be quantified but was felt in every tiny glance or smile.

On top of that, she was enchantingly beautiful, intelligent, and good-hearted. Maybe even too good-hearted. It was why my father had betrayed her, cheating on her regularly with other women: because he knew that she would always forgive him.

"Of course, Judith," he said, passing a hand over his weary face. He gazed at my mother, and it seemed that I could still read a kind of love in his eyes. A love that may have faded but a comfortable love all the same. One that, once upon a time, he had needed.

Why did he marry her when he must have known he couldn't give up his lovers?

It was something I would never understand.

Love created so many different dynamics between human beings and confounded our thinking in countless ways. One thing was for certain:

Cupid shot his arrows wildly, often in the wrong direction, and when attraction collided with emotion, it created confusion.

That was why love was so misleading and illusory.

And I was no exception: I, too, was in love, and I had my own illusions.

Because, secretly, I was still in love with the idea of the two of them together, Matt and Judith. I would have liked to see us reunited as a real family, and I was deluded because that was never going to happen.

Love—illusion. Illusion—love.

It was a dichotomy that was uppermost in my mind, and maybe that's why I struggled to forgive my father and get over what happened years before.

And there, my secret revealed.

A secret that Matt Anderson would never find out about.

Footsteps from the doorway pulled me out of those musings. I immediately turned my attention to the door and saw Logan approaching with Alyssa. She looked as lovely as ever with her snowy skin and nut-brown hair, which seemed longer than I remembered. Beside her, Logan was slim and beguiling. He immediately gave me a sweet smile.

"Hey, bestie," Alyssa began, silently asking my permission for a hug. I nodded, and after we'd embraced, she took a chair next to the bed. Logan pressed a kiss to my cheek and sat down on the edge of my bed.

"Hey, you two," I said, staring at both of them as my mother paced anxiously around the room with her arms crossed.

"How are you? How are you feeling?" Logan asked, turning his hazel eyes on me.

"Like I got into a near-fatal car accident," I groused, making them grin.

"We were so scared." Alyssa gripped my hand and tried not to cry.

"I know… I can imagine…" I muttered, my lips twisting in a grimace of sadness.

"When we saw that you hadn't texted or called about getting home, we were worried, but we thought at first that you'd just forgotten," Logan explained, sounding distressed.

"Or that you were tired and would call us the next day," Alyssa put in.

"No, I would have let you know when I got home." I raised one corner of my mouth in an embarrassed smile.

I stared down at the white blankets covering my legs, and for a second, I thought about telling Logan that my "accident" had been the fault of the same person who ran him off the road. But I bit my tongue and kept quiet instead because something inside told me I needed to save that confession for another time.

"How are you doing?" I asked him instead, because I had noticed that he wasn't on crutches.

"I've got a brace on under my jeans. You can't even see it." Logan smiled and patted his leg, obviously glad his condition was improving.

I was so happy to finally hear some good news, but I couldn't help but think back on what had happened right before I left, to when everything had spiraled out of control before I even realized it. I recalled the moment when Neil's lips pressed against my forehead and his hand slipped delicately into my coat pocket, depositing inside a pearl encased in glass. It felt like I could hear his voice once again, masculine and low, whispering, *"Safe travels, Tinkerbell."* I recalled that fleeting moment: intense and magical but also painful and melancholy.

I wondered where Mr. Disaster was, if he'd ever come to the hospital, or if he'd already erased me from his life. But I'd never been sure of anything before when it came to Neil, and I wasn't going to start now.

I decided to screw up my courage and ask about him. "Neil… He's…" I licked my lips as Logan and Alyssa turned their attention to me. "I mean, has he…" I stammered awkwardly. If he had never come at all, if he had chosen instead to spend the last ten days with Jennifer, the rest of the Krew, and his many lovers, Logan and Alyssa would think I was an idiot.

An idiot who thought she meant something to Neil.

"Yeah, he came here every day, hoping you would wake up. He was here this morning, too, but he left a couple of hours ago to shower and change. You know…" Logan let the sentence trail off, but I didn't need the end of it. By then, I knew all about Neil's obsession with personal hygiene and showering. I knew how much he hated staying in the same clothes for too long and how upsetting it was for him to go hours without washing.

He had never told me about these problems. In fact, he never confided in me at all, despite the many times I had tried to understand or excuse him, trampling on my own dignity in the process.

It was for exactly that reason that I had declared my defeat: I had never managed to gain his trust. He had given me only his body, like he'd always done with all the others, and that wasn't enough for me anymore.

Then, he'd showed me the most twisted and profane side of him, allowing that girl in the pool house to service him while I was right there. He did it to show me exactly who he was and how useless it was for me to attempt to touch his soul. He had made it abundantly clear that the psychological wall he'd constructed around himself was far too thick and insurmountable to be brought down by a naive girl like me.

After all, I hadn't had much life experience. I'd certainly never come across a man like him before. It was very hard for me to figure out a way to make a dent in that steel armor he put up every time I tried to push the limits he'd imposed on me. And he wanted to annihilate me, no matter what the cost. He wanted to make me understand that he would always come out on top and, in the end, he succeeded.

I no longer knew exactly what I felt for him—disgust, frustration, hatred, or attraction. I'd only be able to understand it when…

"Speak of the devil…" Alyssa's comment interrupted my train of thought. Instinctively, I turned toward the door, and my heart rose like a paper airplane, ready to be shredded again in Neil's hands.

My mother's stride slowed, and she gave him an unreadable look. Knowing her, I suspected she'd never approve of someone like him.

Alyssa, though, smiled, and Logan shot him a knowing glance.

"Um, we're going to go get some coffee. Would you like to join us, Ms. Martin?" Logan gestured for my mother to follow them, and my eyes bounced between the two of them. My mother's blue eyes focused in on Neil as he stood there on the threshold. Then, with a deep sigh, she smiled politely at Logan and followed him out.

I was confident she hadn't guessed what happened. She could not have imagined the Selene she knew going so far, especially with Mia Lindhom's son. That knowledge did give me a certain amount of relief, but it also made me feel even more like a horrible person. My mother had such a different memory of me: that shy, virgin girl who was only going to make love to Jared and only when she was really ready. Instead, I had in short order 1.) lost my virginity while blackout drunk, then 2.) repeated that folly multiple times before trying every way I could to use a physical relationship to learn something more about Neil.

Every time you want something from me, you have to tell me something about yourself.

That was the deal I'd proposed to Neil one day when he caught me watching him slack-jawed during one of his workouts. I still remembered the way my heart had throbbed in my stomach, just like it did right then with him standing there waiting for everyone to leave before he'd come talk to me.

I leaned back comfortably in the bed and quickly smoothed my hair. I knew I didn't look good. I was covered in scratches and bruises, and I immediately realized I wasn't going to fix the situation in the next few seconds.

Then Neil strode into the room, all confidence, and I took a moment to admire him. The figure he cut was nothing short of majestic and arresting, almost intimidating. My body tensed because, even though I hated him, Neil was still the most handsome man I had ever seen—would ever see—in my life.

And, right then, he was looking at me. Just me.

As my mother passed him in the doorway, I noticed the stark difference in their heights. Neil was so tall, and as he continued to stride purposefully toward my bed, I felt the way he loomed, overpowering the small space. His body was sleek, perfectly balanced, and even more massive than I remembered. Had he upped his training regimen? Or maybe enough time had passed since our last encounter, and I could see more clearly why a woman would do any crazy thing for him?

It occurred to me anew how everything about him gave off an aura of skill and power, from his potent bearing to his beguiling, masculine face. His dark brown hair was shorter on the sides and longer on top. His forelock, which he usually pushed back, was thick and disheveled. His lips were plush, his nose proportionate, and his eyes…

The closer they came to me, the more their colors bewitched me. Gold as ingots, yellow as two sunflowers. Or maybe twin stars. They were the color of the sand illuminated by the sun or perhaps like ears of wheat in the dawn's light. They were impossible to pin down and completely unique. I thought that every time I saw them.

I really was pathetic.

After what he did to me, I should have gathered up my scraps of dignity and kicked him out of the room, but instead, I lacked the strength to do anything.

Without bothering to ask for permission, he sat down on the side of my bed, the metal creaking under his weight. His every move demonstrated a casual dominance that still had me in awe of him.

I cleared my throat, and my gaze was unavoidably drawn to the way his black shirt strained over his fit biceps and sculpted chest. His light-wash jeans stretched beautifully across the muscled definition of his legs.

I hated myself for the way his very presence intoxicated me, how he could make me forget the thousands of reasons I had to be angry at him.

"Hi," he said, and his baritone sent the same shivers it always did through my body.

Why did he have a voice like that?

"You got your wish," I answered instinctively, letting my pride do the talking.

I even surprised myself.

But wasn't he the one at the Halloween party who had taken me into that room where Jennifer was waiting? Wasn't it all to get me to take that taxi and leave? Wasn't he the reason I had to go?

My hands were sweating, and my breathing had gotten fast for no reason that I could see.

Unexpectedly, Neil smiled, which only made him look more appealing. It wasn't a happy or sincere smile, though, but a nervy, challenging one. As he did it, he stared at me so insistently that it made me redden, but I tried to get myself under control.

"What is it you think I've gotten?" he prompted me, an inquisitive look on his face.

For a moment, I felt incapable of speech, but I wasn't sure whether to attribute that to the trauma of the accident or to the way those golden eyes were staring into me.

"Look at me," I answered in a biting tone. Though my heart still beat for him, I was so disillusioned by everything that had happened, particularly his cruel attitude. My words made him flinch, and his expression shifted and grew darker. He didn't like that I was giving as good as I got. He didn't appreciate anyone trying to stop him from dominating a given situation.

A small frown line appeared in the middle of his forehead, and I realized he was pondering something. He sighed, and his eyes moved to my lips.

"Do you think I wanted this?" he murmured, gesturing to my body stretched out in the bed. Something resonated inside me and a little inner voice reminded me of our sinful interlude on the chaise lounge next to Matt's indoor pool. I recalled the way Neil had let go completely, albeit silently, climaxing inside me. He had trembled between my knees as he gave me a piece of himself that he'd never given to anyone else. I had to believe that he cared about me, even if only a little because, otherwise, I could not have explained that profoundly intimate gesture.

"No, but you did want me to hate you. You wanted to show me how twisted you were. You wanted Jennifer and me both to use you in that room and then…" I paused but did not break our stare. "Then, you wanted me to run away, to leave you in peace because you'd never give me anything more than sex," I finished unhesitatingly.

Neil regarded me seriously and ran a hand through his hair, a sure sign that he was unsettled. The motion allowed me to get a whiff of his good, clean scent, which settled all around me. I breathed it in, instinctively closing my eyes.

When I reopened my eyes, I found his just a short distance away, and I examined his irises. I searched them for undiscovered planets or galaxies, but I found nothing but the vast infinity of the universe.

"That isn't what I told you to take back to Detroit," he said, sounding disappointed. I was beguiled by the movement of his lips, as full as they were devilish.

"What happened at the pool was before you pulled that shit with Jennifer," I told him with confidence. Neil kept staring at me with a serious look, but I could also see on his face that he felt guilty. I had managed to provoke just the tiniest bit of awareness about how sleazy his actions had been.

"I'm not going to apologize to you," he said immediately. "I am the person you saw that night in the pool house and on Halloween. I just demonstrated it more clearly for you." He spoke decisively, making it clear that I was the one who was in the wrong. I was the one who had built up unreasonable expectations about us—an "us" that had never existed for him.

"Then why…" My voice shook and I tried not to cry. I had never been more vulnerable, and my head ached, among other things, but I had to finish this insane conversation with him. "Why did you let yourself go like that beside the pool?"

He frowned, maybe trying to figure out what I was talking about. I was too embarrassed, though, to be more explicit. We were very different people, and my sense of modesty was just one of the characteristics that set me apart from him.

I took a deep breath, though, and continued. "And why did you give me that pearl before I left?" I wanted to get him to admit that he wasn't indifferent to me and our history, but Neil just sat there, staring at me with cold calculation behind his imperturbable face, and that made it all the more difficult.

"I came inside you raw because I'd never done that with anyone before, and I wanted to know what it was like." He took pains to be explicit, and my rising embarrassment made me unable to meet his eyes. But still, I tried to stand firm and waited for him to answer my second question.

"As for the pearl, it's a trinket that I wanted you to have. A lucky charm. Only a girl like you would have assigned some greater meaning to a gesture like that." Again, he sounded cool and apathetic, a cynic who was completely sure of himself and his words. But, before I left, he had clearly told me that he wanted me to take something of his back to Detroit with me. So why was he now trying so hard to downplay everything?

It was confusing.

Part of me wanted to fall on him and bite his lips quiet because all his answers were doing was hurting and irritating me even more.

"You're such an asshole." I didn't raise my voice, but my whisper was so enraged that it echoed like a scream.

My mood was sinking, and I felt like I needed to be on guard to protect myself from him and from the conflicting feelings he conjured inside me. But, perhaps sensing my grim state of mind, Neil got up off the bed. Then, he towered over me, looking down from his imposing height.

I tilted my chin down, examining the wrinkles in the sheet where he had left evidence of his body, and then lifted my face back up to look at him.

He looked like he was struggling. I could tell from the way he kept grabbing his hair and chewing his lower lip.

"You were nothing and no one to me, Selene. Just a girl I passed the time with for a little while. You don't even know how to kiss, let alone fuck. I've always told you that. I thought you understood." He spoke to me with icy severity.

I rubbed my temples and lowered my face away. It was ridiculous for him to be so callous at a time like this. Meanwhile, I was locked in an internal storm: I didn't want him to leave me, but at the same time, I wanted him to disappear—not just from this room but from my mind altogether. Because that was where he had constantly been.

I shook my head, trying to clear it.

What was I expecting?

That Neil was going to suddenly understand the error of his ways?

That moment would likely never come, and I needed to deal with that reality.

Still, I felt a profound sense of anguish that made me wish I was anywhere else instead of right here. With him.

"You might be nothing among the infinity of my memory, or you might be everything in the nothingness of my existence. I can't decide," he added, his tone hypnotic, as though he were trying to keep some unknowable secret from me. His powerful shoulders slumped, and he stared down at a spot on the floor instead of back at me.

Why did it have to be so hard to understand what he was talking about?

Why did it all have to be so convoluted and contradictory?

He looked up at me one last time as he backed away. His eyes locked on mine as though they, at least, didn't want to leave me.

I felt overcome.

Was Cupid messing around again? Shooting his arrows in all the wrong places?

Yes, I thought, *that's exactly what the cheeky little asshole is doing.*

Neil backed away again, and I knew with certainty that I would never forget the brilliant gold of his stare. Not even if I tried to make myself forget, the way I tried to make myself hate him.

My heart seemed to constrict as the distance between us grew. Maybe it was calling to him.

Yes, my heart was calling out to him, looking for the second chance that I suddenly realized I was ready to give him, because I knew that there was something important motivating his behavior.

"Neil, wait…" I stretched my arm out into the air, but all I grasped was the silence that fell over me as his decisive footsteps echoed out of the room and through the door.

Neil was gone.

Maybe I'd never see him again.

Maybe I'd never find out how it might have been between us or if he'd been telling the truth and I really was nothing to him.

There was one thing, however, that I knew for absolute certain: Nothing would ever put a greater weight on my soul than the void he'd left.

3

··

I still struggled to recognize my face.

SELENE

I was back home.

After another week in the hospital, I was back where everything reminded me of the person I was before I left for New York.

I was in the place I'd grown up—Indian Village. It was a historic neighborhood on the east side of Detroit. It didn't exude the ostentatious luxury that Matt's home and neighborhood did, but it was sophisticated and distinctive thanks to a number of noteworthy buildings like the Bliemaster House. The houses and apartments flanked each other neatly with carefully curated gardens and renovated garages. Our neighbors were the Burnses and the Kampers, located respectively to the right and left of our more modest home.

The moment I got out of the car and looked around, it felt like I'd never left. All my best memories were linked to that house, to my mother and my friends, and to the university.

I still felt confused and a little out of it. The doctor told me I might have headaches and sensitivity to light at first and that I would carry the souvenirs of my accident for a long time to come. They were there, carved into my body and soul, but I was confident that, sooner or later, I would recover.

I walked into the house and smiled at finding it exactly as I remembered it.

Our house wasn't very large, but it was easy and comfortable. Antique wooden furniture was featured heavily in the decor, and my mother had even maintained Grandma Marie's old light fixtures. Perhaps, like me, she hadn't entirely gotten over Grandma Marie's death.

My grandmother used to live with us, and I felt her presence so often that it was as though I could still smell the aroma of cherry pie in the air. Cherry pie, like she used to make for me every Sunday. We would always enjoy it together along with a nice cup of tea, a tradition that my mother and I had kept up in honor of her.

I took a deep breath and, at a snail's pace, made my way up the stairs to my room.

As soon as I crossed the threshold, I could see that everything was neat and in perfect order. The carved wooden headboard was flush against the wall, and just above it were shelves displaying books of all varieties.

Beside the bed and night table, there was a desk by the window, two little white poufs, a six-drawer dresser with all my clothes inside, a small vanity with a stool, and a few old photos of me on the wall.

I looked around, drinking in every detail. How I had missed this room.

Then, I focused in on the vanity mirror behind a few bottles of perfume and some cosmetics. I stared at my reflection, taking note of how pale and exhausted I looked. The dark circles under my eyes were very obvious, as was the healing wound that marred the left side of my forehead. They'd taken the stitches out, but the scar was still puffy and slightly red. I probably could have covered it with some makeup, but it still would have been there underneath. It would be there forever to remind me of what had happened.

"So, shall we unpack these bags?"

I jolted when my mother came into the room, looking lovely and smiling as she always did. She gave me a questioning look as she hoisted my bag up on the bed.

"What's up?" she asked.

"Think I'll have to get a new haircut to cover this?" I pointed to my scar, and she frowned skeptically.

Sure, the mark wasn't a huge problem, but I still struggled to recognize my face even as I realized that I was just going to have to make peace with this indelible blemish on my skin. My mother smiled and drew closer, resting her hands on my shoulders with all her fond indulgence.

"It's barely noticeable. And, as far as I'm concerned, you're always beautiful." She kissed my forehead, and I grimaced sarcastically at her.

It was very noticeable, in fact, but she was just trying to comfort me.

"You're just saying that because I'm your daughter," I groused with an ironic smile. Then, I brushed past her to start unpacking. My mother stayed close to me, ready to help. I got dizzy and experienced vertigo fairly often, but Dr. Rowland had assured me that it was completely normal. She said predicting the impacts of a trauma like the one I had suffered wasn't remotely easy. There might be mood swings, anxiety, stress, and insomnia. Any or all of those could change the way I carried out my daily life. That's why she suggested I write everything down in a personal journal to track whether I experienced any strange feelings or symptoms in these early days.

"Don't forget to write down anything suspicious you notice." Like she could read my mind, my mother gestured to the journal I'd just put on the bedside table. I nodded, wiping my hands on my jeans before sitting down on the bed with a sigh.

"What's wrong?" she asked in a worried tone, and I shrugged, not answering. Honestly, I didn't know what to tell her. I felt this inexplicable emptiness inside me. I was happy to finally be out of the hospital, but I also knew that I'd never be able to forget what had happened.

I still hadn't told anyone that the crash hadn't been an accident and had been engineered by some crazy person, and it was making me anxious.

"I'm just feeling tired," I answered, staring at some vague spot on my legs. I felt like crying, but I tried to hold back. After all, I didn't want to scare my mother, who had already gone through so much.

She sat down next to me and stroked my long hair the way she always used to when I was a child.

To be perfectly honest, I still felt like a child.

"The doctor said that feeling of malaise was temporary." She cupped my face gently and looked deep into my eyes, our souls connecting. "You'll see—you're going to be fine, and we'll deal with all of it together." She smiled at me, and I examined her closely, thinking about her words. My mother would always be by my side, giving me the strength I needed to face anything. I smiled at her, and suddenly, she seemed to remember something.

"Oh, I wanted to give this to you." She reached into her pocket and pulled out a small object. "I think this belongs to you." She opened her hand, showing me…the clear glass cube with the pearl inside.

I opened my lips, and Neil's careless words echoed inside my head. To him, that cube was "just a trinket." A dumb, useless good-luck charm that only a naive little girl could have thought meaningful.

To me, though, it had saved my life.

"You were holding it after the accident. You didn't let it go until you got to the hospital," she explained, making me gape at her. I couldn't help but see the profound symbolism in that. It was incredible how an inanimate object could imprint itself upon everything that had happened. It was as though it had taken on a life of its own, watching as Neil gave it to me before I got in the taxi and then everything that had happened after.

I grabbed it with my thumb and forefinger and held it up to the light from the lamp, admiring how the glass became iridescent while the pearl inside gleamed. I got up off the bed and set the cube down on my desk, next to a photo of me and Mom with Grandma Marie. I didn't even know why I put it there. I could have thrown the little thing away or stashed it in a drawer, but my eyes wanted to admire it again. Maybe it was because it was more unique than rare or maybe just because it was particularly beautiful and deserved its place among the souvenirs that decorated my room.

I stared at it again until my vision started to blur and my head began to spin. I rubbed my forehead as a small stab of pain made me unsteady on my feet. My mother rushed to me.

"Selene!" She grabbed me by the shoulders to keep me from falling and touched my cheek, looking into my eyes. "You need to rest and have something to eat," she said in a sternly concerned tone. I agreed with her; not only had I been missing her delicious meals, I also really needed to relax.

Still, it was only noon, and I didn't feel like going back to bed, so I opted for the sofa in the living room. I turned on the TV, and my mom draped a blanket over my legs before retreating to the kitchen to cook.

"What would you like me to make for you?" she asked enthusiastically, fastening a yellow apron around her waist.

She shot me a sly look because she knew perfectly well what I was going to ask for, so I smiled back at her in the same knowing way. The two of us could read each other with just a look.

"Crab cakes!" we said in unison, bursting into laughter. It was my favorite dish, and she knew that perfectly well, which was why she threw herself wholeheartedly into whipping up some delicious crab cakes. The smell of them floated into the living room, whetting my appetite.

My stomach began to growl, so I joined her in the kitchen and hurried to set the table. This part of the house was also functional and casual, just like the two of us. The elm cabinets, stained a deeper brown, popped against the natural stone of the countertop. The smooth tile floor contrasted with the white walls, while a small window next to the stove illuminated the whole scene.

"No, Selene, don't tire yourself out," she scolded, waving a dishrag at me as I opened a drawer. I grinned because it really was cute.

"Mom, I can't spend the whole day doing nothing," I complained as I finished laying out the cutlery. Then I positioned our turn-of-the-century chairs around the table and smiled. I glanced out the window at our little garden; Mom loved to putter in it, growing all sorts of plants. She always said that gardens were tangible evidence of the millennia-old relationship between man and nature.

She'd always been a deep thinker and a bit of a weirdo.

"Crab cakes are ready!" Her voice came from behind me as I stared through the window at the sweet-smelling bushes that separated our garden from the lawn next door. Standing there with my mother, I felt at home. I felt safe. But I also felt a strange sense of anguish at the knowledge that my body was not the same as it had been. My brain wasn't the same either.

After all, no one just went back to their old self after an experience like mine.

We ate lunch, enjoying a tasty meal, the recipe for which had been handed down from generation to generation. I remained quiet as I ate my food, and my mother looked thoughtful.

"What's on your mind?" I managed with a full mouth.

I was as hungry as a bear at that point and had for sure forgotten my manners.

My mother raised her blue eyes from her plate to my face before clearing her throat.

"I should have kept you from leaving…" she said softly, her voice low and upset.

What was she trying to say?

I quit chewing and swallowed hard, focusing on her.

"If I hadn't pushed you to spend more time with your father, this probably wouldn't have happened," she said, soft and sad. She felt guilty.

Did my mother really believe that any of this was her fault? That was ridiculous. Instinctively, I rose from my chair and went over to her, rubbing her shoulder. She shouldn't have had the faintest suspicion that she was to blame. It was nobody's fault but Player's, the son of a bitch who had created the damned game in the first place.

"Mom," I began coaxingly, but she just shook her head and put her face in her hands, letting out the sob that she'd been holding back for far too long. I hugged her close and stroked her hair because I understood what she was going through. It couldn't have been easy trying to look strong so I didn't break down. It was inevitable that she would end up pushing down a pain that needed to come out.

"Everything's fine. I'm right here," I whispered. Sobs shook her shoulders and made her breath hitch. I tried to soothe her, and when she collapsed back down in her chair, I sat on her lap and held her. I was too big to perch on her like that, but neither of us seemed to care.

I wiped tears from her cheeks with my thumbs, and she smiled at me and touched my forehead, right where my new scar was.

"You are everything to me. No matter how big you get, you will always be my little one," she said gently, and I gave her another squeeze.

⋯⋯⋯⋯⋯⋯⋯⋯

After we finished lunch, I set myself to washing the dishes and cleaning up the kitchen. Mom almost shooed me back to my room to rest, but I didn't

release all my frustrations, right as I was tensing up and preparing to give myself over to those fleeting seconds of physical pleasure, my body would throw up a block.

I could feel the rush of rapture all down my spine, and I hoped, as always, it would keep going, straight to the place where I needed it the most. Instead, it bounced back, leaving me unsatisfied.

I sighed in resignation and pulled off the condom, which I always wore with everyone.

Except for Babygirl.

I got up out of the bed, feeling suddenly cold, and threw the empty condom into the trash can. No drips, not a trace of semen. I ran both hands over my face and through my messy hair before letting out a growl of frustration that made Jennifer flinch.

My blond lolled weakly on the pool house's bed, studying me. I was starting to get seriously concerned because nothing like this had ever happened to me before. I had no idea what I was supposed to do, and I hadn't talked about it with anyone because…

Because I was ashamed.

That feeling of shame had been suffocating me for days, keeping me from confronting the problem or confiding in anyone.

"You didn't come…" Jennifer noted, like that wasn't clear to me as well. They'd all noticed it by now, not just her. Though, for the women, not much had changed. In fact, as my stamina increased, so too did the duration of the sessions, allowing me to make them climax several times in a row. The only problem was me and the desperate race toward orgasm that my body refused to let me complete.

My lovers were satisfied, but they began to doubt their own appeal in the bedroom. Several of them had asked me if they were doing a good enough job with the preliminaries because they felt so awkward and helpless. They even apologized to me, upset and overcome with a stress that was solely the fault of me and my inability to come.

Though they tried their best to make me feel good, nothing improved the difficult situation in which I had suddenly found myself. I just couldn't feel that spike of intense sexual pleasure. No ecstasy. No nothing.

"I know, I know, for fuck's sake!" I snapped at Jennifer, raising my voice, and she flinched.

My mood had also deteriorated lately. Everyone went in fear of me because I was full of animal aggression, especially right after sex. I wasn't sure if I could attribute it to recent events in general or only to my new dysfunction.

I stalked naked around the bedroom, searching for my pack of Winstons. I could feel Jen's eyes on me, watching my back and my ass, but I didn't care. I wasn't shy, certainly not prudish.

In all my history with women, I'd never had any kind of emotional connection. Simply put, it made me feel good to force them to submit to me, to satisfy them, and watch them fall apart while I fucked them.

And that was all.

Showing off my naked body was never a problem for me. What was a problem was displaying any vulnerability or losing control. I held my control tight in a protective fist and now I was watching it slip away all because my body had decided to ignore my will and start doing whatever it wanted.

The Boy, the brain, and the body were no longer connected. The last time they had been was when I last took Selene, right before she left for Detroit. That was the last fantastic, freeing, all-encompassing orgasm I had experienced. Every time I relived that moment, I paused to savor the sublime feeling at the end of it all, the one that had left me drained of all energy and completely satisfied.

I couldn't stop thinking about how good I had felt when I was inside her. I was welcomed. Right. Safe.

I felt like a man.

A man who wasn't, for the first time, doing something wrong, immoral, or perverse.

Then, I'd fucked up once again on Halloween. I did something stupid and made Babygirl run away from me and then get into a near-fatal crash. The only time I'd seen her at the hospital, she leveled that crystalline gaze at me, prepared to defend her dignity against the pathetic attempts I'd made to convince her of what I was.

I had gone into that room with the knowledge that she was going to spit poison at me and that she had every reason to do so. It was ridiculous, then, what I felt during that tense conversation: pain at the thought of no longer having any place in her life because I had done everything I could to push her away and the relief that I might have actually done the right thing.

I still wasn't going to apologize to her, though.

If I'd done that, it would erase everything I had tried to show her about my true self. Selene needed to hold on to those memories of us to keep hating me. So she would stay away from me and wouldn't be involved in the clusterfuck that was my life.

Maybe I hadn't gone about it in the best way, but I only had one goal: to protect her.

I wanted her to go back to her life, back to her charmed, brightly colored universe. A world that had no space for the cruelty of human beings. Selene had no idea what people were capable of. She couldn't see the world through my eyes. In fact, I'd often wished I could look at the world through hers. She really was a fairy: tiny but with an enviable strength. Her heart had the capacity for the biggest, most beautiful feelings. Feelings not everyone was able to experience.

Like...love.

Selene was capable of love, and I admired her for that. Love required courage, and she had that in spades. She was definitely braver than I was.

A pain in my chest made the hand on my left pec tremble. It felt like someone had just punched me right in the heart, as if to shake it loose.

Fuck.

Why was I so mixed up?

Hadn't I gotten just what I wanted?

Hadn't I driven her away by showing her what kind of twisted son of a bitch I really was? I wanted her to go back to Detroit, and I wanted her to take something of me with her, but I never wanted to see her eyes so empty.

I had let her down, and there was no way to fix it.

I also strongly suspected that her wreck had been no accident, and I was afraid that piece of shit Player was involved somehow. I was determined to put a name and a face to him, though I still didn't know exactly how to do that or even where to start.

"Let me try to make you feel better." Jennifer's hands meandered from my sides to my groin. I hadn't even noticed her getting out of the bed and coming over to me.

Her nipples poked into my back, and she mouthed greedy kisses on my shoulder. She had to stand on her tiptoes to reach because of my height.

Any man would have been excited by that delicate contact, but not if he'd just been fucking for about an hour without ejaculating. And definitely not if he was in the kind of terrible mood I was in.

I was frustrated, tense, worried, and still hard. Jen moaned when she encircled it with her palm, admiring my dimensions.

But I knew that not even her considerable prowess could solve my problem.

Yes, my fucking problem. I had to admit it to myself by then. Women worshipped me, and I knew how to get them hot, how to keep them satisfied, and how to draw out a clinch. I had a powerful body that often brought a little pain to mix with the pleasure, but none of that made me a superhero or unbeatable.

I was just a regular man, one who was suffering from an increasingly tangible, obvious disorder.

"Don't touch me!" I snapped, violently throwing her hands off me. "You can't touch me when I don't consent. Jesus!" I raised my voice and Jennifer stumbled back. She was afraid that I was going to hurt her; I could tell from the way she lifted her arms protectively.

She'd been afraid of me ever since that time I caught her attacking Selene. I'd grabbed her by the throat and slammed her against a wall. I didn't want to hurt her, just scare her and I succeeded.

I only hit women in bed, usually when they were on all fours in front of me, never in other circumstances.

What was it about me that I could arouse both want and terror? What kind of creature was I turning into? What was I becoming?

Every day, I felt less and less like a man and more and more like a monster.

I couldn't even face my own reflection in the mirror because, whenever I did, the Boy kept urging me to go find his Tinkerbell. But I was never going to listen to him.

I tried to stay calm and empty my head of thoughts. Then, I breathed in the fruity perfume that Jennifer had left on me, mingled with the smells of sweat and sex that we both shared. I felt the urgent need to scrub myself clean even though I had, as always, already taken several showers that day.

My obsession with being clean was especially intense right after a sexual encounter, despite the condoms, the limited kissing, and my refusal to give oral sex. My skin was frequently irritated from my overuse of soaps and shower gels, but I couldn't stop. Kim lived in my head, and sex was the only way I knew to chase her away.

"I need to shower," I told Jennifer in a calmer tone. My mood swung wildly from fury to calm, making me particularly unstable and confusing to be around.

No one in my vicinity was safe when I was going through that kind of thing. So I walked away from her before I did something I might have regretted. After all, Jennifer didn't have anything to do with my issues, and I didn't want to dump on her all the things that were fucking with my head.

Blondie looked at me like I was crazy, but she didn't say anything else, and I locked myself in the bathroom. I stayed in there for about an hour before coming out smelling like bath gel, giving off an overwhelming fragrance of musk.

I went to the bed and picked my boxers and black jeans up off the floor, quickly pulling them on. At first I had no idea where my sweatshirt had gotten to, but then I spotted it in Jennifer's hands. She was still mostly naked, with just a red thong barely covering her tight ass.

She'd done everything she was supposed to do after a fuck session with me: opened the windows, pulled the sheets off the bed, and tidied up the room. And now she was staring at my chest with a dopey look on her pretty little face.

"Give me back my sweatshirt." I snatched it from her hands in my usual rough way, not even giving her a chance to obey, and threw it on the bed. I wasn't going to put it back on because I needed clean clothes, but that didn't mean she could wear it either.

I was protective of my things, habitually possessive.

No one could touch what belonged to me: cigarettes, car keys, phone, clothes, books, and notebooks. Basically, everything that was mine needed to stay mine alone.

Because I was afraid that people would contaminate what belonged to me.

My sweaters or T-shirts had only ever been worn by one woman in my entire life: my sister. Because siblings were allowed to cross certain lines. That's just the way it was.

"What the hell is wrong with you?" Jennifer snapped, mustering up a courage that failed as soon as I turned to look at her. My gaze moved over her firm breasts and pale skin, still reddened from the way I'd worn her out. Her blond hair lay limp and disheveled. I wrinkled my nose at the smell of her and thought about how she should shower as soon as possible.

Fuck. I really had a fixation.

"Shut up," I said, brushing aside her question to retrieve my pack of Winstons. I pulled out a cigarette and wedged it between my lips. "I can't deal with your tantrums right now."

Jennifer's forehead creased up as she stood right there, sizing me up silently. I ignored her and took out my lighter, desperate for that first hit of nicotine. The smell of smoke was definitely better than the stink that still lingered in the room.

"This is about her, isn't it?" Jennifer blurted out, pulling my eyes back to her.

Was she stupid or something?

She ignored my warning and kept talking. "Ever since that snot-nosed brat left, you've treated everyone with nothing but contempt. You're anxious all the time and now..." She quirked a corner of her mouth and pointed at the fly of my dark jeans. "Now you don't even come. Bet you didn't have that problem with her."

Jennifer wasn't just needling me; she was also demonstrating how completely obsessed she was with Selene. She perceived Babygirl as a real threat, an omnipresent ghost even now that Selene was far away in Detroit, living her life. She only called her a "snot-nosed brat" because she knew that Selene was her opposite.

Jennifer was four years older, much more experienced, and had an obvious facility with men. She knew how to wield her tongue, whether she was sucking guys off or spitting venom at them.

I gave her a vague smile and drew closer to her, blowing cigarette smoke in her face.

"You're so afraid of her…" I whispered, close to her lips. "That snot-nosed brat." I hadn't told the Krew about what happened, so they didn't even know about the accident, much less that Babygirl had left because of me.

Recalling it upset me. Every time I thought about Selene, a bubbling energy radiated through my body, coalescing in the middle of my chest. It was a burning, painful thing, something that I knew was deeply wrong. But then, I was always attracted to all that was damaged, all that burned, all that poisoned, all that aroused. That made me feel alive.

And she was all of that, all concentrated in a tiny body and a pair of ocean eyes.

"I'm not afraid of anyone; I just think that you…" Jennifer tried to keep talking, but I quit listening, turning my back on her and leaving the room.

"I don't have time for your bullshit. Clean yourself up," I ordered with frosty calm, trying to keep myself in check.

I walked into the living room, tense as a violin string. My muscles were tensed, my veins were bulging, and the thing between my legs wasn't any better off.

My jeans felt too tight, like I was trapped in the layers of material. If I'd been alone, I would have happily walked naked around the space, like an animal in a cage. But instead…

"Hey…'bout time you two got done! You really did it up, huh? Is she still alive?" Xavier interrupted whatever Luke was saying about some basketball game and craned his neck, pretending to peek into the bedroom. The two of them lounged on the sofa and looked curiously at me.

"She's walking funny, but yeah," I answered in kind, slipping easily into that useless bro banter. I made myself sick sometimes with the way I belittled women, but it was because it had been a woman who'd destroyed me. She'd made it impossible for me to experience emotions or to have normal, healthy relationships with other humans.

As I ground my half-smoked cigarette into the ashtray on the kitchen island, I smelled the aroma of pizza in the air. My stomach grumbled, and, not bothering to ask Xavier's permission, I stooped to grab a slice from the cardboard box on the living room's coffee table.

"What the fuck! Order your own!" he snapped irritably at me.

"Your ass is planted on my couch in my pool house on my property. The least you owe me is dinner." I moved the slice up to my mouth and devoured it in two bites. I avoided the alcohol, though. Xavier and Luke were used to eating garbage and guzzling rivers of beer all the time, but I wasn't. I tried to eat clean and align my lifestyle with my training regimen for boxing.

"Aren't you on a diet, princess?" Xavier sneered, punching me in the abdomen, and I flinched away slightly, worried he might try to hit me lower. He was enough of an asshole to try it.

"Never been on a diet; I just don't eat like shit," I shrugged. Then, Jennifer stormed out of the bedroom, being sure to slam the door behind her so we would all pay attention. She'd gotten dressed again and done her hair back up in the usual braids. She stalked briskly into the living room, hips swaying in her knee-high boots. Xavier gave a whistle of approval, watching her short skirt swing with each step.

"We got one for you too," Luke told her, pointing at the unopened pizza box sitting on the counter in the kitchen, but she just glared at him, jaw clenched.

"I'm out of here," she announced, throwing her bag over one shoulder. She struck a particularly angry pose, and I sighed in irritation. What, did she think I was going to chase her? Delusional.

I never chased anyone, let alone a woman. As far as I was concerned, she could shove off, and I didn't give a damn either way.

"What happened?" Xavier scowled. Clearly she'd piqued his interest, just like she wanted. He was the nosy one, though. Luke, on the other hand, kept his own counsel. He would sit back and listen without putting his two cents in. That's just how he was.

"Ask him." She gestured at me. "That snot-nosed little brat must have fucked his brains out," Jennifer continued, but I remained expressionless.

My patience for this was limited, but Jennifer was still a woman and I needed to rein myself in.

If she had been a man, I'd have already put her in her place. My way.

"Snot-nosed brat? Who's that?" Xavier pressed while Luke kept quiet. He remembered my Babygirl very well indeed. Considering he'd even kissed her once.

"Oh, you mean Matt's daughter?" Xavier guessed with a snicker, and I went rigid. The muscles in my chest pulled tight, and, half-naked as I was, I was worried they might notice it happening.

"What happened to the little doll? I haven't seen her in a while." He made a face, and his dark eyes darted toward me. The fact that they were all talking about her bothered me much more than Jennifer's "brat" nickname.

"She left, and that was for the best," Luke commented finally, breaking the silence. I immediately turned to look at him, wondering what had happened to all his famous discretion. Also…how the fuck did he know that?

"Who told you that?" I burst out, unable to modulate the tone of my voice, which had gone from peaceful to malicious. Jennifer shook her head meaningfully at my suddenly aggressive attitude.

I'd always been indifferent toward women, even sharing them with the rest of the Krew, so the fact that I avoided even talking about Selene and shielded her from them and went out of my way to convince people that she didn't matter to me bothered Jennifer. It bothered her a lot.

Lately, Blondie had been throwing tons of jealous fits, though I'd told her many times to knock it off. She had no right to be busting my balls. We weren't together. She wasn't my woman, and I most certainly wasn't her man. I wasn't anyone else's either.

"Through the grapevine," Luke said, drawing my attention back to him.

"And are you sad about her leaving?" I pressed. I could perfectly recall the way he'd licked his lips after he kissed her. Selene had only jumped him to make me mad after she'd watched some random blond get on her knees for me. Luke and I had talked about it and clarified the situation, but I certainly hadn't forgotten how he'd talked about her in the car that day. *"She is fucking stunning and she smells nice and she has a picture-perfect ass and who knows what else she's hiding under those baggy clothes…"*

"What?" he asked with a frown, pretending he didn't understand me. But I was well aware that he knew exactly what I meant, and he knew that too.

"Are you sad about her leaving?" I repeated. "You wanted to do her, didn't you?" I needled him deliberately. Xavier and Luke both leaped to their feet, though they did it for different reasons. The former wanted to get between us in case of a fight; the latter wanted to start that fight.

"What the fuck do you want from me?" Luke raised his voice, and I grinned at him. I didn't want anything from him, but I was antsy, and I didn't know why.

In reality, there were several reasons: I had built up too much frustration and too much anger, and I was at the point where I needed to explode and take it all out on the first person I came across.

"She's gone! I didn't touch her; Xavier didn't touch her. We followed your orders! You are out of line with this!" Luke continued, stabbing a finger at me, though I wasn't sure why he'd gotten so worked up. "And you only have yourself to blame. She probably left because she needed to get away from a person like you!" he concluded, and I took an immediate step forward, which made Xavier grab me by the shoulders.

"What did you say?" I hissed, trying to understand what he was getting at. Luke knew something, something I didn't know, and he needed to spill, or else I was going to act now and deal with the fallout later.

"I talked with her on Halloween," he confessed, a self-satisfied expression on his face. I tried to advance on him, but Xavier held me back.

He talked to her? When exactly did that happen? And why hadn't Selene said anything to me?

"I ran into her as she was fleeing in tears from the bedroom where you took her to fool around with Jennifer. She told me everything, and she was completely freaked out. All I did was console her," he said with a note of satisfaction. Meanwhile, my brain was stuck on one word.

Console?

I stopped and stared fixedly at him. Halloween had been another goddamned mistake, and I regretted it bitterly even as I realized I'd had to do it. I had to be sure that Selene fully understood who I was. She had to leave me.

So I did something terrible because I knew she would hate me for it, and that would make everything easier for her. I wanted her to go back to Detroit; I wanted her to get far away from me and the many dangers that cast a pall over my life.

And that's what happened. It had definitely happened, just not in the way I'd hoped.

"Console her? How the fuck were you trying to console her?" I asked in a menacing tone.

Luke treated women just like I did. If he told me that he touched her or kissed her again, I would have hit him for real, and, this time, no one would have been able to save him from my fury.

I wouldn't have stopped Selene from sleeping with other men, as long as they were worthy of her body and respected her values. They needed to be a lot more worthy than me, certainly not less. She had to save the best of herself for someone much better than me.

Not someone like Luke.

That was why I told her I'd always protect her from the Krew, because I knew them: I knew what they were like, and I knew how depraved and dangerous they really were.

I tried to get around Xavier again, like a lion throwing himself against the bars of his cage in search of an escape route. But Xavier knew how agile I was, and he never let down his guard.

"Relax," Luke said. "We just talked while you were fucking Jennifer in one of the rooms. But you were the one who decided to show her what you are. How did you think she was going to react? Selene isn't like the women you usually see; she's not used to the kind of stuff we do!"

I hated the way he talked about her, like he knew her better than I did. When, actually, I was the one who figured out the kind of girl she was long before he did.

It occurred to me in that moment that this reaction wasn't warranted—I *was* out of line. But I couldn't help but link this to the physical discomfort I'd been enduring for days and my inability to have a normal sexual relationship, as well as to both Logan's and Selene's accidents. I linked it to the blonds who came to my bed, one after another, and to the Boy who would not give me peace. I linked it to all of my dysfunctions and how I forbade myself a cure for them.

It was all because I was trapped. I had been in a glass prison since childhood, and all my problems were constantly hammering it into my head that they were right there and always would be.

The root cause of all of it was my longing to be free of the suffering that consumed me a little more each day, turning me erratic and violent.

The only things I felt were concealed anger and pure adrenaline coursing through my body, ready to spill out over anyone. Anything to find some relief.

I tried to calm down.

The fact that they'd done nothing but talk allowed me to breathe and rein in my instincts. It was a mistake to show the Krew that I cared in some way for this girl. They already suspected that I liked her, and now I'd just confirmed it.

I had to get ahold of myself to be the indifferent, immovable guy again.

"I'm sorry," I told Luke, taking a few steps back. I ran a hand through my hair, still damp from the shower, and shook my head. "I'm having a rough time. I'm tense," I added, trying to sound convincing. Luke relaxed his shoulders, and Xavier dropped his guard.

We'd never actually fought before. Sure, we were all dicks to each other, but four years earlier, we had made a very specific agreement: We'd never turn on each other over a woman.

"Little too tense, I'd say," Luke grumbled, giving me a suspicious look. I sighed and continued with my script.

"I've got too much on my mind right now. I don't give a shit about that girl," I said irritably, and it was partially true.

Jennifer perked up at my voice sounding so strong and decisive, and a hopeful look spread over her face. Honestly, I really was thinking about how wrongheaded it had been to fight with Luke about Selene anyway. He hadn't ever touched her again, and she'd never shown any real interest in him, and so my reaction had been irrational, even ridiculous.

Was I jealous over some hypothetical, nonexistent "platonic" relationship between Luke and Selene?

Me?

A guttural laugh vibrated my chest, and I leaned on one of the stools at the kitchen island. It was the same one, in fact, where I'd allowed that nameless blond to suck me off not long ago, and…

I burst out laughing. A real laugh, like a lunatic.

The sound of it cut through the deafening silence that had fallen over the luxurious pool house.

Xavier and Luke exchanged looks while Jennifer continued to stare thoughtfully at me.

"There's a screw loose here, folks." I tapped my index finger against my left temple and glared at Luke with a wicked smile on my face just for him. For some reason, my mood seemed to change by the minute that night, and he was apparently my newest target.

Luke.

My hands itched to use him as a punching back to violently banish all those sick thoughts.

Why was I so pissed at him?

I didn't know. I just knew that I couldn't stop staring hatefully at him.

The Krew didn't know about my childhood, what I'd been through, or the disorders I had. They just thought I was weird, sometimes inaccessible, sometimes unfathomable, but none of them even remotely doubted that I'd experienced something fucked up. I drummed my fingers on the island counter and took note of the steel pizza slicer nearby. They'd probably just used it to cut the pizza.

I grabbed it and examined it, lingering on the reflection of my golden eyes in the shiny steel.

"I think today is one of the bad ones," I murmured to myself, running an index finger over the serrated edge of the tool before slowly rotating the wheel.

All the days were bad ones.

Especially since Babygirl had gone away.

I accidentally cut myself, and a tiny drop of scarlet welled up on my finger. I stared at it, then dragged my eyes away and got up off the stool, watching the Krew. They stood motionless, like wax statues with their backs straight and limbs tensed.

Why did they have those disturbed looks on their faces?

I strode slowly but decisively over to Jennifer and looked her up and down. My Blondie was beautiful. Our Blondie, I should say, because all three of us fucked her, not just me.

I stopped just a short distance from her body. She was far shorter than I was, even with her high heels on. Her bright eyes fastened on my lips before moving to my stormy gaze. I could smell her arousal but also the fear that twisted her guts.

I leaned my head to one side and brought my injured finger up close to her lovely mouth.

"Suck," I ordered in a soft voice, and she breathed in sharply.

I could feel her warm, heavy breathing on my skin.

She hesitated for a few seconds, unsure what to do, before gulping and then opening her lips, allowing me to slip my finger inside her mouth. My index finger made contact with the liquid heat of her tongue, and Jennifer teased it, sucking just the way I'd told her to. She did it with uncharacteristic apprehension.

"I've been patient with you tonight," I whispered into her ear, my voice sensual yet menacing. My bare chest brushed the tits covered by her leather jacket, and she shivered. I felt nothing.

"But it's not going to happen again. Don't push me, Jen." I pressed a kiss to the place just under her ear to reinforce the message I wanted her to receive. Then I pulled back, dragging my finger from her mouth with a smirk.

....

I awoke in a foul mood after a sleepless night. Just like every other damn day.

I'd gone to school, attended my classes, and now I was searching the mansion for Logan.

I hurried to his room, needing urgently to talk with him. My brother was the only person I confided in about my problems or any thoughts that were troubling me. I threw the door to his bedroom open but stopped immediately when I spotted Alyssa, grinding intently on him as the two of them kissed passionately.

"What the hell!" The girl turned bright red and immediately leaped off Logan. Fortunately, they were both still fully dressed. I'd interrupted them before they'd gotten too far.

"Neil!" My brother shouted at me, furious. He hated it when I barreled into his room like a tank, never knocking or giving a shit what he was doing in there.

"I need to talk to you." I walked into the room with a cheeky smile and took a look at his girlfriend's bare legs, exposed when the dress she was wearing had ridden up on her thighs.

Logan lay there, hair a mess, his lips smeared with her lipstick, and gave me a threatening look, which did absolutely nothing to intimidate me. Naturally.

"Can't you knock? Jesus!" he snapped, sitting up and fussing with his hair. Alyssa swallowed hard and got out of the bed, fixing the hem of her fluttering dress. I had no idea where they were in their relationship—they'd been dating since Logan's accident—but I doubted it was love. I suspected my brother was just passing the time with her. He was attracted to her, but not much more.

"You'll have other fucks. I"—I gestured to myself—"am more important." And that was the truth.

Logan was always there for me, just like I was always there for him. Women were a secondary concern, and, right then, Alyssa needed to make herself scarce so I could have a moment in private with my brother.

Logan rolled his eyes at me and sat up on the end of the bed, irritated.

"I'll call you later, baby," he murmured, giving her a reassuring smile, and I made a put-out face.

Why did men always use the same pet names for women? I'd never have done that. I would rather find something personal, something unique for the people I deem important. I was a nonconformist; I valued originality. I couldn't have adapted to the typical couple lifestyle or behaviors.

"Okay, sweetie. Later," she answered gently, and I shuddered.

Sweetie...this was worse than I'd thought. I sighed and rested my ass against the desk, waiting impatiently for Alyssa to get out. Once she did, Logan turned all his anger on me, shooting me a glare that had me grinning.

"You've got lipstick right there, sweetie," I taunted him, pointing at my bottom lip. He huffed through his nose as he stood up. Fortunately, he could now walk without crutches and only wore the brace under his pants to keep from pushing himself too hard. He was almost back to normal.

"Not funny, asshole!" he groused, heading for the bathroom.

"You're a total simp," I scoffed, beginning to get seriously concerned. How had that girl reduced him to this?

"You go fall in love, then we'll talk." He vanished into the bathroom, and I heard the water running. He was probably brushing his teeth.

"You can bet that I'm not going to be like you," I said, plucking a pencil from the holder on his desk. I sat down and opened a random notebook of his, doodling senselessly. "I don't get why men become such dipshits whenever they get into a relationship," I muttered to myself.

I heard the toilet flush, and a few moments later, he reappeared with his hair straightened and the minty smell of toothpaste wafting off him.

He glared first at my face and then at the pencil I had between my fingers before marching over angrily to take it from me.

"Don't scribble all over my notes!" He put the pencil back where it belonged and sat down on the bed, waiting for me to talk. I spun around in his office chair and folded my hands over my stomach, stretching my legs out in front of me with one ankle crossed over the other.

There, I had assumed a position typical of the kind of cocky guy that I was.

"So? What did you want to talk about?" he asked curiously.

I wasn't sure where to start. My upbeat, overconfident attitude was just a way of hiding how agitated I was. I'd never suffered from this kind of problem before, and revealing it wasn't easy. For a man like me, feeling like I couldn't fully experience sex was embarrassing.

"I've got a problem…" I leaned forward and arranged my face into a serious expression. I rested my elbows on my knees and stared at him, searching for the right words that would help me confess everything.

Fuck, this was difficult.

"What sort of problem? Neil, you're making me worry," he chided me, unsettled.

I gazed into his darker hazel eyes, a place where I had always been able to find myself. Logan had always been the best part of me, the one who stayed pure and uncontaminated.

I glanced around awkwardly. I was experiencing something that was common for most other humans but rare for me: embarrassment.

"I don't..." The shame was clear in my voice. I hated that awkward, speechless moment. Logan just watched me, perplexed, and I looked like an idiot who couldn't talk.

That's why I hated doing that kind of thing. Words were useless. Most of the time, I only used them to describe problems or express negative feelings. There had rarely been a time when I felt the need to speak out of joy or to tell someone something good.

"You don't what?" he urged me, becoming increasingly concerned.

I had to spit it out. It was now or never.

I needed to confide in someone and I'd always held back with my friends. I didn't like talking about myself or my life. I was introverted and slow to trust. I was never the kind of person to just say what I thought without hesitation. I always thought long and hard about what to say and—most important of all—who to say it to.

Very few people had my trust.

"I can't orgasm anymore," I said in a rush, staring at the toes of his black Air Jordans instead of at his face. I knew he'd never laugh at me for having that kind of problem, but I was still uncomfortable. It didn't feel good, as a man, to admit that sort of thing. I felt incomplete, wrong, and defective.

A Ferrari with a malfunctioning engine.

"What does that mean?" he asked, sounding surprised. "For... For how long?" Now he was the one who looked embarrassed and was having trouble keeping up this absurd conversation.

I jumped up from the chair like there were hot stones under my ass and began pacing nervously in front of him.

"For a while now. I can still feel everything. It feels good; I can get hard. Hell, I can fuck for hours, but...there's no ejaculation," I managed haltingly.

Orgasm was an extreme feeling, a rush of energy followed by a profound state of relaxation and I no longer even remembered what it felt like to be really satisfied. Reaching a sexual climax was supposed to put an end to one's desire and the erotic tension of the act, but the opposite was happening in my body. My frustration was as palpable as my anxiety because my want and arousal were trapped in an endless refractory period.

"Jesus, that can't be easy," he said, rubbing a hand over his mouth in shock.

No, it wasn't. It was terrible.

"Do you think there's something wrong with me physically?" My voice shook. The mere suspicion that this situation could be the result of a physical problem or a serious illness terrified me.

Logan considered this for a moment. I didn't want to dump all this on him, but I didn't know who else I could turn to.

"What the fuck are you talking about? Of course not!" Logan said suddenly, getting to his feet. "There's nothing wrong with your body, Neil. I think it's..." He paused, looking meaningfully into my eyes. "Psychological," he finished.

Psychological?

What he was saying made sense. Ever since I was a child, I'd had a strange relationship with sex. I could never completely let myself go and could never feel truly emotionally involved with my partner. I was always more concerned with "giving" than receiving. I always needed women to feel good, to achieve orgasm. I focused on lasting as long as possible for them, keeping my erection until they were done. I was concerned about "quality" as well as quantity and gave it everything I had without ever getting emotions involved. It was all somewhat methodical, practiced, and carefully calculated. The fact that I almost never gave into requests for oral was a sign of the intense control I maintained with all of them.

Basically, women shattered underneath me while I thought about Kim, about the weeping Boy and my damaged soul. And, eventually, my mind abandoned me. I regressed into the past. Distant but somehow still very present.

"So you think it's like a mental block?" I asked Logan, scrubbing a hand over my face before looking away, out the French windows to the blue sky beyond.

I wasn't dumb; I knew I had mental problems. The constant showering was proof of that, as was the talking to myself, the hallucinations of the Boy, the insomnia, the rage I struggled to control, and the constant thoughts about why all of this had happened to me.

Why me?

Why had Kimberly chosen me?

I asked myself that question every day, even though she was the one I really wanted to ask.

"I think you should talk to Dr. Lively about this," Logan suggested, sounding pained. For once, I agreed with him.

I hated the clinic, my shrink's antiseptic office, and following the course of therapy.

I had been confident in my choice not to go back there, but, at the same time, I knew that my doctor was the only person who could help me shed light on my problem.

It was important that I resolve it.

Sex had always been a tool I used to survive, the only way I had of shutting up the Boy and drying his tears. How was I supposed to do without it? How would I live? How would I keep myself under control?

I didn't know any other way to balance my adult self with my child self: two parts of the same soul that had no desire to work with each other. Sex was the thread that bound them together, kept them connected, and prevented either one from prevailing over and erasing the other.

What would happen if the Boy won that fight?

I was afraid of the answer to that question and the possible consequences, which was why I fought so hard. I fought to keep a war from breaking out and to keep the peace between the two opposite, contrasting sides of me.

"You're right," I told my brother, banishing all my other thoughts. Then, I left him, taking all my misery along with me.

....

That afternoon, I had to take Chloe to her last appointment with Dr. Lively.

My sister was doing much better, and Carter had become a distant memory for her. She had even gone back to school and was getting her grades up again. She was going out with friends and smiling more and more often.

I was happy for her. Dr. Lively had done a great job with her, and my sister had revealed an enviable strength that she'd long kept hidden beneath fragility.

I sat in the waiting room while she finished up. As usual, the pudgy woman at the front desk checked up on me constantly, regularly throwing quick glances in my direction. Meanwhile, I leafed through a car and motorcycle magazine. It was boring, but at least it wasn't some useless gossip or fashion magazine.

I sighed and tossed the magazine down on the low table in front of me. I already owned a Maserati that was the wet dream of any guy my age, so I really didn't need to drool over pictures of other cars. I was happy with my baby, and driving her was one of the few things other than boxing that could relax me. Whenever I got into that driver's seat, I knew I had a marvelous panther in my hands and that it was my responsibility to keep her under control.

"And you can come back any time you want, especially if the anxiety or the nightmares return." Dr. Lively's voice jolted me out of my thoughts. I stood up to meet them.

"We should go. Madison will be here any minute," Chloe said, smiling. She was ready to go out with her friend to celebrate the conclusion of her therapy.

I looked at the doctor, who had, in turn, fixed his bright eyes on me. He was obviously wondering if he should seize this opportunity to talk to me, considering that my sister had finished with her standing appointment. Truthfully, I needed to talk to him, too, and I tried to communicate that with my eyes.

From Dr. Lively's look in return, I knew that he understood.

I walked Chloe out like always and waited with her on the corner a few yards from the clinic to make sure Madison and her parents were actually coming.

"You're being paranoid," she huffed, arranging her woolen hat on top of her head. It was cold enough now that no one was leaving the house without layers of heavy clothing.

"You're sixteen, you're my sister, and I'm high-strung," I said defensively as I resisted the urge to smoke. I was just going to go back inside to talk to Krug anyway, so I wouldn't have had time to finish my cigarette. Instead, I stuck my hands in the pockets of my black jacket and watched the cars speed by on the street.

"You're overprotective." She corrected me with a sly smile.

Yeah, I was that, too, just like any big brother would be.

"Exactly. That's why I need to make sure Madison's parents are with her."

How often did teenagers lie so they could get away with their shit? No way was I going to leave her alone to wait for this "friend" of hers. No, I was going to make sure with my own eyes that she was being honest. Chloe huffed, but when a car pulled up to the curb and honked, I took careful note of Madison's parents driving and the girl herself in the back seat.

"Call if you need anything. And don't be late getting home," I cautioned her sternly, but my little sister just grinned and got up on her tiptoes to kiss my cheek.

"You're a pain in the ass, Neil. See you later!" She darted over to get in the car with her friend. I watched until the car merged into traffic and was gone.

Then I sighed and tried to mentally prepare myself for what I was about to do.

I had no more excuses left.

I went back into the clinic and walked briskly to Dr. Lively's office. His door was open, and there was no one else in the waiting room. I knew he was waiting for me. He'd known me for over a decade at that point; he understood my cries for help, even when they were silent.

"Make yourself comfortable, Neil." Krug Lively stood next to his desk, looking over a document. His glasses were poised on the tip of his nose, and his gaze was fixed on the paper.

I took a few steps into the room but decided to keep my distance from him. Too close, and I might not be able to speak.

"So, what's happening? I'm glad you finally decided to talk to me." He looked up at me and smiled, setting the paper down on the desk. He was always asking me to talk to him and now here I was in front of him voluntarily, just like he'd wanted for the last three years.

I heaved a sigh before spilling my guts. I told him everything, man to man, holding nothing back. Not that it was easy, but the fact that I was talking to a mental health professional and not just some random person had kindled a little hope in me. Maybe he could help me figure out what was happening to me.

"It's called anorgasmia." Dr. Lively pulled off his glasses and propped himself up against his desk, adopting a casual stance. I was still standing, hand shoved deep into the pocket of my jeans while I stared at him. I cleared my throat and pulled down the asymmetrical zipper on my leather jacket. A sudden anxious feeling left me short of breath.

"And?" I asked, trying to keep cool. This wasn't like our professional sessions before, where he analyzed me while I tried to tell him about my history. Now I was the one asking questions, and he was the respondent.

"It's a type of sexual dysfunction. One's response to sexual stimulation is positive, and one can maintain an erection but cannot achieve orgasm. This type of disorder can be divided into various stages and can be or become a chronic condition," he informed me, searching my face for a reaction.

He scratched his chin, which was bristly with the hint of a beard, and I considered his words.

"So you're telling me you think it's a psychological problem?" I tried to keep my voice firm, controlling my agitation.

"I'm sure it is. Anorgasmia is often a secondary effect of other illnesses, but, in your case, it is almost certainly a result of the sexual trauma you experienced as a child," he told me confidently.

All at once, the anxiety wriggled out of my control: I began to have heart palpitations, and my right hand started shaking uncontrollably.

"Neil, you are abusing your body, and it is sending you distress signals. It's rebelling against you. You can't go on like this for much longer. Violating yourself to relive the memories, perpetuating the cycle of sexual encounters void of affection, human warmth, or emotion, unable to place any trust in your partners... It will destroy you in the end. You're putting your body under constant physical and mental stress. Is that what you want?" he asked, his tone severe.

I flinched at his words, raw but truthful.

My conditions were monsters that had managed to tackle me and bind me up in chains. I could have avoided all of this long ago but, instead, I had pushed on to the point of no return. The point where a sexual malfunction was added to my fucking pile of issues.

"Could I become…impotent?" I asked, though it was a struggle.

Christ, just the word sent a stab of pain through me. Impotence was a man's worst nightmare, something that would shatter the image of myself that I had created.

"No, it's not about impotence; that has an organic cause. You have a psychological problem that could have a more severe impact on your body." He moved closer and took a deep breath before continuing to speak. "Neil, it's not about your physical ability; it's your psychological instability. You need treatment," he told me firmly.

He continued talking then, but I struggled to follow our conversation.

After what felt like an eternity, I left the office and the entire damn clinic without saying another word.

Before I left, Dr. Lively advised me to avoid sexual intercourse for the time being and concentrate on working out or other energy-burning activities that might "compensate" for the gratification that I was no longer able to feel in the sack. Despite his insistence, I refused to promise that I would come back to him and actually restart therapy, but I also hadn't denied the possibility that he might see my ugly mug again in the next few days.

I strode furiously over to my parked car, cursing my whole life. I wanted to get away, to disappear and forget about everything he'd told me.

Logan had guessed right. The problem was in my brain, not my body.

I pulled the key fob from my jeans pocket and unlocked the doors. I would have been able to leave immediately if it weren't for the massive, cherry-red Ducati Monster parked perilously close to my Maserati.

"What the fuck!" I burst out, slowing my stride a little ways away from the bike.

I looked around for the dumbass who had parked it so close that I couldn't open my door, but there was no one around. I was on the edge of a meltdown, and I wouldn't have thought twice about breaking someone's face. I knew I'd have to get in the gym and start training the minute I got home, and it would have been nice to warm up my fists on some dickhead instead.

"Oh, sorry, Miller. My baby's out of commission." An assertive and notably familiar voice piped up from behind me.

I turned in the direction of the sound and spotted a head of black hair and a pair of green eyes that I knew very well.

The bike belonged to Megan Wayne. Of course.

I immediately went rigid and internally cursed this day, hoping it would just end as soon as possible because I couldn't go on like this. I had reached my limit with everything that was happening to me.

"Okay, great. I'll go in the other side," I said irritably.

There, I had found a solution, but even if I hadn't, I would have figured out some way to cut off this ridiculous situation.

I examined her feminine shoulders draped in a leather jacket and the star-shaped studs on her lapels. I also looked at her tight black jeans that outlined her slim legs tucked into low-heeled leather boots. She was beautiful, no doubt about it, but her savage, snarky charm would never move me.

"Think you could start her for me? Or at least take a look and see why it won't turn on?" Megan called out again, halting my attempt to escape from her and from the memories that accompanied her. I scrutinized her once again, and I didn't see any hint of malice or mockery in her eyes. She was just a woman alone in a parking lot at eight p.m., asking for help.

I could have told her no and walked away not giving a shit, like I usually did with everyone else. But some human part of me that I hadn't even known I had made me stop. I felt sorry for her, and, with a heavy sigh, I brushed past her to get to the Ducati.

"Oh, thank you. I didn't realize you were nice like that," she teased and tossed me the key, which I caught in the air, ignoring her needling.

I didn't answer; I just made myself useful and got on the bike. Calling it a monster was an understatement. I'd ridden bikes like it before, but I'd forgotten the high of it.

I kicked up the stand and put it in neutral before turning the key. I pressed the red start button, but nothing happened.

I got off the bike and spent a few minutes checking for the problem, which I quickly located: The tank was empty.

"Are you familiar with this thing called gas?" I asked her wryly. "Tank's bone dry." I looked at her, and she frowned back, her green eyes darting back and forth between me and the bike. Then she raised a skeptical eyebrow at me.

She didn't believe me.

The woman really was a head case.

"What? That's impossible," she said, gesturing at the gas tank. I rolled my eyes and moved close enough to her that she had to crane her neck back to look at me. I took in her pleasant scent and examined the long lashes that framed her vine-colored eyes.

"Can't you just drive a fucking pink VW Bug? I think that would be more your speed." I searched her face and quirked the corner of my mouth in a teasing way.

What was she doing on a Ducati when she couldn't figure out when the tank was empty?

"Why do men always act like sexist dickheads, always assuming a woman is inferior to them both mentally and physically?" she snapped back, her voice steady and self-assured.

I would have enjoyed continuing that interesting exchange of opinions if it were literally anyone else in the world in front of me.

Megan was practically a carbon copy of me, except for the pussy between her legs. I knew how she was. If I indulged her, she would make this discussion last forever, and I didn't have time to waste on that.

"I'd love to stay here and break down your feminist ideas, but, alas, I have things to do," I lied. I didn't have anything to do. Except get away from her as fast as possible and go home to take yet another shower. To that end, I tried to walk past her, but Head Case blocked my route with her hands planted on her slim hips.

"I have things to do," I said again, slower and more menacing this time, but Megan just smiled and shrugged an arrogant shoulder.

"If you were a gentlemen, you might say, 'Dear Megan, do you need a lift?'" She tried to mimic my voice and failed miserably. But she wasn't done with her little pantomime. "And then I would say, 'Oh, yes, Miller, you are so well-mannered.'" She pressed a hand to her chest and batted her eyelashes. "And you would be a better man for that good deed." She raised a finger in an instructive fashion, and I glanced around, hoping that no one else was bearing witness to this little scene.

I maintained a serious expression, severe and impassive, until the spontaneous smile that I definitely would not have reciprocated vanished off her face.

I rarely smiled, and when I did, it was for a damn good reason.

"Okay, but you're forgetting one thing: I'm no gentleman. So quit fucking with me and get out of the way." I brushed her aside easily with one hand, my strength far superior to her own.

"You can't run away from me forever," she said, not for the first time, and I halted. I shot her a fierce look, and her legs faltered slightly, making her sway. She knew how prone to rage I was and how poorly I controlled my temper, so continuing to provoke me wasn't a smart move on her part.

"You're the one who should be running from me." Or else, I would destroy her.

I walked around my car and opened the passenger door. I slid in quickly and clambered over the gearshift to get into the driver's seat.

I, Neil Miller, was fleeing like the devil was on my tail.

I started the engine and rolled down the window because I needed a smoke.

I felt around in my jacket pockets, pulling out a pack of Winstons and sticking a cigarette between my lips.

I couldn't stand Megan. I couldn't stand her presence or that feline gaze that was always, always trying to dig deeper inside me.

I couldn't stand her at all, and yet I couldn't stop staring at her.

My eyes were fixed on her through the windshield. She stood, shoulders hunched against the cold.

I should have just left, not bothering about her or the bike, but instead I was inexplicably trapped there in my car. I cupped my hand around the cigarette and lit it. Megan began to walk away, and my eyes slid from her black hair, fluttering in the freezing air, to her high, tight ass that tensed and released with every sway of her hips. She had the kind of well-defined, feminine curves that would have left any man dazed.

Even I, a perfectionist with high standards for women, could appreciate the symmetry of her body. Megan was undoubtedly built to be admired. Among other things.

I let the thick smoke out the window and continued to stare at her.

She'd catch a cab probably, but, in the meantime, she was out there alone, on foot in the cold.

My only consolation was that it wasn't a particularly dangerous part of town, so she could get out of the situation without my help. I hit the accelerator, the engine making a roar like a lion's, and her eyes flew to me. She peered at me as I drummed my fingers on the wheel with one hand, the other resting limp on the window.

I wanted her to know that I was leaving and that I wasn't going to do anything to help her. I reversed sharply and then slammed on the brakes, leaving skid marks on the asphalt.

I needed to leave. Christ, I had to leave and…

"Get in," I demanded, sticking my face out the window just far enough that Megan could hear me.

She jumped, turning in my direction, and lifted an eyebrow at me, thoroughly pleased with herself. Another side of me had emerged—a more compassionate one—and I had no idea why.

Maybe I just wanted to rid myself of any sense of responsibility for her. She was a woman, after all, and if something had happened to her, I would have felt guilty.

Still, I didn't look at her as she walked around the car to get into the passenger seat nor when her orange blossom scent began to mingle with my own inside the car. Instead, I stared fixedly at some point in the middle distance, hoping to understand what the fuck I'd just done.

"Thanks, Miller. So I guess you do have a heart after all." She closed the door and balanced her purse on her thighs.

"I can feel you, you know? Pounding so hard." It was Babygirl's voice. The

Tinkerbell who had quieted the Boy's suffering for a brief period of time. It echoed in my mind, reminding me of her sweet, gentle tone. So different from Megan's more mature, seductive one.

I tried to avoid thinking about Selene because, whenever I did, it stirred up something inside me that I couldn't understand.

That girl had been the most beautiful accident in all of my fucked-up life. A bolt from the blue that had unleashed not only the sick attraction I felt for her but something else as well. Something I could not name.

She was a creature of the divine, a little fairy who had been able to bring me back to life with a wink of her eye. And now she hated me because I'd been such a bastard to her.

Everything is boring now without you, Babygirl, I thought.

"Damn, this car is sick," Megan said, snapping me out of my thoughts and bringing me back to the present moment. She had her seat belt on and was examining the illuminated blood-red dash, the controls on the steering wheel, and those for the multimedia settings.

Suddenly, the display flashed, and she jumped, which made me give her a smug grin.

"I'll give you a ride," I said, growing serious again as I reached for the music player. "But don't talk. I can't stand people who run their mouths." I pressed play on my personal playlist and turned up the volume a bit, the way I always did when I was driving alone.

Megan didn't say anything and just leaned her head back against the seat, making herself comfortable.

I drove off, and we left her bike there. She could pick it up the next day. Then, we plunged into traffic, and almost immediately, I was forced to stop at a light.

Fortunately, Head Case hadn't said a word in the last five minutes.

Good.

She'd followed my order, even though I hadn't thought a woman like her would be so accommodating. I must finally be having the desired effect on her.

"You listen to The Neighbourhood?" Like she could read my mind, Megan spoke up just to ask me a banal question.

"If it's on my playlist, that means I listen to it," I said irritably as I watched the traffic light, waiting for it to turn green. They were my favorite band, actually, but I didn't mention that. Instead, I ran my fingers through my hair nervously.

"My favorite is 'Cry Baby,'" Megan continued, but I still didn't look at her. Green.

I accelerated, and Megan was thrown back against the seat. My car often had the upper hand. It had the power of a wave waiting to take shape, the speed of a rushing wind, and the savage heart of an untamed beast.

That was why I'd picked it out.

"Goddamn! You drive like shit!" Megan shouted, and I grinned, glancing at the rearview mirror before passing another car.

"Next time take a cab or walk, if you'd like that better." I took one last drag from my cigarette and threw it out before rolling up the window. I turned the heater on, and then the song she'd been talking about came on, like it had been summoned with a magic spell.

Without asking for my permission, Megan reached over to turn up the volume and began humming along.

I tried to focus on the road because a ticket would have been just the thing I needed to end this shitty day on a high note, but the woman next to me was a distracting irritant.

"Do you still live at the same place?" I asked her, shooting her a look just in time to see her nod.

I turned down her street, but her voice caught my attention again.

"This is a song about a man who falls in love with the wrong woman," she explained with a little half-smile. "Who knows? Maybe that could happen to you too. You might fall in love with me, Miller, even if you don't want to," she whispered into my ear.

I immediately slowed down and turned to look at her. She wore a sly smile now. Just then, I pulled up in front of her apartment and regarded her thoughtfully. What the fuck was she talking about?

Her green eyes stabbed into mine, trying to grab hold of the darkness that hovered over my soul. The same darkness that I was constantly fighting against and that, way down deep, tied the two of us together. That was why

I couldn't stand being close to her, because she brought back memories that I wanted to erase.

No, I won't ever fall in love with you because I don't want to and because I can't. Not with you, not with anyone else, is how I wanted to answer her. But I had no desire to trade barbs with her.

"We're here." I broke our stare and went back to looking out the windshield.

Why was she looking at me like that?

I could sense her perfume invading my space, and, once again, I turned to find her just a short distance from me. My eyes plunged into hers and could pick out the warm brown striations radiating out from her small pupils.

These were eyes that I had once seen looking dull, terrified, and ashamed.

But now they were pushing my buttons and rekindling all the outrage of my memories.

"What the fuck are you doing?" I snapped in my usually curmudgeonly way, and she chuckled, not at all scared or startled. She just kept staring at me and leaning in, and who knew what kind of thoughts were running through her head?

"I just wanted to thank you," she said innocently with a shrug of her shoulders. I screwed up my forehead and shook my head in confusion.

"And how exactly did you want to thank me?" I pressed because it had looked an awful lot like she was leaning in to kiss me, and the thought of that fucking horrified me.

Me and Megan? Impossible.

She grinned, pretending that I'd misinterpreted her gesture, but I wasn't stupid. I was a sharp man, and I definitely had experience with women. I noticed when they tried to seduce me, and sometimes I allowed myself to be seduced, but only if and when I chose and always with the goal of getting what I wanted.

If Megan had been a regular woman, I probably would have been seducing her myself.

But even though I knew plenty of ways to get a woman excited, to tease her or flatter her or get around her sense of modesty, I never would have tried any of them on her. Touching her at all was inconceivable for me.

"I get you, you know..." I gave her a mysterious smile because I had worked out what was going on in her head.

I stared into her eyes without a shred of uncertainty, and she frowned, showing vulnerability for the first time.

So she wanted to play with me? Well, if I were going to play, I would play dirty.

"You know that I'd never touch you, which is why you like teasing me," I whispered, my voice rough and stern. The voice of a man who wouldn't get fucked up over a pretty face and body, not even one as hot as hers.

Megan retreated but still managed to maintain a confident pose.

I gave her a wicked grin. She was never going to win against someone like me. She needed to accept reality.

"I was going to kiss you on the cheek. You know, there do exist some simple, sincere gestures with which one can convey gratitude to another person," she explained, pausing for effect. "Miller," she finished, opening her door.

I watched her get out of my car and walk toward the apartment where she lived with her family, a sassy smile on her face.

I let my head fall back against the seat and scrubbed a hand over my face. I knew so much about her, things I would have preferred not to remember.

Sighing, I tried to convince myself that it had just been a ride home. A very ordinary ride home. And yet, I still had to promise myself that I was going to stay away from her the way I had done for the last few years.

I didn't want to establish any kind of relationship with her: We weren't friends. We weren't acquaintances. We were nothing. Absolutely fucking nothing.

I was just about to leave when my cell phone buzzed—an incoming call. I raised my hips up slightly to pull the phone out of my jeans and looked at the display.

Tinkerbell.

That was what I'd saved her number under when, in my usual peremptory style, I'd gotten her number out of Logan's phone. I wanted to arrange a conversation before she'd left Detroit.

An unexpected smile made my lips curve. For a moment, I imagined that she'd forgotten what I'd done to her. But, at the same time, I had to hope that wasn't the case because remembering me had to mean remembering the shit I pulled on Halloween. I would rather she had a void where I was supposed to be than have her associate me with a monster or a pervert, as she had so often called me.

I grew serious again, and something powerful seemed to sharply squeeze my chest.

My brother and sister should have been the only people who existed for me, no one else.

I was already too broken, destroyed, and consumed. I couldn't yoke myself to anyone else, especially not a woman.

I couldn't let her suffer or be miserable. I was too fragile, and romantic relationships were for winners. Not people like me who had already been defeated by life.

For people like me whose personal conception of love was incomprehensible to most, women were nothing but trouble. They were a spectacle that I preferred to enjoy intensely but fleetingly and only between the sheets.

My phone continued to ring.

I should have just rejected the call, but instead my thumb hovered over the display, uncertain.

Selene had been the best indulgence I had ever allowed myself to have, but I was positive that it wouldn't work between us in the long run. That was why I'd done everything I could to drive her away.

I'd worked hard to make her hate me so it would be easier for her to move on, but then the accident happened.

The more I thought about her, the more painful that pinch in my chest became.

She should never have come in contact with someone like me. It was better just to never meet men who were so lost, hopeless, and troubled. So filled with issues and secrets.

There was nothing appealing about me.

I had to learn how to walk on broken ground, and I never wanted her to discover everything I tried to hide inside myself. If she did, she would have looked at me differently. She'd be disgusted, probably.

Another ring, and all at once everything became very clear inside me.

I still wanted to hear her voice. I still wanted to touch and talk to her. My desire for her hadn't gone away, nor had my attraction, and there was no point in continuing to tell myself otherwise.

I wanted her.

I contradicted myself; I knew that perfectly well, but it was because, deep down, I was hiding a vast truth: I was ashamed of what I had lived through. Every night, I could still feel Kim's hands on me, her tongue, the filthy things she said, the way she blackmailed me, and all of it made me sick to my stomach. I often dry-heaved, hoping that would be enough to purge that demon from my soul.

It was a war I'd been fighting my whole life, and I didn't want to drag anyone else into it. Especially not Babygirl.

And yet, my thumb slid along the screen.

"Hello," I said, strong and firm because I wanted to put her on the back foot. If she tried to get close to me, I would act like an asshole again until I'd pushed her away and convinced her that I didn't deserve her.

On the other end of the phone, however, there was only silence: no words, no voices.

My Tinkerbell didn't have a single word to say.

I pulled the phone away from my ear to make sure the call was still connected.

Selene was still on the line, but neither of us took advantage of this opportunity to "talk" the way we both wanted.

Wasn't that why she'd called me?

Or was it because she missed me and wanted to hear my voice? Or did she want to scream at me?

I heard a muffled giggling sound, like my beautiful Tigress was not alone, and then nothing again.

It occurred to me then that maybe she hadn't called because she got a burst of bravery that evaporated the moment she heard my voice. Maybe she'd been talking about me and then, egged on by her friends, had done something childish and immediately regretted it. It was this last idea that both thrilled me and made me smile.

A few seconds later, though, Tinkerbell ended the call, depriving me of the agitated sound of her breathing. She was being cute. That might have irritated another man, but it tickled me because it confirmed to me that I could still understand her moves and sometimes even anticipate them.

I liked her impulsive actions; I liked her childlike sense of naughtiness when she gave in to my body. She always did, every time I sought her out with nothing but selfish intentions.

It occurred to me in that moment that I no longer knew anything about her life or what she was doing or even how her recovery was going.

She was far away now, and yet I thought of her. Always. Every moment of the day. Every time I walked past her room to get to mine, I glanced at the bare walls and felt the same sensation: like tons of tiny needles were sticking into my ribs. My stomach would knot up, and my legs would just stop there, forcing me to look at her bed, which still smelled of coconut. All I had to do was close my eyes, and I'd be high on her, on the sweet taste of her and her sinuous curves.

She would always be my Neverland, that place where I lived my fantasy life, the asymptote I would never touch. A girl who was going to grow up and be with some other man.

Still, I'd come to my senses quickly enough when I realized that I wasn't the right person for her. My history was littered with broken fragments, sins, mistakes, and sources of shame, and the present-day me was still too fucked up.

I shook myself free from those thoughts and smiled at how, without even touching her, I had managed to fuck with Selene's peace of mind, getting her to do childish things like the call. And it occurred to me that it wasn't only the Boy who liked Tinkerbell. I liked her too.

But that didn't really change anything at all.

6

Of all the things he could have asked me about,
he picked the very worst one.

SELENE

The shore. We had reached our destination.

Matt picked me up at the airport after a two-hour flight, and we'd navigated through traffic for a few hours until we got to the small seaside town where my grandparents had lived. From there, we headed for the house on the beach.

After the long ride, I staggered out of the car with numb muscles. I couldn't decide how I felt in that moment: I was elated and expectant, but, at the time, I was resolved and wary. It could very well have been just another of my father's unsuccessful attempts to fix things between us. Deep down, though, I always hoped that spending a weekend together could help the two of us make some kind of progress.

"Here we are, our beach house," Matt said enthusiastically, grabbing our bags out of the trunk. I looked around, breathing in the salty sea air. Not far away, I spotted the isolated beach. The sun was high in the sky, and a cold breeze whipped up the waves. They crashed on the shore with a peaceful sound.

"So, how do you like it? Do you remember this place?" Matt's voice brought my attention back to the home in front of us. Dark wood contrasted with whitewash that dominated the exterior. The large front porch came equipped with two wooden benches. There was also a table and a set of chairs out there so one could fully enjoy the fresh air, preferably with a nice glass of wine. I put my hand on the wooden balustrade as I climbed the first steps. It was like I could feel the memories under my fingertips: my grandparents and the childhood summers I'd spent with them.

"Go on, let's get in." My father was clearly much more enthusiastic than I was, but I couldn't deny the new and unexpected feeling of peace I also had.

I followed him to the front door, and, when he opened it, I smiled to see that not a thing had changed since I saw it last. The wood-look tile floor contrasted with the white walls. The linen curtains and cheerful furnishings made the space feel bright, fresh, and airy.

I moved into the room slowly, like a child marveling at something grand for the very first time. In the living room, two couches upholstered with aquamarine fabric recalled the color of the ocean. The kitchen was small but functional. A little deeper in were the bedrooms—five of them and only one bathroom. The whole house was only one story.

Matt set our bags down on the floor, and I grabbed mine to stow it in one of the bedrooms. I picked the one I'd slept in as a child. It was small but cozy, and it looked right out on the water. In fact, the big window gave me an idyllic panoramic view. The sheets on the bed were cream swirled with shades of blue, and the furniture was all blond wood, from the dresser to the headboard, which was decorated in an ocean theme.

"So, what would you like to eat? I'm cooking," Matt announced cheerfully when I returned to the kitchen. I regarded him thoughtfully as he put away some cans in the cupboards.

He was different.

He had adopted a notably more casual, sporty look. His dark sunglasses were pushed up on his forehead, and his black hair was spiked up with gel. He looked younger; maybe the informal clothing gave him a more carefree air.

"You can make whatever you want," I answered flatly. It was his birthday after all, and I hadn't even told him happy birthday yet. He didn't seem to have noticed, though; all that mattered to him was that I'd agreed to spend this time with him.

"Fair warning: I'm not a great cook…" He scratched the back of his head, pulling a jar of peanut butter out of his grocery bag along with a box of pancake mix and several bags of pistachios. He'd bought so many of them, and I had no idea why.

"We could have something basic," I suggested, shrugging.

We decided to eat outside at the table on the porch to take advantage of the ocean view that we'd only have for two days. It didn't matter to us that temperatures were low and we were the only idiots who were choosing to spend time at a beach house long after summer had ended.

An hour later, Matt served up two plates of scrambled eggs and bacon, which would have been delicious had he not completely scorched them.

I was hardly a food snob, but that was the day I learned that my father really was hopeless in the kitchen.

"H-how is it?" he stammered, sounding embarrassed as he poured more water into my glass.

"It sucks, but I am really hungry, so…" I took a second forkful of yellow sludge and washed it down with a sip of water. Matt huffed, putting a dish-towel down on the table. He had tied on a chef's apron for the occasion, which made him look extra ridiculous.

"Anna always cooks for us now, and when I was with your mom, she took care of that. I'm a bit rusty over here." He shot me a tiny smile that I did not reciprocate. The initial peace between us had, once again, been replaced by the familiar tension we both felt every time we tried to have a real conversation.

"We should use this time to our advantage. These twenty-four hours you've given me are going to go by quick," he said softly, his eyes locked on me.

Maybe for him it would pass quickly; it would be far too slow for me. I turned my fork against the plate, shuffling around the burned eggs I was trying to finish. I wanted to tell him to just take me back to the airport, but I had already agreed to this, and I didn't want to ruin his birthday.

"Okay, what do you want to talk about?" I asked in a bored tone.

"Let's talk about you. How are things with Jared?"

Of all the things he could have asked me about, he'd picked the very worst one. My father knew nothing about what had gone down with Jared, much less the secret passion I'd shared with Neil.

I turned my attention back to my food, buying myself some time by taking another bite before I answered.

"We broke up, but I prefer to not talk about that." I was not in the mood to tell him about Jared, and I probably never would be. Because telling him about everything that happened would also mean telling him about Neil and there was no way I could do that.

Neil…

His name echoed in my thoughts. It was ridiculous, how four letters could send my heart roiling.

"Let's talk about you instead and how easy it was for you to cheat on my mother with Mia. I'm all ears." I gave him a challenging grin and watched as he swallowed uncomfortably before clenching his jaw nervously.

"Your mother and I had already decided to separate before I even met Mia," he answered, sounding embarrassed. "Things between us hadn't been good for a long time. My job, her job, the second child I wouldn't give her—it all slipped through my fingers before I'd even realized," he admitted, staring at his own half-eaten plate. Apparently he hadn't liked his eggs very much either.

He stroked his beard with one hand as he stared out past the wooden porch railing. The sea, in its infinite nature, accompanied our voices with the sound of waves, shaking the air at random intervals. Matt stared out into the blue expanse, as though his thoughts were written there.

"Even if I hadn't met my current partner, Judith and I would have broken up because the love was over. The passion was over. She constantly asked me for a divorce. There's still a lot of affection between us, and we have the most beautiful thing in common: you. You are the fruit of our love, but the marriage was destined to end." He sighed. "I've made a lot of mistakes, and I can't turn back time. I can only try to keep the past from impacting my future and yours, which is why I'm trying everything I can to make it up to you." His eyes locked on mine, and I could see the pain that he'd been suffering for so long. I'd stopped considering him my father four years ago, and, for him, that must have felt like an eternity.

"If you made a mistake with someone you loved, wouldn't you want that person to give you a second chance?" he asked.

I considered his question. The person I loved most in the world was my mother, and, yes, if I let her down, I probably would have done anything to have her forgive me. Maybe it was the same for Matt, but something inside made me doubt his sincerity.

"Having a different woman by my side doesn't erase the love I have for my daughter." My father took my hand, and I flinched at the unexpected gesture. "You will always be the woman I love most in this world. No one could replace my daughter, not Mia, not anyone else." He said it with such certainty that I felt it in my chest, like a vibration that made me tremble. In that moment, Matt wasn't lying, and he communicated that fact to me with his whole body, starting with his eyes.

In his gaze, I saw myself, and, for a brief moment, I also saw the bond that once united us.

So I made the decision not to dig up the past and just accept his invitation to spend the afternoon wandering around the small boardwalk that was within walking distance.

Every time I went there, I marveled at how different it was from my life in Detroit. It wasn't just the beach and the water and the food vendors—everything here was an explosion of color, games, and entertainment. Every Friday night in the summer, they would set off fireworks, and I always watched them with my grandparents when I was a kid.

"You were scared of them," my father said gruffly when I reminisced about those nights. We'd been walking for a few hours, chatting about this and that. He took a decisive bite from his hot dog as we walked.

"That's not true," I said defensively, strolling along beside him. The sun was almost down, and I lost myself, staring into the bright spectacle of the sunset. Rays of light broke through the edges of some of the clouds and covered everything they touched in gold and orange.

"Hungry, weren't you? Next time, we'll go out for lunch." Matt pointed to the all-but-finished hot dog in my hand. I'd devoured most of it in a couple of bites because, in the end, we'd given up on the eggs and scraped our plates into the trash. I nodded and balled up the dirty napkin in my hands, waiting until I found a trash can to toss it in.

"I wanted to be a writer when I was a kid. Did you know that?" he asked, apropos of nothing, as we trod slowly down the wooden boardwalk that ran the length of the enormous beach.

"Really?" I tugged my coat tighter around myself and arranged the edges of my scarf underneath my collar, all without taking my attention from him. Despite the low temperatures, the day had been sunny and nice.

"Yes. I even submitted to a few poetry competitions. Won some of them too," he admitted, a nostalgic smile spreading across his face as his eyes turned back to the sea.

"So what made you study medicine then?" I asked.

"Your grandfather," he said immediately. "He was a doctor, as was his father before him. So he wanted me, his eldest son, to continue the family tradition. I kept writing in secret for a while because I knew he'd never allow me to keep pursuing my dream. But when I found myself at a crossroads with regard to my future, I put my passion aside and threw myself fully into my studies." He stuck his hands into his jacket pockets and pulled off his sunglasses to better enjoy the colors of sunset that would so soon give way to stars.

"What about Uncle Robert? Why didn't he have to go to med school?"

My uncle had walked a different path. He'd become a lawyer, and he lived in Chicago now. He was unmarried with no children, and he didn't have a great relationship with Matt.

"He was the lucky one—my father gave him a choice. For me, he already had a whole life planned out," he answered, his voice full of bitterness for a man who was long gone and, perhaps, not as kind as I'd believed him to be.

The ringing of Matt's phone interrupted our conversation. Matt excused himself and answered, "Hey, honey," he said.

It was surely Mia calling; she was the only woman he'd greet like that. I kept quiet and soaked in the peaceful atmosphere all around us. Hardly any people. Hardly any cars. Some places were already closed up. It was perfect.

"Oh, I see. So, it'll just be the three of you? Why isn't he coming?"

I turned to Matt to see what he was talking about, and he shot a brief look at me before sighing deeply. "Well, try to talk him into it. Do you want me to talk to him? I don't get his attitude on this." He frowned and scratched his eyebrow with his thumb. They were probably talking about Neil.

He didn't want to join us? Why not?

Was he so disgusted with me now that he had to avoid me at all costs?

I couldn't hide my disappointment. After we had shared so much, were we now just going to ignore each other? On top of that, I still felt enormously uncomfortable when I thought about what I'd done with him. I didn't regret it, not at all, but it was still difficult, dealing with the emptiness caused by his absence.

But even though Neil seemingly had no further interest in me, something held me back from fully believing that.

He couldn't have been lying the last time we were together. I didn't want to believe he could be that cruel. He'd made love to me; he had given me something of himself, and I had experienced it all firsthand. It hadn't just been some figment of my imagination.

That was the thread of hope I was clinging to with both hands, lest I fall and shatter into a million pieces.

"Okay, we'll be waiting for you." Matt ended the call just as we hit the street that would lead us back to the beach house.

"Mia's coming tomorrow with Logan and Chloe. Neil has apparently decided not to come with them," he informed me, sounding disappointed.

"Oh, why not?" I pretended to be simply disappointed, concealing the anger that was building up in me at the idea that Neil was refusing even to see me.

Damn him!

I'd left New York because of him. He'd hurt and angered me too deeply with his lack of respect for me. Then there was the car crash, and he only came to see me one time. Just once. Like he didn't have the time to bother with me and didn't give a crap about my condition.

"I don't know. I'll never understand that boy. Neil's an odd one," he said.

We climbed the porch steps, and Matt opened the front door for us. But I couldn't stop thinking about how Matt had described Neil, and curiosity got the better of me.

Even when I hated him, I couldn't stop thinking about him.

Something was obviously wrong with me because this behavior was patently deranged.

"Why do you say he's odd?" I asked, shrugging out of my coat and arranging it on the coatrack.

"Because he's a very complicated guy. He had a rough childhood, which, unfortunately, has had serious repercussions on the way he lives." Matt headed for the kitchen, turning briefly to look at me. "Do you want me to make you a hot drink?"

I smiled at his thoughtfulness. I was, in fact, freezing, and I wouldn't have minded warming up with a nice tea or tisane.

"Yes, thank you." I sat down on a stool at the kitchen island and balanced my chin on my hands, watching as my father reached for the small kettle and filled it with water. I quickly dove back into our conversation, though. Maybe Matt could give me some more information about Mr. Disaster that I could add to the few things I'd managed to pry out of the housekeeper, Anna.

"So…" I said, picking up where we left off. "I haven't talked with Neil much; I don't know him very well," I lied. In reality, I had managed to learn about some parts of his nature while others eluded me and no one seemed to be able to give me any damned answers about him. Neil had his own form of communication: He spoke with his body and used sex to create any kind of connection with women. He was unlike any other man I'd ever met and that made it difficult to get inside his head.

Matt turned to look at me, his eyes narrowing into a thoughtful expression that was almost intimidating.

Did I say something weird?

"Selene," he said in the same chiding tone he used whenever something was bugging him. "I'm a man, and I know the kind of guys that women are attracted to." He moved closer to me and rested his hands authoritatively on the kitchen island that now separated us. "And Neil definitely has the looks to reel them in with ease." I wasn't sure where this conversation was going, but I couldn't think of a reasonable response either. So Matt, encouraged by my silence, kept talking.

"He's a very handsome young man; he's not only smart but also very shrewd…"

It seemed like this was all preamble to some sort of warning, but, again, I remained silent.

"I'd be happy to see you get closer to him. After all, you've already lived together, and it doesn't seem like he's made any trouble for you, but there are certain lines you should never cross with him." He hit the word "lines" hard to draw my attention to it. "He's not like his brother, Logan, especially when it comes to women," he concluded severely, and that last statement confirmed what I'd already assumed: My father knew more about Neil than I'd realized, but he was also reluctant to share that information with me.

Damn it!

I tried not to look upset. If Matt had any suspicions that I'd fallen under Neil's spell, he could have easily intuited that something happened between us.

"Could you…" The question slipped out of me too quickly, making Matt perk up. "Could you be a little clearer?" I bit my lower lip to disguise my sudden awkwardness.

I needed to pretend that I didn't know what he was talking about if I wanted to nip his suspicions in the bud.

My father seemed to consider it for a moment before sucking in a breath and answering. "When he's interested in a woman, he'll do anything to have her. Not that it's hard for him to get his targets. Just look at the kid." He rubbed a hand over his face, now looking seriously concerned.

I knew exactly what he was talking about. A woman only had to glance at Neil and she'd be feeling the sudden desire to hit her knees before him and offer up everything.

I was embarrassed by the turn my thoughts had taken.

"The problem is, I don't want you to be taken in by someone like him. I love Neil, but you are my daughter, and I would never, ever want him to think of you as anything other than a member of the family. Besides, he's older than you, and his lifestyle is very different from yours. Is that clear enough?" It wasn't a question but a warning.

I wasn't paying attention, though my brain was too busy going over what Matt could have meant by a "different lifestyle." Was Neil drinking heavily or taking drugs? I recalled asking him about that once, and he assured me he wasn't addicted to anything.

"Is he on drugs? Or something like that?" I insisted. At the same time, my father had just filled our mugs with hot tea, and they nearly slipped out of his hands at my unexpected question. He turned back to me and handed me a cup. I immediately wrapped my hands around it to warm up.

"No, Selene. Nothing like that. He's never used drugs as far as I know."

Well, at least there were some small virtues among the sea of flaws that, in just a short time, I'd already identified.

"He has much bigger problems, problems that go beyond a hangover or a habit. Fortunately, Neil's been smart enough not to fall into that sort of thing, but I still want you to be careful with him. Don't make me tell you again," he warned, sipping his tea as he leaned against the marble counter.

I didn't ask him any more questions and instead just let the subject drop. I had already figured out the kind of guy Neil was, and my father's warnings only fortified the iron shield I'd need to face him someday. Especially now after everything that had happened between us.

Halloween.

Me. Jennifer. Him.

I was fixated on that perverse scene. I just couldn't accept it.

All at once, anger rushed over me, and I hoped I'd never encounter him again. If tomorrow came and he hadn't changed his mind, I probably wouldn't ever see him again. There wouldn't have been any further opportunities for us to come into contact with each other because I would be living in Detroit with my mother, and Neil would be in New York with my father.

Technically, we might have been required to see each other if our parents got married, but there were no plans for that. Thus, he and I were nothing; we led two separate lives, far away from each other.

Knowing that only made me more miserable, though, because deep down I really wished things were different. In my dreams, there was still the possibility of a second chance out there for us.

After we finished our tea, Matt and I decided to rewatch a movie I'd practically grown up with: *Notting Hill*. We'd actually found the DVD by chance in Grandma Lizzie's old things, and it was my father who suggested we put it on because he knew that Julia Roberts had always been my favorite actress.

"You've been a romantic since you were a little girl," he teased me, stretching out on the sofa.

"Or maybe I was just drawn in by Hugh Grant's charm?" I made myself comfortable on the other sofa, curling up under a plaid blanket. My father had said that the heating system was fine, but, earlier that day, we'd discovered that it actually was barely hanging on. We'd have to bundle up with woolen blankets and heavy pajamas.

"Julia Roberts is also quite charming. People say she has the most beautiful smile in the world, but I think that's crap," he grumbled with a silly look on his face. I regarded him, tilting my head slightly to one side, and gave a thoughtful frown.

"Why is it crap?" I asked.

"Because the beauty of a smile is a subjective thing. For me, the most beautiful smile in the world belongs to my daughter," he answered seriously, and I looked down before shifting my gaze to the movie. I tried to hide it, but the corners of my mouth curled up, and Matt must have seen because he immediately threw one of the pillows at my face, hitting me square in the nose.

I sat right up and glared at him while he pasted on an innocent look that made him seem more like a mischievous little boy than a man who was turning fifty.

A moment later, we both burst into laughter and then went back to watching the movie, only occasionally commenting on a scene. Matt dozed off about a half hour later, leaving me alone to thrill over elegant Anna and gentlemanly Will.

When the movie was over, I got up from the couch and took a look at Matt. He was fully dressed, but his shoulders were contracting involuntarily with little cold shivers. He'd left the blanket for me, so I picked it up and slowly draped it over him, careful not to wake him up. Matt grumbled something in his sleep, but, thankfully, he didn't wake up.

I checked my watch: It was eleven-thirty, and, at the stroke of midnight, his birthday would be over. I hadn't wished him happy birthday, nor had I given him anything beyond the gift of my company.

He'd said that was good enough for him, but, in that moment, I had a wild idea.

I went into what used to be my grandparents' bedroom and took a small wooden plaque out of one of the drawers. I grinned, knowing that I would find it there along with the wood-burning pen that my grandfather used for his hobby.

I moved to the kitchen and positioned myself at the kitchen island, then I thoroughly scrubbed the surface of the wood with a cloth so I could engrave words for Matt upon it. Maybe it wasn't a grand gesture, but it was the sincerest gift I'd ever given anyone in my entire life.

So I tried to focus as I imprecisely drew three simple words: "Love, Life, Family," along with my initials in the right corner of the plaque. Aesthetically, it wasn't the best result because I'd never etched wood before. I'd done my best to mimic the technique I'd seen my grandfather use, but it would have taken a lot more experience before I reached his skill level.

I was sure, however, that my father would understand the symbolism of the gift. So I went over to him and put the little wooden plaque on the coffee table in the living room. He would find it when he woke up.

I was careful not to make any noise and, when Matt groaned something sleepily, I flinched and whirled around to look at him, hoping I hadn't woken him up. I breathed a sigh of relief when I saw that he was still sound asleep and leaned in a little closer so I could adjust the blanket around his shoulders.

"Happy birthday," I whispered into his ear, then I pressed a soft kiss to his cheek before fleeing back to my room, embarrassed by my own actions.

....

The next morning, I lingered in bed, curled up under the warm blankets.

I rubbed my closed eyes with the back of one hand and yawned noisily. I was just about to fall back to sleep when strange sounds started filtering in from the living room, and I realized that Mia had arrived.

I felt around on the wooden nightstand for my phone, and I was surprised to see that it was already ten o'clock. My eyes flew open, and I shot out of bed like I was spring-loaded. In fact, I almost went sliding on the smooth floor in my polka-dotted wool socks.

I scratched my neck sleepily, realizing that I was going to have to open the door and walk down the entire hallway in my current disastrous condition if I wanted to use the toilet.

I crept up to the bathroom door, passing my fingers through my long, tangled hair, and swung it open without knocking. I was presented with Logan standing in front of the toilet, really focused on…

"Jesus Christ!" I shouted, immediately clapping one hand over my eyes while the other stayed tight on the doorknob. "Sorry! I didn't see anything!" I shut the door immediately and exhaled the breath I hadn't realized I was holding.

I considered what to do next: I could go back to my room and stay there for the rest of the day, or I could go meet up with the others in the living room, or I could wait for Logan to be done and go in there to get ready like I'd planned. The flush of the toilet made me lean toward the last option. Surely he was done now.

"Selene!" Logan grinned euphorically at me and gave me a big hug as he emerged from the bathroom. I was immobile, my brain still half-asleep and not very responsive but, when I finally registered that it was actually Logan who was hugging me, I returned the affectionate gesture. I could smell his familiar spicy scent. "I hope the Loch Ness Monster didn't freak you out; I really had to go."

Oh god. Was he seriously was talking about his…

"Logan!" I said loudly, finally managing a sincere smile. I absolutely wasn't going to keep talking about that joke, so, instead, I looked him over. He looked great with no crutches in sight. He towered over me; his long legs were straight and strong. His face was beaming and bruise-free.

"How… How are you?" he managed in a halting voice. "God, I really wanted to come see you in Detroit, but I only got off crutches a few days ago, and…" I shook my head and rested a hand on his arm.

He didn't have to apologize to me; we'd both been through a rough time recently. Logan had been far more present for me than his brother had been.

"It's all good, Logan. You've been spamming me with texts, remember?"

I teased, and he reddened, rubbing the back of his neck. It was cute—a big guy like him blushing. I could see why Alyssa was so gone for him. She was always telling me about their relationship and how special Logan was.

Cute or not, though, he was still blocking the bathroom doorway, so I glanced significantly between him and the door. I, too, had some pressing needs to attend to. Logan seemed to get my drift, shaking his head as he stepped aside to let me through.

"You do your thing; we have all day to talk. I'll just be in the other room." He began to leave but, after a few steps, returned and squeezed me again. "It's good to see you again," he said softly, giving me a sweet smile.

Still, I walked into the bathroom with a terrible, anxious feeling. After seeing Logan, I had begun to worry that Neil might actually be there as well.

Yes, Mia had called and told my dad yesterday that he probably wasn't coming, but what if he changed his mind? Neil was nothing if not unpredictable. A small part of me was convinced that he was going to ambush me.

I stared into my reflection in the mirror, resting my hands on either side of the sink just to have something to hold on to. I had no idea how I was going to react to seeing him. I might even pass out and look like an idiot.

I gripped the cold surface of the sink tighter, trying to soothe the burning sensation that was spreading across my chest. If Neil really were out there, was I seriously afraid to deal with him? I snapped myself out of it. I was angsting over a little phone call? What about him, then? Didn't I have plenty to say about his behavior as well?

Neil was the one who should have been worried because, of the two of us, his actions had been far more serious.

Lost in these thoughts, I washed my face and brushed my teeth before attempting to sort out my hair. My bangs covered my scar while the rest of my hair fell nearly to the seat of my pants. I made an attempt at detangling some of the knots but eventually gave up and left the bathroom, still in my tiger-print pajamas.

I knew Neil didn't like these; he'd always told me that.

What did he call them?

Oh yeah… "Horrible."

Well, I was going to show up in those "horrible" pj's just to make it clear to him that I didn't give a crap about his opinion.

I had to laugh at myself. All this pointless overthinking was only making me more nervous. So, instead, I decided to take the bull by the horns, get out of the bathroom and go find out if Neil had actually deigned to join us for the weekend.

I made my way to the kitchen with an uncertain stride, a battle raging inside me. The old me wanted to see him and greet him with kisses; the new me wanted nothing more than to hate him and forget all about it.

Neil caused all of this: anxiety, confusion, racing heart, and… I stopped.

I stopped midway through the living room when my eyes alighted upon a pair of broad shoulders covered in the bright red of a leather jacket. Everything inside me twisted. My heart inexplicably fell into my stomach, and my breath caught in my lungs at the exact moment when he, all six-plus-feet of him, turned to me. Holding a bag of…pistachios?

I cocked my head to one side and actually touched my chest like a dummy just to make sure my heart was still in there pumping because I could feel it everywhere but where it was supposed to be.

His eyes locked on mine, and I remained inexplicably frozen, admiring my nemesis.

I stared into golden eyes that, in that moment, turned to velvet. His full lips turned my brain to mush, and his powerful body sent a voluptuous shiver of pleasure down to my lower stomach, and I blushed.

His eyes moved down to assess my outfit, polka-dotted socks included. Meanwhile, I studied his light brown hair, gently tousled on top and short on the sides.

His hair looked longer than the last time I'd seen him, and I wanted to run my fingers through it. Somehow, Neil was even more attractive than I'd remembered.

How many times had I imagined seeing him? How many times had I tried to relive our memories? But no mental reproduction of Neil could compare to the reality of seeing him right there, in the flesh, just a little ways away from me.

I met his eyes again, and he set down the bag of pistachios on the kitchen island. Then, he turned his attention to a few grocery bags right next to him that I hadn't noticed before. He pulled some cans out and put them away in the cupboard.

He practically ignored me, breaking our fleeting eye contract much sooner than I'd expected.

It occurred to me that if I wanted to get to the fridge for the carton of milk, I was going to have to get closer to him, but I didn't have the guts to take even one step in his direction. Instead, I continued to watch Neil like a patron of the arts encountering a particularly spectacular and imposing sculpture for the first time.

Everything about him seemed to cry pure sex appeal, despite the layers of clothing that covered him. His powerful neck exuded eroticism as it was exposed by the cut of his white sweatshirt. The muscles in his arms exuded eroticism as they jumped with every movement. His raised veins exuded eroticism as they ran along the back of his hands, proceeded along his wrist, and branched out through his body. His firm ass and masculine, well-favored legs exuded eroticism even wrapped in blue jeans. His curated stubble—perfect as the rest of his face—exuded eroticism as it shadowed his powerful jaw. With all of those features, Neil didn't need to show an inch of skin to inspire one particular feeling in women: desire.

"Are you going to just keep standing there, or are you going to give me a hand?"

I sucked in a breath at his voice, a firm baritone that simultaneously scraped my skin and caressed my senses. I watched as his eyes trailed down to my pajamas. He tried to hide the sensual smile that only made him more undeniably attractive, and I immediately knew what he was thinking.

He thought I was preposterous.

"What are you smirking about?" I finally asked. I didn't sound as hostile as I would have liked, but at least I didn't stammer. Neil rested his hands on the kitchen island and leaned forward slightly, exposing the muscled perfection he hid under his sweater. My eyes luxuriated in his amber skin and, for a few moments, I didn't need to blink.

The irritating chaos in my stomach once again made me give up on leaving the spot where, apparently, I had taken root. I no longer felt hungry, and I'd lost the ability to move my body, so now discomfort was the strongest thing I felt.

Neil rounded the island, and, as he did, I realized I wouldn't be able to handle it if he got too close to me. I had never understood why he had such a devastating effect on me but I was acutely aware of the fact that this human disaster had the accursed ability to enchant me completely.

He approached me slowly and then stopped. I leaned my head back to shift my stare from his chest to his lush lips to the bewitching eyes that were, in turn, staring fixedly at my face. At my forehead, to be precise.

I breathed in his smell, the same one that had invaded all the space around us. The same one I'd sensed in the hospital. The same one he left on me every time we made love.

Then he raised a hand to push aside my bangs and get a look at my scar. "It's hardly noticeable," he said. I should have backed up, slapped his hand away, or hurled some insult at him, but instead…

All I could think about was how much I had missed his touch.

I was near tears because the emotions of the moment were overwhelming and they were beating back my good sense.

After a moment, though, I was able to break the trance and get up the nerve to step back. I couldn't help but notice that he looked as disappointed as I did.

Just as a little part of me had expected, Neil was right there in front of me, and now I needed to keep my wits about me and not lose focus. I needed to understand what had really gone on between us.

"Don't touch me," I ordered, harsh and assertive.

Neil frowned and retreated without giving any hint of what he was thinking.

For my part, I wanted to make sure that he understood he couldn't work his magic on me the way he did on all the other women.

He'd ghosted me without so much as a single text or call.

"I just wanted…" He positioned himself behind the kitchen island, and I could breathe again. "I wanted to see how you're doing." He grasped a jar of Nutella in one hand and turned away from me to put it in the cupboard.

He looked tense now and irritated. Still holding my body stiff, I approached him in tiny steps, careful to maintain a distinct distance between us.

I didn't trust myself nor the feelings I had whenever our eyes intersected.

Did he really want to know how I was doing?

Did he just now think of it?

"Bit late to be asking, don't you think? You haven't called or even sent a single text to suggest you were concerned about me!" I said. "Not a single one, Neil," I repeated.

All my insecurity had vanished to make way for the anger that I'd been trying to suppress for days now.

Neil narrowed his eyes until they looked like two smoldering blades, and then he gave me a mocking smile.

"I've been busy," he volleyed back arrogantly. Then he just went back to stowing the groceries in the cupboards and pretended that I wasn't even there.

"For sure, you were busy. I can only imagine the kind of commitments you had. And, after all, I'm nothing and no one to you!" I snapped.

I couldn't even recognize myself. No longer was I the reasonable, docile girl who would never raise her voice at anyone. Neil turned to face me, and the icy glare he sent my way was nothing short of terrifying. Still, I held his gaze confidently and stared him down.

Something seemed to waver inside him. It looked to me like his typical arrogant disregard was getting mixed up with something else.

"Selene," he said softly, and he looked pained. He bit down slightly on his lower lip, and I wondered how many other girls had kissed him since we'd last met. How many had touched and stroked him?

My self-assurance was wavering, getting ready to abandon me to my true emotions.

And what was it that I really felt? Jealousy.

Mostly, I pitied myself. How could I be jealous over a man who didn't even belong to me? And yet…

My gaze sank down to the floor. It was too hard for me just then to hold his stare.

"You really don't get it," he continued. A few seconds later, I could feel him standing in front of me again. I didn't bother lifting my face to look. The smell of him declared his proximity.

"I do get it, though. You don't care about me." I was confident in the words, but my voice trembled, and he grabbed my chin, lifting it until my eyes were forced to lock on his.

I let him do it.

I read sincere shock in his golden eyes along with a tumultuous darkness that made me go weak in the knees.

And maybe dying would have hurt less.

Could you be hurt just from looking into a man's eyes?

"Is that what you think?" he murmured in surprise.

"Could I think otherwise?" I asked challengingly.

His stare shifted to my lips, and the suffering that flickered across his face made me feel terribly guilty.

How could he turn the tables on me so easily?

I was the one who had been let down and was angry; I was the one who was hurt.

"You know what I could do?" He caressed my chin with his thumb and gave me a sad smile. "I could tell you just how much of the sky you took away with you on the day you left, Tinkerbell. But that wouldn't do anything to change the situation."

Neil was so good at sowing chaos in my head with just a few cryptic words, and he was so good at seducing women in general. And yet...

Wait a minute.

He had called me Tinkerbell.

So I was still Tinkerbell to him? Like we'd never even parted? In that moment, he looked so sincere that it brought tears to my eyes.

"Do you remember when I told you that I only wanted to fly in your sky?" he continued, transporting me back in time. It happened in my room—my bathroom, specifically. And of course I remembered it. I remembered everything about the two of us.

"I wasn't lying to you. I never lied to you." He licked his bottom lip uncomfortably. I could see how hard it was for him to talk like this with me.

We were silent together for a few seconds, but I knew that moment of peace would be followed by something awful.

"But?" I prompted him because I knew he was about to tell me more.

Neil looked at my lips again with those voracious eyes that could bite so deep without ever touching me, and, for a moment, I had the sensation of him on my tongue. Stinging and masculine.

"But…I can't." He pulled back, away from me, and took with him the warmth he'd spread to me through that light touch.

His right hand shook slightly before raising up to rumple his hair.

He always did that when he was nervous.

"What do you mean you can't? Why can't you?" I threw up my hands in exasperation. He could have meant so many things: kissing me, touching me, getting close to me, telling me the truth.

"I just can't, Selene. There's no why." He was starting to get pissed off; I could tell by the fluctuations in his voice and the way his whole body tensed up.

"We can't make the same mistakes all over again. You left because you wanted to leave. Do you understand me?" he asked, getting in my face, and I took a step back. Reasoning with Neil was impossible when he got angry like that. His reaction to this conversation was starting to get dangerous, and, after what my father had told me, I was even more acutely aware that I needed to take care in my every word and action so I did not provoke him.

"And do you understand that you're contradicting yourself? What is your actual problem? Are you afraid to give up the other women because you don't have the guts to actually tell me that you want me?" I demanded, feigning like I fully understood the motivation behind his attitude.

Neil just glared furiously at me, though. I tried to back away, but he was faster and caught me by the arm. He loomed over me, making me feel about as big as an ant. I felt both hot and cold where his fingers were gripping me, and I tried uselessly to pull away.

"You're hurting me," I whispered, feeling tears bead on my eyelashes.

"Do you not understand that I would have enjoyed fucking you with Jennifer? I wanted to use you. Both of you. First one and then the other, or maybe at the same time. The only thing that mattered to me was feeling good," he said with a dark power that made me tremble. He was so close to me; I could feel the warmth of his breath. The sense of awe mixed with dread was devastating. Neil was dominating me once again, exerting his unstoppable power over me, and I tried to fight back, not even thinking about what I was saying.

"You're sick in the head!" I shouted.

One sentence and the world went to pieces around us.

Immediately, I regretted it and tried to communicate that to him with a look because I didn't even have the guts to take a breath, let alone speak.

Neil stared intensely at me, first surprised and then confused. He began to breathe noisily through his nose, hatred injected into his stare; his face transformed into a mask of pure fury. If he had looked at himself in the mirror, he never would have recognized himself in the grip of such rage.

"What did you say?" he demanded menacingly, though I knew he'd heard me perfectly well.

I continued to look fearfully at him, admitting my defeat. I had lost the ability to form words—or even thoughts—by that point. In that moment, all of my attention was drawn as if by a magnet to his grip on my arm, which was becoming increasingly hard and painful. Neil looked into my eyes and saw the fear that, like a rapacious demon, had possessed every part of me. In a moment of clarity, he released me and took a step back, scrubbing a hand over his face.

He began to babble nonsense, maybe at me, maybe at someone else who wasn't there. And I truly understood then just how shadowed and tortured his soul really was, trapped inside a deceptively perfect body.

"Fuck!" he shouted abruptly, kicking a kitchen stool to the floor and making me jump. It occurred to me that I had just triggered a bomb that was primed for explosion.

"What's going on in here?" Logan, drawn by the ruckus, burst through the front door and ran to me. He looked from my terrified face to his brother and said again, "Neil, what the hell's going on?"

As he spoke, he tried to wrap an arm around my shoulders, but I pushed it off and freed myself from him as well.

All of a sudden, I felt confused and afraid.

135

"Ask this cunt!" He was railing against me with a previously undiscovered level of anger. Wasn't I the one who should be feeling let down and outraged here?

"She told me I was sick in the head, did you hear that? Sick in the head!" he shouted and then bellowed a laugh full of scorn. "Fuck!" he yelled again, continuing to vent his anger on nearby objects and making me flinch away again.

I squeezed my eyes shut, not wanting to look. I didn't want to see him. I tried to block out the powerful shouts, the violent movements, and the deafening noise. I covered my ears and began shaking like a leaf.

"Enough, now get out of here! You need to calm down!" Logan came to my defense, and I slowly opened my eyes.

"I didn't even want to come here! Fuck all of you!" Neil spit instead, heading for the door. When he left, he slammed it violently behind him.

I remained curled up tightly on the floor even after he was gone, sobs shaking my shoulders and shivers running through my entire body. Tears slid down my cheeks, wetting my neck. I wiped them away with the back of my hands and kept weeping.

"Hey, Selene." Logan's gentle voice caught my attention, but I couldn't look at him.

I tried to regulate my breathing. I'd never had a reaction like this before in my life. I was still traumatized from the accident, though, so everything was amplified for me.

"You really hit a sore spot there." Logan tried to push a bit of hair out of my face, but I inched away from him. He sighed instead and sat down cross-legged on the floor next to me.

"I didn't mean to hurt his feelings..." I mumbled, rubbing my still-moist eyes. It was frightening as well as disappointing—the idea that Neil was a man as well as a beast.

"He's not evil, Selene. He's just afraid of life. You have no idea what he's been through," Logan explained, and I stared at him, trying to suss out more. I had long felt that Neil probably experienced something terrible when he was a child, but no one would give me any concrete answers about it.

"So tell me, Logan. You, at least..." I begged. "Why won't anyone help me understand?" I sobbed, and Logan looked shaken, horrified by the whole situation. Could he help me pin down exactly what had just happened between me and his brother? To understand why he behaved the way he did?

"In his own way, Neil cares about you, Selene…" He paused, giving me a moment to absorb these words. A sudden moment of vertigo made me rub my forehead. My heart felt like it was going wild but I listened carefully as Logan continued to speak. "In his mind, he was just using you, but you know that's not how it really was. He was never just using you. He only thinks that way because, for him, sex is about reducing women to objects. The way his brain works… It's not like ours," he added, searching my face for a reaction.

"Not like ours?" I whispered breathlessly. It was hard to speak; crying had taken all of my energy. Logan licked his lower lip and considered for a moment before continuing. The pause only made me feel more anxious because I knew that whatever I was about to find out, I wasn't going to like it.

"No. There was a woman in the past who really damaged him. It wasn't just a physical hurt; a lot of it was psychological. He was just a little kid when she… She…" He stopped and shook his head. "It isn't for me to tell you this; it'd be disrespectful of him. He'll tell you when he's ready," he said, and my spirit broke. Logan didn't even need to continue, I realized. I pulled my knees up against my chest and wrapped my arms around them, saying nothing. Deep down, I think I had always known, but, until the very last minute, I'd tried to ignore the signs.

The dots connected. The world finally made sense.

The showers, the way he treated women like things, and his distrust of the entire human race.

All of it.

I had seen everything, but I had persistently pushed away every awful premonition, every guess, every unthinkable hypothesis, because I didn't want to believe it.

He had been raped. By a woman.

Just imagining him, small and defenseless, fighting against that kind of monster, was unbearably painful. It was hard to breathe, and, all at once, I thought about the secret room, the one that was always kept locked. I thought about the newspapers in there that I'd managed to catch a glimpse of, talking about a "scandal."

How long had Neil's torment gone on? How old was he? Why had the article referred to child*ren*? Had it been some kind of group? What had really gone on?

I still had too many unresolved problems, too many unanswered questions.

Logan had done nothing but confirm a suspicion that I had long been suppressing deep down in my soul. This was not an unexpected discovery. Still, in the case of Neil, I knew there was still more concealed. Who knew what he had been forced to endure? I felt so stupid and insensitive.

Neil…

I wanted to run after him and hold him in my arms and comfort him, whispering to him that everything was going to be okay and that the world and the people in it still had good parts. And that I would prove it to him.

Logan sat next to me the whole time, watching me collapse.

Sadness fell over me like a shadow, my saliva tasted bitter in my mouth and I began staring off into the middle distance. It felt like I could see an apparition of the evil that a little boy was forced to live through, imposed on him by a mentally deranged woman.

Evil: There was no other way to define it.

It felt like time was suspended between our breaths, between our silent musings and unspoken questions…

....

Matt and Mia returned an hour later. They'd taken Chloe for a stroll around the town while I stayed with Logan.

By then, we were sitting out on the wooden benches on the porch. Neil, meanwhile, had vanished after our short but furious argument. I was hoping he'd come back because I wanted to apologize to him and clear the air.

"How are you feeling?" Logan asked. He was worried about me while all I could worry about was Neil.

He'd run away because I made him feel *wrong*. My hasty words had reopened a wound in him that no one could heal, least of all myself.

For a moment, I considered the immensity of his struggles, and I wondered if I'd ever be strong enough to stand by his side.

Neil was afraid to form attachments to other people because he perceived them as a danger to him. That was why he'd tried so hard to push me away. He'd shown me the degenerate part of himself, intending to scare me off. After my accident, he had refused to visit me in Detroit on purpose. Neil didn't want me deluding myself into thinking he might fall in love with me.

After all, how could he possibly believe in love after living through hell like he had?

For him, love was not salvation but ruination and that was why an actual relationship between us would have been impossible.

"*I don't love,*" he'd told me once in one of our first conversations, and now I understood why. Neil would have to learn how to accept himself, to understand that he had so much more to offer than just his body. Then and only then would he—possibly—be able to be with someone.

"I'm worried about him, Logan," I said for the thousandth time.

I'd been so self-absorbed, thinking about myself all the time, about the attention I wanted and wasn't getting from Neil. I never stopped to think about why he was so afraid to feel human emotions. "I got it all wrong, right from the start." Now more than ever, I knew that by pressuring him, I'd only pushed him further away from me.

"You didn't know," Logan answered with his characteristic kindness, just trying to make me feel better.

"I did, though. I saw all the signs, but I refused to put it together…" I swallowed hard as I recalled how Neil had manhandled me in my bedroom the night Jared visited. The way he'd grabbed me by the hair, his brutal, ferocious thrusts, how he couldn't stop staring at the place where we were conjoined. The way he chased his orgasm as though I weren't pinned underneath him, taking every harsh stroke. His eyes had been so cold and vacant then; I had known that there was some kind of war going on inside him. A war that he'd been fighting for who knew how many years.

Even when I'd caught him with Jennifer and Alexia, I'd never seen him look engaged. He was always impersonal, unflappable, and serious, with no look of pleasure or sexual satisfaction on his face.

"No one is ever ready to face that kind of truth," Logan said, staring out into space.

It occurred to me then why Neil was so attached to Logan. He had such a strong bond with his siblings because what he felt for them was the only real form of love he knew.

"Who else knows about it?" I ventured.

"Just us and now you. Neil's very private; he never talks about it with anyone. He barely talks about it with me," he said, and other, sharper questions began to form in my mind.

Where was his abuser?

She was a psychopath. A demon. A monster.

"And she is...?" I wanted to say "dead" and hoped with all my heart that was the case. Looking into Logan's eyes, I knew he could see the rage I was feeling.

"She was committed to a psychiatric facility in South Carolina," Logan said, intuiting the information I needed.

As he spoke, a frosty wind whipped through the air, and the water grew restless. It was as though by speaking of the devil, we had summoned him, and even the natural world moved at his command.

"What's her name?" I pushed a little harder, chewing on my lower lip. I was afraid that Logan would tell me to quit sticking my nose in at any moment, but he didn't.

"Kimberly Bennett," he said softly, and I immediately committed the name to memory.

I had no idea what to do now that I had some of the answers I'd sought, but I was pretty sure that remembering that woman's name was going to be useful at some point.

I was probably going to spend hours thinking about Neil and about what Logan had told me, but one thing I already knew for sure: What I felt for him wasn't sympathy or pity.

In fact, knowing his nature and how strong he was, I was positive that the last thing he wanted was pity. Neil would never have accepted a woman feeling sorry for him. He would have pushed her away immediately.

What I did feel, however, was a profound anger toward Kimberly and a new understanding of Neil. But my opinion of him had not changed at all. If anything, I found him even more remote than before. If I'd imagined it would be hard to wriggle my way into his soul before, this new knowledge just made it more complicated. Neil wasn't simply some gorgeous, mysterious bad boy, gifted with a volatile charisma that drew women like flies. He was, above all else, untouchable.

I feared I wasn't up to the challenge he presented, but, at the same time, the thought of abandoning him never even crossed my mind.

"He likes you. You know that, right?" Logan cut off my train of thought, drawing my gaze back to him.

Me? He liked me?

My palms began to sweat, and I felt a strange sort of unrest inside me. I wasn't sure whether to be flattered or afraid.

"And you really like him too," Logan added, a knowing look on his face.

I didn't answer him but just looked away, trying to hide the sudden flush in my cheeks. Neil was the only one who could shatter me and then put all my pieces back together. All I had to do was look into his honey-colored eyes, and I felt the earth move beneath me. Indisputably, he was the sort of man who got into one's soul, fusing sex and longing together and creating the most depraved ideas in even the purest of hearts.

Still, I didn't have the wherewithal to confirm Logan's assertion.

....

We were having a cookout for lunch, and I decided to join the family, though I still wasn't done ruminating on everything that had happened. As I stood there watching Logan help my dad with the grill, I tried to smile and look cheerful. The two of them squabbled constantly, and I watched them in amusement, trying to chase away my sadness.

"I could have done it on my own," Logan grumbled as Matt continued to offer him advice in a know-it-all tone.

"That's what he always says, but it's never true," Chloe murmured in my ear, making me snicker.

"Hey, I heard that," Logan shot back, giving her a dirty look.

I had missed the youngest Miller. Even more than that, I had missed the understanding that had developed between us. I looked over at her only to see her looking back at me with a strange softness in her eyes. I couldn't help but notice that her eyes were the exact same shade as the sky. They, along with her bright hair, made her look a great deal like her mother. Her facial features were elegant, just like Logan's and Neil's were. Beauty ran in the family.

Before we sat down to eat, Mia and I busied ourselves with setting the table and prepping various side dishes. Matt and Logan focused on grilling the sausages.

"Where'd Neil go?" Mia put a bottle of wine out on the table and glanced around, looking for her eldest son. It was my fault—my words that had driven him away. I was uncomfortable, afraid to look his mother in the eye. I was afraid she would see the guilt that was twisting my stomach in knots.

"Maybe he went down to the water?" Chloe suggested. Logan gave me a fleeting glance that only made me feel more ill at ease.

Did he also think this was all my fault?

"If you want, I can go look for him," I offered abruptly, which drew my father's attention.

"No, he'll be back soon. He's probably out exploring the local offerings," Matt said lightly before sitting down next to me and rubbing my shoulder. "I found your present. That was a lovely thing to do; thank you so much."

He pressed a kiss to my temple, and I smiled awkwardly, still unused to these weird displays of affection between us.

Then we went ahead without Neil. Logan tried calling him, but he didn't answer, and, at that point, Mia said there was no reason to wait for him, and he'd probably be home later. Logan and I exchanged looks of pure concern.

After lunch, I occupied myself with the dishes and exchanged a few words with Mia. But my thoughts revolved around just one person: her son.

It was ridiculous to be so upset over a man who had absolutely no qualms about hurting me, but deep down, I felt like his behavior had some justification now.

I was lost in thought, basically polishing a glass for almost ten minutes, when Mia called my name and asked me if something was wrong. I was capable of wrangling my emotions, though, and said that I was fine except for a headache, which I'd invented to avoid arousing suspicions. I didn't like lying to her, but I could hardly tell her all about what happened with Neil. I couldn't tell her, and I certainly couldn't tell my dad.

After finishing the cleanup, I ducked into the bathroom for a quick shower. This time, I washed my hair and untangled the knots before drying it. I smoothed it with my fingers and smiled at how soft and silky it finally was. Then I stretched out on the bed in a desperate attempt to get some rest.

I spent the rest of the afternoon like that, immersed in total solitude. When it was time for dinner, Matt suggested the whole family spend the evening on the beach around a bonfire. The idea was appealing to me despite my grim mood. I really needed a distraction, even if it was impossible to completely banish my worries.

So I crawled out of bed and decided to put on something warm because of the cold temperatures. In addition to my dark-wash jeans, I chose a long-sleeved shirt and layered a pink hoodie on over that. I dabbed a couple drops of perfume on my neck and put on a little mascara, making my blue eyes pop.

On some level, I was probably trying to look cute for Neil, to get him to notice me. But I didn't think too deeply about that because it wasn't the time for those thoughts.

I still wasn't convinced by Logan's words, "*He likes you.*"

Maybe he'd been attracted to me at one time, as he had been with who knew how many other women, but I could never be part of his life.

I stopped on my way to the living room when the sounds of Coldplay drifting through a half-open door caught my attention. I frowned, getting closer until I could pick out the melody of "The Scientist," one of my favorite songs. I rested one hand on the lacquered surface of the door and pushed it in, invading a space I shouldn't even have stepped foot inside.

My heart jumped into my throat when I spotted Neil on the bed, focused on sketching in his notebook. I paused to admire the silhouette of his profile. A lit cigarette was clamped between his full lips, and his eyes intently tracked the movement of his hand as it scrawled lines on the paper.

He wore a basic black sweatshirt and a pair of sweatpants. His sculpted body was tantalizing, making me long to tear off those clothes and rediscover all the feelings his expert hands could evoke.

He was so beautiful.

I blushed stupidly at the direction my thoughts had taken. I'd never fantasized about a man like that before I met him.

"You like Coldplay, too?" I asked, all in one breath, hoping to impress him.

Of course, that was a great way to get his attention.

I'd made him go ballistic earlier, and now I was trying to make up for that with something that sounded like a lame pickup line.

Neil turned to look at me, but he didn't seem at all surprised to see me there. It was as though he knew perfectly well how long I'd been standing there in the doorway, spying on him in a daze. His golden eyes roamed slowly and intimidatingly over me. Then he plucked the cigarette from his mouth with two fingers before releasing a cloud of smoke into the air.

He did it in such a confrontational fashion that it made me go stiff. Even God's most devoted angel would have sold their soul, I thought, just for a little taste of that warm, powerful, statuesque body.

"What do you want?" he asked, his voice calm but unyielding. That wasn't a good sign—he was still mad.

I took a few steps into the room, despite the fact that I was wringing my hands like a kid who'd seriously screwed up. I took a deep breath before I spoke.

"I would like to apologize for… Well…this morning." I glanced down at his phone, which he'd plugged into a portable speaker, and my forehead wrinkled thoughtfully. Was Coldplay on his playlist, or had the song just come up on shuffle? A small, insane part of me hoped he had actually chosen to listen to them because they were my favorite band.

Shaken, I tucked a bit of hair behind my ear before turning my attention to him once again. He stared back at me, his authoritative gaze making me feel small and inadequate. His self-assurance and dominating presence were lethal weapons as far as I was concerned.

"I've got no use for your apologies. Piss off," he snapped, returning to his sketch.

His eyes narrowed at the thick wafts of cigarette smoke rising up around him, and it made him look appealing and snarky at the same time. He had a nasty temper, and I knew that I shouldn't be challenging him. Still, I cleared my throat and tried again.

"I didn't mean to hurt you, Neil. You have to believe me," I admitted. My voice had turned pleading, but he didn't respond. He remained seated, ignoring me with his familiar arrogant disregard.

Oh, he was good at that.

He was amazing at making a woman feel insignificant. It was probably his greatest gift, after the way he looked.

If I'd listened to my pride, I would have walked away. Instead, I reminded myself of what Logan had confided in me, and every bit of my anger evaporated. It was impossible to stay mad at Neil after those revelations.

"Neil…" I said in a placating voice as I ran a hand through my hair. The knowledge of what he'd been through made me profoundly uncomfortable and had me reflecting back on everything I'd done since we met. I had complained constantly about Matt and about my parents' divorce, while Neil had never complained about anything, despite having firsthand experience with something truly horrific. The kind of thing that rendered all my supposed "problems" null.

"You said what you were thinking. That's fine." He closed his notebook with a snap and tossed it on the bed, sitting up. "Now I want you to get lost. Do you get that, or do I need to draw you a fucking picture?" he asked, aggressive and insensitive.

So I was no longer his Tinkerbell, and it was all my fault.

He crushed his cigarette butt into an ashtray on his bedside table and stood up. Even from a distance, there was a grandness about him that intimidated me. And after the way he'd reacted this morning, I didn't want to get into another fight with him. I turned my attention to the open bag of pistachios next to the ashtray, trying to escape his uncompromising gaze.

Since when was he so into pistachios? Was that the only thing he'd eaten all day?

It felt like all of a sudden I was noticing things about him that I'd never even thought about in New York. I even wanted to know what other kinds of foods he liked.

"I didn't mean it, though. I only said that about you because you were talking about Jennifer, and whenever you talk about her or I see the two of you together, I can't think straight. I don't want to remember how I felt in that room on Halloween…" I admitted, filled with the utmost sincerity. I wasn't there to play games or get him in bed the way everyone else was. I was there because I was ready to know him.

Reserved and wary as always, Neil regarded me silently before slowly approaching.

No, no, no. Why couldn't he just stand over there? At least then I would have been able to think clearly. Instead, his proximity was bewildering me and putting me on my back foot.

He stopped right in front of me, and his smell, so intensely erotic, wrapped all around me.

And that was enough to have me falling back into uncertainty.

I was irreparably drawn to that man and his doomed aura. I truly couldn't help it.

"But you realize I am sick in the head, though?" A derisive smile warped his plush lips, and I wrinkled my forehead in confusion.

"What?"

"You heard me," he said severely. "I live every day with an abnormal, alarming lack of mental stability. You should pick some other man to spend your time with," he added, sounding amused and wearing a no-fucks-given smile. I still didn't know what the hell he was trying to say, but I felt completely overcome by the way his eyes were locked on my lips.

"But what if that's what I like about you? Your difference?" I crooned the last word, and he frowned, cocking his head to one side.

God, but it was marvelous when he looked at me like that.

"Besides, I'm not afraid of your possible imbalance," I whisper decisively, even though, deep down, I was very afraid of it. But that wasn't going to stop me from getting closer to him.

"You should be furious at me right now. Everything I've said and done to you…" He inched forward, and the smell of him reminded me how much I loved the musky scent he wore, so fresh and sharp. I could have backed up

146

or even walked away entirely, but I just stood there, waiting for him to touch me. Like there was nothing my body wanted more.

"I should, yes. But I'm not anymore." I smiled slightly, because now I understood the fears that lurked behind his every word and action. From now on, I would seek to understand him without letting him bring me to heel. Neil was a master of exerting control, and the line between accommodating him and being subjugated by him could get very thin.

"What do you want from me, Selene?" He searched my face for an answer. I didn't take my eyes off his—so bright, so unique, and so very close to me.

He traced every line of my face as his lips curled into a knowing smile. The smile of a predator sizing up his prey.

As his gaze moved to my lips, staring at them for seconds on end, a jolt of electricity passed from my chest to the bottom of my stomach. My heart turned to paper in an instant, and he could have crumpled it in his fist if that's what he'd wanted to do.

What were we?

What had we been?

We weren't a *we*, but we were something.

There was no category, no label, no definition that could be given to us.

We were what we were. Not everything, perhaps, but certainly not *nothing*.

I tried to think of a reasonable answer to give him. I needed to be careful because I didn't want him to realize that Logan had talked to me. I didn't want him getting mad at his brother for giving me a piece of Neil's past.

"I asked you a question." He wet his lower lip, and I quivered at his deep, authoritative voice.

Instead of answering him, I allowed myself to get lost in the flawless little details of his face, forgetting about everything else.

I was enchanted by the flickers of guile that lit up his eyes like fireworks. Neil knew he could make me vulnerable.

He could feel it.

He could also feel my desire for him, so he inched even closer to me, and I took one step back and then another until my back ran into the door behind me.

"I just want you to know that I want you. Just as much as you want me." I tried to sound self-assured, but I was shaking.

Neil struggled to contain a laugh, digging his straight, white teeth into his lower lip and looking at me like I was deranged.

"You have no idea how it would be, being with someone like me. Do you?" He took another step forward, and his powerful scent was dizzying.

"Where would you be if you could be anywhere right now?" he asked me abruptly, breathing right against my face. He rested an elbow on the wall beside my head and adopted a careless stance over me. Then he examined me from top to bottom, going slow, like I was the most beautiful creature he had ever seen. I could see the gleam of carnal desire in his eyes.

I barely came up to his chest, and my eyes moved from the outline of his pectoral muscles to his powerful throat. I wanted to put my lips there and taste his skin.

"Anywhere, as long as you're there too," I managed, staring up at him from under my eyelashes. Neil smiled smugly and stroked my right hip with his hand.

I gasped.

I wanted him to touch me, but I was afraid to give in to him again. For an endless moment, I looked at his hypnotic face and came to a familiar conclusion: Neil was dangerous.

And yet, I continued to take that risk because, deep down, I was attracted to the danger. I would have allowed his fire to burn every part of me.

"You are sickeningly sweet when you say shit like that."

He wrinkled his nose in disappointment. "But more importantly..." His hand crept slowly up my rib cage, lingering under the curve of my right breast. He bent his face to my ear, and his warm breath brushed against the arc of my neck. "That's not the right answer, baby." He stared into my eyes, and I drowned in his, now heavy with lust.

I tracked the way he licked his full lips, his muscular chest rising rapidly under the sweatshirt that hung from the sculpted edges of his body as he gently rubbed my breast.

My heart was hammering so hard in my chest that I feared he would hear it, and my breath was labored just from that light yet dominating touch. Neil began to stroke my throat with the tip of his nose. Tiny shivers ran down my arms and spine.

He was like a powerful storm breaking against me: His fingers were the lightning that accompanied the thunder, his gaze covered me like the darkened sky, and his every touch fell upon me like drops of rain.

He inhaled my perfume deeply before resting his forehead against mine, closing his eyes.

"Stop trembling," he whispered. I tried to calm myself down, but all I wanted was for him to put his hands on me. That was why I was in his room, after all—to let him use me.

Neil apparently didn't intend to do that, however.

"I'm not going to touch you," he said reassuringly. He opened his eyes slowly until I could see his silent consideration.

Why not?

I was oddly disappointed and ashamed of myself for being disappointed. I—yes, I—had wanted him to...

"I feel it. You know that, right? I feel how you want me. I feel how aroused you are, but I also feel how scared you are," he murmured under his breath, pressing warm lips to my forehead. He gave me a soft kiss and then slowly ran his mouth along the bridge of my nose. He paused at the tip and left another kiss there, followed by a tiny nip that made me smile. "It's always been this way between us, since the very beginning..." he continued softly. His lips touched mine delicately, and I breathed in his smoke-flavored breath.

Neil was seducing me. He would make me crave that kiss with everything I had until I was even dreaming about it.

He was simply letting me know who was in charge between us.

"I've wanted you since day one. That has never changed, and it will never change. I have no idea how I'm going to deal with this fucking situation." He hovered over my throat, and there too he allowed his lips to glide briefly over my skin. A fiery current ran down my spine: the overwhelming desire to let him simply take whatever he wanted from me. I went stiff.

I felt like I was losing my mind, but I knew that Neil was going to torment me until he decided he was satisfied. Still, I couldn't cope with the crescendoing sensations, caresses, and desires. I had to let him know how much I wanted him.

I leaned in instinctively, but Neil pulled back slightly with a smile of delight that had me pouting immediately.

"You want to kiss me? Is that what you want?"

I didn't answer but just stared at his throat again, at the single sliver of naked skin that I could see above his sweatshirt.

Then he put his other elbow on the opposite side of my head and allowed his torso to press ever so slightly against my chest. When he leaned into me, I could feel his swollen erection against my lower abdomen, and I went red.

The thought of being trapped between his well-formed body and the cold surface of the flimsy door was thrilling.

"You've become such a wicked girl. Here you are, wanting to kiss a sicko… But are you sure he wants to kiss you back?" he whispered, laughing, and I swallowed hard, embarrassed. The lusty, carnal sound of his voice did nothing but set fire to the good sense that I was trying to hold on to, the gulf between us that I was trying to avoid showing him. But Neil wanted to annihilate me with his allure, seduce me with his expertise, enchant me with his voice.

"If you don't want to kiss me, then you should walk away right now."

In that moment, I found the strength to push back against him, to regain some semblance of clarity. Neil chewed his lip, more entertained than ever by my reaction, and I pressed a hand to the heart that would not stop thumping uncontrollably inside me.

"Selene! Neil! Where are you? Come on out to the fire!" Logan's voice from the hallway interrupted that insane moment of…of… I didn't even know how to define it. I jumped away from the door and glanced at Neil, who, from the look on his face, was not nearly as disturbed as I was.

This man had managed to set me off on a sensual journey without even undressing.

I stared at him, got lost roaming over the map of his body. Every contour was evidence of a life lived without limits. The defined edges made one hope for impossible things. Those golden eyes were an open road out onto a vast, undiscovered desert.

His face was a model of human perfection and I would have done anything to hold his soul.

Short of breath and feeling a familiar heat spreading throughout my body, I hurried out of the room and away from him.

7

··

I wanted more, especially from her.

NEIL

S ick in the head.
     That was what Selene had called me.

As usual, I couldn't control myself when my brain went foggy. That girl needed to keep that in mind if she wanted to avoid similarly heated arguments in the future.

I knew she'd clocked my frequent, strange, and inconsistent behavior in the past, but I wasn't expecting to hear her say something like that.

She hit the fucking nail on the head.

Like I didn't already know I was sick.

And what about her? Did she actually know? Or had she just been talking out of her ass? Had she figured it out?

In any event, I'd never have the guts to talk to her about my history. I'd never talked to anyone about it, in fact, outside of my family and Dr. Lively.

What was I supposed to tell her? That a grown woman abused me? That I'd been subjected not only to physical violence but also the emotional and psychological kind? That what I had gone through made me essentially dysfunctional in any human relationship?

Kimberly had exercised her power over me, a type of possession that had turned me into nothing but an object.

I was nothing to her and, even now, I still felt like my body was worthless, just like it had been back then.

I couldn't "talk" to Selene the way she wanted because, in my mind, there was only one form of communication: sex. My body, my corporeality, was the only way I had of seeking peace or relief. I could never have had a normal relationship with her.

And that was the problem.

Sooner or later, Babygirl would have demanded a real relationship with me. But she was absolutely perfect, and she deserved better than a man who still lived cheek to jowl with his fractured sense of self. Someone who lived with the memories of blackmail, humiliation, and the wordless violence inside him that nevertheless cried for vengeance.

That's why I had behaved so disrespectfully toward her. It was why I tried to make her feel inferior, to make it clear to her that she could never have me.

And she bolted away from that.

She bolted away from me while I just kept smiling like a total dick as I thought about how I'd made her so weak for me with just the slightest contact.

I rubbed my crotch, adjusting the hard-on that I'd had to force myself to keep in check when I had her pinned up against the door. What I should have done was ignore her completely—from the moment I sensed her presence to the moment I caught her peeping at me to the moment I got a whiff of her coconut scent. But, in the end, I gave up.

I gave up like a fool the moment my eyes met hers—blue as the ocean, deep and so pure that they triggered the kind of lustful thoughts I'd never had toward anyone else. All I had to do was glance at her for a moment, and I was longing to wipe that prim, little-girl look off her face. I wanted to strip her passionately, lick her everywhere, and touch her voraciously—I wanted to fuck her. I wanted with all the visceral desire surging inside me to fuck her.

I wanted more than some boring, childish fumbling because I was accustomed to lewd, filthy, perverse sex. I wanted to bend her over and dominate her completely. I wanted to take my pleasure from her, pounding into her right there against the door without so much as cursory foreplay. No sweet nothings or chivalrous compliments.

Just the way I always did it with everyone else.

Maybe with her I'd even achieve orgasm, as I hadn't in weeks.

I could have performed an experiment, but instead reason prevailed. Instead of taking it all from her, I restricted myself just to touching her and breathing her in. I was still pissed off from the morning—I hated how she'd thrown such a bitter truth in my face—but I also didn't want to use her like an object.

I wanted more, especially from her.

Because she was just a girl. My Babygirl, to be precise.

And it wouldn't have been fair to demand something she wasn't ready or wanting to give me. Like I'd told her, I felt her arousal and her fear as well. She wanted to kiss me, sure. But I could also see the terror in her eyes.

In the end, that was the same reason I wanted to push her away and why I hadn't gotten in contact with her after the accident—a choice that made me feel guilty—because I was still living with the fallout from what had been done to me. All I could do was perpetuate the same pain over and over again using a psychological mechanism that punished me but soothed the Boy.

That's why I didn't want her to get involved in my whole clusterfuck. The women I usually had sex with were always consenting—they agreed to use me and be used in return. But they weren't like Selene.

Lost in my musings, I stared at the door Babygirl had backed into during her weak escape attempt. I smiled again and ran a hand through my hair, still soft and damp from the three showers I'd taken. I'd need to take another right away, though, because that ordinary girl had me ready to erupt.

Under the spray of the water, I once again found myself lost in a vortex of my own thoughts. The world was full of girls like her. And yet, Tinkerbell was something rare as fuck.

She was so lovely, and she felt like a dream. So pure, she reawakened my desire every time.

She was beauty and pain at the same time, seductive and awful, like an angel was awful. She provoked awe.

She was the opposite of me.

It seemed impossible to me that fate had chosen this completely ordinary girl to test me, the boy who had been initiated into sexuality far too early, the one who had been with so many available and experienced women.

She had all my desires etched upon her in the incredible form and curves of her body, all of it coming together to create something larger than life.

Everything.

I wanted everything from her.

I wanted her ocean eyes and her perfect little nose. I wanted her lips, whether bent in a cheeky smirk or the dizzying smile that set the very air I breathed aflame. She was too much of everything, and I wanted her.

I wanted her underneath me as I rocked between her open thighs, losing myself in her heat and…

Fuck.

I needed to knock this off and start acting like a man who wasn't obsessed with her.

A normal man who wasn't constantly having sweet thoughts about her followed by depraved ones. And then more sweet ones, and then even more depraved ones…

I was having a hard time managing all these deranged feelings. I was losing my shit.

I huffed noisily and decided I needed to distract myself with something.

I got out of the shower and dressed quickly, throwing on black jeans and a black sweatshirt before heading out to join my family on the beach.

Matt had this idea that we should have a bonfire by the water, which sounded like bullshit to me, but I didn't say anything when he suggested it. We were there to celebrate his birthday, after all, and I didn't want to ruin it with my shitty mood.

I was feeling pent-up and frustrated.

I'd taken a "break" from the blonds I spent most of my time with because my therapist had told me to; otherwise, my sexual dysfunction would get worse. I certainly didn't want to get to the point of being unable to feel arousal or sexual urges. I'd quit picking up women for sex and taken a pass on more nasty scenes with Jennifer (or Jennifer and Alexia) and had instead focused on myself and what my body really needed.

A ceasefire.

A ceasefire on the self-inflicted violence I'd been putting my body through for years.

It wasn't easy, though, maintaining this self-imposed abstinence. A man like me had frequent carnal urges combined with quite a strong sexual appetite. Controlling all that took a lot of willpower.

I sighed and ran my fingers through the tuft of hair on top of my head, arranging it over my forehead. It was a mess as always, but women seemed to like it that way for some reason. They told me the unruly look of it matched my spirit.

My feet sank into the soft sand as I set off under the starry sky, moving toward the only source of light illuminating the beach: the bonfire.

My siblings were already seated around the fire on a pair of logs that had been repurposed into benches. Mia and Matt were talking happily over a colorful packet that I couldn't identify from a distance. None of that was what I was looking for, though. My eyes scanned the scene impatiently, searching for the object of my desires.

And there sat Selene, radiant and lovely, staring into the eager flames as they rose up toward the sky.

She shone like the moon lighting up a dark sky.

She was a fairy creature who rekindled my desire to imagine a better life. The kind of childlike fantasies and raw emotions that I hadn't felt even when I was a boy.

Sometimes, it felt like she was giving me back the childhood I'd never had.

"Finally decided to grace us with your presence, huh?" my mother chided me sternly. I had disappeared all day after my argument with Selene in the morning.

"Hey, Neil, there you are. Found anything interesting around here?" Matt put in with a sly wink. He was likely talking about women, ignorant of the sexual issues I was having. He was well aware of my ability to find girls even if, as was the case more often than not, I wasn't even looking for them. My looks went a long way in terms of getting what I wanted easily and I never had to work hard to find someone with whom I could share a moment of physical pleasure.

"Yeah, I made the rounds," I lied, sitting down casually next to Babygirl. She sucked in a breath as I settled myself close to her on the log. Then she gulped, working hard to ignore me. I was positive that, were I to peel off that pink hoodie she was wearing, I'd see goosebumps all over her skin. The same ones that rose up on mine when I'd gotten so dangerously close to her in my room.

The next moment, however, I regretted sitting right there because I got a whiff of her coconut smell with every little breeze. I squirmed, resisting the urge to pounce on her like the vilest beast. Fortunately, I was experienced enough to have developed a certain degree of self-control when I wanted to resist a woman who was tempting or seducing me.

Not that Selene was really doing that. Even if she'd tried to seduce me, she wouldn't have been like the bold women I was used to. Still, all she had to do was lick her lips, and I was thinking of lewd scenarios.

I took a deep breath.

I needed to get a grip.

I disgusted myself, so obsessed over having a woman. I couldn't have a relationship of any kind, let alone a romantic one, with a girl like her. Not because I didn't want it but because all my issues would only lead to me dragging her into my fucked-up life, and that wasn't the future I wanted for her. I didn't want her to have a future full of psychologists, medication, and mental disorders. I didn't want her to have to witness my nightmares or my angry outbursts or fall victim to my inability to love. Love was nothing but a curse to me—a painful memory, a noxious dependency. An evil I was fleeing from.

If Selene tried to form an actual bond with me, I would have to make her understand that I wasn't fit for her at all.

"Who wants to toast some marshmallows over the fire?" Logan handed me two sticks with sharpened ends, assuming I'd say yes. I cocked an eyebrow as I looked at the sticks and then back at his face.

"And who said I wanted to, exactly?" I grumbled in my usual truculent fashion, but Logan just smiled and insisted.

"You already missed lunch. Just take them and don't be a dick about it," he said.

I wanted to take exception to being called a dick, but I didn't want to get angry, which is what would have happened if I'd responded to him. Instead, I just glared at him as I snatched the damn sticks and passed them directly to Selene.

Babygirl started, probably still nervous at how close I was to her. She looked from the hand I had extended toward her up to my eyes, and then, after a moment of hesitation, she took the sticks.

"Thanks," she said awkwardly. I didn't reply but only grabbed two more sticks for myself. I turned them over between my fingers and thought about how agitated I was by this whole situation.

I didn't know what the fuck to do either.

I could have ignored her, tried to make it clear that she should stay away from me, but instead, I'd come on to her just a little while ago and now I was sitting right next to her. On top that, I wasn't even pretending to be nice.

What, me be nice to a woman?

I was rarely nice to them even when they were suggesting a threesome or offering to realize any of my other perverted fantasies.

"Here." Matt tossed the bag of marshmallows to Logan, and he pulled out a couple of them and skewered them on his stick. Chloe did the same, and then Logan held the bag out to me. I'd never been the biggest fan of marshmallows, but I didn't complain and instead grabbed two, one to put on each of my sticks.

Selene did the same thing, moving with a very feminine delicacy. I watched her long fingers and perfectly groomed pink nails. I liked women's hands, especially when they were so graceful like hers.

Under my watchful eye, she stretched her sticks out over the fire to toast the marshmallows and immediately made the mistake of getting too close to the fire. One of them went up in flames.

"Damn," she said in an annoyed whisper, and I couldn't help but smile. It made me feel tender toward her when she took on those awkward stances or turned red from fear someone might judge her.

Instinctively, I took her by the wrist to correct the way she held the stick with the still-unburnt marshmallow on it. She flinched and turned her face toward me while I kept my eyes locked on the fire.

"You've got to do it like this." I held her wrist up in front of the flames to show her exactly how. Her smooth skin against my fingers sent a jolt of electricity up my arm, but I pushed that unsettling sensation down and remained blank-faced.

I hated feeling vulnerable with women. I never did it, except with her, and the whole thing made me nervous.

"Right above the coals is the perfect spot for toasting the marshmallow. No sudden bursts of flames to ruin the gummy texture," I explained, and only then did I turn to look at her. I caught her staring at me so intently that she'd stopped blinking entirely.

She looked like she was under a spell, her ocean gaze alternating between my eyes and my lips, and fuck—I wanted to kiss her, if only to replace that goofy look on her face with the satiated one she wore with me and me alone.

"Fire's over there," I said softly, gesturing at the bonfire. Selene snapped out of whatever daydream she was having and immediately looked down at her marshmallow, which was now toasting nicely on the end of her stick.

"Uh...thanks," she said, once again blushing and cowed and drawn in by me.

Shit.

"Quit blushing," I scolded her, maybe a bit too harshly but it was necessary. I didn't want history repeating itself. I didn't want her building up any more illusions about me like she had in the past. Yes, I had screwed up and gotten too close to her, breaking the one rule I'd made for myself before setting foot in that fucking beach house, but I could still turn it around. I could show her I was no one's Prince Charming. Especially not hers.

"What?" she asked, finally emerging from her trance.

"You heard me. You look ridiculous blushing at everything I say. I'm tired of being surrounded by desperate sluts trying to get my attention. So wipe that dreamy look off your face." I went too far, like I always did, and Babygirl's eyes went wide because my fiery arrow had hit her right in the pure, fragile little heart that I would have shattered into a thousand pieces if she'd even considered getting with a son of a bitch like me.

"What the hell is your problem?" She tried to keep her voice low so our

159

parents wouldn't overhear. Her expression had gone from "innocent girl" to "fucking furious girl," and, funnily enough, I found that even more arousing.

"What's my problem?" I echoed. "Nothing. I just want you to knock it off. I hate women who look at me that way," I answered with a narcissist's sense of unassailable superiority. Selene stared at me in confusion, not understanding why I was being so bad-tempered all of a sudden.

To be perfectly honest, it was simply a sick and twisted defense mechanism that I used against her and against the things that I felt when I got lost in her eyes. Now that she'd finally decided to go back to Detroit, I wasn't going to make the mistake of drawing her back into my world or my fucked-up life.

"And what way do I look at you?" she asked sharply before scooting down the log to put some space between us.

"Like you want me to fuck you," I whispered, leaning in close to her ear. Tinkerbell's eyes widened, and she stared at me in horror.

"You are an idiot, Neil. Truly an idiot!" She leaped to her feet, drawing everyone's attention. Matt and Mia looked confused, but Logan just glared at me.

"I'm going for a walk." Babygirl tossed her stick into the fire and stalked indignantly away.

I grasped my perfectly toasted marshmallow between my fingers and popped it into my mouth, chewing placidly.

I needed to pretend that none of that had anything to do with me, and, like always, I did it perfectly.

"What got into her?" Chloe huffed, but no one answered her.

"Dick," Logan mouthed at me, and I brushed him off with a shrug.

I was well aware that I was a dick, but, with Selene, I needed to be even more of a dick so she could see things as they really were.

Matt shot a glance at me, and I held his gaze and feigned indifference.

When we finished eating the marshmallows I hated, my mother, complaining of the cold, went back to the house. Chloe followed her while Matt stood up and shook sand off his pants as he finished his conversation with Logan.

I was the last to get up off the log, and I paused to dig out my pack of

Winstons. I opened it and pulled one out before finding my lighter and holding it to the end of the cigarette. I took my first drag, and, as I exhaled the smoke into the air, I saw Matt coming toward me.

"You not going in?" he asked in a tone I couldn't read.

Was he checking up on me? Was he worried I was going to worm my way between his daughter's thighs? It had happened before, but he had no inkling of that.

"I'm going to finish this first and then head back." I gestured to the cigarette between my fingers, and, with a nod, he walked away.

I could have picked another time to smoke, but it was a plausible excuse to hang around outside for a while.

Once I was alone, I looked around for Babygirl. I found her not too far away on the seashore, illuminated by the light from the dying bonfire.

I clenched the cigarette between my lips and went to her, pushing back a bit of hair that had fallen over onto my forehead. As I approached, I took the opportunity to scrutinize her silhouette while she was turned away from me and distracted. I took note of her slim shoulders, tapered waist, and round, nicely turned ass.

Her body drove me wild.

I thought about how much I enjoyed taking her from behind, how I loved to watch her long hair swing. It had grown out almost to the base of her spine now, and it wasn't difficult to imagine wrapping it lewdly around my fist as I positioned her however I wanted.

A stab of arousal hit me in the lower abdomen, and I needed to think about something else so I didn't get an inconvenient hard-on right there. It would have been tricky to hide that.

"Did you come over here to be a dick and humiliate me some more?" Selene sensed my presence without turning around, so I halted right behind her.

Why *had* I gone over to her?

My goal, supposedly, was to push her away from me. But whenever I did that, I seemed incapable of staying away. I figured that came from the unhealthy protective instincts that she provoked with her naivete and...

No. That wasn't the truth.

The truth was, I couldn't deal with the upheaval that was happening inside me.

I was furious because my mood now depended on her, and it was confusing me.

I took another step forward and then another, and, in no time at all, I found myself brushing up against her back with my chest. Selene trembled. I only noticed because of the almost imperceptible motion of her shoulders. Then I breathed in the sweet scent of her coppery hair, and my eyelids grew heavy. In just a few hours, she'd be going back to Detroit, and I'd be back to my everyday life. Even though I knew she needed to leave, I wished I could bottle up that smell and take it with me.

"Will you stay here with me a little while longer?" I whispered in a tone that was anything but dickish. I'd even surprised myself: That girl could make me do the craziest shit. Like what I was doing right then.

Selene turned to look at me, and her face, even in the dim moonlight, was perfect. The moonbeams, bouncing off a calm, flat ocean, and the stars scattered across the sky were both obscured by her beauty.

"I'm not going to let you mock me." She shook her head and tried to walk away, but I grabbed her arm to keep her there with me. With my other hand, I pinched the cigarette between my fingers and took a drag, blowing the smoke into her pretty little face. Babygirl coughed and shot me an irritated look. Honestly, it was adorable.

"I'm not mocking you. I'm just trying to make you see that this can't work..." I murmured, using the tone of voice that had a hypnotic effect on women. I meant what I said, even if my behavior earlier suggested otherwise. I realized that I was contradicting myself and that my shifting attitudes were confusing. I wasn't sure whether to blame it on my damaged psyche, on what I was going through at the time, or even on what she was going through, which was somehow affecting me as well.

In short, I didn't understand a fucking thing.

"Why can't you just admit that you want me?" She spoke too quickly, and I could tell she regretted it because she looked down, chewing on her lip. I frowned for a couple of reasons. For one thing, I wasn't sure where her certainty on this was coming from and also...

What was that she said? I wanted her.

I did, true, but not the way she was thinking. Selene thought I was like the other boys she'd known, but she'd gotten that all wrong.

We weren't going to walk in the park hand in hand with each other. We wouldn't go for ice cream like a happy couple. We wouldn't talk about books, TV shows, or any other random bullshit over a pizza for hours on end.

"Because I can't be in a real relationship. A woman can't be a...partner in my life." Still, without consciously directing it, my hand remained firmly clasped on her arm, unable to let her go.

I sucked on the filter of my cigarette, hoping for a little more nicotine as I stared at Selene. I stared at her for what felt like forever.

"Oh, no? So what can a woman be to you?" she asked in a low, challenging tone. She had also realized that I was still keeping her there by force, but she didn't fight me. Maybe because she was exactly where she wanted to be.

She wanted to be...with me.

"Revenge," I said softly. Women were a means through which I could take my revenge for everything that had been done to me. A way to take revenge on all of humanity and its evil.

"Revenge for what?" she continued, becoming more and more intrigued at the idea of pulling answers out of me. All I wanted to do was pull off her clothes and put an end to this shit.

After one final drag, I tossed the butt away and concentrated exclusively on her.

"Would you like it if I used you to get my revenge?" I answered wickedly, lowering my tone to a seductive register. I knew the power my voice had over her.

I was confident that the deep, shadowy tone would caress her between her thighs and sneak into her thoughts, igniting her desires, sweeping over her until it reached her brain and caused a total blackout.

As if to confirm her theory, her arm trembled underneath my fingers, and she swallowed drily, putting on a false show of confidence. She surely knew exactly what I meant, and the idea of it thrilled me.

"No, I don't think I would," she answered after considering it for a moment.

"But I did it before and you were the one who allowed me to…" I advanced on her small body, brushing against her breasts with my chest. She was tiny, but she had curves in all the right places. I remembered all of them, and I also remembered the way my hands had to study them to learn where she liked to be touched and how.

"You liked it when I used you…" I whispered into her ear before sucking gently on her earlobe and making her shudder. She smelled so good, and it had me shaking at the thought of tasting her, tasting all of her right there, not wasting any more time.

"Why do you talk to me like that?" she asked, but her voice was shaky, and she was breathing heavily.

The way I expressed myself had provided her with several orgasms, and I was confident it would again if she would only bend to my desires.

"Do you think other men don't talk like this?" I asked challengingly. "Do you think they don't also use women for physical gratification? Sex is just a natural impulse, baby," I lectured, like a professor trying to explain the galaxy to a student who didn't know the first fucking thing about astronomy.

"There are also men who actually love their women," my sweet dreamer replied.

"That's how it goes in those romance novels," I whispered only a short distance from her lips. It was proof of how well I knew her. I paid attention to the details. I knew that she loved to read and that she was deluded by stereotypical, fabulist tales of love.

"Men need to fuck; it's part of their essential nature. For men, love is just a possible side effect of sex. For women, a lot of them need love to fuck, or at least the illusion of it. That's how you are."

Scarlett had been like Selene.

She also dreamed of a fairy tale and lived in her own world when it came to love. It was all in her head, and she projected all her romantic fantasies onto me, ignoring our reality. A reality that didn't have a goddamned thing to do with love.

I used sex to quit thinking, to relieve pressure, and to deaden my problems. The last thing I wanted was a partner who was looking for some affectionate, emotional exchange. I was firmly against any giving or receiving of "cuddles" or "pillow talk" because that could only ever make my issues even harder to manage.

I was firmly convinced that men and women were fundamentally different and that understanding or accepting each other was never going to be easy.

"You say that because you believe your body is all you have to give," Babygirl volleyed back, and I had to smile.

What could she possibly know about life?

All at once, I let go of her arm and sat down in the sand. I leaned back on my hands and made myself comfortable. Puzzled, Selene looked over at me and folded her arms over her chest, clearly unsure of what to do next.

"What are you doing?" she asked in a pouty grumble.

"I'm sitting down, can't you tell?" I teased her cheerfully, and she threw a bit of hair over her shoulder in a manner that was supremely yet unintentionally sensual.

"I'm waiting for you to give me your grand life lessons. How many boyfriends have you had?" I sneered at her, and Selene finally realized that I'd stepped into the role she hated the most, that of the arrogant asshole.

It also occurred to me that I'd never asked her that question before because I'd always refused to have a conversation with her. My preferred method of communication with Selene had always involved our naked bodies and a thoroughly messed-up bed, so this urge I had to open a dialogue with her was new to me as well.

Now it felt like all I wanted to do was hear her delicate voice humming around me. I prepared myself to laugh when she told me that the only man—or rather, boy—she'd been with was Jared, but...

"Three," she said, and my shit-eating grin evaporated, replaced by a flash of surprise.

What did she say?

"Three?" I repeated skeptically.

Where was that number coming from? Maybe she'd been with someone while we were apart? Maybe someone other than Jared. I never would have asked her—I preferred to investigate using my own methods.

"Yup." She sat down next to me, though not too close. She tucked her knees up against her chest and propped her elbows up on them, curving her spine.

"And when did you become acquainted with these three men? Tell me about it." I got the strange feeling that she was lying to me. Or, more likely, that she'd interpreted my question in a different way.

She took her time before answering, sighing with a serious look on her face.

"My first boyfriend was Alain. He gave me a very respectful kiss behind the school when I was about fourteen." She began her story, and I listened, resting my weight on my elbows. For once, it didn't matter to me if my clothes or hands got dirty because I knew I'd shower again later.

"Marlon was my second boyfriend. He was my first kiss with..." She paused and cleared her throat uncomfortably. Was she embarrassed to tell me about a little French kissing? After everything I'd done with my tongue, Selene was embarrassed to tell me about some adolescent fooling around?

She was one of a kind.

I kept quiet so as not to make her even more uncomfortable and waited a very long minute for her to continue talking.

"With tongue," she murmured in the softest of voices, and I only barely suppressed a laugh.

"Sorry, I didn't catch that. A kiss with what?" I pretended I couldn't understand her, and she looked at me like I'd asked if she would suck me off.

She was so cute.

"With tongue," she repeated uncertainly.

"What's that?" I frowned to make my reaction look more authentic.

"A kiss with tongue! For Christ's sake, Neil!" she practically yelled, and I exploded into laughter like I never had before. I struggled not to fall over into the sand and put a hand on my abdomen. Her eyes followed it there from where they had been, staring at my chest.

"Oh, very interesting. That might be the most erotic thing I've heard in my entire life. Truly." I bit my lower lip and looked again at her plush mouth. My mood turned serious because what I really wanted to do was remind her of what a real kiss was, but she turned her face away toward the water. So, instead, I dwelled upon her perfect profile and the little upturn of her nose that I would have happily nibbled.

In that moment, it occurred to me that I didn't want to make her uncomfortable, and, weirdly enough, I didn't want her to stop talking to me either.

We'd only talked like this once before, stretched out in the cushioned lounger by the indoor pool in my house.

And that had been one of the loveliest moments I could recall. Not just because of the intense sex we'd shared but also because of my genuine desire to hear her story. Selene told me about herself and about her life in Detroit and her mother; the whole time, I could tell how enthusiastic she was because I'd finally allowed her to talk to me.

It was a tiny, unexceptional, insignificant gesture for me, but, for her, it had tremendous value.

Before meeting Selene, I was always hostile to conversation. I stayed remote and was reluctant to open up with others. With her, I had begun to discover a new way of communicating, and I was starting to think of it as normal, teasing her and laughing with her.

But I was still a disaster zone, and I hoped she'd be able to see that without too many warnings or explanations. Even if I had given her parts of myself that I'd never given—and, likely, would never give again—to anyone else before.

Abruptly, I sat forward and got out my pack of cigarettes. I lit one up and took a deep drag, like I hadn't had a smoke in days, before exhaling through my nose. I was smoking too much during that time. My throat often got irritated, and I had a cough. But at least the nicotine calmed me down a little.

I turned suddenly somber and reflective, in the throws of a mood swing that I couldn't control.

"Is… Is everything all right?" Selene stuttered, frowning next to me. I enjoyed Tinkerbell, my Tinkerbell, the one who had done everything she could to learn about me and understand me, but I couldn't let myself give in to that body of hers and those eyes. Those eyes the color of the ocean that looked at me, in awe but also enraptured.

I couldn't make the same mistakes again.

When she was lying in that hospital bed in a coma, I'd sworn to her that I'd be by her side, if not exactly in the way she wanted.

I said I would protect her like the shell protects its pearl.

Even if it came at the cost of my own life.

"No, nothing's fucking all right." I didn't raise my voice, but the way I spoke was enough to make it obvious to her that I was agitated. Selene had always had an ability to understand me. Even though she looked at me the way everyone else did and was attracted to my looks, my presence, my face, and even my voice, she also appreciated my essence, my strengths, and my weaknesses. Even my twisted nature and deviant mind.

She wanted me, not just sex with me.

She wanted to use me to get at my soul, not my body.

And that... That scared me.

I wasn't used to people taking that kind of interest in me.

I lifted the cigarette back to my lips and took a long drag before blowing the smoke out into the sharp salt air. Then I stubbed it out and put the long butt into my cigarette pack.

"Neil..." she murmured in concern.

I rubbed my hands together to get rid of some sand before turning to Selene and locking eyes with her lustfully. Her lips fell open, and her breathing was strained as she sensed my intentions.

I approached her immediately, not giving her any time to stop me, and I stuck one hand into her hair, a gesture of dominance meant to disarm her.

"Would you let me fuck you right now? Right here? Because that's the only thing I want from you," I lied.

In truth, I wanted to know about her dreams. I wanted to know her favorite music and ice cream flavors and what color she liked best. I wanted to watch her eyes open as she woke. Would they still be that brilliant ocean color in the dim light of dawn? And I wanted to know if she had any more awful pajama sets besides the ones with the tiger print. And how did she position her body as she slept? What did she look like then?

"Yes," she said, and my mind came crashing back to reality.

I wanted that sense of peace, the same priceless peace that I felt when I didn't care at all about women. Instead, there I was with my mind working overtime trying to think of ways to get some distance from her.

Wait a minute… Did I hear right? Did she say yes?

She was certifiable. How could she not hate me after all the depraved things I'd done?

Instead, she was looking at me like I was the most beautiful man she'd ever seen, worthy of her worship and perhaps even…her love.

But no, I wasn't going to think about that.

Even though I longed to kiss her, and I knew from experience that I could make her succumb to her own desires, I decided to get myself under control.

I pulled my hand away from the nape of her neck and got to my feet. I could feel her pain at the surprise rejection. I'd never successfully resisted her like that before, but, from now on, I was going to be stronger than what tempted me.

Selene looked up at me, disoriented, and then got to her feet, looking alarmed.

In that moment, I had only one thought: escape. Immediately. I wasn't about to stay there and let her knock me for a loop.

I walked past her to the porch, where a small light illuminated the path.

Fuck her and fuck this feeling in my chest.

I wanted to devour her lips. I wanted her to chase after me, but I kept telling myself that all of this was wrong. I couldn't continue to confuse her physical attraction to me for real interest. Every time I got near her, I felt removed.

Even now.

With her, I was always standing outside myself.

"Neil, wait…" Selene called out behind me, but I didn't wait. I continued to stride briskly in the direction of the house until I heard her breathing raggedly behind me. She had to run to catch up with me; she couldn't have kept pace otherwise. I didn't slow down but instead sped up on purpose.

"Wait!" She grabbed my arm, and I swung around abruptly. I was enormous, and she was so little that I couldn't help but soften. She was afraid, but she wasn't letting go.

Tenacity and determination were her strong suits.

"What the fuck do you want?" I'd run out of patience by then, and it was impossible to talk rationally to me in that state.

"I want to know what's going on with you," she answered in an anguished voice.

I jerked roughly away from her, making her stumble a bit. I pinned her with a furious glare. I could feel my pulse throbbing, my blood pressure rising. I felt the sweat, the trembling in my hands, the rapid breathing, and the hatred. So much hatred that I tried to tamp down. Not for Selene but for myself. For what I was.

"You want to know what's going on with me?" I echoed. "For real?" I took a step toward her, and she backed up. "I-I'm…not myself. I'm not myself when you're around. Because you…expand. You are my *more*—my beyond, Selene." The words were dragged out of me, my erratic breathing preventing me from talking to her the way I wanted.

I wasn't good at expressing myself when it came to certain things, and maybe Selene couldn't understand what I really meant: She was not just a boundary I couldn't cross; she was everything beyond.

She was *further*.

I stared intensely at her and realized that she was about to cry. I could tell from the way her eyes had gotten glassy and how her chin trembled.

"I let you have parts of me that I've never given anyone else. I've tried so many times to follow my rules with you, but I just couldn't," I gasped out, and it felt as though my skin were burning under the irritating layers of my clothing. Selene held out a little bit, but, after a few moments, she burst into tears.

She let out all the emotions she'd been keeping inside, and perhaps if I had been a feeling man, I would have held her close and comforted her. But I didn't even know how to convey affection to someone in that way. When I had cried as a child after Kimberly's abuse, I tucked myself into a corner of my room, and no one came to hold me. When I tried to get away from her and begged her not to hurt me again, she never listened. She just ignored me as she continued to satisfy her own wants.

So how could I be human toward a world that had treated me so inhumanely?

"We feel the same things. You don't have to be afraid. It's not anyone's fault. Some emotions are just beyond our control." Selene wiped her face with the back of her hand even as more tears continued to stream freely down her cheeks.

The problem was this: I was a control freak. I always had been, but especially with women.

In my mind there existed a very precise sequence of steps that I followed with all of my lovers. Through that, I had found some equilibrium amid the chaos, and now some random girl wanted to come into my life—into my head—and blow everything to hell.

I scrubbed a hand over my face, trying to calm down.

She had a point.

This wasn't her fault, but it was mine.

It was down to my inability to stay away from her like I'd promised myself I would so many times. If I was being honest with myself, even I didn't know what I wanted from her.

What was I imagining?

That things would go back to how they'd been before the crash? But how exactly were things before?

"I think the solution's pretty clear to both of us," I told her, forcing myself to accept that reality.

It hurt to think about it, but there really was no other option. Time was up.

In a few hours, she'd be on a plane, and I'd be headed back home. I needed to keep her from coming to live with me in Matt's house again on the faint hope of continuing what we'd once started there.

There was nothing I could do except let her go because I wasn't the right man for her.

"What are you talking about?" she asked thickly, wiping her eyes and smearing mascara down her cheeks.

"We can't do this. Look at us…" I gestured at myself and then at her. "You're a young woman with dreams and plans and a full life ahead of you. I'm a complete disaster. I am more fucked up than you could possibly imagine," I admitted, letting my arms go slack against my sides in surrender. Crushed, once again, by the obstacles that bitch destiny had thrown in my path.

171

"I don't have the strength to fight more impossible battles, Selene. In another life, if I were a different man, I would have fought for someone like you," I told her. I wasn't stupid. I knew how rare it was to encounter someone like Selene. I knew the values she possessed; I knew how good her heart was and how pure her soul. But I just had too many demons on my back.

She couldn't see them—no one saw them—but I felt them all the time. They spoke to me regularly, especially the Boy. He constantly told me that if I chose one woman and quit my bad habits, I would be abandoning him and he would die.

"Wait…" she sobbed, but I wasn't going to wait for anything at all.

I wasn't going to wait for her or for a destiny that would likely never be on our side.

I went straight back to my room and locked the door before spending a sleepless night trying to put my head back in order.

....

I went home the next morning.

I'd decided to attend Matt's birthday after wrestling with my own torments, all to get a look at her. Just to spend some time with her, with my Babygirl.

I wasn't expecting us to fuck or to resolve everything between us in two days.

Once, all I needed to do was seduce her. A few touches and that was it—Selene would give in, and I could ease my woes with a straightforward fuck. Now, though, I felt the urge to get close to her in other ways. Ways that I wasn't accustomed to at all.

During our one day together, we'd done nothing but talk, and her eyes, glittering like blue diamonds with her tears, were the only memory I took with me from the beach house. It dragged along heavily behind me, her practically begging me to stay and listen to her.

And yet again, I raged at myself, falling back into that vortex of anger. It was a false friend, company in misery, a whore that fucked me relentlessly in the head, and I couldn't deal with it.

"I've just been waiting for you to get back," Jennifer whispered into my ear, gliding her hand down from my chest to my lower stomach. We were sitting on a bench in one of the school's many green areas, killing time between classes. Her touch was irritating, but I was so absorbed in my own thoughts that I didn't bother putting her in her place.

"So you're telling me you let your dad find the pills in your house?" Xavier was giving Luke shit because his dad found ecstasy in his bedside table drawer.

"The fuck are you laughing about, dickhead?" Luke snapped. "I've got a ten-year-old sister, and he started going off on me about how irresponsible I was because she could've found it. He's right; it could have been a tragedy. And now he thinks I'm a drug addict and a bad example for her and…" Luke continued to blather on and generally lose his shit all because his big-shot lawyer daddy had gotten a peek behind the scenes of his son's life.

Luke used sometimes and got high with Xavier. I was the only one in the Krew who didn't fuck with any of that. I'd always been a shithead for sure, but I could be thoughtful about some things. I'd only given in a few times when I was a kid, curious to know what pot felt like or what cocaine would do to me, but I'd never been remotely tempted to abuse it.

"What, you gonna fucking pussy out now, Luke?" Xavier burst into laughter as he taunted him. Meanwhile, Jennifer continued to pet my chest, running her fingers languidly over the contours of my muscles. She planted a kiss on the hollow of my throat and pressed her breast against my arm. I kept my hand resting lazily on her thigh.

The feel of her saliva was uncomfortable on my skin, but I liked kisses on my neck, so I decided to let her keep doing it a little longer.

"He wants me to take these tests, and if any of them come back positive, he's going to kick me out on my ass. Do you realize what that means?" Luke exploded, digging a hand into his blond hair.

Jennifer, meanwhile, had started moaning and pressing herself against me to signal that we needed to go to my car or somewhere else we could get some alone time. I quit listening to the other two and turned to look at her.

"What?" I asked her in a flat tone, and she grinned, delighted to have captured my attention.

"I want to…" She moved closer to my ear. "…suck your cock," she said in a temptress's whisper.

Anyone else in my position would have jumped at the opportunity, but I couldn't. And not just because we were in a public place either. There were certain indulgences I could no longer allow myself to have while following my therapist's instructions.

The idea of shoving my hard-on into her mouth was enticing and not just a little bit. But, unlike most men, I was capable of keeping my head, even with a woman as seductive as Jennifer.

I decided who I fucked, when, and where.

It had always been like that, no matter what my girl of the moment wanted or offered.

So I didn't say anything to Jennifer and moved closer to her instead, gently brushing against her lips. I needed to find a way to shake her off without arousing her suspicion. I couldn't tell her I was thinking about picking back up with the therapy that I'd stopped three years ago, or that I'd actually been diagnosed with a sexual disorder. Above all else, I couldn't tell her that it was all caused by my intense personal psychological issues.

Instead, I gave her a sensual smile and caught her off guard with a kiss.

The shape of my lips mingled with hers, and my tongue slid into her mouth like it had been waiting for me. Jennifer was a master at giving me pleasure, but even her abilities couldn't remotely compare to the way everything in me vibrated when I got one of my Babygirl's clumsy kisses.

Selene kissed timidly—the touch of her lips was as delicate as a caress. She closed her eyes as she did it and imagined some nonexistent true love. Jennifer, on the other hand, laid claim to me like a seasoned whore. With one hand rubbing between my legs and the other clawing at my back, she dug her nails into my skin.

Her abundance of passion thrilled my body but not my mind. We'd always had sexual chemistry but nothing else. A kiss from Jennifer could awaken my libido. A kiss from Selene awakened my need to taste her soul as well.

I felt at ease with Jennifer, though, because there was no pressure to meet any expectations. She had a jealous streak, but she also knew what she could and could not expect from me.

Selene was a different story. A kiss from her was a sweet, meaningful gesture. A precious treasure and a sneak peek at the theoretical love story she never should have imagined with me.

"Thanks, Miller. I can see you're really taking my shitty situation to heart," Luke grumbled, interrupting my moment of pleasure.

I pulled back from Jennifer and licked my lower lip before stretching my arm out along the back of the bench comfortably. I had achieved my goal of distracting Jennifer, who clearly didn't even remember what she'd been talking about before that kiss. Now I leveled a glacial stare at Luke because I hated to be interrupted during certain moments. It was irritating because even if a basic rubbing of tongues together wasn't enough to get me hard, it was still plenty capable of awakening my sexual appetite.

"If you want to fuck her right now, feel free. I'll just be over here watching you and jerking it like a madman," Xavier cut in, miming the action with one hand. I shifted my gaze to take in his delighted expression and gave him a serious look.

I didn't think there was anything funny about what he'd said, especially not while I was in that period of forced abstinence.

"How was your beach weekend?" Xavier asked, switching to a different topic when he realized I was about to lose my shit. Unfortunately, he'd chosen a topic I didn't want to talk about. I didn't want to think about how tragic my encounter with Selene had felt.

"I was only there for a day. For Matt's birthday," I answered. All of a sudden, Jennifer's proximity and her leg thrown over my thigh bothered me, so I pushed her off. My sudden tension did not go unnoticed.

"Was the baby doll there, too?" Xavier asked, referring to Selene.

I saw Luke prick up his ears, waiting to know more. I stared at him like I could read his mind. He was definitely remembering that kiss he'd had with Selene and I knew exactly what he was feeling: restlessness.

It was the same thing I'd felt when I kissed her for the first time in the pool.

Selene was so far removed from our world, so different from the women we usually saw, that she provoked curiosity. That's why I was sure Luke was hiding a little interest in her.

"Yeah, the girl was there too," I said flatly with an indifferent shrug. Jennifer turned to look at me, scrutinizing my face, but I kept it blank as I balanced one ankle on the opposite knee.

"And? Did you get it wet?" Xavier gave his pants a vulgar rub and grinned at me. "I still think about her cute little ass, you know what I mean?" he continued lightly, and it took every bit of self-control I had not to close his mouth with one of my fists. I bit my lip until I tasted blood, trying to keep my face impassive.

"Nah, I'm not into her anymore. Don't know what the fuck I was thinking, but whatever it was, I'm over it now."

Jennifer continued to study my reaction. I was pretty good at putting on a show, but she was very jealous of Selene. It would be hard to convince her of my indifference to Babygirl.

"Hey, whatcha talking about?" Alexia straightened her blue jacket, which matched her hair, and looked expectantly at us, waiting for someone to answer her. She'd just appeared out of nowhere to butt into this uncomfortable conversation, and, for the first time, I found myself irritated by her presence.

"About Neil's trip to the beach for Dr. Stepdaddy's birthday and how he failed to get his dick wet in the holy virgin of the golden ass." Xavier offered an impeccable summary, and Alexia huffed in irritation.

"Why do you call her that?"

Considering everything Xavier had just said to her, all she could focus on was those last few words because she was territorial over him, even though the dumbass had never noticed. Or maybe he just pretended he didn't. I wanted to tell her that she didn't need to worry because Xavier wasn't going to step foot near Selene while there was still air in my lungs, but I forced myself to keep quiet.

"Because she gives off the vibe: typical little princess who has barely ever been with a man." Xavier looked to me for confirmation, but I wasn't about to tell him anything about what I had or hadn't done with Selene. I already regretted saying too much outside Blanco when her ex confronted me in front of everyone. I wasn't about to make the same mistake twice.

"What about a blow job? Did she at least give you one of those?" Xavier just kept needling me, and I was having a really hard time not reacting.

I continued to stare him down gravely, and Luke elbowed him, trying to get Xavier to stop.

"Knock it off," he chided, having seen something stormy in the gaze that I kept locked on Xavier. I inhaled and exhaled through my nose and continued to stare at Xavier, undaunted.

"Jesus, you should see your face right now; it's legendary," Xavier sneered, pulling his phone out of his pants pocket. "Smile, man."

As he aimed it at me, the memories came flooding back.

It was cold, so cold, and I was shivering.

The blinding flash of a camera hit my face. I raised an arm to protect my eyes, but it was too bright.

All around me, however, there was total darkness. Kimberly sat on a wooden chair and watched me with a characteristically wicked grin on her angelic face.

Yeah, she had the look of an angel, and she used it to hide the cruel demon underneath.

"Stop blocking your face," she scolded me irritably. I was too ashamed to obey her and instead tried to cover the place between my legs with my other hand.

I was completely nude.

"Neil!" she snapped in annoyance, but I couldn't listen to her. I was in a state of complete shock. The only thing I could feel was the rapid beating of my heart. The only thing I could see was the pallor of my hands and the way my fingers trembled.

We weren't alone, though. Someone else was there with us.

The sobs of the little girl beside me rebounded off the walls. She was naked as well, and she kept trying to cover her bare, undeveloped chest with one slender forearm. Her intensely black hair fell in soft waves over her shoulders.

Ignoring our misery, Kimberly ordered me to listen to her, to do to that little girl everything she'd taught me. The little girl was crying, though, and trembling at the harsh voice of our tormentor, who continued to bark orders that neither of us obeyed.

We were stunned, terrified victims of something too big to understand. That camera in front of us was going to be the end for both of us.

More monsters would watch us, our dignity crushed underfoot, drained away by that lens.

But then it all went sideways.

Someone burst into that dark place.

Several men battered down the door, and chaos ensued. I instinctively fled the awful scene, and the little girl followed me. Together, we hid behind a beat-up old sofa. I huddled on the floor, knees tight against my chest. Still naked and terrified, I covered my ears with my hands and squeezed my eyes shut.

Dad said crying was for sissies, so I gritted my teeth and rocked back and forth, singing under my breath so I couldn't hear the noises that surrounded me.

I sang "Imagine" by John Lennon, my mother's favorite song. It was just a simple, familiar tune. . . But it managed to drown out the sound of Kim's yelling.

I wasn't aware of anything; all I felt was a fusillade of blows reverberating up my arms, my two fists like balls of fire. I felt Xavier's body under mine, my arm continuously winding up to hit him over and over again in the very same place. I could hear screaming behind my back, saw his dark eyes roll back into his head and his split lips falling open, but I didn't stop. I couldn't. I ground my teeth and kept hitting him, again and again. With every blow, my body was electrified with more negative energy—energy that had to be released.

It felt liberating, and I liked it.

"Never do that again, you son of a bitch!" I shouted into his face, grabbing his jacket in my hands, which were still crawling with pins and needles.

"Never again, you hear me?" I exploded furiously before letting him slump back down to the ground, where I continued to beat him. Xavier had unwittingly brought a hidden, unbearable part of my past to the surface.

Because there was more to Kim's abuse of me.

She hadn't just been looking for carnal pleasure, the fruit of a diseased mind. She had a purpose.

A goal.

A job.

Kim was part of a larger organization. She was preparing me for more, and if she hadn't gotten busted that day, I never would have been able to stop it.

I wouldn't have been able to save myself or the little girl along with me.

"Neil, stop!"

Someone tried to grab me by the shoulders, but I elbowed them away roughly.

The inevitable had happened: I had lost my self-control, my reason, and my common sense. Everything.

My knuckles began to turn a wet, vivid red, but I still didn't stop. I couldn't control the anger. It was stronger than I was.

I raised myself off Xavier's prone, dazed body and started attacking his stomach with a series of powerful kicks.

My forehead was slick with sweat, my jaw so tight it hurt, and my body was boiling all over. My sweater was completely crumpled, but I didn't care about any of that.

In that moment, all I could feel was the madness erupting out of me as though from a volcano. I was tumbling into a spiral of destruction, and I could feel the darkness flowing. It poured over everything around me, covering the whole world in black, in a darkness with nothing blooming, nothing colorful, and nothing peaceful.

I felt a hot vitality flow uncontrollably through me, making me relish this. It was a feeling that was stronger than any orgasm and more exhilarating than any fuck.

It felt so satisfying, and I didn't care about the consequences. I didn't care about anything except finally unleashing the untamed creature inside me, the insanity of the moment.

I reveled like a true monster in the sight of Xavier's swollen face painted purple.

And I remembered a father's violence toward a child and a woman's abuse of a child.

These were the things that had signaled the descent of Satan into my soul.

"Not laughing now, are you?" I was drained and weak, and Xavier took advantage of the brief respite to fight back. From his place on the ground, he reached out and grabbed my ankle, pulling me down. He hopped on top of me smoothly, holding me down with the weight of his body, and started punching me in the face. The first blow landed on my jaw, the next on my brow bone. I managed to put up a defense, hitting him back and shoving him aside so I could get back on my feet.

I'd lost count of how many punches I'd given him and how many I'd taken in turn, but at some point during the violent, interminable brawl, I managed to grab his phone and throw it on the ground, smashing it to pieces.

Being photographed or filmed unleashed my fury.

Xavier stumbled and coughed, trying to speak, though he was out of breath.

"What the fuck is wrong with you, man? You're acting like a fucking psycho!" He spat blood at my shoes, and I tried to lunge for him again, but Luke grabbed my arms to stop me.

"Don't fuck with me, Xavier, or I'll fucking kill you!" I screamed, out of my mind with my hand clutching my stomach. He'd probably hit me there, too, and I was finally starting to feel the pain.

"I'm not afraid of you," he shot back with a malicious grin, wiping the blood from his lips with the back of his hand.

I'd messed him up for sure, but I was in no better shape.

He'd gotten his licks in.

Suddenly, the world began to spin around me, and pain spread from my ribs up to my head. But I was still charged up, still furious.

"What the fuck did you just say to me?" I yelled, feeling the words scrape against my throat. I thrashed like a lunatic as Luke tried to pull me away from Xavier again. "Let me go!" Finally, he pushed me away while I tripped over my own feet.

"What the hell? Are you insane?" Logan ran toward us, tossing his messenger bag and taking me by the arm, yanking me away from Luke.

I was breathing heavily, and my eyes were wild with fury.

"What do you want? Fuck off!" I spit invectives at my brother as well because I was completely out of my mind by that point. Out of control. Out of bounds.

Out of my head.

"Piss off!" I advanced on Xavier again, but Logan got in my way, pushing me backwards. He was tall and strong but not as strong as me.

"You're not going anywhere. Calm down!" he cried, afraid and worried for me. I could see his fear for me in his wide eyes and alarmed face.

Xavier muttered something then, but Luke told him off, telling him to let it go.

"What happened?" Logan demanded. I glanced around and saw a number of curious students who had gathered to watch the fight like a free show. They certainly weren't there to help in any way.

"Well?" Logan continued impatiently.

My hands were trembling; my whole body was trembling, actually, and my head was spinning. My temples throbbed, and the veins in my neck were so pumped up that I was afraid one might burst at any moment.

I felt abruptly drained of strength, and I hit my knees, exhausted. It was then that I saw the bleeding cuts on my knuckles and realized I couldn't even move my fingers. More blood trailed from my eyebrow and my lower lip. I ran my tongue over it, feeling the metal taste on my soft palate.

Logan rushed over to me and put a hand on my shoulder, but I didn't want him touching me, so I flinched and jerked away from him.

"Don't touch me," I muttered, staring intently down at my hands. Once again, anger had made me do something sick. It removed me from reality and made me unstable and violent, even though I hadn't wanted to lose control.

"Everything's okay, Neil. Relax. I'm here." Logan tried to rest his hand on me again, and, this time, I didn't resist the fraternal touch. I sat down in the grass, blinking. I didn't have the balls to look over and see what I'd done to Xavier or to linger on the horrified faces of the people who'd witnessed the whole scene.

I was ashamed of myself, like I always was when I lost my head, but I was even more ashamed of the way I still succumbed to Kimberly whenever she wanted me.

To distance myself from all of that, I sang "Imagine" softly in a low voice. I almost sounded hypnotized, and Logan kept silent, just listening to me.

"I…saw her…" I breathed, my eyes slowly moving over to him.

My brother understood right away. He knew about all of it, and, hearing that tune, he had immediately guessed what had happened and where I'd gone in my head.

"You know, don't you? You know that you have to go see Dr. Lively?" He gently touched my forehead, brushing back a hank of hair. His frightened, concerned, and sad eyes locked on me, and he knew that I was once again completely subject to the part of myself that wouldn't stop torturing me.

I just nodded.

I knew there was nothing else to do.

I squeezed my eyes shut and then opened them, staring up into the blue sky.

I wanted so much to lose myself in that serenity, to know that light and chase away my demons to make room for something marvelous. I wanted to have a lighter life, to smile more, and to forget about everything that had happened to me. I wanted to be one of those clouds I was staring at: flawless and floating in the air. I wanted to be free.

"I s-saw her, Logan…" I slammed out again, turning to look back at him. "She was sitting in the chair, and the light was in my eyes…and…" My speech was confused. I licked my dry lips and found I couldn't continue.

"I know. Don't think about it; it's over now…" He kneeled in front of me and touched my cheek. He wasn't just my little brother; he was so much more. He was the only shoulder I could burden with the weight of my problems.

"I didn't want to hurt Xavier, but I can't control myself. I can't control myself anymore…" I murmured, remorseful but trapped in a cage I couldn't break. I wanted to get better; I wanted to destroy the toxic part of myself, but it wasn't easy. It would never be easy so long as Kim was still alive in my mind.

Suddenly, I could hear Dr. Lively's voice pulsing in my head.

"Your condition is characterized by extreme manifestations of anger, often uncontrollable and disproportionate to the situation. It's another result of the abuse you experienced and your age when it began. Trauma caused this disorder in you. You've had violence done to you, and now you use violence to take your anger out on others. It's a vicious cycle."

My chest tightened, and I felt the air escaping from my lungs. I stared into Logan's eyes and then back down at my own shredded knuckles.

I was confused; I didn't understand a damned thing, but I did know what I had to do.

....

I didn't go back to the house that day but stayed in the pool house with Logan so he could indulge his need to give at least my eyebrow and lip medical attention. I'd already showered and put on just a pair of basic black sweatpants. My brother had hovered over me the whole time, fussing over me like I was an actual fucking child.

"Hold still," he chided, patting a cotton ball over my injuries.

"Watch it. It stings," I complained, gritting my teeth. Logan also thought that I should go to the ER for the pain in my ribs, but I had categorically rejected that suggestion. I was a boxer; this was hardly my first real-life fight. I knew that the bruises would fade in a few days along with the pain.

I was lucky I hadn't broken my hand and had gotten away with just some visible bruising. I knew how to land a hit on an opponent, especially in a street brawl like the one I'd gotten into earlier. Sometimes I'd knock a guy out with one punch, but Xavier was strong, and he knew how to take a hit as well as how to come back at me.

"Almost done," Logan said as I sat on the pool house's corner sofa with an ice pack on my terribly swollen right hand. There was a huge bruise across my abdomen that kept me from bending or turning.

"Okay, now I'm going to put a bandage on your eyebrow. Be patient." Logan continued to tend carefully to me, and, once he was done, he got up from the coffee table to take the first-aid kit back into the bathroom. I decided to lie down while he did that. I had a powerful headache. When Logan came back, he gave me the stink eye.

"What?" I demanded, annoyed, but he just ignored me and began nervously pacing the room, running his fingers through his thick hair.

"Take a seat. Watching you is making my headache worse," I grumbled again, trying to hold completely still so I'd feel less pain. Every time I tried to get up, even just to piss, vertigo forced me to sit back down. So I'd decided to avoid any sudden movements for the time being.

I was confident, though, that Xavier wasn't doing much better. He might have even landed in the hospital. Maybe I'd broken something. The knowledge that I'd beaten his ass wasn't exciting to me; it was worrying. I'd come across a formidable opponent for once. Members of the Krew were strong. Any scuffle between us always ended badly for everyone.

"How are you feeling?" Logan asked, stopping to give me a concerned look.

"I'm fine. Not the first time this has happened," I answered shortly.

How many street fights had I gotten into?

"Is your head still spinning?" he pressed, and I rolled my eyes at him.

"Shut up and hand me a cigarette." I needed to smoke and to stop listening to my brother.

Thankfully, Logan didn't fight me and just gave me a dirty look instead. He grabbed my pack of Winstons from the kitchen island and handed it to me. I extracted a cigarette and clamped it between my lips, allowing him to light it up for me.

"There, you're making yourself useful for once," I sneered, taking my first drag.

I didn't want him fretting over me. I was fine. My only real problem would be confronting our mother and her irritating questions. I'd rather she didn't see me like this.

"Run interference with Mom. I'll sleep out here. I don't want to deal with her shit," I told him, hoping he'd be on my side.

Logan frowned and sighed.

"And what am I supposed to tell her when she asks me where you are?"

"Tell her I'm out here with Jennifer or whoever. Make sure she knows I'm busy and she shouldn't disturb me." It was the only plausible excuse I could think of to avoid her. My mother knew all about my habits and that I used to indulge in them in my bedroom before moving them to the pool house. She'd never asked me a direct question about my sex life; she was far too embarrassed to talk about it, so I knew that just hearing I had company would be enough to keep her from coming to look for me.

"Okay, so you can dodge her for tonight, but what are you going to do tomorrow morning? Sooner or later, she's going to get a look at you, and she'll see what happened to you." Clearly my brother wanted to discuss future problems while I was still trying to solve the ones right in front of us. I huffed and kept smoking, silently grateful for how the cigarette calmed me like a tranquilizer.

"Logan," I snapped, "tomorrow's another day, and I'll think about it tomorrow."

Huff.

Christ, we were so different, him and me.

I was impulsive, reckless, wild, shameless, and much less prone to worry in advance.

Logan, on the other hand, was Logan: always planning, thinking, analyzing, and being a pain in the ass about all of it.

"Okay, okay, chill out," he said defensively.

"Can you get out of here and leave me alone?" I asked in a bored tone. I wanted to relax in the quiet, have a smoke, and tolerate my aching ribs in peace. Logan glared again because he obviously wanted to keep badgering me, but, fortunately, he walked toward the door instead.

"I'll be back in a little while. I'm just going to call Alyssa. She was supposed to come over an hour ago, and she still hasn't gotten here. Don't move," he warned.

I shooed him away with one hand, and he left, slamming the door behind him.

Good, I was finally alone.

I propped my head up on the arm of the sofa and stared at the ceiling, thinking back over everything that had happened. Everything I experienced during that time was a clear sign that I needed help. Help that I should have just asked for, as I hadn't been doing for the past three years. If I didn't, I was going to have a total breakdown and destroy whatever thread of sanity I still had.

My reaction to Xavier had been abnormal, just like it was abnormal to be unable to orgasm or have a stable human relationship. Little by little, my memories were devouring me; my past self was pushing into my present with the intention of warping my future. I had to fight back. I had to stop him; otherwise he was going to win, and I would lose.

There was only one truth: Nothing and no one else could save me.

I—and I alone—could save myself.

Two raps on the door jarred me from my reflections. I sighed and glanced out the big windows, hoping to see whatever the fuck Logan wanted now.

"You done with your phone call?" I called out huffily, but there was no answer and no sign anyone had heard me.

I tried again. "Logan, just use my key to get in. I'm not getting up to open the door for you." A burst of pain shot between my temples at the too-high pitch of my voice. Even my own voice was getting on my nerves.

Still no answer, except for two more knocks.

Was he for real? I'd asked him to leave me alone in my meditative silence, and here he was fucking with me again.

"Go fuck yourself," I muttered. I gritted my teeth against the flashes of pain along my ribs as I sat up, panting. I tossed the ice pack onto the coffee table and left the still-smoking cigarette on the side of the ashtray. I got to my feet with my hand pressing down hard underneath my right pec. Why the hell was my brother acting like this? He had a key, he could easily have come inside without subjecting me to the ordeal of getting up.

I hobbled over to the door and threw it open wide, ready to tear a strip off my brother.

"What the hell…" I halted when I encountered a pair of green eyes and a wild tumble of black hair. My breath caught in my chest, and an irritated, anguished sensation weighed heavily on the area as I realized I was not hallucinating and that Megan Wayne was actually there. Standing right in front of me.

What was she doing here? Who let her onto our property?

"Hey, Miller." She gave me a once-over and grimaced when she saw my condition. "I'll tell you why I'm here, just in case you were wondering. I drove Juliet to her Romeo because she needed a lift and also so I could take the opportunity to pay you a visit and see what sort of state you're in. Word travels fast; the whole school is already betting on which of you is more messed up. My money was on Xavier, but looking at you now…" She cocked an eyebrow, her gaze lingering on my abs. I almost told her to quit looking at me like that. The two of us weren't supposed to be alone in a room together. We weren't even supposed to get near each other or exchange words. Not given our shared history.

"Thanks for informing me, but you can fuck right off. It's the same path you came in on." I jerked my chin toward the gate. I tried to shut the door in her face, but she blocked my attempt with both hands.

"Be nice for once in your life, Miller. You're in no condition to play gangster right now." She smiled and pushed her way into my pool house. Or, more specifically, into my private space, blowing past the boundary I had always imposed between the two of us.

I remained motionless in the doorway and glared at her. I didn't want her around, getting underfoot, being where I was.

"Megan, don't make me tell you again. Leave," I said in a measured yet firm tone.

She peered around at the living room, like I hadn't just told her to get the fuck out, before bending over to take my still-smoking cigarette from the ashtray and bringing it to her own lips. She turned to look at me. "Somebody got video of you guys. Everyone's passing it around, and the comments are all about what a beast you are and how mad you must have been or whatever…" she said dismissively, waving a hand in the air. "But you…" She took another drag from my cigarette before grinding it into the ashtray and giving me her full attention. "You didn't just get mad at him, did you? There was something else in your eyes. Something that came from here." She touched a hand to the middle of her chest, and I shut the door, surrendering to the knowledge that she wasn't going to leave any time soon.

I could have grabbed her by the elbow and tossed her out, but I wasn't feeling up for it physically or emotionally just then.

"What do you want from me?" I asked in exasperation. I maintained a certain amount of space between us as I moved to the kitchen island and leaned heavily on it. I needed to lie down, but I didn't want to show weakness in front of her.

I'd be better in a day or so, but at that moment, I just needed to shut down my body and mind for a while.

That's how it always was after one of my angry outbursts. They were so intense that they wore me out completely, leaving me weak and helpless.

Megan studied my appearance then, but not to evaluate my bruises. She admired every angle, every clearly outlined muscle, each natural curve, and sharp line. I saw the way her eyes lit up and how she swallowed hard. And I realized she was only projecting the kind of confidence that I actually had.

She was posing as a grown woman, but I actually was a grown man and not just in bed. Someone being attractive wasn't enough to fuck with my head. I was calculating and sly as well as malicious, and I would figure out the purpose behind her behavior one way or another. We had always ignored each other in the past, and now, suddenly, it seemed that my mental health had become her number one priority.

"Yes?" I prompted her when I noticed how her eyes got caught on my pelvic area, right around the elastic on my sweatpants. I wasn't sure what she was studying so hard: the bulge between my legs or the pikorua on my left hip.

"It goes to the base of my cock. If you were wondering," I taunted her, and she started before looking back up at my face. "Tragically, you'll never get to see the whole thing." I tugged my waistband down just a bit, giving her a peek below, then I pulled it back up over my hip and gave her a challenging grin.

I decided that prolonged discomfort would be the price she paid for invading my privacy.

"You have a great body; I already knew that," she answered, not remotely embarrassed. "And I could have guessed your tattoo ended right about there. I like the toki better, though." She shrugged and turned her eyes to the Māori-style tattoo on my right bicep. It was the first time she'd seen me without a shirt, so she was taking the opportunity to scrutinize me thoroughly. The tattoo talk was just misdirection, but I was too clever for that. Not even a savvy girl like her could get one over on me.

"What do you want, then?" I moved toward the couch, and she backed away from me. Was Megan afraid of me getting too close?

As I moved past her, I saw how my large frame made her go rigid, and I recalled how, once upon a time, she hadn't been afraid of me at all. She'd considered me a friend, a playmate in the garden, both of us ignorant of what was about to happen.

I sat down, holding my ribs, and leaned my back against the soft fabric of the couch as I took deep breaths.

It was getting too exhausting to make any unnecessary movements.

"Can't a friend pay another friend a polite visit?" It was my turn now to scrutinize her as she stood in front of me. She wore a pair of high-waisted black pants with a crop top and a long coat over all of it. Her voluptuous yet firm breasts were clearly visible, despite her attempt to conceal them under that awful coat. They, along with the curves of her hips, gave her a perfect hourglass silhouette. She had a woolen scarf wrapped around her throat and tall leather boots that lengthened her form.

It was the second time I'd found myself watching her so blatantly, yet I felt no sexual pull toward her, and I was happy with that.

No part of her demanded my attention, and that was proof of how much stronger I was than her constant provocations.

"You and I are not friends," I said pointedly. I looked back at her and caught her staring at me. I was sitting there on the couch covered in cuts and bruises, and, still, she was looking at me like she'd never seen a shirtless man in sweatpants before.

"We could always become friends." She crossed her arms over her chest and blew a bubble with the gum I hadn't even noticed her chewing.

This ballsy attitude of hers was unbearable.

"Never. I don't give a fuck about being your friend." I raised my voice before another stab of pain made me lean my head back on the sofa and breathe deeply. I stared at the ceiling and tried to get a grip.

Calm down. I needed to stay calm.

"You're pissier than usual today." She glanced around in a bored sort of way, infusing her words with all the confidence she was trying to hold on to.

I started pondering ways to get her to run away from me and the pool house. It wouldn't be hard to come up with something evil enough to wound her.

"Do you hear yourself? You're talking about me like you know me," I said derisively, trying to ignore the way my body was screaming in pain.

Megan stopped looking around, and her green eyes homed in on the dismissive expression on my face.

"Do you know what I see when I look at you?" she asked, seemingly at random as she stared me down. "I see a man who has failed to overcome his past, someone who has obliterated himself by letting his memories defeat him. The same memories he reenacts by having sex with different women, believing that they will be the solution to all his problems. I see a man who is unable to admit even to himself that he is trying to self-destruct. Someone using only his body to communicate because he's too afraid that his own feelings might wound him. I see a good, smart man who has armored himself to hide his weaknesses because the truth is, he is incapable. He is incapable of healing himself and, most of all, of loving himself."

The corner of her mouth curled up defiantly, and I was frozen, staring at her.

I could try to pretend otherwise, but as much as I hated to admit it, she'd gotten me good.

I got up, unexpected strength flowing from my head to my legs, and approached her, still holding my stomach tightly. I let myself loom over her. I knew her intentions: She was trying to provoke me into a reaction and now I was going to do the exact same thing to her.

"And how about what I see when I look at you?" I murmured in a diabolical tone. Megan gulped, and finally, I saw her confident facade falter. But that wasn't enough for me: I was going to make it collapse entirely.

I took another step forward until her face was even with my chest, and then I inclined my head slightly to look into her eyes. It was there that I would find every fear I needed to seriously injure her. "I see a woman who thinks she's gotten over her past but, in reality, still bears the scars. I see a woman who is always dressed in black, in her best bad-girl cosplay. A woman who hasn't been in a relationship with a man in God knows how long because she can't stand to be touched. Do you think I haven't been paying attention to you all these years? Do you think I've failed to notice how avoidant and untrusting you are?" I whispered, never taking my eyes off hers, which were now growing stormy with a feral rage that she was struggling to control.

"How long has it been since you actually slept with a man? How long since you had a normal relationship? How many nights have you dreamed about Ryan? How many more do you spend imagining his hands on your body?" I asked, feigning curiosity and she stared hard at my chest rather than continuing to look at my face.

"You can fool your shrink and mine, but you can't fool me," I concluded. A little tremor in her shoulders told me how powerful my words had been. I'd rubbed her face in the truth, a truth that no one could ever understand better than me.

Just for a moment, her fears surfaced, but Megan shoved them back down immediately, faking a smile as she did.

"It really gets you off, hitting people in their weak spots, doesn't it?" She recovered her air of self-assurance immediately and lifted her chin in challenge. I might win the battle, she was saying, but she wouldn't let me win the war.

"Just as much as it gets you off, hitting my weak spots," I answered in kind, taking a step back from her.

Megan advanced on me, raising herself up on her tiptoes until she could reach my ear. For a moment, her breasts were pressing against my chest, and her hips lined up perfectly with mine. I found myself between her thighs.

"Let me tell you a secret," she said in a sensual whisper. "You are undoubtedly a difficult man, Miller, but I've already been through hell, and I'm not afraid of any devils. Least of all you." Her warm breath caressed my shoulder, then she pulled back from my ear and smiled. Instinctively, I looked down at her full lips.

After a moment, I shook myself and stepped back again, putting more necessary distance between us.

"Don't play with me, Megan, because if I start playing with you, you're going to get hurt for real," I warned her sternly. She was smart; she would understand what I meant.

A derisive smile twisted her lips, and then, without another word, she turned and walked resolutely out the door.

8

....

I blamed it on his eyes.

SELENE

I couldn't stop thinking about Neil.

Ever since I'd gotten back from the shore, I'd been reliving that moment against the door when he touched me, when he'd reawakened my lust with his burning gaze. I recalled his hot breath creeping between my lips, making me crave his mouth.

If he'd tried to kiss me then, I would have let him. Because I wanted him.

This was a new sensation for me—I'd never been so attracted to anyone before.

When Bailey or Janel had talked to me about "chemistry" I'd always thought it didn't really exist. But that was only because I'd never experienced it for myself.

Now, though, I knew exactly what they were talking about. Even just a brush of his fingertips sent chills down my body.

I blamed it on his eyes and how they shone like oxidized gold and his deep, manly voice, all to avoid thinking about the fact that Neil was becoming a genuine addiction for me.

Something had changed inside me after Logan told me about Kimberly. I couldn't judge Neil or his behavior (though it was often unacceptable).

Instead, I wanted to be on his side. I wanted to be with him and make him understand that love meant total acceptance.

Did I say *love*?

Yeah, I did.

I didn't have the first clue what love really was, but it was the only word I could use to describe this calamity. I was confident, though, that something had changed in him as well when it came to me. I'd never seen him so confused.

Usually, Neil always seemed so self-assured, with a casually dominating presence that would have made another man falter. But he hadn't been like that on the beach that night. He'd seemed lost then. Unstable, struggling with all the conflicting emotions trying to burst out of him. I'd seen it in his eyes.

I had learned how to read him a little bit, how to look deeper. Now, even when he refused to talk to me, his actions, his facial expressions, even the different tones of his voice told me how he was feeling.

"You are my beyond."

I didn't know exactly how to take a confession like that. He'd said the words angrily, but I had the feeling that, in his own way, he was trying to tell me something important. But what was it that made him run away from me all the time? Why was he so afraid of me?

Sure, Neil wasn't in love with me—he didn't even believe in love—but there was a fine thread linking us together.

It was undeniable.

But he was very good at closing himself off to others and keeping all his fears inside so he didn't have to expose them. Usually, a woman wouldn't even notice them, but I did because I was the one he had permitted to peek into his soul.

And, ever since then, I could do nothing but wonder about what Kimberly had put him through. How much shame had she inflicted upon him? How many colors had she snuffed out of a child's life—a child who was never allowed to have a childhood? My heart wept every time I thought about it.

But there was another problem on top of all of that: Mr. Disaster was the son of my dad's girlfriend. What would happen if Matt and Mia found out about us?

"Hey, earth to Selene." Janel waved a hand in front of my face as I stared, lost in grim thoughts.

I hadn't said a word since we walked into our favorite café near my neighborhood.

"You've been spacey ever since you got back from your vacation," Bailey tutted, sitting beside me. I hadn't told them anything about what had happened.

For some reason, I felt the inexplicable need to protect Neil, to safeguard those moments we had shared in that room and on the beach and to honor Logan's confidences.

When it came to Neil, I felt like a butterfly.

A little butterfly that, despite having the entire sky through which to roam, always chose to land on one particularly damaged flower because that's where her heart was.

"She's right. You're different; you seem…" Janel paused to suck some orange juice through her straw. "…thoughtful," she finished.

I moved the spoon around slowly in my coffee and watched the dark liquid, considering.

"What is love to you?" I asked abruptly and looked at both of my friends, who both wore unsettled expressions. They probably weren't expecting a question like that from me. I was the one, after all, who always tried to dodge that kind of conversation.

"There are so many ways to define love. The only thing I know for sure is that none of us will ever really understand it." Janel answered first.

"Love is like lightning. You never know when it's going to strike until it hits you right here." Bailey touched her chest and smiled as I looked back to my coffee cup. I ran an index finger around the rim as I pondered their answers.

"What do you think love is?" Janel asked me, and I turned my eyes back to her. She was frowning in concentration with her chin balanced on her palm. I'd never seen her look so focused, not even in class.

"For me, love is…" I mumbled awkwardly. I was always embarrassed when I had to talk about my thoughts on such personal subjects, but I was the one who had started this conversation, and talking to my friends could only help me.

"It's when you see the one you love and your hands start to sweat and your legs get weak and your heart starts beating. You like everything about him, even the little things. Even the flaws. Love is when you can see a whole universe in his eyes. It's when you can smell his scent even when you're sitting on a park bench and you look up from your book because it suddenly feels like he's right there, all around you. Love is when his face is constantly sneaking into your thoughts. Love is when he makes himself at home in your head with no intention of ever leaving it and, for the microscopic bit of time, you get to go somewhere else. Love is when the days pass slower because he's not there. When you look for his eyes in other people's faces, but his color is too special, too rare, so it could never belong to anyone else. Love is when, for better or for worse, you can let go of all the bitterness and hate. Love is when you're willing to shoulder your beloved's baggage from the past and ease some of the burden as he moves into a better future. It's when you accept him unconditionally because you just…love him."

I opened up and gave voice to everything I was feeling in that moment. The emotions were so powerful, so intense, that I couldn't control them. Talking them out should have felt like a weight off, but instead it did nothing but confirm something I'd been suspecting for a long time: I didn't just have chemistry with Neil; my feelings for him were strong and inevitable.

"Wow," Janel whispered as though she'd just witnessed some dazzling spectacle.

"If that's the Neil Miller effect, I've got to meet this guy," Bailey put in. What neither of them knew, however, was that there were a lot of Neil Miller effects, and most of them weren't positive.

Like the bonfire, for example, where he'd made me feel two inches tall with his condescension and cutting "jokes" that would have made anyone lose their cool. We'd gotten into a heated argument and then I'd cried in front of him because I realized that Neil was struggling. He was struggling with himself.

It had taken me too long to really understand, but, now that I did, I couldn't really get angry at him. Even if it did make me look like a girl devoid of pride or dignity to outsiders. I had finally figured out that if I wanted to break through the shadows that surrounded Neil, I couldn't use rage or distance from him to do it.

We needed to take to the skies together, united against adversity, just like Peter Pan and Tinkerbell.

Quickly, before I could overthink it, I got out my phone and typed a text to him.

I figured out the answer.

That night in the bedroom of the beach house, Neil had asked where I would be if I could be anywhere I wanted, and I had finally, if belatedly, understood what he'd been getting at. Neil was unusually deep as well as complex and he always hid a part of himself in the things he said. That was why he never wasted words. I often felt inadequate, unable to keep up with him or immediately intuit his meaning.

I stared uncertainly into the darkened screen of my phone. Neil might not even reply. On the beach he had rejected the possibility of any sort of relationship between us, after all. But I knew I wasn't the only one who felt certain things when we got too close, when our eyes communicated wordlessly in a way others couldn't understand.

Janel and Bailey had started talking again by then, and I heard Tyler's name. Apparently Bailey was still obsessed with him. I just kept checking my phone and imagining Neil getting that text and thinking it was from some crazy person or, even worse, from a girl who had a crush on him.

When my phone vibrated against my thigh, I jumped. Then I immediately unlocked the screen to read his text.

And what's that, Babygirl?

He had responded to me with the nickname that I loved. He usually called me that when he was in a good mood or when he was trying to seduce me. So maybe he wasn't mad at me? Had his meltdown on the beach simply been a moment of…weakness? Confusion?

Mr. Disaster was a mess of contradictions, and I was getting to be the same way.

A faint yearning made me clench my legs at the memory of all the times I'd given in to lust with him, but the guilt that usually followed was gone.

Gone completely.

Neverland. I would want to be there with you, and I know that you would too.

I smiled slightly because I loved to tease him.

Aren't you mad about the things I said to you?

There he was—the childish version of Neil who tried every trick he knew to get away from me. But now I knew his game.

If he were living another life, he would have fought for someone like me. In this one, he didn't have the strength to fight another impossible battle. He thought I was going to judge him. He thought all women were like Kimberly and would only ever use him as an object. He lived his whole life confined by these beliefs and deprived himself of the most beautiful parts.

And those parts did exist. Happiness was for everyone, after all; one just had to know where to look for it.

I am, yes, but I've also forgiven you, I wrote.

I'm not going to apologize, he texted back immediately, like he'd just been waiting for my message. Maybe he was glued to his phone just like I was. Maybe his heart was beating hard too. Maybe he was missing me, though he never would have told me if he were.

I don't expect you to, I tapped out quickly. This was a clear sign that I was starting to get him: I didn't need his apologies. Neil knew that I wanted to dig deeper into him, and he was trying to protect himself.

I still believe what I said. It won't work between us, he wrote with his typical candor. I made a face as I read the message. He was talking about how it was impossible for us to go back to how things had been before, despite the fact the neither of us had ever been able to make much sense of what we'd had in New York.

But even though we were now living separate lives far apart, we hadn't forgotten any of it.

Above all else, we hadn't been able to forget each other.

A few moments later, I grabbed my phone and got up from the table. But even as I paid the bill and followed my friends out of the café, my mind was still anchored to my chat with Neil. I did everything like an automaton. I nodded my head at Janel and responded to Bailey distractedly, but in reality, I just wanted to be by myself so I could talk to him again.

Was this also one of love's side effects?

It's what you believe, sure, but it's not what you actually want, I wrote back to him.

Maybe I was pushing it but Neil could be incredibly arrogant and presumptuous. He was convinced that he knew everything and that refusing to allow himself to forge normal human relationships was the only solution to his problems. Above all else, he was convinced that he was unworthy of receiving true, pure love.

He was convinced that there was something wrong about him, that he was a monster.

Why had it taken me so long to see this? Because no one—certainly not Neil himself—had told me anything about his past.

We don't always want the right things.

I told my friends goodbye and headed home. I walked, glancing between my phone and the sidewalk. Every now and then, I would stumble over my own feet, distracted by our conversation. It was rare to get the opportunity to have an actual conversation with Neil, so even if he was only present virtually, I was going to take full advantage of the temporary talkativeness.

The right thing isn't always what's best for us, I wrote out with both thumbs flying.

And what do you think is best for you? He asked, and I stopped in the middle of the sidewalk. I adjusted the scarf around my neck with one hand. A woman passed me pulling a little girl along by the hand, and her face looked numb from the cold. It occurred to me that my own fingers were practically frozen around my phone, but I couldn't wear my gloves if I wanted to keep texting with him.

Being with you. It was a confession, and I sent it without any further reflection.

I wasn't sure if that could be considered a true declaration of love, but I regretted writing it almost immediately either way. Suddenly, the cold all around me was replaced by a heat that was emanating solely from my cheeks.

I bit my lip and began walking again, hugging my long coat around me. I shook my head at the ridiculous thing I had just done. Neil was never going to text me again. How many more attractive, more experienced women was he surrounded by at all times?

A lot.

He wasn't going to choose me.

Neil often thought that I couldn't handle him and sometimes I thought so too, but there was something inside me that shooed those doubts away. Because I knew that I could accept him for who he was.

My phone vibrated, and I read it immediately. I wasn't expecting a response but I got...

I already let you be with me.

I snarled angrily. That's what being together meant to Neil: hopping into bed. His mind could only envision a sexual relationship between us, nothing more. His body was a merry-go-round, and he'd already let me have more than one spin. Now it was time for the next girl in line.

From every angle, Neil was unbelievable. He had a deep soul and a brilliant mind but sex was the only way he knew how to communicate. He expressed himself physically so well that women, enthralled by his power and skill, didn't see what was hidden behind his enigmatic air and seductive smile.

Now I understood that he'd been turned into an object when he was a child, and even now, he was still objectifying himself because he believed that was all he had to offer.

I wasn't talking about sex, I typed, my fingers numb from the cold.

How could I make him see? It wouldn't be easy to change his way of thinking; it had been developed over the course of his entire life.

Fifteen minutes later, I was home and still lost in my thoughts. He hadn't responded to that last message, though I'd seen that coming. I walked up my driveway and lifted a hand to wave at my neighbor, Mrs. Kamper, as she headed to her car. I smiled at her, but then a sudden feeling of vertigo forced me to grab hold of the porch railing. My heartbeat sped up, and powerful throbs of pain in my head made me close my eyes and breathe in deeply.

I was having these dizzy spells and getting headaches more and more lately. I'd already told my doctor, and she assured me it was nothing to be concerned about, just more fallout from the trauma of the accident.

I tucked my phone into my coat pocket and paused for a couple of minutes before climbing the last few steps to my front door. That miserable feeling had come back, weighing heavily on my chest. My body frequently felt weak; I wasn't getting much sleep at night, and the headaches only increased in frequency. I honestly didn't know who to talk to, besides the doctor, or how to cope with the situation. I wanted to keep my suffering under wraps to avoid freaking my mother out, so I tried to get through the worst moments by myself. Unfortunately, they seemed to just show up without warning throughout the day.

Once I'd calmed down a little, I went into the house with a forced smile on my face.

"I'm back, Mom." I put my bag on the shelf in the entryway and shrugged off my coat, hanging it neatly on the rack. When I turned to the living room, though, I immediately noticed a stranger there, and my look of feigned cheer gave way to total confusion.

"Oh, hi, sweetheart." There my mother stood, looking as lovely as ever and graciously entertaining a man. I moved toward her, glancing back and forth between the two of them. Finally, my gaze settled on the man, who couldn't have been more than forty. He had notably intense gray eyes and neatly coiffed black hair. His angular jaw was covered with a dark layer of beard. His nose was straight, and his lips were thin. His charcoal suit matched his eyes, and his body looked slim yet leanly muscled.

"Is this your daughter?" His voice was low and scratchy, and it made me halt a short distance away from him.

"Yes, Anton. This is Selene." My mother smiled at me, and I tried to smile back at her, concealing my obvious surprise.

"A pleasure to meet you, Selene. I'm Anton Coleman." The man stuck out his hand, and after just a moment of hesitation, I shook it.

"Well, Judith, as always, time flies when I'm with you, but I have some errands I have to get to." Anton nodded briefly in my direction and then headed for the door, my mother accompanying him. I watched him all the way. The two said goodbye in the doorway, and when my mother closed the door and turned to look at me, I pulled off my scarf and tossed it onto the sofa.

"Do you have something to tell me?" I asked her immediately. Mom knew that I would be fine with a new man in her life—my father had moved on, and it was probably best for her to do the same—but she was likely still a little worried about my reaction. For my part, I knew I was protective and possessive of her, though I'd never tried to dictate her life or her choices. I had to admit, though, that this was a big reversal for her. She hadn't dated at all since the divorce.

"He's just a colleague," she said immediately—and defensively—before fleeing into the kitchen to escape any more of my questions.

"He has beautiful eyes, your *colleague*, Anton," I said teasingly, following her around the kitchen island. Mom turned her back to me and started shifting things around randomly on the counter, pretending she was cleaning up.

"Mom," I called out to her, taking a seat on a stool. "Mooom," I said again, and she turned around, hands on her hips. Her cheeks were pink with embarrassment, and her eyes glowed with a new light.

"Selene, I told you—he is a colleague of mine. And he's too young for me, anyway," she babbled, waving a hand in the air.

"How old is he?" I asked, trying to stifle a laugh.

"Forty," she answered. He was only four years younger than her.

"And what was he doing here?" I smiled, trying to put her at ease. I didn't want her to feel like she couldn't talk to me about this sort of thing. I was her daughter, and understanding had always been a big part of our relationship.

"I forgot my agenda in the classroom, and he was kind enough to bring it back to me," she answered, but something wasn't adding up for me. First of all, wasn't it interesting that Anton apparently knew where we lived? Second, my mother was blushing again.

"Uh-huh, I see," I said. "So he's also a professor?" She nodded.

"So how do you feel about each other? Are you dating? Tell me everything," I insisted, and it occurred to me that the messages my mother so often read with a dreamy look on her face were from this guy.

"We went out one time; it was while you were in New York," she began.

"But nothing happened," she added immediately. "Plus, at my age…" she continued with a gloominess that I didn't like at all. My mother was a cultured, intelligent, and enchanting woman. Her beauty had not faded at all with the passage of time, and more importantly, she had unique qualities that would be sure to impress any man.

"You should get to know him, see what happens. I have faith in you, Mom, and in your choices. I know you'll do what's right for you." I gave her my blessing and was happy to see a quiet spark of hope in her eyes.

We talked for another hour about Anton Coleman. My mother recounted every detail of their first meeting and all the things about him that had captivated her from the moment she saw him. She also told me that she was going to be very sensible and think long and hard before getting into a real relationship with him. Either way, she would take her time now and deepen their pleasant acquaintance.

I kept asking questions and listening to her answers until she switched to another, decidedly less exciting, topic: Matt Anderson.

"Give him a call. He said he called your phone, but you didn't answer. He wants to talk to you." Mom handed me my phone and urged me to call Matt.

Okay, yes, we had spent a day together, and I had even given him a handmade gift, but as far as I was concerned, he was still Matt Anderson, asshole father, even if my hatred of him had dulled slightly.

"C'mon," Mom smiled at me, and I grabbed the phone, rolling my eyes.

I got off my stool and went into the living room to call while my mother got dinner started.

"Selene." Matt answered on the second ring, like he'd been waiting to hear from me. I sighed and looked out over our neat little lawn, wondering what I could say to him that wouldn't sound rude.

"Hey, Matt. You were trying to get ahold of me?" It wasn't very polite, but it wasn't overly rude either.

"Yeah, I wanted to suggest you come over to my place this Saturday," he said immediately without hesitation. I frowned because I hadn't been expecting anything remotely like that. He wanted me to fly out and spend more time with him? There, in the house I had barely escaped last time?

Heat from the memories I associated with that house warmed my cheeks, among other spots on my body.

God, I had to get my head on straight.

"I've already talked to your mother about this. I'll pay for your plane ticket, and, of course, I'd pick you up from the airport. What do you think?" he added, sounding enthused, and I paused to consider his offer.

Neil still hadn't responded to my text and had just cut off our conversation, as was his style. He always had to be the one making the decisions. Sometimes, I could appreciate the domineering part of him, while other times I detested it.

Still, I could choose to go back to New York. Not just for Matt but also for a chance to see Neil again.

I blushed.

The real question was, would he want to see me again?

We would be sharing a house and a family again. Our relationship had taken a firmly negative turn after the car crash, though, so maybe going back wasn't the best choice. I didn't want to be all over him—I didn't want to smother or suffocate him. I knew how he was: Neil was a free spirit, firmly independent and rebellious.

He would have fled from me again and that wasn't what I wanted, but… I hadn't said anything yet about Player being behind the crash. I wasn't sure what to do about that and when or if to tell anyone.

"Selene? Are you still there?" Matt's voice jolted me, and I cleared my throat.

"Yeah," I said, sounding uncertain. I didn't want to go back to New York or set foot in my father's mansion again. Yet, the thought of seeing Neil's golden eyes again, of getting to smell him and feel his presence in the room next to me, was a kick in the chest so powerful that it made me gasp for air.

I needed something to hold on to so I didn't just give in to the lightning-fast feeling of fatigue that rendered my whole body weak whenever I merely recalled the feeling of his hands on me, his brazen mouth, his fiery passion, his dominance…

"So, are you coming?" my father insisted, wary of my silence. Meanwhile, I was trying to reconnect with reality. I should have refused; my answer should have been a decisive "no." I couldn't live with Neil, not now that I'd realized I had real feelings for him. I would have to hear or see it every time he brought Jennifer or one of his other blonds to his room, and then I'd be miserable and crying again.

No.

I shook my head rapidly.

I couldn't go back there.

Except...didn't I say I could handle someone like him?

Yes, I did. But the fear often came back to torment me.

I was afraid of what I felt when he looked at me or when he touched me in that confident, expert way of his. I was afraid of the things I felt even at just the sound of his voice.

Thus, my internal struggle between reason and feeling began.

Then, instinct won out.

"O-okay," I agreed.

I was nervous—terribly nervous—at the thought of seeing Neil again.

Ever since I accepted Matt's offer, I'd done nothing but think about Neil all the time.

I saw him in my head as clearly as if he were actually standing in front of me. I'd never be able to forget those mysterious eyes, especially not after our encounter on the beach.

I felt like I'd been stripped of all my certainty, left vulnerable and weak.

Weak when it came to him.

Neil really had become an obsession for me, his face a marvelous fantasy that ebbed and flowed like waves on the sea. The memory of him was a slow, constant torment, a sad yet passionate nostalgia that dulled and obscured all other thoughts until I had no space left in my head for anything but him.

Mixed in with all of that was the guilt I felt toward my family. Whenever I remembered that Neil was practically my stepbrother, I knew just how wrong it was to want to kiss him. But that wanting, that mental image, was like a wild storm that blew through my days with its fury and rendered all my other worries small, because just the thought of him became a constant rumble that I wanted to banish.

I spent the five days before I left at the mercy of these feelings.

Five goddamned days of thinking about making up some excuse to avoid going to see Matt only to inevitably change my mind again.

"You're deep in thought." My mother walked into my bedroom as I sat in front of my vanity mirror, combing out my hair. I had covered my scar again with my long bangs, and now I was trying to untangle the irritating knots at the bottom.

"Come here," she said gently, patting the spot next to her on the bed. I held the comb out to her, knowing she would want to deal with my long, untamable hair.

"I still remember combing your hair when you were a little girl." My mother's voice emerged from behind me like a sweet melody. The canopy of the bed with its ivory curtains surrounded our figures. I stared out the window as the soft, warm light of the bedside table lamp gently illuminated my room.

"I know... You made me go to school with those embarrassing pigtails until I was fourteen," I grumbled, staring down at my legs where they hung over the edge of the bed, swathed in basic pj's.

"Hey, don't denigrate your mother's talents. They looked lovely on you," she mock-warned me as she brushed my hair. I relaxed under her gentle, affectionate touch.

"You still need to tell me all about your trip. You've changed the subject every time I've brought it up, but I'm sure there's lots to tell," she said curiously.

She had asked several times about how I'd spent those two days with Matt and his family, but I had always avoided discussing it. My mother knew me very well, and I was afraid that, somehow, she was going to suss out what I was trying to hide from her.

"There's not much to tell. Matt's a terrible cook, but you probably knew that. He managed to reduce the eggs to carbon, so we got hot dogs at the boardwalk instead." I smiled and turned my head a bit to look at her, but she just turned my face back around and continued to work delicately through my hair.

"Selene, a mother knows everything before a daughter even opens her mouth," she noted, making my forehead wrinkle in a frown. This time, I didn't try to turn around and stayed stiff and motionless, listening to her. "Can I tell you a story?" she asked in a fond tone.

"Don't you think I'm a little old for fairy tales?" I tried to make my voice light and hide how inexplicably nervous I suddenly felt.

"For sure." She continued combing out my hair. "That's why I said I was going to tell you a *story*, not a fairy tale," she continued.

I glanced at her in confusion, and she gave me a sweet smile.

"Once upon a time—" she began, but I cut her off.

"That's how fairy tales start." I rolled my eyes at her, and she sighed.

"Then let's call this a slightly different kind of fairy tale." She cleared her throat and picked up where she'd left off. "Once upon a time, there was a princess left lying in a sterile bed after she had fallen into a deep, deep sleep. Her pale skin recalled the purity of snow, and her full lips the red of a cherry." She took my hand and rubbed the back of it with her thumb. I turned to her then, and the identical blues of our eyes met.

"But the princess was not alone. A mysterious, captivating knight spent all his time with her, warming her cold body the way the sun shines down to slowly melt the snow. But the young man's heart was a hidden treasure box to which no woman possessed the key. Many feared him because he certainly didn't have the appearance of a good man..." She shook her head, smiling and lulling me with her voice. "He was not courteous or kind; in fact, he was so unfriendly and arrogant that no one knew what was hidden in the depths of his soul. His eyes were full of darkness, and his spirit was imprisoned by a shadow," she went on, looking at our clasped hands. Then she lifted one corner of her mouth slightly, as though remembering something beautiful.

"Where are you going with this, Mom?" I murmured.

"But one day in that barren room..." she continued, ignoring my question. "He watched that princess as though she were the most beautiful creature he had ever seen. Then he crouched down next to her and took her hand, staring into her face," she said softly. "He rested his hand on her chest and, taking advantage of the girl's slumber, told her everything he felt but was too afraid to confess. He cracked open the secret chest that was his heart for her, revealing everything inside." She lifted her eyes to mine and stared deeply into them. Her story had fully captured my attention.

"And what was inside?" I asked, making a face.

"The monsters he was fighting. The monsters he wanted to protect the princess from, even if it came at the cost of his own life. The monsters that he needed to destroy so he might live his dreams. Perhaps even live them with her," she answered and tucked a lock of hair behind my ear. I gulped, getting lost in her words. Words that, oddly enough, I had heard before. Someone, somewhere else, had said them, but I couldn't recall who or when.

"That seemingly rude and hot-tempered knight had, in reality, an immense heart as well as an unassailable strength and a noble spirit. But no one had ever tried to look beyond the shadows in his eyes. He sheltered true love inside himself, though he didn't even know what it meant. Once the princess awoke, she needed to be strong enough to help her knight win his battles. Both of them needed to unite against the darkness to destroy it once and for all. Only then would they both find true love, which often hides itself in the shadows, under a black cloak and behind enigmatic eyes that might appear to have nothing to give. Bear this in mind, Selene: True feelings are often silent and imperceptible, hidden in an action, a word, a touch." She smiled again and stroked my cheek. I just sat there in shock, considering her words.

"Why did you tell me that story?" I asked, visibly moved.

"Because we shouldn't run away from the things that scare us. Or the people that scare us." She stood up from the bed, and I once again found myself looking up at her.

"Remember, Selene—a mother knows everything before a daughter even opens her mouth," she added, giving me a little peck on the nose before she left my room. All at once, my face went up in flames.

Was she talking about...Neil?

No. I shook myself.

How could she possibly know?

I pondered her story. Was I afraid of Neil? Yes. Even though I wanted

him with all my heart, I still feared the way he could completely desta-
bilize me.

Maybe my mother did know something, but how?

I tried to sleep on it, but a powerful headache along with my general
anxiety kept me from sleeping.

The next morning, I was going to leave and see my Disaster again. Just
thinking about it made my legs shake and my heart…

My heart cried his name.

9

He punished himself not just because he had suffered,
but because he thought that suffering was his fault.

SELENE

The next morning came all too quickly.

Matt was as good as his word: He picked me up from the airport,
and we drove to his house.

Returning to that place brought back the same familiar feelings: anxiety,
awe, and curiosity.

When I went inside, rolling my suitcase along behind me, I breathed
in the vanilla smell that spoke to how well-kept the house was. The crystal
chandeliers glittered, light bouncing off the silvery marble of the walls and
floors and turning it almost golden.

"Miss Selene, it's so nice to see you again. How are you doing? I heard
about your accident." Anna, the housekeeper, gave me a hug and immediately grabbed my suitcase to carry it upstairs.

"I'm doing well, Miss Anna, thank you." I smiled at her, and she pressed
a tender kiss to my cheek. Her eyes lingered on my forehead. Even though
I'd gotten bangs to cover the scar, it was still there—a constant reminder
of what had happened. Anna was discreet, though, so she didn't ask me
about it.

"Anna, please take Selene to her room and let the kids know she's here."

My father rested a hand on my shoulder, urging me to follow the older woman up the stairs.

I climbed the enormous marble staircase with bated breath. I hadn't heard anything more from Neil after our brief exchange of text messages, so my opportunity to convince him to look at the situation in a new way had come to nothing. Once again, I found myself thinking how awfully pigheaded and generally exasperating the man was. It wouldn't be easy to get him to understand that I wanted more than just his body. Plus, I had to be careful never to let on that I knew about Kimberly. If he found out, I'd not only lose all the trust Logan had placed in me, but I also risked alienating Neil entirely.

I needed to wait until Neil was ready to tell me about his past himself. Maybe he'd never be ready, but a part of me still hoped he would one day decide to confide in me and open himself up without any reticence. It would be a huge turning point for him, and it would give me the opportunity to chip away at the ice around his soul and maybe even transfer some human warmth to him. The kind of warmth that had little to do with sex. The kind that, perhaps, no one else had ever offered him. Or maybe Neil had always refused to receive it out of a desire to punish himself.

He punished himself not just because he had suffered, but because he thought that the suffering was his fault.

"Thank you, Anna." I smiled at her as she left me alone in front of the door to my room, where I could wash up and change my clothes after my trip. I watched her go, and then my eyes instinctively slid to the room next door: Neil's room. His door was open.

With just a few steps, I was standing in front of it with a trembling hand on the doorknob. His bed was made. The sheets were clean and so strongly scented that I could smell them even at a distance.

Everything was in perfect order—impersonal, cold, like a room no one used anymore.

I frowned.

Had he stayed out all night?

He preferred to send his lovers home and never spent the night with them. In fact, in the period right before I left, he'd stopped bringing them into his room at all.

"Look! She's here!" someone yelled, interrupting my train of thought.

I didn't even have time to turn around before a superexcited Alyssa threw herself at me, making me sway on my feet.

"She's been asking me constantly when you'd get here. I might actually be a little jealous." Logan appeared behind his girlfriend, ruffling his curly hair with an ironic smile.

Alyssa, meanwhile, had wrapped herself around me so tightly that I was having trouble breathing.

"Oh my God! You look amazing!" She grabbed me by the shoulders to get a better look at me. "What did you do to your hair? And that bod! It's different, but you look so good. Wow!" She hugged me again, and I grinned at Logan, who was rolling his eyes.

"Give it a rest, Alyssa," he groused, grabbing her by the arm as he approached to scrutinize me more closely. "Though I completely agree with my girlfriend, you're a knockout." He gave me an affectionate hug and kissed my cheek.

Logan had always been very brotherly toward me, and I'd never felt uncomfortable or embarrassed with him. After the talk we'd had at the beach house, I felt like the understanding between us had only grown deeper. I was honored that he'd trusted me with something so important.

I wasn't going to let him down.

After saying our hellos, we went downstairs for lunch, all of us sitting in our customary places from when I'd lived there. I took a seat next to Chloe and was surprised by how natural it felt to do so. It made me feel like I'd never left. Apparently, even here in New York, among Matt's new family, I had carved out a little place for myself.

"Are you still having frequent headaches?" Mia looked at me with concern as she sipped her water. Anna moved around the table, making sure we were all content with our meals, while Logan and Alyssa bickered about something I didn't understand.

"Yeah. My doctor says it will just take time to fully recover from the trauma I experienced." I smiled reassuringly at her and glanced around, waiting for Neil to make an appearance.

Where the hell was he?

On one hand, I wanted to push our meeting off for as long as possible. On the other, I had an enormous desire to see him again.

For a fleeting moment, my brain played a trick on me, making me think I could sense his musky scent in the air. I knew it was only a bizarre hallucination, though. A figment of my own imagination.

"Did they prescribe you any medications?" Chloe asked. I snapped out of my musings and turned to look at her.

"Only on an as-needed basis." I only used the painkillers when my headaches got particularly bad.

"It was an incredible stroke of luck that the hematoma was completely reabsorbed. The brain is one of the most delicate parts of the human body and—" Matt stopped when he heard the front door slam.

We all jumped.

Decisive footfalls told me exactly who had just arrived.

Neil burst into the dining room, and the moment I saw him, I stopped breathing.

He looked furious.

His black sweater only highlighted how his chest was heaving in time with his labored breath. His light-wash jeans, on the other hand, clung to his stiff, solid legs. Neil was capable of communicating so much with his body and, as he loomed over the room with every inch of his more than six-foot frame, he radiated anger without ever saying a single word.

We all stopped what we were doing. All eyes were fixed on him, and it was only then that I noticed the purple bruises that punctuated his face around his lower lip and one eyebrow.

They looked like souvenirs from a fistfight.

What had happened to him?

Despite his beaten-up appearance, I felt an untamable yearning inside me, a fire that consumed my skin.

He was beautiful, even like this: angry, exhausted, and all in disarray.

Especially his mind.

In fact, the disarray was mostly in his mind.

He approached us in a few strides, and I felt the urge to flee like a coward because I knew something bad was about to happen.

Neil stopped and went still, just watching us. Then he held up a note-book in one hand.

"Who fucking ripped up my drawings?" His powerful, livid tone made us all flinch.

With a grunt of rage, he ran a hand over his face and through his chestnut hair. He looked confused, pained, and unstable.

Extremely unstable.

"Neil, what are you talking about?" Mia was the first to get up the guts to talk back to him. None of the rest of us could because, just then, Neil seemed capable of anything.

"Who fucking ripped up my goddamned drawings?" He repeated the question with such a frightening anger that it made my blood run cold. I could see the tension in his body, and so could everyone else. None of us knew how to handle this. Neil, meanwhile, looked at each of us in turn, then at the table generally, not focused on anything in particular.

It seemed like his brain was somehow unable to process the things his eyes saw.

This whole time, I had kept still, determined not to move a muscle.

"Chloe," he said. "Was it you?"

His sister clutched my hand under the table, and I looked at her. She was trembling. Her eyes were huge, and her breath came in pants. She shook her head slowly, and Neil turned his attention to Logan. Alyssa had gone white as a sheet next to him while Logan had wrapped a comforting arm around her shoulders.

"Neil, why would any of us rip up your drawings?" Logan slowly got to his feet; every one of his small movements was carefully measured. Neil watched his hands warily.

He looked like a wild animal put on the defensive, ready to tear apart anything that made a false move in his direction.

Logan raised his hands in surrender, a gesture I'd seen him make in the past. He'd done it outside of Blanco to get Neil to throw away a shard of glass that was cutting into his palm.

"You can't touch my things," Neil hissed, lowering the arm holding the pad of paper. Logan nodded and moved away from his seat to stand closer to Neil.

"Neil, you're the only one with access to the pool house right now. Your drawings have been in there lately. And none of us would do something like that." Logan continued to approach him slowly. Mia tried not to cry, but she let out a small sob, catching Neil's attention. As he looked at her, a cruel expression came over his face, and she looked down, unable to bear the chilling gravity of her son's stare.

"Neil, try to get ahold of yourself. Please." Logan spoke to him in his usual calm, tolerant fashion. A few more steps and he would be able to touch Neil, but instead he paused a little ways away, perhaps seeking permission to continue. Neil gave him a suspicious look and backed up.

"Okay, I'm stopping here," Logan said, correctly interpreting Neil's standoffish look. "Can I... Can I just see what happened?" He stretched out an arm in Neil's direction, open palm face-up.

Neil's golden eyes flicked down at him, but once again, he didn't seem capable of communicating normally. He somehow looked like a scared child and a dangerous man at the same time. His imposing frame loomed over Logan's and his broad shoulders spoke his insurmountable strength.

His whole body was a tight bundle of muscles and nerves. The bulging veins on the back of his hands showed the rising rage that he was trying to tamp down in any way he could. He shook his head again and touched his hair nervously. A move he always made when he was feeling anxious.

"I'm going to go... I... I... I'm going," he muttered confusedly. He stepped back and took a deep breath.

"Neil..." Logan tried to call his brother back, but he raced out of the room.

None of us commented on what had just happened after Neil left. We were all shocked speechless.

After lunch, I went to my room to chat with Alyssa. I found out that she couldn't stand Neil but that Logan didn't know that because Alyssa was afraid she'd lose her boyfriend if he found out how much she disliked his older brother.

"I think he's completely off his rocker." She twirled her index finger around her temple, and I glanced at her in the mirror. I was brushing my hair while Alyssa talked about Neil.

"We don't know what might have happened to make him that way," I responded shortly. I was irritated by the flippant way she was talking about Neil. First of all, she barely knew the man. Second, I felt this primal urge to come to his defense, especially now that I knew some of the truth about him.

"I get why the girls at school are content just to fuck him. I mean…that's all you can really expect from a guy like Neil. They say he's a beast in the sack," she said boldly as she lay on my bed and perused her red fingernails. Though I'd told Alyssa a lot about me and Neil, I'd never gone into specifics about his skills in bed. She'd tried to get me to spill the beans in the past, but I was deliberately vague, and I recognized this as another attempt to coax more details out of me.

But Alyssa, like most everyone else, was making the mistake of judging Neil solely on his physical appearance. Neil was more than what he showed to the world, though.

"He's not a sex object." I quit brushing my hair and switched to applying makeup.

"How are things going between you two anyway?" Alyssa watched me curiously as I applied mascara.

"They're not going at all." I sighed. I hadn't told her what happened at the beach. If I had told her that Mr. Disaster had treated me like crap and then rejected me, she would think I was an idiot for continuing to pursue him. Sometimes I even thought that about myself but then I thought about what Neil had gone through during his childhood and my anger gave way to understanding.

"I figured," Alyssa murmured. "I've seen him with Jennifer a lot since you've been gone," she added. I froze with my mascara wand in midair and stared sharply at her through the mirror's reflection. I had long suspected that Jennifer was back in the rotation, but knowing it for sure hurt.

I turned to Alyssa and fought for a breath. Jealousy had my lungs locked up. My stomach swam with nausea.

"Where?" I asked in a small voice.

Alyssa chewed on the inside of her cheek and gave me a shamefaced look. She obviously regretted telling me.

"Enough about that guy. Come on!" She hopped up off the bed and approached me, looking beautiful as ever. Sometimes I really admired how charming and confident she was. "Why don't you come out with us tonight?" She took me by the shoulders and gave me a vigorous shake—the way she always did when she was trying to convince me to say yes to one of her suggestions.

"And be the third wheel while you and Logan cuddle up and make out? No, thanks," I said teasingly, and she arched a disappointed eyebrow.

"Oh, come on. We've never made you feel like that," she huffed, and that was true, but I still didn't want to crash her night with Logan. They were a couple, and if they decided to switch it up and spend a few hours alone, I would have been in the way.

Just then, there was a knock at the door, and we both turned to see Logan, who had poked his head inside to peer at us.

"There you are. I should have put money on finding you in here." He walked in, grinning.

"I'm trying to convince Selene to come out with us tonight." Alyssa put her hands on her hips, trying to recruit her boyfriend to the arduous task of changing my mind.

"I agree with you completely. Selene, be ready at nine, no excuses," Logan ordered, making me roll my eyes. Then he went over to Alyssa and wrapped his arms around her waist. He made a few affectionate movements and whispered something into her ear. His girlfriend giggled mischievously and winked at me.

"You know, this is exactly what I was talking about when I said I didn't want to be a third wheel." I went red and slipped out of the room before I was forced to witness something much more embarrassing. I went down to the kitchen in a huff; thoughts of Neil were still spinning around in my head. After his outburst at lunch, he'd vanished. Maybe he went out? Or maybe he'd fled to the pool house?

Who knew?

Maybe Anna could help me out with that question?

After grabbing a pack of shelled pistachios that I knew he'd like from the pantry, I left the kitchen and found Anna in the living room, focused on polishing the silverware. I joined her.

"Miss Anna, do you know where Neil is?" I asked bluntly, which made her turn to face me. She looked at me with a kindly expression and smiled when she saw the packet I was holding. She jerked her chin toward the garden.

I thanked her and went outside. I rubbed my arms, clad only in a basic white sweater. The air was cold, and I hadn't thought to put on a coat. The sun had already set, and it would be nine in about an hour. I was supposed to be getting ready to go out with Logan and Alyssa, but I decided then and there that I was going to make up some excuse to get out of it.

I wasn't in the mood for parties or clubs.

With my mind made up, I looked around for my Disaster, but there was no sign of him. The chaise lounges by the pool where he often sat and smoked were all empty.

I frowned as I paused in the middle of the patio and looked over at the pool house. The light was on, which meant…

A sudden bout of nerves made my legs tremble.

I had no positive memories of that building, which was where Neil used to go to be with his lovers. I vividly recalled the two episodes I'd witnessed in there, and I definitely didn't want to repeat that experience.

I sighed, undecided about what I should do. I knew that he was furious, and I just wanted to make him feel better.

Wait, though…

Who in the family would have torn his drawings up?

It seemed impossible and yet someone had done it and incited all his fury.

Almost without noticing, I had brought myself to the front door of the pool house. I clenched my hand into a fist and raised it, ready to knock and alert him to my presence, but then I hesitated.

What if Jennifer opened the door in sexy underwear or, even worse, completely naked?

I let my hand fall slowly and took a step back because I knew that I wouldn't be able to take a sight like that. My disappointment would have been too obvious. I might have even cried, and that bitch would have just laughed at me.

No, it had been a stupid idea to go looking for him in the first place. I needed to get out of there.

I looked down at the bag of pistachios I held in my hand for him, and I felt so small. Just a girl trying to act like a woman with a man who carried his own hell around inside him. It was one of those moments when I vacillated between full courage and complete insecurity. I took a deep breath, trying to remind myself of all the things that had driven me to come back to New York, even if only for a weekend.

Then I managed to make myself knock. Three soft, fast raps, and I hoped deep down that there wasn't a woman in there. It made me feel pathetic, and the wait that followed was all the more terrible for it.

How much time passed? Two, three, or four seconds? And yet it felt like forever.

I shrugged and was about to leave when…

The door opened, and Neil stood before me in just his black boxers.

He radiated a rare beauty and an eroticism so intense that it completely annihilated my ability to speak.

I opened my mouth, intending to say something, anything, but his seminude body was just too distracting. I couldn't get a single word out as my eyes roamed over every bit of him, ending on the only piece of clothing he was wearing.

I forced myself to look up at his face and found him staring back at me.

My soul was drawn into those golden eyes and I felt an inescapable weakness moving over me.

I swallowed, but my tongue felt thick and my throat was dry, and I couldn't get out the speech I'd prepared.

A tick in his jaw and the tension of his muscles told me all about how enraged he still was. I'd made a mistake coming for him, I realized belatedly. He wanted to be alone. Or maybe I had interrupted him with one of his blonds and pissed him off.

"Uh…"

Come on, Selene, you can do better than this, I thought.

I jerked my chin toward the bag of pistachios I was crushing in my hand and then looked back at him.

"Can I come in?" I asked uncertainly.

It wasn't exactly what I'd planned to say, but at least I got my point across. I realized something then: Neil had done nothing but ignore me since I arrived. He didn't give me the warm welcome that everyone else in his family had. At lunch, he hadn't even looked at me.

Had he known that I was coming back?

Did he know I was going to be there for two days?

I assumed he did because Matt always called ahead to announce my arrival because he couldn't contain his excitement.

But Mr. Disaster hadn't even acknowledged my presence.

I tried to keep those fears at bay and focused on Neil, who was looking me up and down. I could never tell if he liked what he saw or not. He was good at concealing his thoughts. After a moment that felt like an eternity, he stepped aside and gave me his answer without words: *Yes, you can come in.*

I stopped a few steps inside when I heard the door slam behind me. I flinched, swallowing hard.

There was no one else in the pool house.

Everything was in perfect order.

Silence enveloped us.

I sniffed the air, and…there was no fruity Jennifer smell. No sex smell.

Neil was alone, and a part of me delighted in that and felt relieved. I felt him lurking behind me then, and I turned to face him. I considered the breadth of his shoulders, the toned arms that spoke to his incredible power, and his defined pectorals. His body had changed; it had become somehow even more powerful and vigorous.

Had he stepped up his training?

I watched him admiringly—I really couldn't help it—and frowned when I spotted a purple bruise near his ribs. It was a true hematoma, spreading out into a visible darkened spot.

Who did that to him? What happened?

I took a couple of steps closer and reached for him. Neil did not reject my touch by any means. So, I gently explored the spot with my fingers, and his abdomen twitched in pain. Once the immediate stab of pain faded, I stroked his smooth, warm skin. My hand looked very pale on his luminous, bronzed chest.

"Did you get this looked at? It's a bad bruise." I continued touching him, and he breathed gently through his nose. I had to tilt my face up to look him in the eye. He was staring fixedly at me, and he still hadn't said anything. Maybe he didn't want to talk to me. I chewed my lower lip, more embarrassed now than ever, and I timidly handed him the bag of pistachios.

"I brought these for you. I noticed that you seem to like them, right?" I whispered, staring into his luminous eyes again. Neil just watched my hand, and for a second, I thought he was going to go into a rage. Maybe I was pushing too hard? I could never be sure of anything with him.

To my surprise, though, he snatched up the bag. He looked it over, frowning, and I couldn't tell if he was pleased, surprised, or irritated. Then, he tossed it onto the couch, leaving me uncertain.

He hadn't appreciated my gesture.

I shook my head, trying to push past him, but I didn't get far before Neil, with his characteristic dominance, grabbed my face with both hands and stopped me in my tracks. His eyes bored into mine, and I knew immediately what he was going to do next. Despite my previous angry outburst, I had always felt protected when I was with him. I could feel his warmth and his desire, and it was enough to have me melting in his hands.

He licked his lower lip and breathed in deeply, closing and opening his eyes. He looked like he was struggling with something insurmountable. There was so much in his eyes, so many things that Neil would never tell me but that I would nevertheless try to learn.

My heart began to throb in my stomach. I was at his mercy, not only physically but mentally as well. He had gotten into my soul, and I belonged to him. It was over for me every time when he looked at me like that: lusty, angry, fragile, and confused.

With a groan of exasperation, he surrendered to his desires. He bent down until he could reach my lips and kissed me urgently. He pressed his mouth hard against mine, and I felt it, warm and lush.

He closed his eyes, and so did I. I was starving for him.

We were both starving, starving for kisses, for bites, tongues and touches, for an embrace. We were starving for sex and for love, dreams, feelings, and unspoken words. But Neil immediately broke contact, even as he remained way too close to me.

I looked at him in confusion and put my hand around the back of his neck to stroke him there. He hadn't taken everything he wanted, but in his gleaming eyes, I could see what he was feeling.

I felt it too.

These shared emotions of ours sometimes pushed us apart, while at other times they drew us together like magnets.

With one hand, Neil grazed my thigh, and I shuddered. He smirked and kept going.

His hand moved along my flank and then around to my ass.

His fingertips delicately traced the contours of my spine, making me arch my back and exhale. He stopped at the curve of my throat, his palm completely engulfing the nape of my neck. His thumb moved to caress my lips, and his eyes lingered there. He stared at my mouth like it was something entirely new to him.

He traced the outline of my mouth, and I kissed his fingertip, never lowering my eyes.

We were closely intertwined, perhaps for the very first time, and words had become superfluous.

As he moved closer, his breath moved over my face, and his lips touched mine again.

It was a light contact, just a hint, like the flutter of wings. But it awakened in me the desire for more.

I needed to feel him inside me, inside my soul.

I groaned in frustration when he pulled away and gave me a superior smile. Neil was really making a meal of this seduction. He made me believe that he was about to kiss me for real, crude and carnal, but instead he pulled back, just to drive me crazy.

"Quit it," I muttered in a low voice. He drew closer again and licked my lips with the tip of his tongue. My knees went weak, and I had to hold on to his sides to keep from falling to the floor. The rush of arousal made my nipples stiff and sent chills down my arms. My head spun.

The taste of him, so masculine and intense, was an aphrodisiac.

I licked my lips clean so I could take it all in and even shut my eyes as I savored it.

"Feeling eager?" His baritone, slightly raspy, forced me to look at him.

Yes, I was eager to have him. I was eager to have all of him, in fact. I would no longer settle for just his body.

I stood up on my tiptoes to reach his mouth, and Neil didn't pull back.

He dug a hand into my hair and wrapped it around his fist, pulling it slightly. I gritted my teeth against the minor pain, but I loved the violent, dominating way he touched me.

"Very eager, I'd say. Welcome back, Tinkerbell," he whispered with a sensual smile before he leaped on me like an animal, kissing me. And this time he kissed me with all the fire that raged inside him.

He unleashed his true self: the greedy, possessive one. The one who was no shame and all lust. I could finally recognize the old Neil and, even more so, the old me. The one who struggled to keep up with his rapacious and all-too-expert kisses.

This was the way he'd always been.

He imposed himself on me and left me stunned.

While I'd been thinking, he'd been using his other hand to palm my ass, driving me closer to him. I could feel his erection against my lower stomach, and I pressed my thighs together, fighting the pang of yearning I felt between them. All the while, his tongue sent jolts of electricity all over, short-circuiting my brain.

Like always, I wanted more.

I felt his masculine power; I felt it in his lips, in his hands as they caressed me, and in the tension of his muscles. Without ever breaking our kiss, we began to back up. I was inundated with waves of desire, coaxing moans out of me.

God, how I *wanted*.

My stomach twisted, my chest grew tight, and the swell of lust became unbearable.

I clung to him, and he groaned when my nails bit into his skin.

This was all his fault—his alone. It was how he kissed and smelled and was so desirable. So magnificent. It was all his fault for hypnotizing me and waking up a part of myself I barely recognized.

It was all his fault that I had...fallen in love.

Neil fell back down on the couch and took me down with him. I found myself straddling his pelvis, his swollen erection between my thighs. He had one hand on my ass, the other clasping my hair in his tight fist. In turn, I put my hands on him, worshipping every bit of him. I stroked his firm biceps and his powerful shoulders before traveling down to his pecs. When I accidentally grazed his ribs, Neil squeezed his eyes shut and quit kissing me.

He let out a grunt of pain and let his head fall back, trying to catch his breath.

"Oh my God. I'm sorry," I whispered in horror through swollen, painful lips. I was sweating, and my heart throbbed in my temples. I moved my hands up to his face and felt along his jaw, covered with the short layer of scruff that looked so good on him.

His fingers spread out over my hips, and his golden eyes opened slowly, coming back to me.

Neil was not in good shape, and that rictus of pain on his face was a clear sign of how much he was hurting.

"What happened?" I asked, carding my fingers through the long hair at the top of his head until it was arranged just the way he liked. A hank of hair had tumbled over his wounded eyebrow and hung in front of his eye, so I brushed it aside with my fingertips. Oddly enough, he let me do it. He allowed me to touch him without objection. I stroked the shorter hair near his ears while Neil watched me gravely, accepting every one of my touches.

"How long are you here?" he asked, licking his lower lip. My eyes tracked the motion of his tongue—it was sexy as hell. I blinked, coming out of my daze.

"Two days," I answered, and, instinctively, I began to trace his bruised eyebrow as I examined all the lines of his face: the straight, symmetrical nose, the lush, sensual mouth, and the eyes, which might have seemed cold to others but were, to me, the most expressive I had ever seen.

It was a surreal feeling—only a few hours earlier, Neil lived only in my imagination, and now here he was, right there with me.

Everything was real; it was not a dream.

He touched my hair, letting his fingers slide down to the ends.

"This is getting long," he said thoughtfully, watching his hand instead of me. Then he let the auburn strands fall over my breast before selecting a single strand to toy with, wrapping it around his index and middle fingers.

"Yeah." I smiled. His eyes got caught on my lips and stayed there even longer than they usually did.

"Don't cut it," he ordered, and my heart swelled in my chest. He liked my hair. Neil took me by the nape of the neck and drew us closer. I felt his hot breath on my lips and I swallowed nervously, quivering with the longing that coursed unstoppably through my veins.

"I'd love to show you why I like it long, but I can't right now," he said, his tone angry yet sensual. Then, his grip loosened, and he gave a weary sigh.

He said "can't," not "won't."

I dearly wanted to follow up on his statement, but then it occurred to me why a man might appreciate long hair, and I went red, naturally.

"No, for fuck's sake—no blushing," he said severely, positioning his hand between our bodies, right over his boxers. I glanced down, seeing first the tattoo on his left hip, and then grimaced when I noticed the head of his penis, dark and swollen and peeking out from under his tight elastic waistband. Neil squirmed around on the couch, trying to get comfortable. It must have been difficult, dealing with such a hard, stubborn erection. Then, like always, I got embarrassed at the knowledge that I was the one who had provoked this reaction.

For the first time, I felt the overwhelming urge to taste him in a way I'd never tasted anyone else before.

My blush deepened. The idea of doing that with a man had never occurred to me before and I knew I'd never have the guts to offer it to him.

"Why are you so embarrassed? What's going on in your head?" Neil tucked a strand of hair behind my ear, and I looked up at him.

Why did he always have the ridiculous ability to look right through me?

I cleared my throat and inched back further on his lap. I needed to get some air and clear my head.

"Why didn't you reply to my last text?" I asked him. Switching to another topic of conversation would give me a chance to recover.

His eyes studied me closely. Then, glancing around the couch, he stretched out an arm to scoop up the bag of pistachios he'd discarded there earlier. He opened it, looking like a little kid presented with his favorite ice cream, and pulled out a handful.

Though he was so beautiful even when he was just munching pistachios, I refused to be distracted and continued trying to extract a few more words from him.

"Because you were spouting a bunch of shit, Babygirl." He chewed slowly and rested the bag on his stomach, periodically slipping a hand in so he could keep eating them. I was pleased that he seemed to appreciate my gift.

"A bunch of shit?" I repeated indignantly. "So you're telling me I'm wrong? That you don't want me and that it wouldn't be right doing what we both want to do?" I folded my arms over my chest and awaited his response. But Neil just kept eating his pistachios, oblivious to my need to have a conversation. I considered the totality of him, not sure myself how I was resisting this Adonis. Here he was, half-naked and underneath me with an enormous erection that was barely contained by his boxers, and I somehow hadn't demanded he make love to me.

He watched me in turn, savage and irreverent. Then he shook his head, making me frown.

"I want you, but not in the way you're thinking, Selene. What I really want to do is fuck you without any obligations." He pulled his focus away from his pistachios and raised his torso up slightly so our eyes could meet. Up close, wary, and inquisitorial. He was trying to get a reaction out of me. "Is that what you want?" he asked in a soft, challenging voice. "You want to fuck me and get fucked by me? Don't you think we've used each other enough?" He gave my thighs a squeeze, signaling that I should get off his body, but I didn't move an inch.

Again with this using each other thing?

225

"You didn't use a condom with me. You let yourself go; you even gave me one of your firsts. Did I just dream that up, or did it really happen?" I asked, but before I could continue, Neil took me by the hips and lifted me up with incredible ease. He got up off the couch, and I slipped back into the spot he'd just vacated. I could still feel his warmth in the soft fabric, and I rested a hand on it, looking up at him.

He was running away from me again.

Why couldn't he admit it to himself? It was different with me.

"I'm your beyond. That's what you said. What did you mean?" I chased him, determined to get him to crack. Neil scrubbed a hand over his face and paced irritably in front of me. His tight shoulders and tensed core indicated just how uncomfortable he was.

He looked like a wild beast trying and failing to free himself from a curse.

Then he turned to me, and I sucked in a breath. His face was so shadowy, brooding, and dark.

"It means that you go beyond my limits, and I can't follow you, Selene." He said the words firmly. Adamantly.

"Explain more." I got up from the couch and stared him down, determined not to give up.

"We experience things differently," he sighed in irritation. "For you, sex means joining together; it means understanding, a relationship, fidelity, and God knows what else. For me, it's…" He paused, rubbing his forehead. "It's just sex for me. Whether I'm having it with you or someone else, it makes no difference to me. You're just a body that I can use to pleasure myself. Is that what you wanted to hear? Well, there you go. Hope you're happy," he burst out furiously. I took a step back and pressed a hand to my heart. I was not prepared for his barbs, which stabbed me in the chest like so many needles. No. Not prepared at all.

"Okay," I whispered, trying not to cry. I wasn't going to give him the satisfaction. Where had the scrappy woman who would do anything to convince him gone? I knew she was still inside me somewhere but, just then, the girl who'd been deeply hurt by his words was in control. "You know what I should do?" I asked him, my voice shaking.

"I should just stop running after you. I know that one day you'll realize you made a mistake, but not until you've lost me for good. Not until you see me happy with someone else and you know that someone else is touching me. Not until you no longer mean anything at all to me!" My voice went higher on the last sentence, and Neil stared intensely at me. I couldn't figure out what was going on in his head, but he did look thoughtful. Serious, uncomfortable, and awfully thoughtful. He stood there, his arms slack at his sides, his posture and expression both grim.

Why wasn't he reacting?

"Answer me! Is that what you want to happen?" I moved closer. He had kissed me, and he'd done it in a way that contradicted the words he'd just said. I hadn't imagined the longing way he touched and claimed me, wanting to take more but, for some reason that remained unknown to me, stopping himself. He hadn't acted like an indifferent man but rather like one who was troubled and deeply conflicted.

"That would be the right thing for you." He licked his lips and stepped back, moving toward the bedroom. He was demonstrating his lack of interest in me. Or, at least, that's what he wanted me to believe. "I need to shower now." He ruffled his hair and walked away again. All I could do was stand there silently, watching him.

I realized that Neil had rescinded his attention. I was like a cigarette that he could light up or snuff out whenever he liked. He breathed me in deep and then pushed me right back out because my presence was too heavy; the things we made each other feel were too dangerous.

"I hate you, I swear I hate you. I can't stand you! You're such an idiot!" I exploded in exasperation, but there was nothing. Neil just hid in the bedroom, where he used his blonds, and slammed the door abruptly in my face.

He liked to spark and then stifle my desire before disappearing entirely.

Sometimes, he looked at me with a profound passion, while at others he seemed detached and removed from me.

He was a hedonist.

Everything revolved around his theory of pleasure, and he wouldn't acknowledge the existence of anything more.

And still…I was crazy for him.

10

I felt a void open up beneath me, a chasm
ready to pull me down.

SELENE

So? Are you coming?" Alyssa asked again for the millionth time.

I'd been back in the house for about ten minutes, returning furiously after my fight with Neil. I stationed myself on the couch in the living room, trying in vain to find something to watch on TV.

"Why are you so mad?" Logan asked, swinging his leg back and forth over the arm of the chair he was sprawled in. I looked first at him and then at his girlfriend and gave them both a huff. I didn't want to admit that the cause of my bad mood was just a few yards away in the pool house, taking one of his numerous showers.

Neil wanted me to use him, did he? Well, what I really wanted to do was burst into that shower, slam him up against the cold tiles, and kiss him. I wanted to touch every part of him, trace his every natural relief with my tongue, and show him that I, too, could act like Jennifer. I could have taken pleasure from him and his body without feelings.

I could have, but, of course, I never would have.

"Your brother!" I snapped at Logan, which only made him snicker at me.

"It's not his day today. Whatever he said or did to you, try to be understanding," he answered, turning serious again.

"What are you talking about? Neil is always out of his head, and he always treats her like shit. Stop defending him and try to be impartial for once," Alyssa cut in, scolding Logan. He turned his attention to her, giving her a sharp look. Alyssa had crossed the line. Everyone knew, after all, that Logan didn't allow people to talk about Neil like that.

Alyssa must have sensed that because she drew her knees up tight against her chest. She curled into herself next to me on the couch, looking timid in the face of her boyfriend's reaction.

"I'm sorry, love. I didn't mean to be tactless," she murmured immediately, trying to disperse the tension that had arisen between them. I looked between the two of them and decided to intervene. I never wanted them to get into a fight because of me, and I was the one, after all, who'd brought up Neil.

"Weren't you two supposed to go out?" I cleared my throat and turned off the TV. There was nothing on anyway.

"Are you coming with us?" Logan asked in a placid tone, turning his attention to me. I was glad he was calm again.

"I don't know." All at once I was unsure again about what to do. Just ten minutes before, I had convinced myself that I was going to turn down their invitation, and now I wanted to go out. I wanted to distract myself and, more than anything else, get away from Neil. Staying in the house with him so close by wouldn't have been appropriate. I felt too vulnerable, and my mood swung too violently whenever he lavished his attention on me. It didn't matter whether it was to actually talk to me or just to bother me.

"Oh, come on. Come out with us. Please." Alyssa batted her eyes sweetly at me, and I smiled. At the same time, I heard the sound of a key turning in a lock. The front door opened, and Neil's now unmistakable footsteps echoed in the space around us. Alyssa fell silent, and I turned to watch him as he let the door fall shut with a thud.

Immediately his scent overwhelmed my nose.

How much bath gel did he use?

He smelled so good.

Additionally, his hair was surprisingly neat, with the longer quiff arranged in an orderly fashion, though still casually enough that it gave him an impetuous look.

He was beautiful, like he always was.

He was dressed all in black, from his tight jeans to his hoodie, while his leather jacket (undoubtedly from some expensive brand) had fiery-red trim along the sleeves and zippers. That was another small characteristic of Neil's: He always dressed simply and casually. He didn't need to look ostentatious to get women to notice him.

His body had a carnal impact on a woman.

"Finally, you emerge from hibernation," Logan teased, giving him a wolf whistle. Neil paused for a moment to glance at him. It was the first time he'd deigned to pay attention to anyone in the room. Then, his gaze shifted to include the rest of the living room, and he cast an uninterested glance at Alyssa, ignoring me completely.

Dick.

I knew that he saw me. I mean, I was right there.

Either way, Mr. Disaster chose not to answer his brother and moved toward the kitchen island instead. He circled it casually and opened the refrigerator to retrieve a container of pineapple juice. As he lifted it to his lips, I saw him look at me. But I was determined to reflect his own indifference, so I turned to Alyssa in a fit of pique and continued talking to her.

"What were you saying?" I asked, pretending to be interested in our conversation. "Oh, yeah. The party. I think I will go. I really need to get out for a little bit." I looked at her and Logan, who had started frowning, wondering what had made me suddenly change my mind. I gave him a smug smile and kept talking. "Will there be hot guys there at least? I'd like to..." I tapped my index finger on my chin, pretending to be deep in thought. "Blow off some steam," I concluded firmly, trying my best to sound convincing. I knew Neil was listening to our conversation, and I'd decided to get a few things off my chest. Far too much had built up there.

"Wow." Alyssa nudged me with her elbow, grinning. "And how do you intend to blow that steam off?" she asked with a wink, and I hoped I wasn't blushing.

"What does one usually do at a party with hot guys? I am single, after all..." I shrugged one shoulder, flashing a mischievous grin as I tried to look confident.

In reality, I didn't even have the guts to turn and look at Neil for any reaction or sign that I'd achieved my goal of getting under his skin.

"So you're trying to get laid?" Logan arched a surprised eyebrow.

"Of course, what else?" Alyssa blurted out, a delighted expression on her face. I was about to tell them that this wasn't the case because I didn't want them to think I was that kind of girl. I still had my principles; I was still the prudish little girl who was incapable of fully satisfying a man. I was still the girl who had lost her virginity far too recently to have learned everything about sex. I was still me, the person who associated sex with feelings and would never be able to tolerate the touch of anyone who wasn't...

The sound of the refrigerator being slammed shut made me jump.

I quit thinking and even "performing" when I turned in the direction of the sound.

The gold of Neil's eyes had all but disappeared, and he was staring fixedly at me with a gravity so dark that it chilled me to the bone.

I felt a void open up beneath me, a chasm ready to pull me down. He breathed in deep and exhaled through his nose, pure hatred in his eyes aimed at me.

Only at me.

"Neil, is everything okay?" Logan watched him intently. He planted both feet on the floor but remained seated as he considered the situation. Neil, meanwhile, leaned back against the kitchen island and crossed his arms over his chest, making the muscles in his biceps flex.

"What sort of party are you taking the Babygirl to?" He spoke in a derisive, singsongy tone, especially on the last words. He looked to Logan for an answer, chewing his lower lip with a strange look of cruelty on his face.

"Why? What's it to you?" Alyssa cut in, intrigued.

"Was I talking to you?" Neil snapped in irritation. He shot her a dirty look, and Alyssa gulped, shrinking back into her seat.

"Well?" Neil turned to his brother again, drumming the fingers of one hand on the opposite forearm impatiently.

"You want to come with us?" Logan offered. "You could keep Selene company. She might get bored with just the two of us," he said drily, and I frowned at this ridiculous suggestion.

What the hell was he trying to do?

In the depths of my heart, I wanted Neil to accept Logan's offer.

"I don't take sluts out," Neil said baldly, an insolent smirk curving up his lips. For a moment, I thought I must have imagined his words. Maybe I'd heard him wrong? But no...

"Neil!" Logan scolded him, leaping to his feet. "What the fuck are you saying?"

"Slut? You mean me?" I got up from the couch, fists clenched at my sides. I couldn't believe he'd actually said that.

"Aw, Tigress, sheathe those claws. It's not like I mentioned you by name," he answered slyly and even gave me a wink. He was making sport of me, completely unashamed. He was trying to needle me until I lost my cool and tipped over the edge into exasperation.

"You were obviously talking about me!" I raised my voice, determined to defend myself. Oh, today was the day. I was going to slap him or give him a kick in the downstairs that he'd remember for the rest of his life. Neil just chuckled.

"As far as I'm concerned, a girl who goes out looking to get fucked is a little slut." The confidence in his voice was almost as infuriating as his over-the-top arrogance. I walked over to him with no fear and looked up at him.

"You do nothing else with your blonds, and now you're going to lecture me?" I shook my head, smiling sarcastically. We were at the edge of absurdity. He of all people was daring to judge me? I didn't like getting so aggressive, but Neil drove me crazy; he made me lose all inhibitions.

"But I don't take them out. Never," he answered calmly with a mischievous smile. He was keeping himself under control, but his every word cut sharper than a knife. I stared at him, determined not to bend to his will. If I was being honest, though, I didn't actually want to provoke him. I didn't want a war between us. I just wanted to...to kiss him and touch him. To mess up his hair and get him out of his clothes.

I wanted him to tell me something true about himself. I wanted him to open up and trust me.

I wanted everything from Neil Miller.

But I interrupted this train of thought by boldly, unthinkingly asking him, "Are you maybe *jealous*?"

He sucked in a breath, clearly not expecting that question. Logan's mouth fell open, and he came up to stand next to Neil, but neither he nor Alyssa interfered in what had become a no-holds-barred beatdown.

Neil let out a guttural sound that was extremely seductive and something like a laugh. His chest and my entire body vibrated with the dark notes of his baritone. He dropped his arms to his sides and inched closer to me, obliterating the space between us. His musky scent seemed to sink into my skin, and I knew that it would linger there for hours, mingling with my own smell. He smoothed a lock of hair behind my ear, and I shivered.

It was a move that might have looked sweet on the surface but was really anything but.

"Get ready, Babygirl. Put on your best dress and your sexiest underwear. We're going to go out together, and I'll find you tonight's fuck myself," he whispered, highly amused as he showed me just how little I mattered to him. "Are you down for that? Or are you going to start whining when it comes time to satisfy the lucky guy's demands?" he added sneeringly.

"Neil! What the—" Logan attempted to intervene, trying to make his brother see reason.

"Can it, Logan," Neil scolded him sternly before turning back to give my body a quick once-over. He was rubbing it in my face how wrong I had been to test him.

"We'll take my car. I'll meet you at the car in half an hour." He pulled out his pack of Winstons and walked out the French doors to the garden.

I was stunned by what had just happened. I blew out a shaky breath and stared out the large glass window where his imposing frame had just disappeared.

"He won't do it," Logan said softly, breaking the silence.

"What?" I turned to look at him, and he moved toward me.

"He didn't really mean it. You provoked him, and he reacted. That was what you wanted, right?" He smiled at me, and I refused to meet his eyes. I bit my lip, considering. Neil had clearly been upset at the idea that I would actually go out with the intent of…

"He insulted her." Alyssa folded her arms over her chest and looked at her boyfriend, annoyed. "You do realize that, right? Your brother is a total asshole. I've seen for myself how he's constantly coming out of the pool house with Jennifer. So why can't Selene be free to have fun however she likes or with whoever she likes?" she continued, coming to my defense.

"Because..." Logan tried to explain but just ended up sighing impatiently and giving up. "Eh, I don't know! Neil is twisted; he's just...Neil. That's just the way he is," he muttered in exasperation.

"No, your brother is a sexist jerk. He's arrogant, domineering, and gross. He—" Alyssa retorted, really laying into him, and although there was a part of me that agreed with her, the other part—the irrational part—resented her for running him down.

"Let's just go get ready." I cut her off, walking toward the marble staircase without another word. I didn't understand myself. I should have been mad at him, but, instead, I was frightened of him and drawn to him at the same time. And although I fought those unhealthy emotions with all my might, I couldn't win.

He was becoming an addiction, something that had already thrown me into an abyss of chaos. Neil's eyes were my obsession, and I smelled his scent whenever I breathed in.

You want to play with me? Then I'm going to play too.

Moments later, Alyssa and I were posted up in my bedroom, focused on making ourselves presentable. Forty minutes later, and I was still huffing as I tossed aside yet another dress.

"Try this one." Alyssa showed off another option.

She'd already chosen the perfect dress for her: a lacy blue sheath that fit her like a dream, highlighting her sinuous shape without being too short. The back, however, made up for it. It plunged almost to the base of her spine, which made her look irresistibly seductive.

"Pink?" My face twisted into a skeptical expression. Pink looked fine on me, but it also made me look angelic, and I was feeling anything but. I rejected her suggestion and plopped down on the bed, surrendering myself to the idea that I simply didn't have anything adequate to wear. I'd have to settle for a sweater and a pair of jeans.

This was exactly why I hated parties. You always needed to dress to impress, show off, and go over the top…

"Hmm…" Alyssa strode on her stilettos to the walk-in closet that Matt had set up for me, though Mia had mostly likely done the actual clothing selection. I'd never worn most of the clothes. Honestly, I'd never even imagined I would need them.

"What about this one?" She came back to me with a little black dress on a hanger.

It was…stunning.

I got off the bed and ran my fingers over it, admiring the soft fabric. It consisted of a bodice with a sweetheart neckline, two thin straps, and an embroidered band just below the bust, which was covered in small, bright stones. The skirt draped softly over the hips, and there was a little bow on the back.

"I like it," I said, not looking at her.

"Try it on," she prompted me before turning to look for a matching pair of shoes.

I took off my clothes quickly and slipped the dress on over my head. I didn't know what brand it was, but I was pretty sure I'd never worn anything so expensive and eye-catching in my life. If I somehow ruined it, I knew I'd never be able to pay Matt back.

I paused in front of the mirror to consider my reflection, tilting my head to one side. The skirt was short, and the neckline was low, dipping down to the base of my sternum. My firm breasts were clearly visible, my push-up bra only making them more eye-catching.

"Oh my God, Alyssa! No way. I need something less…" I didn't get to finish that sentence because she approached me then with a wicked smile and a pair of sky-high heels in her hands. I felt naked, uncomfortable, and…

"Try these on with it." She arranged them beside my bare feet, and I shook my head.

No, I could never go out dressed like this.

"Get a move on, Selene." She huffed and crossed her arms over her chest, waiting for me to do as she'd ordered. Delicately, I climbed into the pair of stilts she'd given me, trying not to lose my balance.

"Oh my God! You're a bombshell!" Alyssa positioned herself behind me, and I looked myself up and down in the mirror. I was a few inches taller than her now. My extra-long hair fell over my shoulders in soft waves while my wayward bangs covered my scar. My makeup brightened me up without being too heavy. I'd put some basic pink lipstick on my lips and used mascara to darken my thick lashes, making my eyes look bluer and more compelling.

"You look elegant-sexy, not vulgar-sexy," Alyssa reassured me when she noticed my obvious discomfort. I wasn't used to dressing up; I still preferred jeans and T-shirts.

"Maybe I should…" I wanted to peel it all off and get into bed. I'd changed my mind once again. I didn't feel like attracting inappropriate stares or cheeky comments from some passing idiot. I knew there were men who went to these parties to "hunt," and dressed like this, I would look like prey.

"Selene, we'll be with you. You won't be alone. Besides, you know that dickhead deserves to eat his heart out over your incredible legs. Now, get that round ass in gear so we can leave!" She gave me a gentle, encouraging nudge, and I smiled shakily at her.

I grabbed my clutch and followed Alyssa out of my room. I needed my black winter coat, but I'd left it on the coatrack in the living room, so I was going to have to walk down the stairs under Logan's and Neil's watchful eyes, and there was nothing I could do to hide from them.

I sighed and gripped the railing on my right, my fingers tight around it. Alyssa walked in front of me, bold and self-assured. She carried herself beautifully in her high heels, unlike me, who only seemed to get more awkward and clumsy.

As I watched the movement of her hips, I wondered how any woman could truly *like* heels. They were unbearable; I could already feel my big toe throbbing in pain.

"Finally!" Logan groused, turning in his girlfriend's direction. He stared at her with deep admiration, and as soon as Alyssa reached him, he kissed her and told her how beautiful she was.

"Hope I don't have to fight off some assholes tonight," Logan said, frowning slightly at Alyssa's tight-fitting dress. Then he pressed another kiss to her temple, handed her coat to her, and turned his eyes on me.

"So, Selene, are you read—" He stopped.

I couldn't tell what he was thinking, but Logan seemed to be momentarily dazzled. His eyes drifted down my body, and I realized he approved of the bombshell dress his girlfriend had picked for me.

"You… I mean… You look great." He rubbed the back of his neck, maybe embarrassed or maybe just confused. Then he heaved a sigh and politely handed me my coat, just as he had done for Alyssa.

"Did I do a good job? What do you think? Selene doesn't know how much potential she has. She could have any man she wants falling at her feet with a snap of her fingers." She snapped her fingers and then headed for the door, Logan's arm draped around her shoulders.

"I agree," he answered, grinning at me, and together we walked out onto the porch, where we shivered in the cold air. My coat kept my top half warm, but my legs were freezing. The sheer pair of thigh highs I wore certainly did nothing to protect me from the cold.

Once outside, Alyssa and Logan went on ahead of me to Neil's Maserati. The thought of him looking disdainfully at me or tossing some insult or cruel joke my way made my legs shake. Still, I silently followed the loved-up couple. Inside, however, I wanted nothing more than to scream, letting out all the frustration that had built up in the last few hours.

"Don't be a dick. They're running late because they're women, and women need more time to get ready," Logan said preemptively, anticipating what his brother was about to say. Then, he stopped abruptly.

Neil was leaning against his car door, looking bored. He had a lit cigarette clenched between his lips, and he looked peeved.

He'd waited too long for us, and he wasn't used to it. Neil didn't like to wait; he wanted everything, and he wanted it now.

"Can we go?" he asked Alyssa, looking seriously at her. He studied her outfit and raised an eyebrow without comment. Luckily, he couldn't see me because I was still hiding behind Logan, where I planned to remain. Except Neil craned his neck to the side, looking for me, and when Logan realized that his brother was specifically trying to see me, he moved, showing me off to the devil himself.

I clutched my bag as his bright eyes slowly moved from the pronounced neckline down to the too-short skirt. Then on to the high heels that lengthened my figure unnecessarily.

My cheeks were scalding, and my breathing was rapid.

Traitorous feelings.

I looked around and focused specifically on a small bush nearby—anything to avoid looking at him. But I could feel his stare hot on my skin, burning the flesh upon which it rested.

Little by little, he was branding me, and I could feel the full power of it.

"Beautiful, isn't she?" Alyssa commented, though I wished she would have stayed quiet. Compliments always made me feel shy, and I needed to feel strong just then, not weak.

Neil took a step toward me and then another. I could smell smoke as he got closer and closer, mingled with his regular pleasant scent. I lifted my chin to look at him when my nose nearly made contact with his chest.

I saw everything in his eyes.

I saw his audacity. His strength.

I saw his power. His fury.

I also saw his lust. The desire to bite into my flesh; the desperation to make me his immediately. I saw the yearning and the clash between his determination to resist me and the heat that had set him aflame—an exhausting torture.

I saw the urge he had to be inside me and his furious need, which had to be satisfied.

We were going to lose our minds just from looking at each other.

"So you're serious about this?" he whispered, his voice rough. I knew that tone; it was the same one he used when he whispered obscenities into my ear in bed.

"Looks like it," I said challengingly. I wanted to brush past him and get in the car. I wanted to appear confident, but instead I just stood there. Motionless, helpless, and intimidated. If he had tried to kiss me then, my legs would have given out from the sheer intensity of the moment.

This was the Neil Miller effect.

"Let's go." Mercifully, he pulled away and passed a hand over his face. I went back to breathing again.

I was surprised at his sudden surrender, and I was positive there was something strange going on that stopped him from going on the attack.

I didn't say anything, though, and simply got into the car with everyone else.

The brothers sat in the front with us girls in the back. I was visibly uncomfortable, and I hadn't said a single word while Alyssa continued to chat with Logan. I envied how attuned they seemed to each other. Logan was so attentive and kind. Neil, on the other hand…

I glanced at him. He drove in silence with a characteristic thoughtful frown on his face; his self-assurance was showing in the way he gripped the steering wheel one-handed. He didn't say anything more because, like usual, he wasn't feeling chatty. There were times when Neil displayed an inclination to talk but other times—like right now—-he clammed up, needing to be alone as he navigated his chaotic inner world.

After a few minutes in the car, it occurred to me that I didn't even know where we were going. Logan and Alyssa told me the party was being thrown at a private club by someone named Bryder Janson, but I had no idea who that was.

After about ten minutes, we arrived at our destination.

The sight of all the people queueing up at the entrance of the enormous club took me back to Halloween—an evening much like this one that had ended in disaster. Logan, Alyssa, and I got out of the car and waited for Neil to park it and meet us.

A feeling of anguish stopped me in my tracks, and I stared at the club like I was looking into the void.

"Selene…" Alyssa called, trying to get my attention.

"Are you okay?" Logan asked, staring at me. I'd gone pale, and, what's more, when I touched my cheek with one hand, it felt frozen.

"Yeah, of course." I smiled.

"Let's go." Neil appeared behind me, and I stiffened. I had to quit being so tense.

Logan linked hands with Alyssa, and together they walked to the entrance. Neil, on the other hand, lit another cigarette and paid me no mind. He looked irritated and bored.

Without exchanging words or touches, we followed Logan and Alyssa toward a white LED sign reading NEW LION, the name of the club. I'd never heard of it, but Alyssa told me it was a haven for New York's richest people. They threw all sorts of parties there.

The place was so exclusive that the bright red door only opened if security approved someone to enter. We watched as several people without the proper invitations were turned away and left grumbling indistinctly under their breaths.

I knew Logan had gotten a special invite, and I sincerely hoped that the exclusivity meant that it would be a nice place, but even more than that, that it would be low-key.

"They say that beyond the cocktail area, there's some kind of playroom and suites where you can spend the night," a young man ahead of us commented as he stood in line with his group of friends while we all waited our turn for the door.

"Yeah, and they have table dancers after midnight," said another man.

Oh great, just what the place was missing—hot dancers with perfect bodies shaking their asses in everyone's faces.

What kind of place had Logan taken us to?

I snorted and rocked back on my heels, feeling the discomfort in my back and calves. I wished I could take off my shoes and walk barefoot. I sighed, turning to see Neil.

He stood behind me with his phone in one hand and his eyes locked on the display. He was messaging someone; I could tell by the rapid movement of his thumbs. I wondered who it was—maybe Jennifer? Maybe someone else? I'd never looked through his phone, but I knew what I would find if I did: lewd photos, sexts, come-ons, and offers to hook up.

"Why are you staring at me?" Neil grumbled. Somehow, he'd noticed my gaze even though he'd never even lifted his eyes from that damn screen. He was incredibly sharp.

"I'm not staring at you; I'm just trying to ignore the stabbing pain in my feet," I answered with a wince of pain.

Never again.

Never again with the high heels.

"Quit whining. We need to find the lucky guy who's going to fuck you," he retorted, casting a bored glance over the line before looking back down at his phone. Despite my heels, Neil was still taller than me, and it was easy for him to look down on me, just the way he wanted.

"I actually wore my favorite thong for that very reason. Can't wait," I said breezily, faking a smirk. Actually, I was just wearing my usual cotton panties, but I enjoyed provoking him. His gleaming eyes immediately shifted from the phone screen to my face. He looked earnestly at me for a moment before hiding behind his armor again, determined never to appear vulnerable or let me know what he was thinking.

"Why do we even have to bother with these door checks?" A familiar voice from over Neil's shoulder drew my attention, and I spotted a girl with bright blue hair in a high ponytail. She was facing away from us, leaving us with a view of her black leather skirt and a jacket in the same color that was tight across her narrow shoulders.

Neil didn't hesitate. He stretched out an arm and, with complete confidence, smacked her ass. She jumped and whirled around, ready to retaliate against whoever had made a move like that. When she met Neil's eyes, however, her expression softened, and she gave him a bright smile.

"Asshole! Your smacks hurt like hell, did you know?" Alexia whined, massaging the area that had been hit. I breathed in deep, trying to conceal how much Neil's behavior actually bothered me, especially with Krew girls.

"Oh, he knows perfectly well," Luke—whom I hadn't even noticed next to her—cut in. His blue eyes popped against the darkness of the cold night, and his blond hair perfectly framed his evenly featured face.

"Shut up, Parker. Where's the other one?" Neil stuck out his hand, and they greeted each other with grips of iron.

"If that's me you're referring to, you giant asshole, I'm right here." Xavier popped out from behind Luke's back with a cigarette between his lips and a nasty look on his face. My eyes went wide as I spotted his black eye and slightly swollen nose. I examined his bruises—definitely more obvious than Neil's—and surmised that the fight must have been between the two of them.

"Glad to see you're alive," Neil said drily, taking in his friend's appearance as though nothing had happened between them. I frowned and kept watching—those two had a truly incomprehensible relationship.

"You, too, apparently," Xavier replied, looking at the purplish splotches that dotted Neil's eyebrow and the corner of his mouth.

"Okay, let's not start this again," Luke intervened, looking directly at me. His forehead wrinkled, like he didn't quite recognize me, and he stared down at me, lingering over my face.

"Selene?" he said uncertainly. I wasn't sure how to respond or how I should greet him. Luke and I had shared one fiery kiss and a brief conversation on a bench that tragic Halloween night, which meant...

"Oh, look who came back. It's the doll with the golden ass. Welcome back, kitten." Xavier looked me all over in his typically sleazy fashion. Next to him, Alexia stared at me like I was some kind of leper.

"Don't start that horny shit, you jackass!" she elbowed him, trying to break him out of the daze he'd fallen into, staring insistently at my breasts. Xavier snorted.

"If the girl is looking fuckable, I'm gonna look. I always look at hot bitches, whether you like it or not. You're not my woman, and you don't control me," he answered, sounding annoyed. Alexia sighed, and sadness swept over her face, making her look down. Was it possible that everyone—me included—had noticed that this girl had feelings for Xavier, and he was still oblivious?

That wasn't any of my business, though.

When it came to the Krew, trouble was always just around the corner.

"Is it done yet?" Neil turned his attention to Luke, jerking his chin at Xavier, who now had his eye on a nearby brunette, all curves and piercings. I shook my head as I watched him. The dude was obsessed with any living female.

"Not yet," Luke answered with a sigh, and he caught me watching him. My gaze had lingered distractedly on the dimple in his chin. It was a detail I'd never noticed before.

Indeed, Luke had charms of his own. I couldn't deny that...

"So you came out from Detroit to go to New Lion?" He smiled at me, and I smiled back. I had never been afraid of him. Sure, he was a member of the Krew and surely not as angelic as he looked, but I had always thought he was different from the likes of Xavier.

"I'm only here for two days and..." I didn't have time to say more because Neil put a hand on my back and pushed me forward.

"What are you doing?" I snapped in vexation. A wall of testosterone now stood between me and Luke. There was no way to escape him so I turned my face slightly to look at him. He was so beautiful, and my anger gave way to the familiar yearning sensation between my thighs. I gasped and stiffened up when I felt his pelvis against my backside. I was wearing my long coat but I was very confident that the thing poking into the base of my spine was the huge bulge he kept in his pants.

My throat suddenly felt dry, and I had to lick my lips.

"Walk," he ordered, shoving me again. After the small group of men ahead of us got through, it would be our turn. But that didn't mean he needed to push me or act like some surly barbarian. I looked to Logan for assistance, but he was talking with Alyssa and not paying attention to anything else.

"What is wrong with you? Stop forcing me forward," I grumbled irritably. I turned to look at him and was about to say something else before Neil bent down to my ear.

"If I were really forcing you, Tinkerbell, you'd be screaming for me to stop," he whispered provocatively, making me shiver. It had been a while since I'd heard that name fall from his lips. I gulped and tried not to break, not to show what he could have easily seen in my all-too-transparent eyes. They were too sincere when it came to him.

I mustered the strength to turn around and gasp for air before following Logan and Alyssa into the club after the bouncer let us pass.

We walked down a long, black-walled corridor faintly illuminated with red lights.

Neil stayed behind me the entire time and put both of his hands on my hips when we moved into the crowd. The gesture left me stunned, and I found myself wishing he'd stay close like that forever. I could actually feel the fizzing as our souls connected, the collision of our joint desires. I shot him a brief glance, barely moving my chin, and he pulled me close with a possessiveness that I'd never felt before.

My heart felt like it was going to explode out of my chest.

"Start looking around. We need to find that lucky guy," he hissed into my ear, and my anger flared.

"This place is dope," Logan said, turning to me just then and smiled before he walked away with Alyssa pressed to his side.

Intrigued, I did take a look around.

It was, in fact, a very strange place. It felt like we had crossed some border into a world of sin, lust, and the forbidden. The walls were blood red, contrasting starkly with the black leather couches. Round black tables with a single central leg made of highly polished steel were arranged around enormous dancing platforms. The surface of each one was covered with illuminated frosted glass, and there was a chrome-plated metal pole in the middle for exotic dancing.

We all proceeded to the bar, which was lit up with alternating lights and provided a dramatic play of colors.

Neil walked past me and leaned an elbow on the bar, perusing the illuminated shelves where numerous bottles of alcohol were arranged.

Then the inevitable happened.

His golden eyes succumbed to the blond bartender, who looked back at him with a wickedness that immediately irritated me.

I wasn't his girlfriend; we weren't together, but I simply couldn't contain the jealousy.

Nothing like it had ever happened to me with Jared, but Neil was elusive, he didn't belong to me. Maybe that was why I was afraid I might lose him at any moment.

I noted, then, that his things for blonds had clearly not diminished.

"What can I get you?" The bartender rested her hands palms down on the bar, tossing her long hair over one shoulder. She had a jeweled septum piercing and was notably beautiful. Although she had directed her question to Logan, her brown eyes immediately slid over to Neil. He remained serious, but I didn't miss the way his eyes flicked to the girl's generous breasts.

I didn't stand a chance against the kind of girls he slept with. He hadn't even said anything nice about my dress. It was impossible to get a nice word out of him. Or maybe he wasn't as attracted to me as he used to be.

Sometimes I was certain we had a connection, while other times my insecurities rose up to make me doubt everything.

"What do you want, Selene?" Logan asked.

"I don't—" I started to tell him that I wasn't drinking but I stopped.

"Do you want to order something to share? I don't want to drink much either," Neil asked me. Me specifically and not anyone else. I nodded, and he smiled at me. "I'll choose. I'm not going to ask what your drink is because you don't know them anyway," he teased me, and the bartender giggled. I blushed, of course, because Neil had succeeded in humiliating me, but what he did next astounded me. He glared severely at the woman for daring to laugh at me. He stared her down ominously and we all watched him in awe. The bartender quickly took the rest of our orders and made an awkward exit.

Too often, I had no idea what his actions meant.

Had he been trying in his own way to defend me?

"Since when do you 'not drink much'?" I dared to ask, and Neil turned to look at me. He took a seat on a stool, elbow against the bar, one knee bent and the other stretched out, supporting his weight.

He was such a rare beauty, the most attractive man I had ever seen.

"I hardly ever drink," he answered, looking me slowly from top to bottom. We'd left our coats at the entrance, and my body was now completely exposed for his wicked eyes. He let them trail easily down from my breasts to my legs before coming back up to look at my face.

"Here you go." The bartender handed us our drink, and I realized I didn't even know what Neil had gotten for us. I moved to get a closer look at our cocktail, and Mr. Disaster took me by the hips. At first, I didn't understand what he was trying to do.

Did he want me to sit on his lap? Sure seemed like it.

Neil was big and strong; he could maneuver me in whatever way he wanted, so he didn't even bother asking my permission and instead just pulled me down onto him. I sat, and as my butt met the hardness of his muscled thigh, something lit up inside me. It was impossible to feel such a powerful arousal every single time he touched me. My body could not simply go up in flames he put his hands on me.

I shot an embarrassed look at Alyssa and at Logan, who was standing next to the stool she was perched on, and I caught them exchanging a knowing glance.

"You've had a margarita before, right?" Neil gripped the glass, its rim decorated with a lime slice, and brought it to his lips. He took a sip as he waited for me to answer.

I shook my head, preparing myself for one of his insults or snarky little quips, but he just tightened his hand on my hip and pulled me closer to him. It was suddenly hard to breathe.

"Taste it." A faint smile tugged at his sinful lips, and his stare became all-encompassing. He moved the glass to my lips without ever breaking his stare, and I did as he'd requested. I put my lips on the exact same spot where his had been moments before and took a sip. At first blush, the drink was delicious. But then I felt the tequila aftertaste on my tongue along with an intense burning in my esophagus.

"How is it?" he asked and took another drink after me, and I lingered on the way his Adam's apple bobbed up and down. I wanted to kiss him, and it felt like I was already drunk.

Drunk on him. On his smell.

No drink could ever have such an effect on me.

I acted on my impulses and did something truly stupid.

"I'd rather taste you," I whispered in his ear, and he froze with his glass in midair, staring at me.

He frowned and set the drink down, giving me a mocking smile.

"Babygirl, you don't know the first thing about…" He inched closer to my lips. "…my taste," he continued in a seductive murmur. I looked at him, bewildered. I had been talking about kissing him, but maybe he meant…

My eyes bugged slightly, and I shifted awkwardly on his knee as I realized what direction this conversation was taking. Neil pulled me closer to him, tightening his grip around my hips. I was a genuine naïf, and now I was playing with fire.

What an idiot.

"Hey, we're going to go dance. You coming?" Logan took Alyssa's hand and gestured to the center of the dance floor, between the still-vacant platforms. I had forgotten those two were still present.

That was how it always happened.

Whenever Neil let me into his world, I forgot my own entirely.

We were completely defective together but, sometimes, in some moments, I felt like we understood each other completely. I could feel the energy between us, the incandescent fire that brought us together. I could feel our thoughts linked by a single thread, a subtle understanding that was slowly peeling away his armor.

"No," Neil answered, and I agreed with him. Logan gave us a wicked look before walking off with Alyssa, as though he'd known from the beginning how this was going to end. A moment later, I turned to Neil and caught him examining my dress. Specifically the plunging neckline. I bit my lip and decided to finally ask him the question that had been on my mind for hours.

"Do you like it?" I asked, all in a rush. Even I didn't know where I got up the courage. Neil took another sip from the margarita and licked his lips thoughtfully. No emotion and no flicker of weakness or vulnerability crossed his face.

"Yeah, it'll do," he said, glancing around out of boredom.

And what the hell did he mean by that?

"It'll do?" I echoed indignantly.

"You got it. I mean, you look pretty and…" He deliberated for a few moments before adding, "Fuckable." He tried to hand me the margarita, but I shook my head. His words had hurt me, and he didn't even notice.

He took the last drink and left the empty glass on the bar with a sigh.

"Fuckable is an insult. You do realize that?" I retorted. It was especially insulting considering the way he'd said it.

"Is that not what you wanted?" he taunted me again. "Have you picked one yet? Oh, that's right, I'm supposed to do it for you. Tell me what you like." He glanced around, drumming his fingers on the bar. I watched his hand, taking note of the steel ring on his middle finger. Reflexively, I stroked it with my own finger, and he went rigid.

He wasn't used to those little spontaneous gestures.

"Brown-haired," I answered, resting my hands on my thighs. He didn't want to be touched just then, so I forced myself not to.

"Lots of guys with brown hair here," he commented, contemplating some of them. Had he lost his mind?

Neil was seriously looking for tonight's lucky winner. I kept playing along, but the longer the charade went on, the more offended I got that he actually believed I was going to go through with it.

"Tall. Very tall and strong. With a perfect nose and full lips and strangely colored eyes," I continued.

Neil stopped examining his surroundings and finally looked at me with that haughty frown that made him so irresistible.

"Oh, and he has to have gleaming amber skin," I added, raising a finger while he watched me in the most devastating way. He was serious, reflective, and could turn me to jelly without uttering a syllable.

"That's a pretty tall order." He smiled, stroking his lips with his index finger. He leaned comfortably on one elbow and had adopted such a sexy stance that I couldn't look away from him.

I didn't care about any of the other men there.

I wanted him.

"I'm particular. I'm not interested in just anyone," I said. It was true, I wasn't attracted to empty, superior, or self-absorbed men. I had always valued substance over style. I could appreciate outer beauty, sure but what really drove me wild was the beauty inside. Neil was the sum of all those things, which was why I was so fascinated with him.

He bit his lower lip and, once again, looked at mine.

Why wasn't he kissing me if that's what he wanted?

It looked like he was trying to control himself, just like he had been in the pool house.

He chuckled, apropos of nothing, and moved his eyes over my shoulder. All at once, I watched his face change. The levity of the moment evaporated. I could tell that insidious thoughts were filling his mind. I followed his gaze, looking for whatever had caused this lightning-quick change, and spotted a woman, black-haired and beautiful, walking into the club.

Though the place was packed, she drew almost all of the male attention. She wore a simple pair of leather pants and a black, low-cut top that was tied off around her rib cage, leaving her midriff exposed. She was with a blond girl and had an arm draped over her shoulders. The girl in black turned to smile at someone, her wavy black hair fluttering with the movement. I looked back at Neil and found his eyes still locked on her.

It seemed ill-advised just then to keep sitting on his lap, so I moved over to the next stool, the one Alyssa had vacated. Neil seemed to agree with my instinct because he did nothing to stop me. He did nothing—absolutely nothing—to keep me close to him.

"Shoot your shot. I doubt she'll reject you," I said testily. There it was—jealousy pressing down on my chest like a boulder. Neil turned his gaze to me and frowned.

Was he pretending not to understand?

"What?" he murmured absently.

"The black-haired girl you're staring at. If you try to pick her up, she's not going to say no," I repeated more clearly. It seemed like a fairly obvious observation.

Who would say no to him?

I was positive that Neil had never been rejected by a woman in his entire life.

"You think?" he said mockingly, though he didn't seem to have any plans to seduce her. He absolutely could have but instead remained right there in front of me looking like a god: beautiful and out of reach.

"You're just sitting here staring at her. I don't want to hold you back. You've found tonight's lucky girl. Do what you gotta do." I gave him a smile, but it was tight and forced.

"What I gotta do?" he repeated, sounding amused.

"Yup. Bonus: She has great breasts. Big, like you like them," I grumbled. I was going too far, but I was so terribly nervous. My legs had even started shaking. Neil managed to keep from laughing in my face and leaned against the bar to get closer to me.

Here he was—Neil the seducer.

Handsome, shameless, and sensual.

"Your breasts aren't so bad," he said softly, casting an approving glance at my chest. "I'll remind you that I've felt them, licked them, and sucked on them. I don't usually give that kind of attention to anything I don't like," he asserted.

"Could you be a little less…explicit?" I blushed and looked around to hide the redness in my cheeks. I could feel myself getting hot, and my underpants bore the evidence of my body's weakness: I was aroused.

"I'm usually even more explicit, Tinkerbell." He smirked at my reaction, and I avoided meeting his eyes again. He was too close; I could feel his breath on my skin. So I shot him a sideways glance and saw that he was still watching me.

"Why are you staring at me?" I huffed. Neil was definitely looking at me now and not at the beautiful girl in black.

"Because I prefer the black-haired girl, right?" he shot back wickedly.

I automatically glanced at the lovely green-eyed stranger and then back at him. He was still focused on me.

"I'm the one you're staring at, though," I answered thoughtfully. There was a hint of an enigmatic smile on his face and…

Damn it, he had to stop smiling like that.

"So…?" he whispered. He couldn't possibly mean he liked me better than that woman. No, the idea was absolutely absurd.

"You cannot prefer me to her." I shook my head. I could not be what he wanted. Whatever happened between us, Neil would always be attracted to other women, women like the total smokeshow who had just come in. I wasn't delusional; I knew he didn't feel the same way about me as I did about him.

"Did you know men don't like it when a woman's too insecure?" He smiled at me, and it actually seemed like Neil Miller was flirting with me.

"Doesn't matter. I don't want you to like me." I hoped I sounded convincing. His eyes slipped down to my hands, which couldn't stop shaking, and he instantly had all the confirmation he needed.

"Such a liar," he said in a soft, amused voice.

I found myself squirming awkwardly on my stool because my body was apparently responding to the siren call of his stare.

He could have stripped me naked right there on the spot.

"Look who we have here. Hey, Miller." A feminine voice broke the spell. I immediately turned to see the gorgeous black-haired girl giving Neil a casual smile.

It hadn't occurred to me that these two might have already known each other, and my shock was obvious.

She touched Neil's side, and he did absolutely nothing to remove her hand.

"You're here, too, Megan?" He heaved a sigh of annoyance and finally moved away from her touch. Megan checked him out just like every other girl in the club had, but Neil remained cold and apathetic.

"You remember Britney?" The beauty gestured to the small blond girl at her side, and as I examined her huge eyes, sensual lips, and long, light hair, I remembered precisely where I'd seen her before: in the pool house.

It was her. The same girl who'd given Neil a blow job right in front of me.

A sudden storm of emotions had me wobbling on my stool. I tried to project indifference, but the dark-haired girl saw how upset I was. Her gaze moved to me and immediately slid down my body. Was she actually checking out my legs? Embarrassment washed over me.

"I gave you my number. I thought you'd call." Britney faced Neil directly, clearly disappointed. Neil, however, just kept wearing the same grim, uncaring expression.

He had already used this one. Once was enough for him.

"Must have lost it somewhere," he answered vaguely. "Maybe in the toilet? Who can say?" He was truly sneering at her now. I couldn't help but pity her even as I also felt relief. Neil hadn't seen her after the pool house so they'd never slept together again.

I knew I was being irrational, but that discovery pleased me. Fortunately, I couldn't recall any of this girl's specific gifts because I'd been trying not to look in the pool house specifically, so I wouldn't have those obscene images burned into my mind. Still, I felt a burning sensation in my stomach at the knowledge that this girl had touched Neil.

She knew his taste that we'd discussed earlier while I'd never experienced that particular intimacy with him. The very thought of it made me tremble with jealousy.

"See, Britney? Never put your faith in assholes, because this is what happens," Megan cut in, shaking her head.

Neil stood up from his stool and managed to make them both flinch with the sheer imposition of his body. These women both feared and desired him, and it was frustrating to watch them become so enthralled with his presence.

"I can't stand you, and I can't stand these stupid theatrics," he snapped at Megan.

"I'm going to the bathroom; I'll be right back," he said to me, his voice softening. The other girls furrowed their brows, perhaps wondering why Neil Miller was bothering to tell me where he was going. I just nodded and watched him walk into the crowd.

"Are you his girlfriend?" Britney asked me.

I turned to her and caught her watching me haughtily.

"You must be Selene. My sister has told me so much about you." Megan, unlike her friend, stuck out her hand for me to shake. I gave her a puzzled look.

"Yeah, that's me. Have we met?" I reciprocated her handshake, and she smiled at me.

"No, I'm Alyssa's sister," she explained. Oh, so *this* was the famous Megan whom Alyssa had told me about so often. I felt my attitude toward her shift immediately and become much more friendly. She was my friend's sister, after all. The only friend with whom I'd really established a close relationship here in New York.

"Oh yeah! We're really good friends."

"She told me." She approached the bar and signaled for the bartender to bring her two beers. "You want something?" she added kindly.

I shook my head as she confirmed the two drinks with the bartender. Her perfume smelled really good, and her green eyes were very appealing. A little mole next to her Cupid's bow caught my attention. She didn't look much like Alyssa. She grabbed the two beers the bartender handed her. I was about to make conversation and pass the time while we waited for Neil to come back when an outraged Jennifer stalked toward me in her signature boxer braids. Her skinny jeans were ripped at the knees, and her white shirt was cut way too low. She looked as beautiful as she was dangerous.

She halted in front of me and stared wrathfully at me.

I hadn't seen her since the night of Halloween, and I had been hoping to continue not seeing her for a long time.

"Where is he?" she burst out, not caring at all that she was interrupting a conversation. I sighed, determined not to let her steamroll me.

"Who are you talking about?" I asked, playing dumb. No way was I going to tell her where Neil was. The bitch would probably have followed him into the bathroom and offered him a BJ on the spot.

"Don't give me that shit, you snot-nosed little brat," she hissed, and my eyes widened. I wasn't going to let her attack me like she did before. If she tried to put her hands on me, I wasn't just going to roll over.

"Where the fuck is Neil? I've been calling him for hours, and he hasn't answered. He's spent this whole night with you, hasn't he?" she continued angrily. She sounded like a hyena. Apparently it still wasn't clear to Jennifer that Neil was not with her—he wasn't with anyone.

"You're a slow learner, aren't you, honey? Neil can spend the night with whoever he likes. You two are not together," I needled her. Megan stood next to me, sipping her beer but watching Jennifer with the same level of animosity the blond girl had shown to me.

Jennifer shook her head and licked her lips, preparing her counterassault.

"While you were off in Detroit, he was with me. Want to guess what we were doing? Do you want me to tell you all the details?" She laughed with gusto, and I wanted to slap her so badly. I'd been pretty confident that there had been more sexual encounters between the two of them—Alyssa had basically told me as much—but hearing it from the Queen Bitch herself had a cratering effect on my mood. All my confidence wavered, and I could barely keep from crying.

Tears were the way I vented everything—love, disappointment, and anger—but I had to control myself just then.

"Miller only ever looks you up when he wants to get it wet. Doesn't seem like much to brag about, does it?" Megan put in, coming to my defense. She brought the beer up to her lips and stared Jennifer down with a cocky grin. It was only then that Jennifer noticed the other girl's presence.

"And where did you come from, Xena Warrior Princess?" she heckled. Megan set her beer down on the counter and moved toward her, cocking her head to one side, and she scrutinized Jennifer carefully.

"Play nice, you little bitch. Or else you're gonna go home with these pretty little braids shoved right up your ass," she said in a menacing whisper, grabbing her by one of those same long braids. For the second time since I'd met her, I saw Jennifer look afraid. Megan loomed over her. "I don't give a shit whether you run with the Krew or fuck Miller or play the queen fucking bee. I'm not afraid of you or your little gang. So piss off!" she snapped, releasing her abruptly. Jennifer stumbled back, and Megan continued to shield me with her body as she stared the other girl down fearlessly.

Jennifer straightened up and glowered at both of us.

"You're going to pay for that. Both of you!" She pointed threateningly at us and left.

I got up from my stool, finally able to breathe again. I just wanted to go home. Jennifer wasn't the type to give up easily, and her being in the club made me feel unsettled.

"Thanks," I murmured. Megan turned back to me and smiled, grabbing her beer and taking a drink.

"Don't mention it. You're not like her; that's why she's jealous," she told me, sitting down on my stool. "Plus, you're beautiful. The beautiful ones always want assholes like Miller, and Jennifer is obsessed with the guy," she continued, looking up at my face.

"We're not together," I clarified quickly. Neil hadn't given Jennifer up, after all, just like he hadn't chosen me. Jennifer's jealousy was unfounded.

Megan was about to answer back, but someone interrupted her.

"Selene!" called a male voice.

I whirled around to see Luke hurrying toward me, looking concerned.

"Are you okay?" he skidded to a stop in front of me, panting. He even had to lean on the bar for a second to get his breath back.

"She's fine, Parker. But do try to keep your poodle on a leash. She's very annoying," Megan answered for me, shooting me a grin.

"Fuck, I told her to just let it go, but Jennifer..." Luke sighed and scrubbed a hand over his face. "She loses her shit when it comes to Neil," he explained.

Over-the-top charisma, sexual dominance, magnetic stare, beauty—everything about Neil was unusual. Unusual enough to attract the obsessive interest of women, and I was no exception.

The pattern was simple: Neil used a girl, she fell in love with him, and then she paid the price in unrequited feelings.

What about me? Was I going to pay as well?

"Oh, there you are." Megan's green eyes looked over my shoulder. Instinctively, I turned to find Neil's marble chest right in front of my nose. How good did his sweater smell? How good did *he* smell?

I lifted my chin and met his eyes, which were already aimed at me. He observed me in that unknowable way that always muddled my thoughts.

"Everything okay?" His voice—his lovely voice—caressed my senses. Every fear and worry melted away in the face of the ardor he made me feel.

"Keep that shrew you're pseudo-dating away from her. Who knows what she would have done to Selene if I hadn't been here?" Megan groused. Neil breathed roughly, and then he made a bizarre move. He looped his arm around my body and rested his palm on my ass. In an instant, I found myself pressed against his body. I stood frozen, embarrassed by the protective gesture.

"Tell Jennifer to knock that shit off, or I'm going to get really pissed off," Neil said, addressing Luke. I sucked in a breath at his surly tone and noted that Luke wasn't paying attention because he was too busy staring at Neil's hand on my backside. I wrinkled my forehead in confusion.

"If you'd quit fucking her, she'd probably get the message faster," Luke shot back. Neil smiled and pulled me even closer to him, sliding his hand down to my thigh. My short dress allowed him to graze the tops of my thigh highs and I... I was going to die or maybe just faint. I wasn't sure.

My breathing grew labored, and I felt a familiar warmth spreading between my legs, the kind that only my walking disaster could elicit.

"You seem uncomfortable, Luke," Neil said, positioning himself behind me. His chin brushed against the top of my head, and his pelvis was pressed tight against my ass. I began to sweat. Neil knew exactly what was going on inside me. He was joining our desires together, wanting me to feel his powerful erection in the exact place I wanted it most. He really was a son of a bitch.

"And you seem…" Luke looked from my face to his friend's. "Stiff," he concluded, looking disconcerted.

My cheeks burned, and I clenched my lower lip between my teeth.

Neil leaned over my neck, gently moving my hair behind one shoulder.

"Do I seem stiff to you, Tinkerbell? Tell Luke, he'd really like to know," he whispered into my ear slyly, and I gulped. He knew what I was feeling. He knew that I could feel everything. If it wasn't for my modest nature, I would have answered his question yes, without a doubt. He was stiff and hard. Male and ready to dominate. He was a gloriously aroused man. I could vividly remember what he was packing in his boxers.

"Want to play a round of pool?" Megan finished her beer and got up, interrupting my extremely uncomfortable moment. She'd felt the tension between the two boys—the same tension that I had observed. Luke frowned while blond Britney went off with some other girls, promising Megan they'd meet up later. Then there was Neil, who…wouldn't stop staring at Luke.

"Come on, Miller. It'll be fun. You and me against Luke and Selene," Megan suggested, sashaying toward a room I hadn't noticed before. Neil retreated with a bored huff, and I rubbed my forehead.

I was actually sweating.

Luke followed Megan, brushing past Neil and me without saying anything. I didn't understand the sudden shift in the vibe—they had been talking about Jennifer, and then the whole situation took a different turn—but I needed some air. I tried to take a deep breath, but Neil's musky smell overpowered the air all around me. He was still too close. I turned to look at him, gorgeous and cheeky with a tempting grin. My eyes drifted to the fly of his pants and I couldn't help but notice the pronounced bulge. It was enormous. I imagined all the women who had gotten a look at it and couldn't hold back a scowl. Neil must have sensed the direction of my thoughts because he pulled down the hem of his sweater with one hand and tried to adjust himself with the other.

"He's a gentleman. He stands up when you enter the room," he said sardonically, gesturing to his lower half. I stood stock-still, staring at him.

Had Neil just made a joke?

I shook my head and hurried after the others.

"Cover that up!" I snapped automatically. Neil watched me with a strange look on his face and I went red.

He'd figured me out.

He knew that I was jealous and the concern in his eyes didn't please me at all. Embarrassed, I cleared my throat and continued walking. Neil, thankfully, didn't say anything and just walked behind me.

"You're not looking at my butt, are you?" I asked him impulsively as we proceeded down a short hallway that separated the club from a quieter room. The music grew muffled, as did the noise of the crowd.

"Of course, just like you were looking at my co—" he began, but I whirled around, skewering him with a look.

"Stop. You already ridiculed me in front of your friend." I stabbed a finger at him, and he grinned, not at all worried or regretful.

"Were you embarrassed because Luke was there?" He cocked an eyebrow and looked probingly at me.

"Of course not. I was embarrassed because you were alluding to *certain things* for whatever ridiculous reason…" Instead of answering, Neil just snorted and brushed past me, no longer listening. He had already gotten tired of talking to me.

With a heavy sigh, I followed him through a black curtain and into a game room. It looked like a real arcade and was decidedly less crowded than the rest of the club. It had everything: coin-op machines, video games, pinball, and various pool tables. I spotted Megan at one of them and joined her, pasting a wide smile on my face.

"About time, Selene. What'd Miller do?" She laughed, picking up a cue and chalking its tip.

"I can't stand him sometimes," I said in a low voice because Neil was right next to us, intent on picking out his own cue.

"Nobody can stand him when he's not naked in bed." She gave me a mischievous wink, and we giggled together. Neil turned to look at us then with a frown, so we straightened our faces.

"Good, good, good. Now let's see if you boys can get it in the hole," Megan chuckled, drawing the attention of both men.

"I don't know how to play," I grumbled while I watched Luke pick out a cue. Neil already had his, and he stood there looking bored, waiting for us to be ready.

"Here, take this one." Luke came up beside me and handed me a cue. It was a different size than his, and I frowned questioningly at him.

"Each player needs to use a cue that's appropriate for their height," he explained with a shrug. I took the opportunity to get a better look at his leather jacket; it was black and had a skull wreathed in red flames on the back. Luke had an aggressive sense of style that clashed with his milder affect.

"Are you calling me short? Thanks," I joked, and someone cleared their throat. I turned Neil's way and found his golden eyes watching us. He had his elbow balanced on his cue and looked irritated with us.

"Are you going to get a move on?" he asked harshly.

"Don't start, asshole," Luke muttered with a huff.

"Prepare to lose, Parker," Neil chastised with an expression of such confidence that it immediately punctured any hopes I had of winning.

Hopes that were already pretty meager, as I had never played pool and had only watched friends play a few times. Slightly worried about breaking something, I examined my cue and considered how to position it.

"Hold on, let me show you." Sensing my discomfort, Luke approached. Not for the first time, I wondered how a nice guy like him ended up with the Krew. He was unquestionably a member of the gang, but the way he acted was nothing like Xavier or the girls.

Then he put a hand on the base of my spine, and I froze. "You need to lean slightly forward." He urged me to follow his instruction with his hand, and I did so automatically even though I was a little afraid my dress would lift up too high in the back. Not to mention my heels, which were decidedly uncomfortable. "Hold the end of the cue in your right hand and balance the narrow end on your left," he continued patiently. His breath grazed my cheek, and his chest was pressing into my back, and it occurred to me that I couldn't tolerate physical contact with any man but Neil.

I couldn't even focus on what he was saying because my body was rebelling against his proximity.

"Luke, I think she gets how to hold the fucking cue," Neil cut in, irritated. I looked at him, noticing his tightly contracted jaw. He peeled off his leather jacket in a hurry and threw it on a nearby stool. Then he rolled the sleeves of his sweater up to his elbows. Pronounced veins traveling all over the backs of his hands were the only thing I could see. My grip on the cue went slack and I forgot all the rules of the game Luke had just explained to me. The power of that Adonis's body was unreal.

"Just giving her a hand," Luke told him with a sly smile.

Neil just licked his lips and gestured for Megan to rack the balls, not even giving me a chance to do a practice shot.

The game began.

Neil took the first turn, and I stood there, admiring him. He was nothing short of dazzling, leaning forward intently with that serious frown on his face and a lock of chestnut hair tumbling down over his forehead. He ran a hand through his hair to push the strands back up before going back to the colorful ball he'd decided to go for.

Seconds later, he hit the ball with an expertly controlled strike.

"Wow." Megan patted his shoulder flatteringly, but he just stared at the table, adjusting his back like a cat. He looked at Luke with a grin of defiance. Rather than a simple game, it was looking more and more like a competition between the two of them.

I looked to Megan for some female support, but she just shrugged.

"Men," she snarked, rolling her eyes.

Half an hour later, the other team was clearly in the lead.

"Well, Luke? What's going on? Don't tell me you can't get it in the hole." Neil sneered at his friend after he'd missed several shots in a row.

"Maybe I'm distracted," Luke answered, and there was something wicked in his tone. I looked at him and caught him ogling my ass as he circled me like a predator. For the first time, I recognized another side to him: perverse and dangerous. I supposed that was the reason he was with

259

the Krew. Despite what I'd foolishly thought, he couldn't be that different from Xavier if he was hanging out with him all the time. Luke cut his eyes at Neil and gave him a challenging smirk while my Disaster stared at him, unmoving, not remotely intimidated.

Instead, he seemed a little antsy.

Abruptly, Luke stationed himself to the left of me and stopped checking me out like he was trying to undress me with his eyes.

"Your turn," he smiled, and I bent forward, immediately breaking eye contact with him.

I positioned the cue where he'd suggested, but I wasn't feeling very confident. Our opponents were clearly more at home on the green felt. They held the cues correctly and knew all the lingo and the rules, while I could barely hit anything. I tried not to grip the cue too tightly, just enough to keep it steady as I took my shot. I kept my wrist soft, just like Luke had told me, and I concentrated.

"Come on, Selene. You've got this," he murmured, but my eyes immediately sought out Neil and found him watching me. His eyes crawled hotly over me and made it very difficult to maintain my concentration.

I struck, but weakly and inaccurately.

The ball didn't go into the pocket—it didn't even get near it. We really were losing miserably.

"Sorry," I said softly to Luke, who just smiled at me, not at all bothered. I didn't know this game, and I felt foolish for agreeing to play. Especially since Megan was amazing at it. Even worse, every time she leaned forward to expertly position her cue, Neil would sneak a peek at her butt. He did it very discreetly, but his eyes were undeniably tracking the woman's enthralling form. I had seen right away that Mr. Disaster was not immune to Megan's wild charms. Anyone would have been captivated by someone like her: strong, confident and extremely attractive.

"Let's swap. We're destroying you," Neil suggested, pulling me abruptly from my thoughts. I didn't know why he'd made this sudden request, but Luke didn't object and walked over to stand next to Megan. I stayed where I was until I caught the scent of musk in the air and realized Neil was right behind me.

"Now I'll show you how to hit it right, Babygirl," he whispered in my ear. His strong torso brushed against my back, and his long arms wrapped around me, encircling me. Then, Neil forced me to bend forward and draped himself over me, not caring about all the stares we were attracting. I could feel his hips bump against my ass in a bold, uninhibited way. His hands covered mine, moving them into a better position. "It just takes patience, dedication, and precision. You're a quick study; I'm sure you'll get it this time," he added, breath hot on my neck. If he kept talking to me in that low, thrilling voice, I would lose my mind completely. Neil—a man who could provoke such storms within me and upset my equilibrium—made eroticism into a deadly weapon, and I was his target.

In that moment he was using some strange erotic strategy to get me to yield inexorably to him. I swallowed a mouthful of saliva, and as it burned down my throat, I looked at the end of the cue. Neil's fingers were long and firm over mine. I stared at them and licked my lips, surprising myself with my intense desire to feel them all over my body.

"Come on," he murmured. I focused on not letting him down, on striking the little colorful ball in the best way possible. I jabbed the cue forward with just the right amount of force.

I saw the ball spin, and then… It went into the pocket.

I stood frozen for a few moments, wondering whether I'd actually done it. But then my lips curved up into a grin, and I instinctively jumped for joy.

"Yes!" I let out a squeal of happiness and turned to Neil, who gave me the loveliest smile I had ever seen.

And that was the real victory: getting to see him smile.

We continued the game against Megan and Luke until we won.

United, simpatico, strong. Together.

I still knew that Neil had demons but, somehow, those demons had managed to communicate with me.

I no longer feared him.

I felt protected by him.

And it felt like each day I discovered a new part of his personality that did not require words because I was learning to read his silent signals.

I could sense the purity of my own feelings and the strength of something else that was being born within him.

Maybe this thing that brought us together would never blossom in full. Maybe we'd never have a real romance or be a real couple. Maybe we'd just keep bumping up against each other forever.

Maybe we'd keep finding each other whenever we wanted to get lost.

11

No other girl ever mattered that much to me.

NEIL

What the fuck was happening?

I had no idea either.

Selene and I had just come back from the club, and I brought her to the pool house with me for no reason that I could think of.

That was where I took the girls I fucked.

The blond girls. Always blond.

Selene, apparently, was the exception to the rule.

"I didn't know you were so good at pool," she commented from behind me, her voice echoing off the walls of my lair. I still couldn't believe she was there with me.

Babygirl had arrived from Detroit that morning—Matt had been talking about it constantly for days on end. But I'd welcomed her much differently than the rest of my family because someone had ripped up my drawings, and I'd lost my cool, like usual.

I hated it whenever anyone touched my things or made a mess of my space. So, I had stormed into the dining room like a rabid dog, heedless of the familiar fear I was so used to seeing in the eyes of everyone around me.

Selene, though, stayed sweet as fuck. She brought me a bag of shelled pistachios, and I'd let her come into my pool house with her ocean eyes, coconut smell, and shy smile. I only kissed her once before, fortunately, I managed to get control of myself. It took more than that to make someone like me lose his mind.

Except then she'd put on that indecent little dress, and all I could do was stare at her. It's like she was begging me.

"Come over here and tear this off me."

Or maybe, *"Throw me down and fuck me."*

I found myself questioning my own self-confidence. I'd thought myself so immune to her charms and then turned around to find myself hanging on her every word.

Shit.

I passed a hand over my face. I was tense. I had been tense for hours because I wanted a release. I needed a release, but I couldn't have one. I was still following Dr. Lively's instructions to resist my sexual urges because of the issues I'd been having in that department.

What would happen if I gave in to Selene and then wasn't able to come?

I would have made her feel inadequate, like the other ones. Even worse, she would start in with her talking thing again, and I'd have to explain to her why my body was reacting so weirdly.

Babygirl was never satisfied with just using me. She always wanted more and that scared me.

It made me feel uncomfortable and confused and I didn't know how to handle it.

"Why did you agree to come out here?" I sat down on the couch and tousled my hair. I was going to take a shower and then kick her out. Or maybe I'd kick her out and then take a shower. I wasn't sure exactly what order it would happen in, but either way, she was going to leave.

"What?" She stood there with her coat draped over her shoulders, her thighs clearly visible, and her seductive cleavage on display.

"Why are you here?" I asked again. "Usually only people who've agreed to pleasure me come in here. Do you want to fuck?" I looked at her, trying to make my stare as icy as possible. Meanwhile, inside me there was an incandescent fire I struggled to contain.

Selene screwed up her face and shrugged. My mood had shifted on her again, and she was looking at me like I was a lunatic. That was understandable, really. The evening had actually gone quite well. I had been nice to her and unusually protective, especially when Luke looked at her a little more than he should have. I had been the one to make her think there might be something more going on with us, and she had followed me like any woman in her place would have done.

We'd had one of those moments when I felt this inexplicable understanding with her, a kind of attunement I'd never experienced with anyone else. Worst of all was the bizarre feeling I got around my chest area whenever a man at the club looked at her. It bothered me when people stared at her, which was absolutely an abnormal reaction for me. No other girl ever mattered that much to me; I'd regularly shared women with Xavier and Luke.

Luke, who played white knight the whole time when we both knew perfectly well that he only wanted to sneak into that tight spot where only I had ever been.

That place belonged to me: my Neverland.

"Why are you talking to me like this now?" she asked as I took in her very long hair draped over one shoulder and her firm tits.

Did she really think I only liked them huge? I was a man. It didn't matter if they were little or big, round or teardrop-shaped; the only thing that mattered was that I got to do what I wanted with them.

In fact, I actually preferred the small ones.

No.

I preferred hers.

Babygirl was too naive to know how the male brain worked. Plus, she had no idea how beautiful she was. If she had figured that out, everything would have made a lot more sense to her.

"Because you're here in my pool house, half-dressed, without having found this evening's lucky guy. Maybe you'd like to replace him with me?" I was toying with her. The one-night-stand story was just a game I enjoyed playing with her. I knew her too well to think she'd fall into bed with just anyone. Selene valued herself. She valued her kisses and embraces. She couldn't give herself to someone until she'd gotten to know them or at least gone out with them a few times. Never on the first night.

Selene demanded a lot; it was why it was so difficult for me to be around her.

"Do you think one is just as good as another?" She grew more annoyed as I stared at her thighs like a desperate man, trying not to get distracted from our conversation.

Yeah, I thought one was about as good as any other for everybody else. But not for her. She wanted me; she had been wanting me all night long.

And that was a fucking problem.

"I'm the only one you want, Tinkerbell, and that's no good. Why don't you go find a man who can make you happy?" I let my head fall back on the couch and splayed my legs, adopting a comfortable position. If she had actually found him, I would have accepted it.

Or maybe I would have just killed him.

No—I would have accepted it.

Selene shook her head, a cheeky little smile passing over her face. A little dimple always appeared on the right side of her mouth whenever she smiled. It was really tiny, but I spotted it. Just as I had also noticed the two other moles she had in addition to the one next to her right nipple. She had one shaped like an upside-down heart on her knee and an identical one at the base of her spine.

It occurred to me that I'd like to take another look at them, just to make sure I wasn't mistaken. Her body lived only in my memory now. It had been so long since I'd touched her.

And dammit if I didn't want to do it again.

I sighed, undoing my jeans with one hand. I couldn't tolerate my hard-on anymore. It had been like that for hours, compressed by my pants. Sometimes I even felt breathless from the stabs of arousal. It got so bad that I couldn't even sit up straight.

Selene tracked my movement and swallowed hard, embarrassed. I knew that I was making her uncomfortable, but I was used to being shameless, especially with women.

I did what I wanted, said what I thought, and had no scruples.

"Would you tell me what happened with Jennifer?" I asked. I didn't really care, but I needed some distraction, or else I was going to succumb to my animal urges. I would have fucked her over that kitchen island and then failed to come, making her feel like she wasn't enough for me. Selene was still too inexperienced and insecure, especially when it came to sex, so getting down with me in my current condition would only make her more neurotic. She would have felt used and dirty, and I didn't want that. I wanted her to enjoy whatever we did, not feel even worse about herself.

"You're still thinking about her...even now," she answered in irritation. As usual, Tinkerbell was letting her insecurities get the best of her. She didn't understand that thinking about someone meant something different to me than it did to her.

"I want to know what she did," I admitted, adjusting my erection under my boxers. I wished I could just strip them off and be comfortably nude.

Could I do that? Or would she think I was a sicko even if I never touched her?

"She made a scene because you ignored her calls. She thinks I'm distracting you somehow," she explained, tucking a strand of hair behind her ear. I looked her up and down again, lingering on her legs.

Just how high were those heels?

They looked heavenly on her. If I could have, I would have fucked her just like that, completely naked except for those elegant stilettos.

"I'll have to talk to her," I observed. Again. Just because we'd been screwing for four years did not mean that I was serious about Jennifer or that I wanted to be in a relationship with her. I'd have thought she would have taken the hint when I didn't return her thirty-five calls. She did not. Even though I'd told her repeatedly that I wasn't her man and that there was nothing between us, Jennifer only accepted the things she already believed.

Maybe if I'd ever had the balls to tell them about my past, they'd understand what I really was.

"You'll have to remind her that the only thing she really enjoys is your co—" Selene paused, pressing her hand to her mouth. I grinned and stared intensely at her, trying to make her blush.

"I'm a bad influence on you, Babygirl," I said. Selene turned and slipped

267

off her coat, putting it down on a stool in the kitchen area. Finally, I could appreciate the swell of her hips and that high ass under her swishy skirt.

What would she look like without it? What kind of underwear was she wearing?

She'd said she was wearing a thong, but she'd probably been lying. I wouldn't have been surprised to see her hiding a pair of those awful cotton panties. Almost as bad as her pajamas.

"You already *influenced* me more than a month ago," she said, standing there at a distance from me. "And now you're talking to me, finally," she added, sounding pleased. That was another issue. I had started talking to her way too much. I never told her anything about my past, but I was more talkative in general. Sometimes it was just to flirt or tease her, other times to explain things she couldn't just intuit.

"It won't work between us," I said casually, trying to clarify again for her one of those things that she refused to accept. But I didn't like the melancholy I saw in her azure eyes. All I wanted to do was protect her from me and get it through her head that there could be no relationship—that I could never give her what she wanted.

I didn't want to drag her down into the abyss with me. I wanted the best for her, and I was not the best. We both knew that.

"Why?" she insisted, and I felt my nerves beginning to fray.

"Why, why, why… It's always fucking *why* with you, Selene!" I burst out, even standing up to emphasize my point.

"Why don't you just take off your clothes? Why don't you just put your hands on me and use me? Why?" I raised my voice as I walked toward her. "Why don't you push me down on that couch and fuck me like the rest of them? Like they've always done? Why? It would be a lot easier, you know. I could accept having you with me, but only my way, never in the way you want." I'd gotten too close, and she'd backed up until she hit the wall. When I saw her tremble, I cursed my inability to be rational like a normal man and stepped back. Who knew how hard her heart was beating or what she was thinking of me. I scrubbed a hand over my face because I'd never been in a situation so difficult before.

Women had never been a problem for me. I could take what I wanted—a momentary high—from them and then move on, almost indifferent to even the most obscene acts. Yet even when I'd had multiple bodies to enjoy at once, I'd never felt what I felt with Babygirl. To be honest, the sex we'd shared hadn't been anything special but I'd liked it because it was simple, genuine, natural, and, above all else, true.

Really goddamned true.

"Because, to me, you are not an object," she said in a low voice.

I turned sharply to scrutinize her. Why would she say something like that?

I automatically searched her face for a hint of the feelings I despised, like pity or compassion. I would have put her out on her ass if I'd seen them there, but I didn't.

Then I smiled wickedly.

Did she believe that women used me like an object?

Did she think of me as some kind of victim?

She was dead wrong.

The exact opposite was happening. I was the one who used women as objects. I was the one projecting Kimberly onto each one of them and taking revenge for what she'd done to me.

I was the one who broke them with my dominating attitude, making them like it and then tossing them aside, just like Kim had done to me.

I was on the other side now.

"You really are an innocent, Selene. Too much of an innocent." I took another step back, getting further away from her scent, which only confused me.

"You sure? You use them, and they use you. It all comes from the same place." She pushed off the wall and advanced on me. She walked slowly on those high heels and a little awkwardly, showing none of the confidence that usually irritated me in other girls.

With her perfect, well-proportioned body, she looked like an innocent fairy and a bewitching siren all in one. Not a single man at that club had failed to notice her.

Everyone—truly everyone—had looked lustfully at her.

And what about back in Detroit? How many guys were looking at her when I wasn't there?

"Neil…" Babygirl prompted. "Are you listening to me?" she continued cautiously.

No, I wasn't listening to her anymore.

And she had noticed my absence—that I was lost in my own reflections.

Acting on instinct, I grabbed her by the nape of the neck and pulled her to me. I clutched her hair in my fist and brought my lips to within a hairsbreadth of hers.

"You need to be gone in the next five minutes. You really need to get out of here," I said in an angry whisper. Her slim little hands rested on my chest, and I could barely breathe.

"Okay," she managed, sounding intimidated. Was she afraid of me? I rubbed the end of her nose with mine and pressed a kiss to its small, upturned tip.

She was perfect.

"Make that ten. Ten minutes." I descended on her mouth. Ten minutes would be long enough to satisfy the sick need I had to taste her all over.

"Agreed," she answered.

Good. I liked it when she was accommodating.

Still holding her by the hair and trying not to hurt her, I wrapped my other hand around her waist and groped her ass hard. Selene let out a tiny hiss.

She'd just have to get used to me and it wouldn't be for the rest of our lives, after all. Just the next ten minutes.

After a moment's hesitation, she bit her lower lip and shut her eyes. She was ready to submit to me, the devil himself. So I kissed her.

My tongue slid impatiently into the paradise that was her mouth and was immediately met by hers, ready for me.

Timid and uncertain.

Yes, that was the kind of kiss I wanted to receive.

Then, Selene slipped her hand into my hair and drew me closer to her, so I started kissing her my way.

The way that hurt her.

The way that hurt me.

Selene was the only one who didn't just arouse me; she made me actually lose control. She didn't know anything about pleasure, yet I liked everything about her, even her shyness. I was dominant—not just in bed—she seemed to appreciate that part of me, though she'd never admit it.

"Make it fifteen. Fifteen minutes, and then I'm booting your ass. And I will boot it, you know. Your ass will be bright red tomorrow," I whispered, irritable and terribly confused, but all she did was nod.

I went back to kissing her. My thoughts were swarming, crowding together chaotically.

Too chaotically.

The more I kissed Babygirl, the more I searched the meandering pathways of my brain for an escape route, of which I found none.

All my blood was concentrated in my cock, and it was getting very difficult to think rationally. Her sharp moan further inflamed me and only made me lay claim to her with more force.

All at once her hands were pushing at my shoulders because she couldn't breathe.

She never could kiss very well, my Babygirl. She was too awkward.

I looked into her eyes as I paused to let her get some air. Selene rested her forehead against my chest and breathed.

She breathed me in.

"You still can't kiss," I mocked while she stood still, breathing deeply.

"You… You…" she babbled, trailing off.

"I… I…?" I asked derisively, stroking the back of her neck soothingly. Slowly, she looked up at me. In her eyes, I saw seas of pleasure, oceans of arousal.

I could feel her hot breath curling over my skin, on my flesh, and along my muscles.

"You have to go." I felt like a prisoner of my senses, delirious. I was actually delirious.

"You don't want me to go," she answered with certainty.

The blood began to race in my veins, and the combined scent of us hung in the air.

I was enjoying being hers in that moment, in those fleeting fifteen minutes. But I had to make her see it was just an unworkable illusion.

271

"I'm going to fuck you," I said then, hoping it would make her understand the kind of trouble she was getting into.

"Okay. Do it," she said challengingly.

She'd lost it for sure. We were caught in a storm of destructive desire, and neither of us could think straight.

"I'll do it like I do it with the other girls. No feelings," I insisted, sure that this would finally make her back up.

I remembered what Dr. Lively told me: I had to abstain from sexual intercourse, from violating my own body or else…

"You seem to *feel* pretty strongly about the lack of feelings." She smiled at her own joke, and I gave her a puzzled look. What was that silvery glint in her eyes? Was she looking at me with…adoration? I licked my lips, gathering a bit of her flavor. That sweet, irresistible feminine taste. Then, I stroked the soft skin of her cheek, and she kissed my fingers.

Her every breath produced shivers.

In me. In her. In the both of us.

"On the couch," I ordered her abruptly, pulling back. I was doing it all wrong once again, but I wanted her. I wanted a little taste of her, at least.

Selene looked at me for a few moments, hesitating before finally obeying. I frowned at her body—she was wearing too many clothes.

"Undress. Slowly," I demanded before sitting down on a stool to enjoy the show. I needed to keep my distance from her, or I wouldn't be responsible for my actions. I ran a hand through my hair and tugged on my sweater. I wanted to take it all off.

Selene turned my way and gulped. She watched me thoughtfully and took a deep breath, gathering enough courage to make herself bold. Her hand shook as she slid down the first strap of her dress. I looked at her collarbone and then at the perfect curve of her neck. She repeated the action on the other shoulder and allowed the dress to slowly fall to the floor.

In an elegant movement, she lifted first one leg and then the other out of the dress until she stood there, balanced on her high heels, displaying herself for me proudly. She wore nothing but a pair of cotton panties, white and angelic, along with a matching bra and some sheer thigh highs.

I looked her all over. I ate her up from head to toe. Her pale skin was milky and luminous, free of imperfections. Her small breasts were high and firm, her stomach flat, and her legs slim and defined. Her hands were locked together, and she watched me timidly.

I rested my chin on one palm and continued staring at her, noting the redness of her cheeks.

"Are you embarrassed to have me look at you?" I asked her, forcing myself to stay seated because if I'd gotten any closer to her, I would have devoured her whole. She shook her head, but she was lying. She couldn't even hold my gaze for more than two seconds.

I had changed my mind. I got up from my stool and approached her slowly, letting her desire build.

I could feel how much she wanted me. And it was a lot.

I kept staring at her, and it occurred to me that I'd like to take a picture of her. I'd tuck it into my pocket and keep that image with me forever. Selene chewed her lip and lifted her eyes slightly, giving me a slow, sensual flutter of her eyelashes. I stopped right in front of her then and touched her chin, tracing the contours of her lips with my thumb. They were full and rounded, slightly chapped in the middle.

"Lie down," I whispered, pressing a kiss to the space underneath her ear. Babygirl shivered, and I smiled at her. She sat down slowly on the couch but hesitated a few moments before lying down. When she finally did, her auburn hair fanned out around her. She kept her legs pressed together and her hands in her lap. Her eyes were apprehensive.

I moved closer to her and took a knee. I wanted to be on top of her, next to her but, most of all, inside of her.

"Relax," I stroked her ankle and gently took her foot so I could slip her shoe off. I let it fall to the floor and cradled her foot in my hands. I massaged it with my thumbs, and she groaned approvingly.

I proceeded to give the other one the same treatment until I felt her muscles relax. I locked eyes with her to show her what was on my mind as I caressed her knee.

Selene gave a slight gasp, but I didn't stop. Nothing could have stopped me then.

I kneeled down, parting her thighs delicately. I resisted the urge to be rough with her because she was already trembling.

"Will you tell me something more about yourself?" she asked. I tilted my head to one side and considered her question for a moment.

"No," I answered decisively. I wasn't going to talk about myself this time either. I fixed my eyes on her white panties, noting the place where the fabric was darker with her wetness.

My Babygirl wanted me.

I stroked up and down her thighs. All I wanted to do was plunge my tongue into her center and do to her what I did to no one else, but Selene unexpectedly pushed me off her.

"Then stop. I don't want this." She clamped her legs back together and bent her knees to the side, protecting herself from me. I could hardly believe it—no one ever rejected me. Women threw themselves at me, craved me wildly, and I wasn't at all used to getting a categorical "no."

"You really are stupid, aren't you?" I blurted out, wounded by her rejection. "Do you think it's easy for me to talk about myself?" I got up and backed away from the couch, leaving her there half-naked and humiliated. I glanced around for my cigarettes before remembering I'd left them in the pocket of my jacket.

"And you think that's what a woman does? Just goes along with whatever you say?" Her voice behind me sounded sharp. I didn't bother looking at her as I retrieved my Winstons, extracting one cigarette with my teeth and immediately lighting it up. It was nothing but a desperate attempt to calm myself down, but the nicotine did help.

"No, but a woman should be able to figure out when a man wants to fuck and when he wants to talk. You, on the other hand, have terrible timing." I took my first drag and blew the smoke out into the air. Selene sat up and folded her legs underneath her.

"You're the one who's terrible," she answered, watching me as I smoked and prowled the room like a caged animal, a giant erection under my jeans as I was forced to listen to her and unable to touch.

What the fuck was going on?

"What are you doing here, then? If I'm so terrible, go find someone nice. Go find Luke," I said with a dismissive wave.

"I'll consider it. At least he's less of an asshole than you!" she shot back at me. I continued smoking so I wouldn't blow up at her.

"Fuck you," I hissed.

Selene could make me lose my patience like no one else. Not that it was particularly difficult to do, but she was an expert in the field.

Hot and uncomfortable, I pulled off my sweater and prepared to take a shower. I'd lost count of how many I'd taken that day, but in my head it had been way too long since the last one. I threw the sweater onto the kitchen island and then walked shirtless through the living room with just my dark jeans on.

Cigarette clamped between my teeth, I stole a glance at Selene and found her staring at my chest. Her big blue eyes trailed from my pecs to my abs. I heaved a sigh. I knew she liked what she saw, and I couldn't do anything but accept that, but I took no delight in knowing she thought me handsome.

I considered my body a punishment and a tool: Sometimes I used it to seduce, while other times I just wore it like a suit of armor to protect me from the world.

There were two of us, after all, living inside that perfect shell. The Boy and I. And we were both so afraid.

"Come over here and stop acting like I'm your enemy. I would never hurt you."

I looked at her, perched there on the couch and only saw a danger to myself. Selene didn't know what was in my head, how petrified I was of trusting women after Kim had betrayed me so deeply.

I ground the cigarette butt into the ashtray and waved away the last cloud of smoke, remaining aloof. Babygirl didn't stop watching me like she couldn't understand why I was acting that way. Maybe she was wondering how I'd recovered my self-control after her rejection, why I wasn't imposing myself on her the way I usually did, or why I wasn't trying to talk her into it.

The answer was simple: I couldn't.

I passed a hand over my face, fighting my body's instinct to do anything except what my brain had been urging it to do for hours. My hard-on was still there, and Selene had clocked it; it wasn't difficult to make out. She knew that I wanted her as much as she wanted me.

But I couldn't tell her about my problem.

"You need to leave. For real this time, you need to listen to me," I told her, more calmly but still severe.

If she hadn't, I would have gone over there, picked her up, and tossed her out.

One hand slipped into my undone jeans, and I adjusted myself again. The head of my dick was now protruding from the elastic of my boxers, but I didn't care. I just left it that way. Selene's gaze dropped again to that exact spot, and she swallowed hard in embarrassment.

Enough of this.

The truth was, I couldn't resist her, but I still didn't want to open myself up to her. Selene demanded emotional connection while I insisted on the purely physical kind.

All at once I was furious with myself, with the tumult inside me that I couldn't manage, the control I was about to lose, and the effect Babygirl was having on me.

Moments later, I advanced on her, drawn to her now more than ever.

"You don't want to leave?" I said, melting down once again. "Fine, then. Lie down. I'll show you why you should have gone when you had the chance," I burst out, enraged.

Selene slid back on the couch, but she couldn't escape.

I decided by that point that I was going to show her all about the sick way I wanted her so she would once again see me for the depraved person that I was and forget any possibility of being with me.

As soon as I reached her, I grabbed her hard by the wrists and forced her down. Selene didn't fight me, but her widened eyes were full of unspoken feelings: disappointment, hope, desire, and fear. I straddled her, bending over.

I immediately began kissing her neck in that greedy, carnal, dominating, fiery way that she could never resist, and Babygirl arched her back, pushing her still bra-covered tits against my chest.

Fuck, it felt fantastic having her underneath me.

Our bodies began trading heat, want, lust, everything.

I grazed my lips along the velvet softness of her neck and watched as goosebumps spread across her skin. When she tried to move her wrists, I didn't let her.

"What are your intentions here?" she asked, afraid but also aroused.

"The worst kind," I answered without shame.

Perversion, after all, was an important aspect of what I considered true romance to be.

Without hypocrisy.

Without self-righteousness.

Without any fake fucking Prince Charming.

Instead, it was me.

A mind that was deep but also soiled.

A man convinced that there was no profanity except what was made that way by eyes that saw it or ears that heard it.

I was a romantic. In my own way.

One of those bad-tempered romantics, one of those who refused to hide behind some angelic mask and was never afraid of showing his real imperfections.

One of those romantics who stripped women of their modesty along with their clothes and brought out the whore in them.

A *real* romantic, in short. Realer than most.

"I want you," I whispered, my breath controlled but my arousal running wild. I should have held back, but I was too hungry by then.

I was hungry for her, for her mouth and her eyes.

I was starving for her body, her little nose, and the funny faces she made.

I was hungry for her delicate curves and velvety legs.

I wanted to devour her warm heart.

I wanted to get inside her and befuddle my darkness with her light. I wanted her screams to be the soundtrack to all my cursed fantasies.

"Me too," she admitted in a gasp. I let her wrists go and moved my hands to her sides. She clung to me, spreading her legs so I could grind myself against the apex of her thighs. Selene shook from head to toe, her palms sweating and her eyelids flickering in time with the waves of pleasure that I drew straight out of her soul.

"I'm not going to fuck you," I warned, though the hoarseness of my voice suggested just the opposite.

Selene emitted a tiny groan. It always got her going when I talked to her under my breath like that, with that low timbre, even if it did embarrass her too.

That's how she was.

Still shut up in her prudish little world despite everything we'd done together.

She could have had me kneeling at her feet with the crook of her finger but she never would.

She wasn't like Jennifer.

She was seducing me slowly with her mind, to who knew what end. I had long known what she really wanted from me but I was working hard to keep her from getting it.

She was something pure, something lovely that made me feel alive.

"Neil…" My name emerged from her lush lips as a moan while I unhooked her bra and began to pull it away from her small breasts. My hand cupped her firm flesh. I could even feel her rapid breathing underneath.

"Ditch the bra." My movements grew impatient and I tugged it off her quickly because it was still dangling from her arms and I wanted see her free from any restraints.

"I've thought about nothing but sucking on these," I confessed, biting her neck. Selene raised her hips to meet me, growing bolder. Little by little, she grew ready and hot. My cock twitched, and I felt my glans, exposed and overstimulated, rubbing hard against the fabric of my underwear.

"Do it," she whispered. Apparently her good sense had abandoned her. I could tell by the tone of her voice, the way she was moving and her hands, which were now clutching my ass.

Her curves fit perfectly into the sharp angles of my body, like we were one being. I grinned sensually at her and sat up on my knees, positioning one on either side of her torso, caging her in.

"Now I'll show you what I've been wanting to do to you all night," I said in a provocative whisper.

I couldn't wait.

Maybe we didn't have enough time; maybe we never would.

Right then, she was there with me, but one day she would leave.

Selene fluttered her long eyelashes, ensnaring me with those crystalline eyes.

I hovered eagerly over her lips and pulled her up into an urgent kiss. Carnal.

It was not love. It was not sex. It was ecstasy.

Need.

It was fucking war.

My tongue pressed against her, swirling around in her mouth.

I used her hair to pull her head up slightly so I could deepen the kiss. Selene was panting as usual. She'd put her hands on my ribs to slow me down, but I did not relent. I continued showing her all the passion I could let loose on her soul.

The power, the dominance, the sheer control I had over her.

Once again, my animalistic frenzy contrasted with the delicate way she returned my kisses. Selene was trying too hard to keep up with me, and I felt a wave of tenderness for her.

Suddenly, a soft intake of breath, weak and damnably feeble, made my hard-on even more insistent.

I should have stopped myself, but I couldn't. I couldn't do it anymore.

By then, the urge to fuck her was throbbing in me, tearing through my stomach and every other part of my body. I pulled our hungry mouths apart and registered the confused look on her face.

Soon, she'd understand.

Selene lay spread out before me, cheekbones flushed, panting rapidly, her arms over her head.

I pulled down my jeans and boxers and freed the erection that was pulsing, pleading, and demanding my attention.

"Neil, what are you do—" She didn't even finish her sentence before her eyes slid to my member.

It was hard and jutting forward. It was pointing right at her, in fact. I smiled and grasped it with one hand.

"Just watch, Selene." I began to jerk myself off while staring unblinkingly into her eyes. I saw confusion there—and awe as well as arousal—as her gaze flicked from my face to my hand. I pulled down my foreskin to fully reveal the flushed, swollen glans and sighed in relief as some of the tension eased from my body. I continued stroking myself while Selene watched me raptly. The look on her face only generated more indecent thoughts. I moved my hand quickly over my entire length, and Selene examined the protruding veins under the thin skin with approval.

Her face was blazing in embarrassment, but she was also enthralled and aroused. And she never looked away from me.

She licked her lower lip, and I stared at her breasts, and then a truly *romantic* idea popped into my head.

I stopped masturbating and leaned over her chest. I took one of her sensitive nipples in my mouth and swirled my tongue around it. Selene arched her back and dug a hand into my hair, practically vibrating underneath me.

I knew how to pleasure a woman; I knew where to touch and how. Soon, I'd push Babygirl over the edge, and she'd lose her mind, melting into my twisted world. That was how it worked: I pulled her into my world of shadows, and she brought me into hers in exchange.

She allowed me to spread my wings and raised me high above the world's concerns.

Her body was all that existed.

Her coconut smell.

Her ethereal voice.

It felt like there were no obstacles before me.

My spirit was at peace.

I felt free.

Kim wasn't there.

The Boy wasn't there.

It was just me in my Neverland with my Tinkerbell.

"How much did you miss having my mouth on your body?" I raised my eyes to glance at Selene while flicking her nipples with my tongue. They got stiffer and stiffer with my every touch.

"So much…" She let out a moan of arousal. Then she shut her eyes, fighting against the pure lust that I'd injected straight into her veins with nothing more than a touch.

"And you like having it right here?" I continued wickedly. I abandoned the nipple and ran my wet tongue down the cleft between her breasts, both hands fondling them passionately.

"Yes, I… I like it," Tinkerbell managed, struggling with the sensations that always seemed to be novel to her. She watched me from beneath her eyelashes, staring at the part of her chest I was lapping at.

"I have no doubt…" I climbed on top of her with a sinister smile and inched my knees up the couch until they were on either of her naked ribs. I could feel the fabric of my jeans cutting into my thigh muscles, but I didn't give a shit.

I clutched her to me again and watched her eyes widen as her breathing sped up. Babygirl looked like she was being eaten up with anxiety, fear, arousal, and curiosity. All of them were waves crashing in her ocean.

"Raise your chin," I ordered insolently, watching her stunned expression as I let my member slide along her sternum, into that lethal valley between her tits, and let my testicles rest on her stomach.

"Yeah, there, stop. Do as I say," I whispered in a low, seductive voice that made her pupils dilate. Slowly, I began to rock my hips back and forth between her breasts.

And discovered what my heaven was.

"Squeeze your tits together, Selene, and look at me," I demanded, and together we watched everything I was doing. Maybe it was a mistake, a whim, or another one of my sick perversions, but whatever it was, it felt incredible.

I felt bolts of pleasure moving down my back. My muscles were tight and rigid; my abs were contracting with each slow thrust of my hips. Meanwhile, her breasts were pressed tight between our hands, creating just the right friction to give me pleasure. Never, ever had I watched a woman's curves more closely than I did in that moment.

"Good job, baby." Beneath me, in my power and my possession, she didn't say a word, only alternating her splendid stare from my face to my member. Her eyes tracked me, luminous, ecstatic, and enchanted.

It suddenly became harder to breathe as every muscle swelled with arousal, and my nerves tingled at each thrust. Unfortunately, I was being blocked by my own damned inability to let go.

"You're going to have a new sexual experience to tell your little friends about, Tinkerbell," I said insolently, trying to rile her. Just then, I felt my back burning, along with my glutes, my legs, and every other part of me. The urge to increase my pace got more intense. I saw the tip of my cock getting wet as pearly, semi-transparent beads of moisture accumulated on its slit. I swiped my thumb over it, feeling the light, viscous liquid between my fingertips; I kept thrusting, though I knew I'd have no further physical reaction.

I squeezed my eyes shut, and it seemed that I could feel Selene's heart beating. Her hands underneath mine cupped her firm breasts, her rosy nipples. A chill ran down my spine, followed by another and another until it tore a gasp from me. My balls were tingling. The pressure was rising. My heart rate was increasing until it felt like it was beating in my throat. I stopped breathing. I went rigid, and my veins swelled so hard it felt like they were on the verge of bursting. My body was boiling, shaking, and humming, but just as I was on the precipice, just when I was about to purge my frustration, pain, and bad memories—the moment when I came within a hairsbreadth of orgasm—I was instead left hanging on the edge of a chasm with no ability to throw myself into the void.

I licked my lips and dwelled on Babygirl's ocean eyes, which were ravenously following my every move. Then, with a growl of anger, I stopped.

I gave up.

I couldn't do it, not even with her.

Now I was sweaty, tense, and profoundly unsatisfied.

Selene frowned and looked at me, her beauty disarming, a potent mixture of innocence and sensuality.

"Fuck!" I burst out, hurling myself away from her. "Fuck this!" I got to my feet and angrily tucked my erection back into my boxers, pulling my jeans on over them. I was on the edge of a meltdown because I was still aroused, and I had a different scent on me. It was my own scent mixed with Selene's, but I still felt like I needed to clean myself. I ran my hands through my hair and over my face as I fell back into my usual dark reality, my usual confusion and chaos.

"Neil." Her delicate voice hit my ear like a melody, but I turned my back to better ignore her. "Are you okay?" she asked, her voice shaky.

No, I was not okay. Nothing was okay.

"I'm pure insanity. No fairy tale here, princess. Piss off." That was what I wanted to say to her, but I kept silent. I hid once more behind the mental wall that kept me from telling other people what was going on inside my head.

On top of all this, I felt a vast disappointment. A part of me had been hoping that I was going to have a strong, overpowering orgasm with her like I'd had before, but my body refused to indulge me.

What was I thinking? That Selene was going to wave a magic wand and solve all my problems?

More importantly, why was I even having this problem?

I had to laugh at myself and at my hopes that had been dashed into nothingness.

I turned to look at her. Babygirl was watching from the couch, where she sat in just her panties. Her hair gleamed like copper, her skin was white, her breasts were shiny with my saliva, and her cheeks glowed pink. There were reddened spots on her chest from the crude touch of my hands. Had I hurt her? I hoped not.

Either way, even all disheveled, she was more beautiful than ever.

I stood there and stared at her, dumbfounded. My throat was dry, my body hot, and my thoughts had twisted up into a knot that was impossible to untie.

"Risk it, Neil. For once, just take the risk," she murmured then, apropos of nothing, and I sucked in a breath. "Don't be afraid. Stop keeping yourself under such tight control. Do what makes you happy without hesitations or regrets. Do you want me? Then take me. Be selfish. Do what you feel. It doesn't matter what other people think is right or wrong. This is the only life we get, so live it the way you want." Selene swallowed hard and cupped her chin in her hands. I wanted to go over to her and soothe her.

Hold her and then fuck her.

I wanted it with my whole self, with everything I was deep inside.

"Enough," I spit instead, stubborn as ever. "You don't know me; you don't know a thing about me!"

She flinched at the force of my words. After all, I was the one who had made sure she couldn't know me. I was the one who refused to show anything but the worst of myself to her, the bestial one. All because my heart was too frozen and full of suffering.

"You're wrong, though." She stood up, smiling at me. Naked, confident, and breathtakingly beautiful. I breathed in deep so I didn't make the mistake of reaching out to her.

"You always mess up your hair when you're nervous," she began, forcing me to bend my neck down to look at her. "You chew the inside of your cheek when you're uncomfortable. You look down when you're feeling guilty or actually sorry about something. You get this different light in your eyes when you talk about Logan or Chloe. You hide your true self behind this cynical, cocky persona and hide your intelligence behind weird or incomprehensible behavior. You hate nosy or pushy people. You are reserved and don't like to speak your thoughts aloud very often. So you often keep quiet and let your eyes do the talking. You have a good side—but you won't admit it to anyone—and a dark side that you warn everyone about. You love pistachios. I just found that one out recently, and…and honestly, you smoke way too much, and you should quit." She said it all without stopping, all in one breath. When I continued staring at her, not saying anything, Selene blinked uncomfortably and took a few cautious steps back.

Was she afraid of how I'd react? That I'd get angry? Probably.

My mood swings had become increasingly frequent and inexplicable.

I turned my back on her and her tiny body. In that moment, Selene looked to me like a giant ready to stride right through my soul. I felt naked without a shield strong enough to protect me from her. My walls were weakening, but I still tried to hold everything together, to gather up every piece of me so I wouldn't get steamrolled.

"Go." I managed to get to the kitchen island and press my hands to it, propping up the weight I suddenly felt on my shoulders. Selene's taste was on my tongue, and her smell was on my skin. I was more and more hers and less and less the Boy.

"I'm going back to Detroit tomorrow and—" My sardonic laugh cut off her words.

Was she really that naive?

I tasted her coconut smell in the air.

She was right behind me, too close to me. Why couldn't she just stay away from me?

"For fuck's sake, Selene." I whirled around furiously, and she jerked backward. "I meant go now. Right now. Leave!" I pointed to the door of the pool house. She was naked, shaking, and ashamed that I was treating her like some random skank. I'd taken what I wanted from her, got to live out one of my male fantasies, and now, like the son of a bitch that I was, I wanted her gone.

"Whatever you want," she conceded, though I hadn't expected her to do that so quickly. She walked over to her bra, abandoned on the floor, and bent down to grab it. I watched the curve of her spine as it melted into her firm, perfectly proportioned ass. Inexplicably, I felt annoyed by her sudden surrender. I hated it when she chased me, but I hated it even more when she ran from me. Still, I was the one who drove her away; all she did was listen to me…

I sighed heavily. I was unstable. I couldn't just act like a normal person.

I walked furiously over to catch her by the wrist and yanked her around to face me just as she was about to put her dress back on.

"'Whatever you want,'" I repeated her words with a sneer. "What the fuck kind of answer is that?" I allowed myself to get angry at her so I didn't have to admit to myself that I'd made the wrong call. Selene's lips opened, red and swollen, and I wanted to lick them. I wanted to lick her all over and taste her again until I felt like throwing up the way I did when other women asked me for certain favors. The kind of nausea that had never come up with her.

"You really are nuts," she answered, trying to wriggle out of my grasp. She wanted to leave now; I could see it in her eyes. Selene was an open book for me. I saw all her feelings, felt her desires, and knew her thoughts. Everything about her.

"Yeah, I'm nuts. Troubled. Fucked up. You should find someone more like you. Someone who wants you the right way and can give you the happily ever after you deserve." Because in my head, it was just Kimberly and the kind of love that tied us together. And that kept me from really living.

Selene stared at me in shock; her wrist was still clenched in my furious grip. Her long bangs were messy, as was the rest of her wild hair.

She looked rebellious and savage in that moment. I stared at the scar from her accident, which was already less noticeable than the last time I'd seen her, and I loosened my grip on her.

She'd already gone through so much recently, and here I was, the giant asshole who hadn't even asked her how she was doing. Even though I'd thought about her every day, I hadn't wanted to show her the attention she really deserved.

"I'm going, okay? I'm leaving. I'm putting a stop to this, Neil!" She raised her voice, getting angrier and angrier. "And you have to let me get dressed." Was she seriously thinking she'd just put her indecent little dress back on and walk out of my pool house? Sure, that was what she wanted to do and what I wanted her to do, but...

"Shut up, baby. Shut up." I grabbed her and pulled her into me. I wrapped one arm around her sides, and the other I ran along the back of her neck. Her face pressed against my bare chest. She was freezing cold, and I would have tried to warm her up, but Selene went stiff and did not return my embrace. She was motionless as it dawned on her that I was...hugging her.

I couldn't believe it myself.

Was I really hugging her?

It wasn't my style at all. I couldn't even remember the last time I'd given someone a hug.

An endless moment passed while we both took stock of the situation. Then, Selene slowly put her trembling arms around me and pressed her cheek to my chest. I could hear her sobs, and her tears washed over her and me both. They were sweet and sticky like cotton candy. It was the thing I hated most: making someone cry.

Selene wrecked herself against me and allowed herself to be hugged. Or maybe I was the one who was being hugged—I had no idea what the fuck was going on anymore.

"I'm not going to apologize," I clarified again.

I wouldn't do it because I wanted to save her from me, to push her away and give her the chance to choose someone better. My desire for her was becoming more and more explosive, triggering more insane outbursts, but that didn't mean that I was her man. And she was not my woman. We were not a couple.

I rubbed the back of her neck with one hand, slipping my fingers into her hair while the other remained on the soft skin of her back. Babygirl smelled so good, intense, and irresistible.

"Shh, enough." I wanted her to stop blubbering, but I had no idea how to console her. I wasn't good at that sort of thing. Selene let out a deep breath and, little by little, began to calm down, though she did continue to cling to me. And then the inevitable happened: a long, lethal exchange of glances.

What did she want me to do?

Did she want me to sleep on my pain?

Did she want to burn along with me?

What do you want, Tinkerbell?

Do you want to hold my hand while we fly elsewhere?

But my wings got ripped. Where did she expect me to go with her?

What did she really want? Did she want to kiss me, or bite me, or burn me?

Did she want to love me the way Kim had?

Neither of us said anything. We didn't need to. I stared at the reddened tip of her nose, her swollen lips, and shining eyes. On instinct, I planted a kiss right there on her pert little nose before sinking down to her mouth; I left another chaste, fleeting kiss there too. Her lips were warm, soft as silk, and wet with her tears. With this vivid bit of sweetness, I was letting her know how much I wanted her, while Selene thought I was preparing to fulfill both of our fantasies. But there was something inexplicable that kept me from unleashing the beast within me and urged me to lock him up tight, lest I give in to temptation.

"Do you want to stay here tonight?" I wanted her to stay with me, to spend more time with her. Selene wiped away her tears with the back of her hand, and I cupped her face, looking deep into her eyes.

"Here?" She sounded surprised. I was also surprised, but I had realized by that point that I was no longer in control of my thoughts.

Selene made too much noise inside my head.

"You don't want to leave. So..." I trailed off. I was actually suggesting that she stay and spend the night with me, so there was really no more to explain. I shocked myself. I never slept—literally slept—with a woman unless I was really drunk. If they tried to stay the night with me, I'd kick them out. Sleeping next to a woman was an act of faith, an extremely personal and intimate one. I could only see it as putting my unconscious body at the mercy of a woman who might do anything to me.

Selene looked around, casting a thoughtful glance at the couch.

"Okay, I'll sleep here. You take the bedroom," she answered, a sour note in her voice. She didn't want to sleep in the bed where I'd fucked other people.

I watched Selene vacillate. All her questions about me rose up in my mind, making me feel uncomfortable in my skin the way I had since I was a child. Then, Babygirl turned abruptly away from me and plopped down on the couch, looking tired and cold. Once seated, she looked first at her dress abandoned on the floor and then at me. Although her face usually kept no secrets from me, this was not a situation to which I was accustomed. So I was in trouble.

"Do you... Do you have anything I can borrow?" She bit her lower lip, and I looked at her, horrified. I looked at her like she was some enormous monster crowding my pool house when, in reality, she looked like a tiny fairy.

"Women never wear anything of mine," I answered. If she thought I was going to break one of my nonnegotiable rules, she was dead wrong. Instead, I found a woolen blanket and tossed it to her.

Selene grabbed it out of the air and draped it over her thighs before pausing thoughtfully again.

"I'm not used to sleeping naked," she complained, arranging her long hair behind her shoulders.

Why should I give a fuck?

Sometimes I felt like slapping her just as much as I felt like devouring her lips.

"Well, tonight, with me, you're going to." I was already breaking my rule about never sleeping with a woman, just like I'd broken so many others for her. Babygirl made a face, and I snatched the blanket from her with a huff.

"Come on, lie down." I gestured for her to do as I said, but she just kept looking at me, annoyed.

"Don't order me around," she lectured.

"Just do it," I said, sitting down next to her. There was nothing for Selene to do but to lie down naked next to me. I arranged the blanket over our bodies and settled into position beside her, where I could feel her warmth creeping over me.

Her pointed nipples pressed against my ribs, and I slipped my forearm under her neck to make her more comfortable. Silky hair tickled my skin all over, and her hand rested on my chest.

I looked at her, planning to tell her not to push it, but she just smiled and hooked her ankle around mine. It had never happened to me before, sharing this kind of intimacy with someone, and I felt discombobulated by it.

"You're forcing me to sleep naked, so I'm going to need your body heat to keep warm," Selene said before yawning so widely that one eye winked. I tried to conceal a smile as I breathed in her good smell. I felt like I was drunk on that damned coconut scent.

Then, her hand trailed slowly down to my stomach and drifted, little by little, back up to my chest. I had no idea what she was doing, but I liked it, so I allowed her to repeat the same movement several times. Her touch was gentle, light, and soothing. So soothing that I soon had to fight sleep so I didn't go down before she did. After a little while, her eyes closed. I couldn't tell how many minutes went by as I lay there watching her. But I did discover her preferred sleeping position: on her side with one knee wedged between my legs and one hand clenched into a fist right next to her mouth. I stroked her hair, letting my fingers glide through the soft mass, and she sighed.

She liked being touched by me.

I was learning to linger over details that had never mattered to me before.

I found myself wanting to understand her and know her in all ways, not just sexually.

I stiffened when she moved, putting her head on my chest. Her nose was wedged right between my pecs, and I laughed. She was funny even in her sleep.

Funny and beautiful.

I adjusted myself so I could hold her better, and my erection brushed against her hip. I sighed as I reflected on the fact that my physical desire for her would probably never fade, especially not in an intimate moment like this. I wanted to take off my jeans and sleep in my boxers like I always did, but I didn't want to wake her up, so I closed my eyes and tried not to think about it...

She had made a wreck of me and didn't even know it. She was drowning me in her ocean, and that was why I was always afraid to look into her eyes, with their little striations of iron and silver. I was afraid of the way her small fingerprints were all over my soul. But my heart didn't know how to start over; it didn't know how to give itself to another person and that's why...

That was why I should have told her I was sorry and why I probably never would.

....

I woke at dawn and let out an irritated groan.

Sweet-smelling hair tickled my nose, and I opened my eyes slowly, letting them adjust to the sunlight streaming in through the glass doors. I tried to shift position, but to no avail. Selene was still asleep on my chest with her pink lips slightly parted and her upturned nose that perfectly matched the rest of her small, delicate features. Finally, there was a little furrow on her forehead that gave her a concerned expression even as she slept.

I yawned and stretched out my arm, which felt numb from being in one position for too long. I watched Selene sleep some more and rubbed a hand over my face. All at once, my paranoia came back, assailing me from all sides before I even saw the colors of the sunrise. I was afraid of the shit that would come from staying on that crappy little couch with her. Selene might decide to take us sleeping together as something more than physical attraction on my part. She might be convinced that I had feelings I didn't have and might have even thought I was in love with her and that a relationship could happen between the two of us.

"Fuck," I grumbled, my mind packed with worries. After I fucked her by the indoor pool I had told myself over and over again that I wasn't going to make the same mistake again. I wasn't going to give her another piece of myself. But now I'd done it once again. I shook my leg, trying to get her off me. My morning wood was pressing up against her, and I needed to get away. Now.

"Mmh…" Selene moaned as she moved, the blanket slipping down her stomach and giving me a great view of her firm breasts.

I watched her with the intensity of a starving predator. Her shoulders were narrow but defined, her breasts rounded, her nipples were small, perfect cylinders surrounded by areolae so light pink that they almost blended in with the rest of her skin. I lifted my torso up slightly and slowly moved her arm away from my pelvis. She muttered something unintelligible, and I smiled.

I positioned myself over her, using my elbows to hold myself up, and bent to give her neck a lingering kiss. I didn't want to do it, but my instincts somehow overwhelmed my good sense. I had planned to wake her up and kick her ass out, but then Selene turned her head in the other direction, exposing more of that interesting spot. So I kept kissing her.

She smelled like coconut, sleep, arousal, and everything else we'd shared.

I moved down to her breasts and grazed one with the end of my nose.

Selene was still sound asleep while I was acting like a perv who couldn't control his sexual urges.

I flicked her nipple with my tongue, trapping it between my lips. It was small and stiff and simply magnificent. I moved my eyes up to her relaxed face and saw that her forehead had creased up involuntarily.

I drifted still further down to her belly, where I experienced the strange sensation of smelling myself on her skin. Finally, like the demon that I was, I made for the place between her thighs.

She reached her arms out over her head and stretched her muscles. She was going to wake up at any moment, and I was ready to delight in her shocked expression when she found me nestled between her thighs.

I pushed her panties to one side and kissed the top of her mound before moving down to the magic button. I delicately teased her clit, hidden in the folds of her labia minora, and glanced up again at her closed eyes. Her mouth had fallen slightly open, and she emitted light huffs of air.

She looked like a goddess.

The most beautiful things are not necessarily the ones that are perfect, I thought, *but the ones that are special.*

She was special.

I traced the contours of her outer lips, already soft and plump. I licked them all delicately before blowing on the spot where I knew she'd most like to feel my touch. She sighed in pleasure, and her back arched on instinct, raising her pelvis to my mouth. The need to satisfy my savage urge and devour her completely kept nagging at me.

But I knew that if I did it, I wouldn't be able to stop there. Her taste did not dampen my craving; it only intensified it.

My body reacted to hers in such unpredictable ways, it was a struggle to control it.

I stared between her legs, stared at that gleaming chalice, now polished with my kisses and ready to welcome me inside.

I was burning up inside, holding my breath, only the thinnest of threads connecting me to sanity. I was hanging in midair. I wanted to throw caution to the wind and fuck her, to lose myself in every curve, and try once more to see if I could allow myself the orgasm I hadn't experienced in so long.

I was going crazy, but I could still hold back.

I had always maintained full control of myself, and I wasn't going to let one girl destroy that.

"Neil…" Her voice sounded, fluting in my ears; I looked up and caught her staring at me in bewilderment, just like I'd imagined.

Her cheeks were red and she was breathing fast. She was aroused, I could feel it.

I smiled and stretched myself out over her, bearing my weight on my forearms. I deliberately pushed my hips against her so she could feel just how much I wanted to possess her. She gasped, and I could see shivers of anticipation traveling down from her neck. She sighed, trembling.

Did she think we were about to have sex?

I would have liked to but I had no intention of giving in to temptation.

"You need to leave," I whispered then in a placid tone, like that was the best good morning I could possibly give her. She looked down, specifically at her pushed-aside panties, and she bit her lip, embarrassed.

"What… What were you doing?" She looked confused and stunned, but I didn't answer her. Instead, I looked into her eyes and found she had the sky in there, or perhaps a field of wildflowers.

"They're cornflower blue right when you wake up," I commented. Babygirl didn't get it and blinked several times, tilting her head slightly. "Your eyes…" I explained.

I'd always wondered what color they would be in the early light of morning, and now I knew.

"And…you like them?" she asked mischievously.

Yeah, I liked them the way I liked everything about her. And that was the real problem.

I shook my head, trying to get a grip, and lifted myself up off her body. I had to take one of my showers and change clothes. I passed a hand through my hair and turned to Selene, still lolling on the couch. I caught her ogling my ass, and when she noticed me looking at her, she turned red immediately.

"What do you usually eat for breakfast?" I asked her, walking over to the kitchen island and the coffee maker. I would have to shower later because just then I needed my cup of bitter black coffee. Her eyes continued to track my every movement. If she thought I was going to make her breakfast or bring it to her like some gentleman, she was sorely mistaken.

"I usually have orange juice and some toast with cherry jam. That's my favorite." She smiled back at me, then sat up on the couch, looking disoriented. She spotted her bra on the floor nearby and got up to grab it. She had wild hair, a perfect shape, and a tight ass, where my sinful gaze got caught. I stared at her as I placidly sipped my coffee, giving a masculine grunt of approval at that dream ass. I wanted to look at it every morning, and the realization startled me.

"I'm not making you breakfast. There are oranges if you want to juice them. No toast, I don't think, or jam." I said gruffly, finishing my coffee.

Miss Anna was the one who made those perfect breakfasts; it certainly wasn't me.

I didn't need much to start my day.

Selene wasn't listening to me, though. She'd put her dress back on and was looking thoughtful.

She walked barefoot toward me, looking at my empty cup.

"You aren't just going to have that, are you?" She sat down on a stool and ran a hand through her hair. It was wild, but even when sleepy and disheveled, she was glorious. If I'd listened to my instincts, I would have already bent her over the kitchen island.

"We slept together," I said, dodging her question. I had far more important things to make clear to her. "But it doesn't mean anything. So don't get ideas." I leaned on the kitchen island and looked seriously at her so she could see how real my words were. She nodded and smiled, not at all offended or upset.

"You have this irritating habit of changing the subject," she complained calmly, and her demeanor confused me. "Also...you didn't need to specify any of that. I know it perfectly well. Just like I know that you've never slept like that with anyone else and that I was your first in this too." She gave a one-shouldered shrug, and I stood up straight.

I considered her words. I actually had slept platonically with someone before but never voluntarily, as I'd just done with Tinkerbell.

Selene really did understand how many things I was sharing with her for the first time. Or maybe she was just trying to get me to talk.

She wanted to hear me say it, to admit the effect she had on me.

"What do you know?" I sneered at her, taking up my characteristically arrogant stance. Babygirl smiled again and fixed the neckline of her dress, where my gaze immediately zeroed in. There was my breakfast, right there under that flimsy layer of fabric. I'd had her there next to me all night long, and yet I'd restricted myself to some adolescent dry humping that left me with nothing but an unsatisfied longing that would linger inside me for a long time to come.

"I've learned how you are now." She gave me a wink, and I stepped back. She didn't know the first thing about me, unless she had somehow learned what happened to me when I was kid, which was highly unlikely. She might think she knew me, but that wasn't at all the case.

"I have to take a shower. By the time I get out of the bathroom, you need to be gone," I ordered firmly. I was being a real dick. First by kissing her, touching her, wanting to fuck her, and crossing lines with her that I absolutely shouldn't have been crossing with anyone. And now I was giving her the fucking boot because I was incapable of keeping myself under control when she was around.

I felt like I no longer knew myself.

"I'm going back to Detroit tonight." Selene got up from her stool and walked past me without a glance, heading straight for her shoes. She bent down and grabbed them, pinching them between her fingers. "And who knows when we'll see each other again?" She brushed her bangs to one side, revealing part of her scar, and again I had that numb feeling of deep wrongness. But I didn't make any attempt to keep her there with me. I watched her walk toward the door, saw her open it and cross the threshold, and still I remained motionless, just staring as she walked away.

"Oh, fuck you," I whispered to myself. "You total dickhead."

I knew exactly where I'd gone wrong. Selene didn't deserve that kind of treatment, but I couldn't be any different than I was. If I'd let her get into my soul, I would have come out the other side destroyed. Every beautiful thing came to an end, and she could very well be the beautiful thing that would spell *my* end.

I headed into the bathroom, her coconut smell still in the air. I could smell it everywhere I went. I undressed and quickly got into the shower. Cold water would clear my head. The solitude would give me a chance to gather myself.

I stayed under the spray for about an hour, but my yearning for her did not go away. Nor did the thought of running after her and making the most of our last moments before she left for Detroit.

"I like her, but you can't be with her. If you choose her, you're abandoning me," muttered a high, childlike voice, and I turned sharply to the glass door of the shower. Drops of water snaked down my body, dripping into a pile of soap suds on the floor below me. I smoothed my wet hair over the back of my head and tried to focus on the vague figure I could just barely glimpse through the frosted glass. With one quick movement, I shut off the water and grabbed a towel to wrap around my waist.

I saw the Boy in the bedroom doorway. He was standing there with his basketball under his arm, an Oklahoma City basketball jersey draped over his skinny torso, and blue shorts that skimmed his scabby knees. He was covered with dirt, his hair was an unruly chestnut mess, and he watched me with a sad, listless look on his face. I was not surprised to see him. He almost always showed up in the bathroom to talk to me.

"I can't be your host forever." There, I said it. I had finally admitted that two souls could not coexist in one body. Sooner or later, one will have to give way for the other. I knew this interplay between us was becoming a true problem.

"You're evil," he answered sullenly, fleeing into the bedroom.

"I'm just being honest!" I snapped back impatiently.

I followed him, trailing water everywhere, but I didn't care. I stopped short when I found him on the bed, the basketball clutched to his chest and his gaze locked on something on the floor. I looked down to see several sheets of paper, torn in countless pieces. I felt my heart pound in my throat. My hands were shaking. My head spun, and I clamped my lips together, looking furiously at the Boy.

"What did you do?" I asked in a menacing whisper. He popped up on his feet and backed up, never taking his eyes off mine. They were my drawings. He had ripped them up and tried to hide them under the bed.

"What did *you* do?" he yelled back accusingly, and a sudden vertigo made me clutch my forehead. I struggled, unable to get a breath.

"Go away!" I yelled, and he flinched away from me. I was in a fog of rage. I immediately began hunting for my phone. This situation was getting out of hand, and before I tried to cope with it in my usual mis-guided way, I decided I needed to talk to the only person who could understand me.

I found my phone and hunted for my therapist's contact. It was hard to keep my fingers steady—every muscle in my body was being rocked by inexplicable tremors.

"Hello? Neil?" He answered on the second ring.

"Dr. Lively," I rubbed my face and glanced behind me to see if the Boy was listening.

"What's going on?" he asked, sounding alarmed. Indeed, it was rare for him to get a call from me, especially on a Sunday. He used to see me every other Thursday, though I hadn't gone to therapy for three years and I was paying the price now. But now I needed his advice because he was the only one who could help me.

"Someone ripped up my drawings. I found the pieces in the bedroom. I didn't even know they were in there, but it was him. The Boy did it!" I explained rapidly, my voice also trembling. There was a long silence on the other end of the line. I started to wonder if he'd hung up on me, but then he sighed, and I knew he was still there.

"Have you been using any controlled substances, Neil?" he asked skeptically.

I was horrified at the very thought of taking that shit. I'd never be that stupid. I squeezed my eyes shut and then opened them, trying to keep my temper under control.

"No, I don't do fucking drugs. You should know that!" My voice was getting louder. I was feeling anxious, and my therapist's insinuations were only making things worse.

"Neil," he sighed. "This is your abandonment issues combining with your need for attention." The doctor got to work, analyzing me and presenting his point of view. As I listened to him, I moved into the living room to find my Winstons. "You had these problems even as a child. You would destroy your possessions and claim that someone else had done it," he explained. I unearthed my pack of cigarettes and lit one, sucking smoke deep into the bottom of my lungs in a useless attempt to calm down.

"What are you talking about?" I scrubbed a hand over my face, clenching the cigarette filter between my fingers, and began to pace nervously. I left wet footprints everywhere.

"Neil, we both know about the conflicted relationship you've always had with your father and mother, the need you had to feel loved, and how they were unable to understand you during the time you were being abused. Self-destructive actions are a way of expressing that need to draw the attention of others, which was caused by the extreme lack of affection that characterized your childhood. Your parents were always working, you spent all your time with Kimberly, and…" He kept talking, but I had stopped listening. I let the towel drop to the floor and stood there naked. Naked both physically and psychologically with a shattered heart still pounding in my chest. Blood rushed through my veins at top speed while my brain categorically rejected everything he was telling me.

I went back into the bedroom as Dr. Lively's voice called out, trying to get my attention, but I was already gone. I avoided the bed and sat down in a corner of the room. My muscles twitched slightly on contact with the cold floor, and I stared into the emptiness in front of me.

The emptiness inside me, actually.

"Neil, are you still there?" Dr. Lively asked, but I slowly let my arm fall and ended the call.

I brought a cigarette to my lips, continuing to smoke as I stretched my legs out in front of me. Did Dr. Lively think I'd lost my mind? He was wrong. Sure, I had a whole heap of problems and obstacles to get over, and my mind wasn't like other people's, but none of that made me some kind of psycho.

Suddenly, I could hear light footsteps approaching me. I didn't look up and just continued to clench the filter of the cigarette between my lips, blowing smoke out the side of my mouth.

"He doesn't understand you," the Boy affirmed. I was still wondering then how I might get rid of him, but I was also realizing that his presence was exactly what I needed.

I watched thoughtfully as the Boy approached me slowly, gauging my mood. I continued smoking casually as I watched him, and he observed my naked body. I was sitting on the floor, my back against the wall and my hair dripping wet. I couldn't have looked great.

The Boy decided to sit down next to me, and I didn't object.

"Remember when…" He pushed a hank of lighter brown hair off his forehead, and I stared at his filthy knees. It looked like he'd fallen; the skin was red and peeling. "Remember when we used to watch the Peter Pan movie while she was…" He stopped because it was difficult for a little boy to remember such awful things. "While she was doing that stuff to us?"

I remembered…

It was a particularly boring Saturday night.

My parents had gone out to dinner with people from work, and Logan was already in bed sleeping. Kimberly asked me to sit with her on the couch in the living room. She said she had my favorite cartoon, and we were going to watch it together. So I sat down next to her in my favorite pajamas and locked my eyes on the TV. Her hand was wrapped around a can of beer she'd just opened. She took a gulp and looked at me. She was always looking at me in that unrelenting way.

Smiling, she bit her lip and rested her hand on my knee. I started to tremble because I already knew what she was going to do. I couldn't push her away, though, because she would hurt my brother instead.

Her hand slipped into my shorts just as Peter Pan was trying to convince Wendy to run away with him. He was telling her about Neverland, where all the Lost Boys went, and I focused hard on him, trying to ignore the woman's hand now stroking me.

I shut my eyes when I felt her fingers push under the elastic band of my underpants and tried to think about something else.

I imagined a Neverland.

I imagined I was inside my favorite movie and focusing on Peter Pan through those agonizing, inescapable minutes of violence.

Peter was insisting then and telling Wendy he could take her with him, but the little girl must not have wanted to leave her parents behind, because she told him she couldn't fly.

Peter's tenacious voice, assuring Wendy that he would teach her to fly, sank into my brain just like Kimberly's hand sank into my soul and shattered it into a million pieces.

"Open your eyes; watch your favorite movie," she whispered to me, and I focused on the sounds, the voices, and the words Peter said even as I felt Kim everywhere.

Inside me, outside.

She was in the sped-up beating of my heart, in the pulse throughout my body; she was in the sweat that snaked down my forehead and my panting breath. She was in the eyelids that I kept clamped shut so I wouldn't see, the lips that parted to let out sighs I couldn't control. She was in the groans, in my submission and coercion.

She was in everything except Neverland.

There, I was alone.

Kimberly would never be able to reach me there.

I left my body behind and took refuge in a place that didn't exist.

I tried to protect my soul.

I created a parallel world, an illusion that could save me.

Like I did every time.

Only when the torture was finally finished did I come back to the real world and open my eyes again.

Invariably, I found myself naked and sweaty on the couch because she had used me again the way she always did.

"I remember..." I took a drag from the cigarette and blew out the smoke, bending one knee so I could balance my elbow on it. With a sigh of sadness, the Boy rested his head on my shoulder.

His touch was cold but gentle.

"You won't forget me, will you?" he whispered fearfully, leaning away to look at me. I took one last drag and then ground out the butt in an ashtray. Normally, I was a clean freak, but in that moment, I couldn't care about anything.

"I could never," I answered defeatedly, not looking at him.

I would have liked to forget about him, about my abuse, and about my childhood. I wanted to forget about Kimberly and even Peter Pan, but I never could.

The past was going to hang on to me forever, hindering my future and making my present into a living hell.

That was my reality, and I needed to accept it and learn to live with it. After all, I was a grown man and knew all too well that Neverland couldn't save me anymore.

12

The connection between us was undeniable
and we both knew it.

SELENE

I ran to my room.

I was still wearing my dress from the night before, and I hoped I wouldn't bump into anyone.

It would have been a disaster if Matt had found out.

I arrived at my destination without incident, though, and locked myself inside, resting my back against the door.

My cheeks were still burning. I'd felt so perverse the previous night. It was incredible watching his muscles flex, feeling his thrusts against my breasts, seeing the look of ecstasy on his face, and hearing his guttural groans.

Neil was always sexy. Shameless and glorious, a true sex fiend. I smiled and covered my face with my hands. Thinking about certain things still embarrassed me, despite everything we'd done together. He'd even invited me to sleep with him and, when I woke up, I found him with his head between my thighs, a hairsbreadth away from my sex, ready to pleasure me.

Neil was gorgeous first thing in the morning, obviously. I lingered for a long time on his perfect face. The full lips curved into a mischievous smile, the chestnut eyelashes framing golden eyes, the messy hair I loved to run my fingers through, and the little wrinkle he always got in the middle of his forehead when he was particularly pensive.

As always, he was too complicated for me figure out.

First he tried to kick me out; then he asked me to stay.

I learned a little more about him and I knew that trust was a precious commodity for him. He allowed me to have little bits of him, only in small doses, so I would be too eager for what he did offer to demand more from him.

He was sharing his soul with me in his own way, but he was afraid of what drew us together.

The connection between us was undeniable, and we both knew it.

With this new understanding, I smiled as I bounced around the room, happier than I had ever been before. I needed to shower and change, so I stepped into the bathroom humming a Coldplay song. In the shower, I scrubbed myself, washing away his scent even though it was so deep in my head by then that no soap would ever have the power to erase it. When I was done, I put my hair into a high ponytail and tugged on a sweater and a pair of jeans.

Half an hour later, I was still unusually joyful, feeling like we'd had a breakthrough in our relationship.

Neil was starting to trust me, and that was already a huge step forward.

Of course, I couldn't delude myself about anything. I knew I wasn't the only one, and my confrontation last night with Jennifer had only confirmed that they were still having sex. Which meant that I still wasn't important enough for Neil to give up the other girls.

The more I thought it over, though, the more my happiness faded as it occurred to me that I was living a fantasy, something that didn't actually exist, and soon I would need to wake up and come back to reality.

Feeling bleak, I went over to the bed to grab my phone out of my purse. I had the sudden urge to call my mother, the only person who could chase away some of the misery I was feeling.

I sighed and tapped her contact, waiting for her to answer.

"Hi, sweetheart," she said on the second ring.

"Hi, Mom. How are you doing?" I didn't have anything of particular import to tell her, but I wanted to hear her voice.

"I'm fine. How's it going there? Did you get some quality time with your father?" she asked, and I rolled my eyes. I knew she was going to ask me that. She was stuck on the idea that Matt and I were going to work out our issues, while I was firmly convinced that it would never happen. At the time, we were living in a kind of armistice. I'd put down my hatchet after his birthday, but that didn't mean I was ready to bury it completely.

"Not really," I admitted, choosing to omit the detail about how I'd spent the night with Mia's son. I suspected my mother knew something was going on with Neil, but I was still afraid of her reaction to the whole truth. I was afraid she'd be so disappointed in me that she'd kick me out of the house and cut contact forever.

What had I done?

"Mom..." I added immediately in a shaky voice. I sat down on the edge of the bed and rubbed a nervous hand over my jeans.

"Tell me, sweetheart. What's wrong? Are you having headaches again? Did you get sick to your stomach? Did you have another nightmare last night?" She immediately flew into a panic, and I instantly felt guilty. I didn't want to make her worry, especially when I was far away. Knowing her, she'd hop on the first plane out to bring me home.

"Would you stop loving me if you found out I'd told you a small lie?" I whispered, tears in my eyes. I tried to keep my voice steady because I knew my mother had an uncanny ability to sense my mental state. To be perfectly honest, I didn't know why I'd asked her that question. Maybe because, for the first time, I'd actually thought about the repercussions if my parents found out about Neil and me.

"I could never stop loving you, Selene. What's happened?" she asked anxiously, and I chewed my thumbnail, trying to release some tension. Was I actually considering just telling her everything? Of admitting the whole truth and asking her for advice because there was no one else I could talk to, no one else who could help me?

"Remember that story you told me about the princess and the dark knight?" I asked her, getting to my feet.

"Yes, of course I do," she answered, bewildered.

"What if the dark knight doesn't fall in love with the princess? What if he eventually picks someone else or just decides to disappear entirely?" I blurted out in one breath, feeling agitated and melancholy at the same time. Just the thought of Neil connecting with another woman or asking me to end whatever was going on between us for good made my chest feel like it was being squeezed.

"I told you that wasn't a fairy tale, remember? There may not be a happily ever after," she said, and I stopped my anxious roaming of the room. "But, still, it might have an important lesson to offer that the princess goes on to carry with her for the rest of her life," she continued with her usual wisdom, and I shook my head.

The only lesson I'd be taking with me was how miserable it was to fall in love with the wrong man, but I couldn't tell her that.

"The princess has to be a strong woman, ready for anything. She has to have a warrior's heart," my mother continued, and I pictured her blue eyes, identical to my own, and her fond smile. The loving arms that I wished I could have wrapped around me right then.

Contrary to my mother's beliefs, I wasn't strong. Instead, I felt like I had a heart of glass that anyone could shatter. The need to feel my mother's love was just as powerful as the knowledge that I would never be able to fully grasp the soul of a complicated boy like Neil.

Mr. Disaster was constantly pulling me to him and then pushing me away, so being with him meant putting up with his mood swings and dealing with his extremely difficult nature.

Not to mention, I had to cope with what he had experienced as a child. I still didn't know the whole story, but Logan had made it clear to him that Kimberly Bennett had abused him. I'd never judge Neil for what happened to him but, at the same time, I wasn't convinced that I could stay by his side and handle the fallout from such severe trauma. I understood why he couldn't trust me and I even understood why he pushed me away. I just wasn't sure such deep wounds could even be healed.

Maybe a doctor, a psychiatric facility, and medication could have done it, but not me by myself.

Neil's demons were too big to tame.

Which meant that whenever I was with him, I was constantly

flip-flopping between moments when I thought everything was going to be okay and that we'd eventually make it through and learn to understand each other. That we'd be able to join our very different lives together. And then there were the moments when reality beat down the door to my self-awareness and told me to stop clinging to my delusions.

I felt defeated when I hung up with my mother, reminding her that I was coming home that night. So I spent some time on my laptop, listening to music to distract myself.

I chewed my lower lip as I searched YouTube for "Fix You" by Coldplay, but before I could start the song, two raps on the door stopped me. I muttered, "Come in," and immediately Anna appeared in her uniform, her blond hair pulled back into a bun.

"Miss Selene, your father wants to see you," she told me, her hands folded in front of her. It seemed like she was worried about something, judging from the sad smile she gave me.

"It isn't time for lunch," I answered, shooting a glance at the clock. I didn't know what could be so important that Matt needed to send Anna to fetch me.

"I'm afraid you need to join him in the living room right now. It is urgent." She sighed, turning to leave without giving me a chance to argue. It seemed like it was an enormous effort for her to say those few words to me. I quickly got up and shut my laptop.

I left my room and took the stairs down into the living room. I was afraid Matt was going to suggest another beach weekend, and if he did, I was definitely going to decline. I had no desire to repeat that experience.

I got to the living room slightly out of breath but stopped in my tracks when I saw Matt standing with his arms crossed. Neil was leaning against the big glass doors, his hands tucked in the pockets of his jeans. His golden eyes were glassy and cold, however.

"Oh, there you are," Matt said in an arch tone. He looked at me, his stare growing sharp, and I stiffened. I frowned, having no idea why he was being so weird, and shifted my gaze to Neil, who hadn't stopped watching my father.

"What's going on?" I managed to ask, though my voice came out small and uncertain. My father stroked his beard with one hand and cocked an eyebrow, his thoughts unreadable.

"I've just asked Neil a simple question, but apparently he's struggling to give me an answer," he said scornfully, his manner stern. I glanced at Neil, but he just stood there, all arrogant bravado.

"I... I don't understand," I stammered. A strange discomfort tortured my stomach. My heart swung back and forth in my chest and my breathing sped up, an unbearable knot forming in my throat.

"I asked Neil to explain why you two spent the night together in the pool house. Doesn't seem like such a difficult question to me. What do you think?" He cocked his head to one side, studying me. I swallowed automatically, feeling short of breath. I hoped this was all just a bad dream and looked around, trying to see if I was actually there in the living room of Matt Anderson's house. Unfortunately, everything looked to be absolutely real.

Did my father know everything or did he just suspect?

I shuddered at the thought of him watching us through the glass kitchen doors.

"Listen... I..." I said, barely a whisper. My voice was fluctuating, and my hands were shaking, but I was still trying to maintain some control. I hadn't been prepared to face Matt with this, but I had known it was going to happen sooner or later. I glanced to Neil again, maybe searching for support, but he remained still and silent, locked in his own misery.

"Well?" my father prompted, alternating his gaze between us. Then he shook his head and rubbed his face. His whole body was tense, and his eyes were clouded with a frightening anger. Frightening because while I had only seen my father get angry a few times, I remembered every one of them. "I told you at the beach house to stay away from him!" he shouted suddenly, and I flinched. He stabbed a finger at Neil, but his threatening gaze remained fixed on me. His eyes were like the barrel of shotgun, ready to fire. "I told you not to cross the line with him!"

"And what did you do? You ignored me. You did what you wanted. Do you think I'm stupid?" He advanced on me, and I took a step back, bumping into Anna behind me. Matt looked furiously at her, and everyone could tell that he didn't want any spectators at the moment. "Anna, go do your job. Now," he ordered curtly, and the housekeeper nodded, scurrying away.

I swallowed hard. It felt like pins were stabbing me in the throat, the same ones I could feel in my chest. I tried to keep my eyes down—for the first time, I was afraid of my father.

"Goddammit! What's actually going on between you? Is it a relationship? Are you together or what?" he asked anxiously. He cleared his throat, probably because of all the yelling. He ran his hands over his face again and began to pace. "Do you even know? Do you understand the gravity of what you've gotten yourself into?" He shook his head and began muttering broken sentences under his breath. He looked like he was losing his mind: All of his muscles were tense under his fitted suit ,and beads of sweat formed at his temples.

"How long has this absurd little affair been going on?" he asked, turning then to face Neil. "How long?" he shouted again, and I gasped. My heart sank; it felt like it wasn't even beating. Neil, however, just stood motionless and looked back at Matt, entirely unintimidated.

"Since about a week after she got here. I was the one who came on to her; it was my fault. If you want to be pissed off, be pissed off at me, not her," he answered. It was the first time he'd opened his mouth since I'd gotten there. His firm baritone betrayed no hint of insecurity.

I wished I had even a little of his indifference to stifle some of the anxiety that was making me feel faint. My father concentrated all his attention on Neil and walked slowly toward him, clearly struggling to believe what he was hearing. "A *week* after she got here?" he echoed shakily. He squeezed his eyes shut and shook his head, visibly angry and disappointed. "I put my trust in you. I thought that at least when it came to my daughter, you would be able to keep your damned urges at bay, but no. You were selfish, like always. You had no respect for me or your mother. And why, Neil? A whim? A desire? Just what the hell was going on in your head when you were trying to seduce my daughter, huh?" Matt was an inch from Neil's face, ranting. Neil's jaw was tight, his features drawn, but he didn't react the way I had feared he might. No emotion showed in his eyes.

"How far did it go?" Matt asked, and I moved closer to him, trying to keep the worst from happening. "How far did you go with her? Tell me!" Suddenly he grabbed Neil by the sweatshirt and yanked the boy into him. My father wasn't as powerful as Neil, not as young or athletic, but he was fully capable of hurting Neil, especially when he was out of his head like that. I couldn't just stand there, motionless and afraid to act, so I ran to Matt and grabbed his jacket.

"Matt, no!" I screamed, pulling him away from Neil. I was trembling like a leaf, and there were tears in my eyes.

"Tell me! Have the balls to tell me just like you had the balls to do it in the first place! You disgust me! Your mother should be ashamed of you!" Matt stabbed his finger at Neil again, looking at him with so much outrage. Every word, every insult was like a slice on my skin. It was as though Matt had a knife and was using it to carve wounds not just into Neil's heart, but into mine as well.

"You're right" was all Neil could say. He stared into Matt's eyes, grim thoughts clouding his own until his pupils were almost imperceptible and the gold had been replaced with something much murkier.

"For four years, I have never meddled in your relationship with your mother or your sister or your brother. I haven't said a word to you even when I watched all those girls going in and out of your room, despite the fact that this is also my house. And, believe me, I would have been well within my rights to complain," my father continued, sounding increasingly crestfallen. "I never tried to replace your father. I knew from the beginning that it was hard for you to accept a relationship between your mother and me, so I tried my best to be a good partner to her and a positive presence for you and your siblings. I have always accepted the meltdowns, the constant disrespect, and the verbal abuse. I have tried to be understanding because I know your history and what you've been through. I have even tried to give your mother good counsel so your relationship could improve. I did everything I could to maintain the right balance in this family. So why would you do this to me?" Matt asked, on the verge of tears. I had never seen my father so devastated, and it was a heartbreaking sight.

"That wasn't my intention," Neil answered, his voice firm and his posture unyielding. I wondered how he could possibly look so apathetic at a time like this. "It all started as a game..." he continued. I watched his eyes. "I like to provoke, and I've always been attracted to the taboo, the forbidden, whatever's just over the line I can't cross. I realize that's a bullshit justification, but I never wanted it to go this far. The situation got out of hand and…" He didn't finish because Matt lifted a finger to silence him.

"The situation got out of hand?" he echoed with a bitter smile. "Was that how it happened with Scarlett and all the other ones, too?"

I put my hand over my mouth to suppress a sob, but Neil heard it, his gaze flicking to me. He stared at me with the kind of heat that I could actually feel on my skin. I felt like I could sense his sadness, and he was feeling my pain. We were connected without ever needing to speak.

"I'm sorry, but we went about as far as anyone can go, Matt. We…" He left the sentence unfinished, confirming what my father already suspected. Then he straightened out his wrinkled sweatshirt and licked his lower lip.

"I…don't know what to say," my father mumbled, in shock, staggering back like he'd just been punched in the chest. He leaned against the couch as though he might collapse at any moment and shook his head repeatedly.

"I'm also at fault, Matt." I said, intervening for the first time and pulling his gaze to me. "He didn't have to twist my arm," I mumbled as I stared back at him. "We acted on instinct and made a mistake, but we are both to blame." I took a deep breath, trying to project a confidence I didn't really feel. But my father just turned his attention back to Neil, still trying not to break down in front of us.

"Do you even care about her? Do you have any feelings for my daughter? Or were you just passing the time?" he asked, all the strength drained from his voice. He didn't seem fully lucid, nor able to cope with the possibly negative answer he'd get. I looked at Neil as well, waiting to see what he said. His eyes were a mixture of emotions. I tried to read into them, and I didn't like what I saw.

I saw a man who was trying to communicate wordlessly with me. A man who was trying to apologize in advance for what he was about to say. I shook my head and stepped back, trying to shield myself from the cutting words that were about to fall from his beautiful lips.

"No, Matt. I was attracted to your daughter the moment we met. As soon as I saw her, I planned to use her. And I did. I satisfied my urges, and then

I disposed of her, just like the rest of them. At the end of the day, I always knew I wasn't the man for her, and I still believe that. I don't love her. I've never loved her, and I never will love her...because I just don't believe in love." His voice was austere and his demeanor so frosty that I bent over in pain. Matt closed his eyes, and at the same time, I closed my heart and decided I was going to throw away the key. Silent tears slid down my cheeks as my soul was subsumed into nothingness. All the while, Neil just stood there, motionless, witness to my annihilation.

I looked at him for an unknowable amount of time, hoping I would hear him say something else. But the longer I looked into his face, the more I knew that wasn't going to happen. I felt like I was drowning, and I was cold, so cold. I had fallen into a deep chasm of pain and had no idea how I was going to get back out. My heart was pounding so hard I thought it was going to burst from my chest.

Delusional as it was, I couldn't help but think back on what we'd shared. *"I'll call you whatever I want, Tinkerbell,"* he'd said the first time he used that stupid nickname after. I had only been in New York a few hours and had gotten lost on my way back from an ordinary trip to a bookstore. I ran into him and his unruly pack of friends on the sidewalk. It was like fate was playing a joke on me, dropping the most beautiful angel I'd ever seen right in my path. I allowed myself to be enthralled by him, not realizing that he was the kind of angel that got kicked out of Heaven because he was destined to live in Hell.

"My bed smelled like coconut this morning," he'd said after we made the dire mistake that we would go on to make again and again.

"The truth is in the details, Selene." I thought that "truth" was the sentiment he hid from me so I'd never see his human side. But I'd been an idiot to hang on his every word, to think that we might possibly have a future together.

Love makes a person blind and crazy—that's what it had done to me. I needed to just give him the freedom he wanted so badly. I should have let him go long before then. He deserved to live his life without me if that's the way he wanted it, and I'd have to accept that. Especially if that's what made him happy.

"I should have seen this coming," my father said, soft and blistering. "I am so profoundly disappointed in you," he added bitterly.

Suddenly, an unexpected sob came from behind us. I whirled around to see that Mia had joined us. Her blue eyes looked stricken, and she stared at her son in disbelief, one hand clamped over her mouth to keep from crying.

"Neil…" she murmured, but there was nothing else to say. Nothing more to add. Silence lay heavy all around us; not a single sound was disturbing the air in the living room.

"You hurt me, Neil," I said after what felt like an endless minute, and both my father and Mia turned their attention to me. I could feel their eyes on me, but with the last ounce of strength I possessed, I kept going. "You hurt me when you touch me, when you kiss me, and especially when you talk to me. You provoke the kind of devastating feelings that would destroy even the strongest woman in the world. And we both know that I'm not her." I rubbed the back of my hand against my cheek and, taking a deep breath, went on.

"You're troubled. You're a mess. Definitely not the kind of guy you take home to meet the parents. But you were the only guy I could both laugh and cry with, the only guy my heart woke up for. The only guy who made me feel alive. Yeah, alive. You may be flawed and unbearable at times…" I gave him a weak smile, praying I'd be able to finish my little speech. "But I felt your heart pounding more than once when you were with me and not from the stupid arousal response you're always talking about. Maybe you'll never be ready for a relationship; maybe you'll always need more time. Or maybe I just won't be the one. But I do know that there is goodness inside you, a part of you that just needs to be loved.

"I've learned it all by heart, you know? Every mistake, every need, every false move, every personality defect, and even your weaknesses. But in spite of your cruel words, I still think that you are incredible just the way you are. I'm going to remember everything we experienced together; I will carry it all with me. And maybe this makes me look like an idiot right now, but I want to thank you. Thank you for everything you've taught me." I sighed and licked my dry lips before continuing. "You taught me not to believe in fairy tales and how to rebuild a dream when the storms come and destroy it. You taught me how to be stronger, to face life head-on even with all its pitfalls and obstacles. You taught me how to be a woman. You taught me patience because sometimes it takes more time to understand the really

311

special people." I finished in a small voice, my words evaporating into the air. I didn't even care if I'd touched his heart; the important thing was that I'd said it. In spite of everything, I couldn't hate him because hate was the opposite of love, and I couldn't associate either with Neil.

I was heartbroken and disillusioned, but I finally understood.

I realized that I'd been deluding myself. I had meant nothing to him.

If I mattered to him, he wouldn't have touched any other women. He would have had the guts to go against my father to defend what we had. He was all I wanted, but he felt nothing for me.

The people who loved you shouldn't hurt you, and Neil was constantly hurting me.

I'd been a fool to imagine that he was mine, even in those brief moments when he gave himself over to me. He wasn't, he never had been. It dawned on me that I had done all the wrong things, because I was never going to save him or fix him. Love was not enough to save someone who was truly damned.

I was willing to fight for Neil—for us—but I knew that there was no point if he didn't reach out a hand for me. I'd done everything I could to get close to his heart, but the truth was he wasn't letting anyone in there, not even me.

My love would never be reciprocated because his suffering would always be stronger than anything else.

Neil was like a black eagle: He flew high and far and was impossible to reach. He'd never stop because he was searching for infinity, not the finite. Love was nothing but a prison for him.

I had dreamed of our life together, even during my coma. But I knew then that it would remain just a dream. A lovely dream. I understood that then, and I hoped that sometimes Neil might dream of me too. I hoped that there, at least, in our Neverland, life might exist and we could be happy.

Was that how the story went?

Didn't Peter choose Wendy?

Well, I hoped that in his dreams at least…he would choose Tinkerbell.

I returned home that evening with a new sense of understanding, ready to take control of my life again. I was never going to stop thinking about Neil entirely because he was going to be with me forever, but I was going to try to move on.

My mother didn't ask me any questions when I got back. I knew Matt had told her everything because I'd eavesdropped on the call he'd made to her before I got into my cab and left. Still, Mom greeted me with an affectionate hug and kiss to the forehead, right over my scar. "I made cherry pie," she said. Then we spent the rest of the night huddled up on the couch watching comedies, eventually falling asleep together in a completely bizarre position.

More than a week passed after that. Neil never sought me out, neither by text nor phone call, but I was still trying to get used to his absence. I wondered every day about what he was doing and how he was doing. I was positive that he wasn't missing me at all and that he'd never apologize for what he'd said.

Neil had just been honest, after all. He told my father what he really thought—what he had repeatedly tried to make me understand. I had known from the jump that loving someone was a risk, but I had taken that risk, and now I was going to have to deal with the consequences. In addition to the devastating way Neil had talked about me, I was also shaken up over Matt's reaction. He had been so broken that I worried he might never recover from the shock.

"Why so thoughtful?" Janel asked as we stood in the library at Wayne State. I had been tagging along with my friends when they went to campus because, according to my doctor, I was cleared to go back to my everyday activities, and I wanted to see if I'd be able to reenroll for the spring semester.

"You know, ever since you came back from New York, you've seemed really far away," Bailey put in, twisting a lock of red hair around her index finger.

How could I tell them what happened without completely going to pieces?

"It's all good. I've just been getting my ducks in a row. Trying to make up for lost time, you know," I answered with a forced smile. I wasn't lying. I had thrown myself into planning my courses and refining my study plan. Spending hours bent over my books kept me from thinking.

"Hey, if you do need anything, we're here. You know that, right?" Janel reached an arm across the table and patted the back of my hand. It was one of those moments when I felt my heart lurch and my eyes prickle. I shook my head and tried to reassure her with another smile.

"Figured I'd find you here. Who the fuck gave you permission to take my car?"

All three of us gasped as Ivan, Janel's twin brother, popped out of nowhere to berate his sister. His problem was the same as it always was— he didn't want her to touch his precious car.

"Are you nuts? We are in a library?" she snapped back in annoyance, and I laughed softly. Some things never changed, and Ivan was one of them. I'd known him for two years, since the day I'd become friends with Janel. The two of them were too alike, so they could never get along. They were fraternal twins, and Ivan had green eyes that Janel was always envying. Plus, he was ten minutes older than her and particularly eager to remind her of that in every argument.

That day, Janel's brother was wearing one of his usual tracksuits, which, as always, looked great on him. He played basketball and was as tall and athletic as that implied, with a thick fall of black hair that framed his masculine face.

"I missed the bus. What's the big deal?" Janel added, huffing as she shrugged her shoulders indifferently, a move that only served to infuriate her brother.

"I had to come here on my motorcycle because I couldn't find my car parked in my spot. That's the big deal," Ivan retorted, pointing a finger at her. Bailey and I could barely suppress our laughter.

"Oh, come on, don't be a baby. I even cleaned the seats, and who knows what kind of bodily fluids were on there?" Janel made a disgusted face, and with good reason. Ivan was extremely popular with the female portion of the student body, and his car was where he spent the most time with them.

And that was when we actually burst out laughing. Bailey tried to hide her face and go unnoticed, and I gave her a teasing kick under the table.

Ivan just cocked an eyebrow at us with a serious expression, folding his arms over his chest.

"And what the hell are you two laughing about?" he asked, looking back and forth between us.

"Nothing, we're just sympathizing with Janel. It takes guts to get into your car," I joked, and he reached out to ruffle my bangs. He always did that, and I couldn't stand it.

"Come on, knock it off." I slapped his hand away, and he gave me a snaky smile.

"There, you're definitely more attractive now," he teased, showing off the dimple in his right cheek, a little detail of his face that had knocked many a girl for a loop. I genuinely thought that dimple might be cursed: It made everyone fall in love with him.

"And you! We're going to talk about this at home." Ivan rounded on Janel and then left, though not before giving me another furtive look and a wink. Despite his buffoonish show-off persona, I knew that he was actually a very quick-witted guy. He spent any time he wasn't at practice studying, and he'd actually been nice enough to pass his notes along so I could decide which classes to take.

Bailey watched me with a mischievous smile, and I frowned at her.

"What?" I asked. She adopted a suggestive stance and drummed her fingers on the table. She always did that whenever she was about to say something really absurd.

"I could see you with him," she answered, and Janel raised her head up out of her book to look at her.

"With Ivan?" I laughed, shaking my head. He was a nice guy, but his reputation wasn't much better than Neil's. He changed girls about as often as he worked out, and I had decided I was done with guys like that. I wasn't going to fall for it again.

"No, absolutely not!" I added severely, trying to put a quick stop to that nonsense.

"You're gorgeous and smart, and I think you might like him. I certainly wouldn't mind having you for a sister-in-law," Janel noted wryly, but I was never going to change my mind.

"Ivan's a nice guy, but…" I stopped. But my heart was somewhere else. I wasn't ready to date someone new and might not be ready for a long time.

"Selene, you can't rule out even the possibility of dating other dudes just because you knew a giant asshole in New York," Bailey scolded me, and I gasped.

"Yeah. Sure, you lost your virginity to him, but maybe just chalk that up to experience," Janel added airily.

"You can't live the rest of your life chained to his memory," she added, sounding more concerned. I just stared down at the table, considering her words and lost in thought.

How could I forget Neil?

When I first met him, I thought the same things everyone did: that he was beautiful but uninteresting. I thought he was living his perfect life, sleeping with all those different women just because he could. After that first night, when I hadn't been able to sleep because of Jennifer's screams, I had bought some ear plugs, not that he'd ever known or cared. And then on the couch when he grabbed a handful of my popcorn? I realized how overbearing he was.

I'd hated him, couldn't stand him at all. Especially when he treated me like a kid and tried to lord his greater experience over me. He sneered at me whenever I didn't understand something; when I wasn't on his level sexually; when I blushed at dirty jokes.

I had even been with someone else, but after I met him, I couldn't do anything but want him.

It might have started off shallow and careless, but I always knew there was something different about him.

Every day was a new discovery.

He was special.

A total disaster, which is why I couldn't hold a grudge or really hate him.

I couldn't bring myself to hurt him even after he'd hurt me so badly once again.

All I could do was…thank him.

13

It disgusted me, what I had become because of her.

NEIL

We were lost, she and I.
Yes, truly lost.

For fourteen days.

It had been two weeks since I'd let her walk away, since I'd made the best possible choice, and since I'd freed her from the spiderweb she'd gotten herself wrapped up in. Two weeks since I'd last smelled her coconut perfume or saw her ocean eyes.

"Neil! Are you getting up? You need to go to class," railed Logan, bursting into my room.

No, I didn't really feel like getting out of bed. Logan had been nagging me, and I'd been giving him the old "five more minutes," but the truth was, I didn't feel like doing shit.

I didn't want to get up and face my days, which felt monotonous and dull. I didn't want to go out to a club or a party. I didn't want to be surrounded by women just waiting to open their legs for me. Not that I could actually have a real fuck with my anorgasmia. I was still following Dr. Lively's advice to avoid sexual intercourse, and I was getting good at it.

Truthfully, I didn't want any eyes on me except a specific pair of crystal-line ones, deep as the ocean.

I simply did not feel like doing anything at all and I didn't know what was going on with me.

"Five more minutes, Logan," I muttered for the umpteenth time, burying my head under the pillow.

"You already said that. Five minutes ago. And it's been thirty minutes since I came in here to beg you to get your ass out of this bed!" he snapped and then sighed. I required a lot of patience.

But I didn't care how many times Logan scolded; all I wanted to do was sit there alone and wallow in my correct-but-shitty decisions.

I really was rotting.

And that wasn't like me.

I wasn't like me.

Matt quit talking to me after Selene left, and my mother made it clear how deeply disappointed she was in me. I was trying to live with the awful things I'd said as best I could. I had rubbed Matt Anderson's face in the fact that I'd screwed his daughter. I told him straight up with zero respect or consideration that I'd lusted after her and considered her just one of many. And, at the same time, I had also hurt Selene.

The truth was, I lied and I acted that way just to get her far away from me, but I could never tell her that.

"Logan, quit busting my balls; you're starting to piss me off." I pulled my head out from under the pillow and gave a look that brooked no argument. Except he wasn't looking at me but rather at the ashtray on the nightstand next to my bed, and I knew another one of his lectures was about to pop off like a machine gun.

"How long did it take you to smoke those?" He narrowed his eyes at the twenty-some butts I'd smoked the night before, looking back at me sternly.

"I couldn't sleep. Don't start." I put the pillow back over my head, sighing in irritation when I felt a sudden draft on my naked back.

"Get up!" Obviously Logan had pulled the blankets off my body, but I still had no intention of listening to him.

"Piss off!" I blurted out angrily. "You've got three minutes to get lost."

"Neil, this has been going on for two weeks. You barely eat; you're chain-smoking like you're possessed, and this place looks like the inside of a fucking chimney. And you've practically destroyed that wall!" He heaved a worried sigh. Two nights before, I'd had an angry outburst that, unfortunately, I was unable to control. I'd woken everyone up by making multiple holes in the walls.

"I had one of my nightmares." I took my head out from under the pillow again and rolled over on my back, rubbing a weary hand over my face.

"Sure. You've gotten used to the nightmares about Kim, but the ones you've been having aren't about her, are they?" Logan put his hands on his hips and studied me closely. A few moments later I got up wearing only my boxers and brushed past him, yawning. "Neil!" He called out. Obviously, he wasn't going to shut up, which did nothing for my head. It was already throbbing from another sleepless night. I went into the bathroom and examined my reflection in the mirror. My hair was messy like always, and the deep shadows under my eyes spoke to the stress and mental exhaustion I was feeling. My beginnings of a beard only looked semi-presentable because I'd decided to trim it the day before. My eyes were dull, and my body was tense. I was a fucking bundle of nerves, primed to explode.

"No, Logan. They weren't about Kim," I said. I washed my face, trying to wake up and get myself together. The problem was, I just couldn't get Babygirl out of my head.

I'd even dreamed of Selene the night before, in bed with Luke. He'd kissed her, stripped her, and touched her like only I had done in real life. But that wasn't easy to admit.

My brother, naturally, followed me into the bathroom to invade my privacy.

"I need to piss," I said, trying to get him off my back. I waited for him to leave, but he didn't. He leaned on the doorframe instead and cocked an eyebrow at me, waiting for me to tell him what was going on in my head.

"Your tricks don't work on me. Tell me about your dream," he urged.

"No, it's none of your goddamned business," I snapped and stalked toward the toilet, patience gone. I did what I needed to do regardless of his presence, and after flushing, I brushed my teeth. I brushed them neurotically and then did the same with my tongue.

I could still taste that whore Kim in my mouth, and Logan knew it, which was why he just stood there silently, watching me with a thoughtful look on his face. He would give me all the time I needed. He knew that whenever I brushed my teeth or took a shower, I would punish myself. I would make the water freezing or burning, rubbing my skin until it turned red because I could still smell my abuser on me and hear her filthy words inside my head. It disgusted me, what I had become because of her. Sometimes I even imagined scraping all the skin off my body and somehow managing to sew on a new one. But a part of me knew that, even then, I wouldn't be able to forget her.

That woman had put down roots so deep in my head.

"So?" Logan continued, resuming his interrogation in a calmer, more measured tone. "Why are you smoking so much? And how did you make all those holes in the wall? Let's hear it…" He jerked his thumb at the damage I'd done to my room and the full ashtray.

I brushed my teeth again, rinsed my mouth, and spit into the sink. Then I sighed heavily.

"The little one I did with a lamp, which I hurled violently at the wall after I had a dream about Luke's tongue between Selene's thighs. The big one was from throwing a chair when I dreamed he was fucking her. Happy now?" There it was. My confession.

Luke smiled a faint, wry smile.

"That's…uh…interesting. So you don't care about her at all? And you aren't jealous, right?" he taunted me. His words gave me pause, though. Never before had I felt jealous over one of my lovers. I didn't even know what the hell jealousy felt like.

I shoulder checked Logan on my way back to my room, though my nerves had twisted up even more because of our conversation.

"That's right. I'm not," I answered. "I even told Matt I was just messing around with his daughter," I informed him.

"I know, you fucked up huge," he retorted.

I'd never admit it. I'd never tell anyone, least of all my brother, that I had lied just to make Selene hate me and go back to Detroit. I was very stubborn, and I had already made up my mind. End of discussion.

I angrily pulled on a black sweater and a pair of jeans. Logan watched my every move carefully, determined not to give up so easily.

"You did it because you're convinced you don't deserve her, right? Do you think she'd judge you if she found out about your past?" he asked, but I didn't answer him.

I knew exactly what he was trying to do. He was trying to sneak his ideas and his thoughts into my head. He wanted to convince me to go after Selene and keep her from hating me—which she already did, but whatever.

"I'm not the type to get stupid over a woman, Logan. I'm no Romeo climbing the balcony to get his Juliet. I'm not going to go to Selene with tears in my eyes and crawl like some worm. If you want to watch a big love scene, then get a DVD or take your girlfriend to the movies because my life is not a fucking romance movie. Now, is that clear to you, or do I need to spell it out in big letters?" I tried to catch my breath after practically vomiting my rage all over him. He was my brother and should have understood me better than anyone, but he didn't. He *couldn't* understand me.

He didn't understand that there was no way I could be with Babygirl, not with all the problems I had to solve.

I wasn't in my right mind.

I didn't even know where my right mind was, but I was pretty sure I was outside of it. Outside of normal.

And until I could control myself, I could not intertwine my life with hers.

"Would you rather I keep hurting her? Or would you prefer it if she stayed away from me and was happy? Huh? What's the right choice?" I advanced on him confrontationally. I was trying to back him into a corner and disarm him. "Answer me—which choice was more right, Logan?" I shouted before looking into his eyes and holding that stare. He seemed to consider my question for a second before shaking his head sadly.

"You need help, Neil. You know that, right?" His question was like a knife to my stomach. I felt a cold chill run down my spine.

"You can't handle this situation on your own anymore. You're consuming yourself and letting yourself be consumed by your past. Either you save yourself or…" His words went straight to my brain but also to my chest. They clawed, they stung, and they hurt me.

My brain rejected them and chased them away, refusing to accept them.

"I… I… It's fine… I've got it all under control." My certainty wavered, but I didn't fold. I didn't break. I stayed on my feet. Because I would never again allow anyone—not even someone in my family—to control my mind like Kim had done.

Confronted with the idea of being manipulated like that again, I knew I'd rather die than "save myself." Perhaps I had already subconsciously started down a dead-end road because I knew that it would lead to my demise and also to my liberation. I didn't like to say it out loud, I didn't want to admit it, and I never would have told Logan or Chloe because it would hurt them too much, but I had no other choice.

I had come to believe that it was the only way I'd ever completely rid myself of Kim.

"You don't have shit under control. The life you're leading is not normal, and you aren't—" I didn't let him finish. My voice overlapped with his presumptuously, full of anger but also resignation.

"My life has never been normal. Since I was a kid and everything changed. I've always lived this way, and I can't keep fighting anymore. Not now. It's too late, Logan," I said, my voice breaking.

I felt defeated, like I'd already lost the war. Too often, I wondered where I found the strength to hold on, and more and more lately, I felt like even that strength was failing me. I was on the edge of the precipice. I walked carefully, trying not to fall, but I was beginning to waver. I could no longer bear the weight of my suffering, and with each day that passed, the weight of reality crushed me even more.

"The meds didn't help me, and neither did years of therapy with Dr. Lively. There's nothing else to do…" I looked him in the eye. I was telling the truth. I never pretended with Logan. I could be myself with him and actually admit how I was really feeling. His eyes shifted, becoming bright and clear, and I could read real love in them, the only kind I believed in. The kind that had kept me standing for so long and continued to do so even now. But I knew that even that love wasn't enough.

This life of mine was a great illusion.

A dangerous game.

I'd passed through all the levels and now I'd reached the final one.

I had run.

I had run for years, trying to flee my enemy but now I was slowing down.

I was getting tired.

I was losing.

And my monsters were going to win.

At the end of it all, there was an enormous flashing GAME OVER waiting for me.

I knew it now.

Love could not save me.

Only medicine could do that.

Except that, with me, even medicine had failed.

"You've interrupted your therapy lots of times, Neil…" Logan moved toward me almost fearfully. It was obvious he didn't like what he was seeing in my face or the darkness in my eyes. Still, he had to face fucking facts: I was fading. And, for the first time, I could admit it.

"I'm tired, Logan. I'm tired of dreaming about Kim and feeling her on me. I'm tired of going back to my child mind. I'm tired of being back in that house over and over again. Every time it's torture. It's a prison. And there's only one way to break the bars…" I looked away from him. During the past two weeks, I'd been having more and more moments of panic, nervous breakdowns, or even just weak periods like this one. They were signals my mind were sending to me. Incontrovertible signals that I needed to understand.

"No!" Logan shouted, throwing himself at me. "You don't even think about that. You've got to put all that bullshit out of your head. I don't like the way you're thinking at all, Neil, and it's not like you. You're strong; you've always been that way, and you can't just give up…" He held my face in his hands; his eyes were locked on mine. I could feel his heart pounding. Fear radiated off his body and sank into mine, and I felt guilty. I hadn't meant to scare him. I didn't know what to do about it. I felt truly unstable, and that hadn't happened to me in a while.

"Neil, it's no good, what you're thinking and what you're saying. It's no good at all." Logan gave my face a shake like I was drunk or high, but unfortunately I was neither.

"Boys, what's going on?" My mother came into my room in one of her elegant pantsuits. She stared at me in alarm, like I was some fucking psycho on the loose. I brushed Logan's hands off my face and felt my mood shift again. This, too, happened to me all the time.

"Aren't you supposed to be at work?" I grumbled, grabbing my packet of Winstons and slipping it into the pocket of my jeans. I couldn't manage without my cigarettes, especially in my current condition.

"Neil, can I talk to you?" she asked before turning to my brother. "Logan, could you give us a minute?"

My brother rubbed my arm, reminding me to stay calm. He was truly afraid; I could see it in his eyes. He left the room with one last look of concern, and I was alone with her.

"If you're here to bust my balls, I need to let you know that today is not the day," I said, looking her right in the eye.

"That's what you say every day, Neil. Do you have any idea what this situation is doing to Matt?" So she was worried about her partner, not me. It was just like when I was a kid and she never noticed a damn thing that wasn't directly about her.

Her blue eyes never left my face, but as usual they felt distant and cold to me. Incapable of communicating with me.

"Dr. Lively called me. He told me you've started talking to yourself again and having hallucinations of a little boy who makes trouble for you…"

"Sounds like my shrink has forgotten the meaning of the term 'doctor-patient confidentiality.'" I laughed uncomfortably even as I realized I'd never be able to trust him again.

"He only did it because he believes the situation is grave. You are out of control," she murmured in concern, and it took an enormous effort not to throw her out of the room.

"Mom, why don't you go back to what you do best?" I said, looking over her perfectly made-up face with all the disdain I could muster. "Thinking exclusively about your own life, I mean," I added in a low voice, looking

324

away from her. I tried to brush past her to get out of the room, but she took my arm, her pink fingernails digging into my flesh like she was trying to hold on to me. Too bad there was no way to cling to a broken thing without getting cut herself.

"Is that how you talk to me? I'm trying to understand what's going on with you. You sleep with my partner's daughter without even thinking about the consequences. You go out every night with your unruly friends. You're aggressive and unreasonable. You need to start listening to me or—"

I raised a hand to stop her. I had no interest in her threats. She'd always thought I was a freak, and she had never been able to help me.

And if that was how one loved a son, then love was nothing but bullshit.

"Or what? You'll ground me?" I grinned sarcastically at her, knowing she had no real power over me. She couldn't handle me; she never could.

She was a failure.

"Neil, I'm your mother. I just want to help you and—" She stopped when I tore myself abruptly from her grip. My mother flinched away from me and pressed a hand to her chest.

"You want to help me?" I asked, then I laughed right in her face because that was the biggest fucking lie she could have told me. "Then where the fuck were you when your husband was 'punishing' me and calling me a little pervert? Where were you when my babysitter was fucking and degrading me? Where were you then, Mom? Huh?" I raged, close to her face. My mother was the only woman—other than Selene—who could make me completely lose my tether to sanity like that.

"You can't say those things to me…" Her eyes began to well with tears, but I didn't care. Right then, I felt pity for no one, not even the person who had brought me into the world.

"No, you have a point. I can't say those things to you because you don't have the balls to admit your giant failure to yourself. But the result is standing right here in front of you. Take a good look and accept it. I may be a total asshole, but you were a terrible mother, and you continue to be a terrible mother." I stared grimly into her eyes. I wanted her to look into my face and see what I truly thought of her. I wanted her to understand that our relationship had been in the toilet for years. I wanted her to stop hoping for some sort of gesture of love from me because it was never going to happen.

"I know, Neil. I know you suffered so much, and I know that you've been hurt, but I would give my life for you and your siblings. I think about what happened to you every day, and if I could go back in time and erase it all, I would. I miss you so much. I miss getting a hug or smile from you or any other little affectionate gesture a son might give a mother. I know you aren't okay. I can see it. You can't go on like this... Not anymore." She tried to move closer to me, but I stepped back, giving her an indignant look. She was ridiculous. For years she'd begged me for something that she could never have. I felt nothing for her except a profound sense of disappointment.

"You must not care about my life..."

I continued to ignore her words, though I knew now that I was too far gone...

I was falling.

And ever since I let Babygirl go, it had gotten worse.

Everything had fallen in on me.

When I was with her, I could see a light far in the distance.

That light gave me a sliver of hope.

Just a little hope that I might catch up to her... One day.

Now I was surrounded by total darkness.

I couldn't see anything before me.

Just a deep tunnel.

Interminable.

Obscured.

There was nothing for me.

I was drowning.

I was losing.

My soul was dying slowly, and I was doing nothing to save myself.

"You can't cling to your pride when it comes to your mother, Neil. Do you understand that? You're too rigid; you don't give anyone a second chance. I have been begging you for years to just let me love you, and you always deny me. You are not okay, and if you think I'm just going to stand by and watch while you destroy yourself, you are wrong!" She'd started to cry, but my only reaction was a mocking smile, bitter as poison.

"You don't need permission to love your son. That was your first mistake." I looked gravely at her and saw that she was musing on my words. I didn't waste any time; I took advantage of her distraction and left.

I left her alone in her silent suffering and left the house entirely.

Taking classes again and actually studying was the best thing I'd done in the last year. It was the only way I had of getting my mind off things.

It wasn't easy, though. My problems had wrapped around me like threads. Kim, my history, my father's violence, Scarlett, my relationship with my mother, my pride, my inability to trust, my behavioral issues, and, finally, Selene. Each thread had dug painfully into my flesh, all except the last one, which I had just severed two weeks before.

If I had been selfish, I would have kept Babygirl with me instead of letting her go. But I didn't want that grim future for her. I wanted the best for her. Kicking her to the curb like that had been my insane way of protecting her and making her happy.

I had realized a long time ago that I was always going to have to live with my wounds. That I would always feel the pain of them on the inside. I knew that there was no cure for me. No medicine, no escape, no light, and no salvation.

I could only ever bring darkness and evil into Selene's life.

Sure, Babygirl might have enjoyed my body and the things I gave her in bed. She liked the kisses and touches but even she wasn't capable of loving someone like me. I was convinced whatever feelings she thought she had were an illusion.

People like me couldn't be loved.

Soon even Selene would have to realize that love was just a bunch of big talk without any real significance. It was a set of rote actions and pat, empty phrases.

People "loved" without really loving.

Selene had this illusion of love that would never really exist.

Lost in thought, I took the Maserati and drove to campus.

After three hours of classes, though, I felt the need to get away from everything and be by myself.

So I walked out of the lecture hall, bored as hell and desperately needing a smoke. Walking down the hall, I pretended that everything was fine; I acted like I was my usual self, giving zero fucks. I avoided the wicked glances from girls who would have given it up to me in the bathroom if I'd asked. All I had to do was jerk my chin, and they'd be waiting in a stall, but I had no desire to do any of that.

I would have definitely shot down anyone who tried coming on to me.

As I headed for the exit, I took my phone out of my pocket, my thumb automatically scrolling through my contacts until I landed on one name: Tinkerbell.

That was how it always happened.

I wanted to give her a call or a text. I thought about her every moment of the day, but I wasn't going to do anything to make up for how I'd treated her. I wasn't going to give in. I wasn't going to lose my mind over any woman, least of all her.

Firm in my convictions, I made it outside, where I lit up a cigarette.

"Hey, Miller. Aren't you supposed to be in class?" A familiar female voice caught my attention. Standing before me was the last person I wanted to see—Megan Wayne.

"Aren't you supposed to be on another campus?" I waved my smoke away and looked her up and down. She was wearing too-tight leather pants and a black T-shirt with a large silver skull printed on it, right over her bountiful tits. The rocker-chic look never got me going, but she looked good in it.

"What? You don't like my look?" she asked when she noticed my eyes on her body. She arched an eyebrow in challenge.

"Look, Head Case, I'm not in the mood for conversation," I told her glumly, trying to get her to stop bothering me.

"Always so taciturn, Miller." She tucked a lock of her black hair behind her ear and looked intently at me. Her ivy-colored eyes were always trying to encroach on me, always trying to look past what I showed everyone else.

"And you're always a pain in my ass." I took another drag and looked around at everything but her. Her very presence bothered me.

"Wow. Such courtesy." Megan gave me a fake-surprised look, and I cut my eyes at her. I watched her eyes drop to my lips, where I'd stuck my cigarette. "Makes me wonder how someone like Selene puts up with you for more than ten minutes," she taunted, not realizing that bringing up Babygirl was a mistake. I was trying my best not to think about her.

"What does she have to do with anything?" I snapped irritably.

"You two were cute during that game of pool." She smiled slyly at me, and I decided I needed to nip any ideas she might have had in the bud.

"We're not together," I said clearly, shifting my gaze to a nearby gaggle of blonds. I studied them carefully, hoping one might pique my interest, but once again, nothing happened.

I was bored with women, and my body wasn't reacting to them.

"Yeah, she was quick to say that too." Megan shrugged before going back on the attack. "Alyssa told me she went back to Detroit after you acted like a total dick to her dad," she continued, sounding curious, and I stared at her in confusion.

"Don't you and your sister have shit to do? Besides gossiping about me, I mean," I said carelessly. Megan always seemed inexplicably up-to-date on what was going on in my life, which annoyed me.

"Logan told her everything, and she told me," she said casually.

"One of these days I'll have to tell Logan to shut his trap," I answered, annoyed. I hated people who tried to stick their nose in my business or analyze me the way Megan did.

"You like Selene," Head Case said abruptly, sitting down on a low wall nearby. I looked at her as blank as ever, and she gave me a sarcastic smile in return.

"What do you know about that?" I stood up straight and continued staring her down. I wasn't about to let her get inside my head.

"I could tell by the way you looked at her."

"Oh, yeah? And how did I look at her?" I brought the cigarette up to my lips, and again her eyes seemed to get caught on my mouth.

"Like you were in the middle of the best dream you'd ever had," she answered, and my impenetrable affect disappeared. My Winston dangled from my mouth, and I breathed the smoke out my nose, having no response.

"Bullshit," I managed finally, watching a girl walk past us. Her auburn hair was the first thing I noticed. Her eyes were just a regular shade of blue, though. A color just like any other. There was no sea, no ocean in those eyes.

Nothing like Selene's.

Still, the girl in question returned my glance avidly in the vain hope of catching my eye. My awful reputation preceded me—I'd fucked so many women that I couldn't be bothered by girls looking for exactly what I'd always given them. But this time, I had no ulterior motive. There was no lust, no perversion. The only thing I really wanted was to see Selene magically appear in front of me. To see her cock a hip as she yelled at me to quit smoking so much and stop being such a dick. I wanted her to pounce on me and give me one of her awkward, unpracticed kisses. All at once, I had the urge to taste her full lips, which always had a hint of coconut, and her tongue that filled my mouth with sweetness.

"You got all riled up about Luke Parker being there. You can lie to other people, Miller, but never to me." Megan spoke again, and I mourned the few seconds when she'd been silent. I scrubbed a hand over my face, swearing under my breath.

"Why does it fucking matter to you? What, are you studying me?" I had begun to lose my patience with her nonsense, and she just laughed. Like always, she made light of my dominating nature and wasn't afraid of me in the slightest. I hated that about her.

"Chill out. I like aggressive dudes only in bed." She splayed her legs wider, making herself more comfortable on the little wall.

"If I took someone like you to bed, you wouldn't be walking for a week after. You deserve to get punished for real," I burst out, thinking about how satisfying it would be to tie her ass up and leave her alone in some hotel for a few days. Maybe then she'd learn not to push me.

"You have all the charm of a caveman. Has anyone ever told you that, Miller?" She bit her lip to keep from bursting out into laughter. At me. I advanced on her, and Megan didn't stop laughing, not even when she could clearly see that my control was slipping. So I pushed my way between her legs and took her by the throat.

"You're fucking with the wrong person, Head Case." I dragged her close until she was just a breath away from my lips. I stared hard into her eyes and realized that there were little brown spots among the emerald green. I paused to evaluate them, and while I was, I noted that Megan did not blush, bite her lip, tremble, or appear to fear me at all. She wasn't like Selene.

"Is this any way to treat the woman who gave you your first real kiss?" She batted her long eyelashes and pretended to pout.

"That was a game," I answered calmly, using the tone of voice I always adopted when I was trying to talk some woman into bed. In this particular case, however, I had no intention of sleeping with her.

And yet…

"But you liked it," she whispered, plush lips moving slow. Suddenly, I was launched into the past.

Megan and I were fourteen years old, sitting on the floor at a birthday party. We were playing a game called "Seven Minutes in Heaven." We all wrote our names down on slips of paper and put them in a hat. As fate would have it, Megan and I were picked together, and moments later we found ourselves shut in the birthday boy's room, alone. After some initial awkwardness and nerves, we'd kissed and kept kissing for ten minutes, overshooting the limits of the game because neither of us wanted to stop. It had been the first kiss for both of us since the violence we'd experienced at Ryan's and Kimberly's hands. In fact, up until that moment, neither of us had ever kissed someone without being forced. It had left both of us nauseous at the idea of putting our lips on someone else's. We felt so in sync—and so completely not nauseous—that it surprised both of us. We'd chalked it up to our similar histories. Megan never needed to be told anything.

She already knew all about me.

"You liked it too," I answered seductively. I tried not to grip or maneuver her throat too roughly—I didn't want to actually hurt her, just intimidate her. But Megan seemed perfectly comfortable in spite of my tight hold on her.

"I've never forgotten it, actually," she admitted before giving me a gentle shove backward. She hopped off the wall, dusting off her pants. "Call Selene, Miller. Tell her you're sorry, give her one of your head-spinning kisses, and stop being such a dick. She doesn't deserve it." She smiled at me one last time and walked toward the entrance of the building, swaying her hips confidently. I shook my head and licked my lips, reflecting on what she'd said.

I wasn't going to look for Babygirl.

I was just going to keep protecting her…

From myself.

14

He of all people wanted to talk?

SELENE

It takes some precision, so be careful," my mother whispered as I attempted to sketch out a tulip on a glass plate with paint. Since coming back to Detroit, I passed the time by preparing for restarting school, spending afternoons with Janel and Bailey, and having long chats with my mother over a glass plate or cup to be painted. Though we could usually talk about everything, my mother and I still hadn't addressed what had gone down in New York, and I was grateful for that. Still, she knew me very well and could see that I wasn't okay. It wasn't just the post-accident headaches; it was my actual state of mind.

All I did was fantasize about Neil and me in some alternate world where we could be together, ready to fight off his demons and bring our chaotic souls together. I'd heard it said that dreams were deceiving while also being manifestations of our deepest desires. For me, that was true. I dreamed of him, imagining us finally together, happy and ready to kick the past aside.

How could I not hate him after everything that happened?

I didn't understand him, but unfortunately, I still wanted him. I wanted every part of him. I wanted to kiss the good parts of his soul and caress the flawed ones. I wanted to embrace not just his perfection but also his imperfections, to share memories of the past and make plans for the future. I yearned for him to belong to me and for me to belong to him, today and every day after. Like we were the shell and the pearl who had found each other after searching for so long through the worst of the storms.

I was afraid, though, of hurting again. I was fighting alone for a love that was never going to bloom. I was also afraid of being crushed again, of finding out that Neil was still screwing his blonds. Of Neil once again using his razor-sharp words to shred my heart.

He had been perfectly clear with my father: "*As soon as I saw her, I knew I was going to use her.*"

"Selene..." My mother roused me from my thoughts, and I turned to look at her. She stood, lovely and elegant as always, in front of the door, preparing to open it. "I think you have some visitors." She smiled, and I frowned.

I got abruptly to my feet, leaving the paintbrush and glass plate I was working on at the table. I patted my loose hair, afraid I wasn't sufficiently presentable. I wiped my hands nervously on my jeans. All the while, my mother was smiling like she'd already known we were having guests that afternoon. She pushed the door open wide, and moments later Logan and Alyssa walked in beaming.

"What?" I shouted, immediately shrugging off my initial concern. I hadn't seen them in weeks, so discovering them here in Detroit was a totally unexpected surprise. I ran to them and tackled Alyssa.

"We wanted to come see you," she explained as I wrapped her tightly in a warm hug. Logan, standing next to her, patted my hair and pressed a tender kiss to my cheek.

"How are you doing?" he asked as I motioned for them to follow me into the living room. My mother immediately fled to the kitchen to get some juice from the fridge. In the meantime, I sat down on the sofa with Alyssa. Logan took a seat in the armchair opposite us.

"I'm good. I wasn't expecting to see you. What are you doing here?" I asked, looking at both of them. After Matt found out about everything, I'd left right away without even saying goodbye to Logan and Chloe. I apologized to them both later over text messages, but I didn't tell them what happened. I knew they were informed shortly after I left, though.

"You left without even saying goodbye. We know about everything; Matt's still wrecked," Logan said with a soft sigh. I knew that finding out about my pseudo-relationship with Mia's son had put my father in a state of shock, but that wasn't why I was hurting. Instead, it was Neil's words—they were so cold and heartless.

"My brother didn't really mean those things he said to you," Logan continued as though he was reading my mind. How did he know that? Had he actually talked to Neil about it? A faint, ironic smile spread across my face, and I immediately shook my head.

"Oh, he did. He meant exactly what he said, every word. I know you want to come to his defense because he's your brother, but—" But I didn't get to finish because Logan interrupted me.

"I would be the first to tell you that he's a dickhead, Selene, but believe me—he likes you. He likes you a lot, and that scares him." He sighed, and Alyssa gave a snort of displeasure, but Logan ignored her and kept talking. "He hasn't been doing well lately," he continued sadly, and something strange vibrated in my chest. It felt like those same contrasting emotions—confusion, fear, lust, and love—that I felt whenever I thought about Neil.

"Did something happen to him?" I asked in alarm. I never said anything about Player being behind my accident. What if he had hurt Neil? Right at that moment, my mother appeared, holding a tray with three glasses of juice on it. She set it down on the coffee table in front of us and smiled.

"I brought you all something to drink. If you need anything, I'll be right over there," she said as she took her leave, giving us the privacy we needed to talk. I immediately focused on Logan again.

"Neil has to deal with his issues, and lately it seems like he'd rather give up entirely instead of fighting like he always had before. Matt's anger and our mom's disappointment have been like the last straw for him," he continued miserably. Logan assumed that I understood exactly what "issues" he was referring to but, in reality, I only had a vague idea. He hadn't really told me much at the beach house, so I could only imagine the full scope of the trauma Neil was forced to deal with every day because of what he'd suffered at the hands of Kimberly.

"What about now? Where is he now?" My voice broke, and my instincts urged me to grab my phone and call him, but pride stood in my way.

"We offered to let him come here with us," Alyssa informed me. "But he absolutely refused to see you. Tell her the truth, Logan." Then she glared at her boyfriend, and I looked down at my legs. I'd rather not know that kind of information, actually.

"I know my brother better than anyone else. He cares about Selene, and if he's not here, it's because he has a good fucking reason!" Logan snapped back, annoyed at her. Alyssa cleared her throat uncomfortably. No one, but no one, was allowed to rag on Neil in front of his brother. Not even his girlfriend.

After that little tiff, we continued talking about nothing in particular while sipping juice. I steered the conversation toward college classes to dispel some of the tension still lingering between Logan and Alyssa. Once harmony was restored, the time went by too fast. When, after a couple of short hours, they had to leave because they were planning to stay with some of Alyssa's cousins in Ann Arbor, I was feeling melancholy.

In the doorway, Logan advised me to message Neil, while Alyssa told me to have some fun with someone new and get Neil out of my head. She couldn't seem to stand him at all and, as time went on, her distaste for him only seemed to increase.

"When will they be back?" my mother asked when we were alone again.

"No idea," I said thoughtfully. I sat down in a kitchen chair and watched the sky outside the window. It had just started sleeting, and the glow from the streetlight rendered the tiniest water droplets visible, like thousands of pinpoints of light. The drops raced down the glass, and the sky overhead was as dark as my mood.

"Sooner or later, missy, you are going to have to tell me about you and Neil. You do know that, don't you? I'm just giving you some time before the inevitable mother-daughter discussion," my mother said in a stern voice, and I turned to look at her. It had been a long time since she'd talked to me like that, and I'd almost forgotten how uncomfortable I got when she looked at me the way she was now: frostily.

"Yes, I know, Mom," I murmured, trying not to look annoyed. I was well aware that I had screwed everything up and that my relationship with Neil had ended exactly the way I should have expected it to; I didn't need her lecture as well.

"Okay, I'm going to take a hot bath," she told me before vanishing through the kitchen doorway.

I snorted and returned to staring out the window. I used my index finger to draw funny faces on the fogged-up glass, like a kid. The first had his tongue sticking out, the second one's eyes were crossed, and I drew a little heart in the middle between them. I smiled to myself at my silly little drawing until the ringing of the doorbell interrupted my art appreciation, which was very annoying.

"Who the hell is it now?" I got up reluctantly and walked slowly toward the front door.

"Selene! Get the door!" my mother shouted from the bathroom at the back of the house, and I rolled my eyes.

"Yeah, I've got it," I groused as the doorbell continued chiming impatiently. "Hold on a minute, for God's sake!" I said acidly and put my hand on the doorknob to pull it open in a bored fashion.

"I don't know why I came all the way out here either. I'm just hoping you aren't going to immediately kick me out and will give me a chance to explain why I said that stuff to your dad."

My eyes bugged slightly when Neil's deep baritone rebounded off the living room walls, like the kind of powerful thunderclap that gave me goosebumps.

I shivered, and my pulse sped up.

That was Neil: butterflies in the stomach and a racing heart.

The most seductive lie, the most refined torture.

His face was wet, as was the messy hair that straggled over his forehead. A leather jacket made his shoulders look even wider and highlighted his fit biceps. Underneath it, a basic white V-neck sweater was completely saturated with water, plastering it to the sculpted shape of his pecs and stomach. My eyes flicked then to his powerful legs, swathed in black skinny jeans, before moving back up to his face. Specifically to the swollen, slightly parted lips that had so often inspired my most sinful desires.

I stared at him in shock: I hadn't expected to find him at my front door. I tried to breathe steadily as I considered my options. I could give him the boot and show him how angry he'd made me. Or I could invite him in and hear what he had to say.

"I take it this is your bizarre way of saying hello? Hi to you too," I answered in a shaky voice. I wished I could have projected more confidence, but my agitation showed. My heart was bursting from my chest and my body trembled under his dark yet terribly arousing stare.

"Can I come in?" He ran a hand through his hair, messing it up. It was incredibly sexy, and I couldn't help but watch his muscles in the white sweater he wore under his leather jacket.

I tried to get myself together and think about what I needed to do. Neil deserved to be left out in the freezing rain or to have me scream "Go back to New York!" at him. But, instead, what I said was…

"Yes." I cleared my throat and stepped aside to let him in. A hint of a smile played at his lips, and the honey of his eyes lit up with all the splendor of the sunrise. That moment was confirmation of how completely gone I was for the man. His stare was enough to bring me back to life. His presence was enough to keep from giving up in most hopeless moments. His smile was enough to light up the night sky. I wanted to hate him; I wanted to stay far away from him. I had tried to burn my love for him out of my soul, down to the roots. But all I had to do was see him again, and the feeling bloomed again: overpowering, untamed, and even stronger than before.

"Are you by yourself?" His voice pulled me out of my daze. Neil came forward a few steps, and I watched him wipe his shoes on the blue, crescent-shaped rug just inside the door.

"Logan and Alyssa came by today." I ignored the question, and out of nerves I said the first thing that popped into my head. I was also confused—Alyssa had told me that Neil didn't want to see me, yet now he was here, right in front of me and not in one of my dreams.

"Yeah, I know," was all he said, sounding slightly irritated. I closed the door behind him, and he touched his wild hair with one hand. My eyes tracked a trail of droplets until they vanished into his short beard. It looked good on him.

"I'd like to talk," he answered, catching me off guard.

He of all people wanted to talk?

"So you can tell me that I mean nothing to you and you were just using me? Trust me, I got it," I snapped indignantly, drawing on the anger I'd been suppressing for far too long. He hadn't gotten in touch, he hadn't apologized, and now he wanted to just swan into my house with his smug attitude and careless air like he knew he already had me in his grasp? Well, he didn't.

"Sweetheart. Who was at the do—" My mother appeared behind me in a pair of black pants and a blue sweater, the long sleeves of which she was rolling up over her forearm. She turned her blue eyes on the boy in front of her. A lock of hair slipped from her orderly bun, and she moved it aside with her index finger.

"Hello, Ms…" Neil looked to me like I was going to supply my mother's last name, which he had surely forgotten. But I remained silent.

"Ms…" he said again, less confidently this time. He rubbed an eyebrow with his thumb and looked my way again, seeking my help, which I cheerfully denied.

"Ms…um…Calvin?" He hazarded a skeptical look. I held myself back from laughing outright, and he must have seen that because he immediately started glowering at me.

My mother, however, continued to watch cautiously as Neil licked his lips in a particularly uncomfortable way. I'd never seen him look so nervous before.

"Martin," my mother corrected at last, a faint, amused smile on her face. "Judith Martin," she elaborated gently, and unable to control myself any longer, I burst out laughing, even resting a hand on my stomach. They both turned to look at me, and my mother cocked an eyebrow in confusion. Neil, by contrast, just clenched his jaw.

"Yeah, pardon me, Ms. Martin. My memory's not so great," he explained before turning back to me with a look so severe that it immediately extinguished my laughter.

"Selene, is this how I taught you to welcome a guest?" my mother admonished me, letting me know I needed to get it together. Then she turned back to the walking disaster who stood before us. "You're Neil, right?" A warm, welcoming smile lit up her face, and she looked him top to bottom.

"Yes," he answered, standing motionless there with his clothes all soaked and his powerful body exuding a breathtaking beauty. I knew he wasn't going to be particularly chatty with my mother either. In fact, he'd probably already said more than he'd like.

"Well, Neil, I think you need to change your clothes, or you're going to get yourself a bad cold." My mother lifted her index finger, and Neil looked down at his sodden clothing and sighed.

"Does it always storm like this in Detroit? This freezing rain is a real motherfu…" He paused, looking from me to her, and I gave him a minute head shake. "Fluffer… A real motherfluffer." He cleared his throat and forced a faint smile that somehow turned out sensual.

"I agree with you, Neil. I'm going to go get something for you to wear. I think I still have some of Matt's old things," my mother explained briskly, tapping a finger on her chin.

I looked at Neil and immediately saw that he was very nervous, so much so that I could feel how difficult it was for him to keep talking to her. By now I knew him better than he realized. As soon as my mother retreated, Mr. Disaster's golden eyes turned on me, looking irritated.

"You done fucking with me now?" he chided me, his eyebrow raised.

"Calvin," I repeated mockingly, still trying to keep from laughing.

"So immature," he muttered with a roll of his eyes.

"And you're an asshole. I still haven't forgotten about what you told Matt," I said, making a challenging face, and he smiled at me, amused.

"Looks like you missed me, didn't you, Tinkerbell?" He gave me a seductive wink, and I felt my cheeks blaze with heat.

"If I'd really missed you, I would have gotten in touch with you," I answered firmly, determined that I was going to act just like him. He was the one who taught me, after all, how to give biting answers and act like I couldn't care less. But something changed in Neil's eyes, and he strode toward me determinedly until he could take my hair in his fist. Surprised, I let out a cry of pain, and he breathed against my lips, making me go rigid. My arms twitched with tension. I looked defiantly into his eyes.

"You can't lie to me, Babygirl. Remember that," he whispered. His pupils had dilated enough to reduce his irises to a thin, golden ring.

"Here you go, Neil." I winced at the sound of my mother's voice, and he pulled away, restoring his composed equilibrium. Oblivious to everything, my mother handed him some clean clothes and smiled.

"Many thanks," Neil said, almost imperceptibly, as though he weren't accustomed to such gestures. Then my mother pointed out the bathroom, and we both watched his imposing figure walk in that direction.

"Well, he's undoubtedly very sexy, but that doesn't justify you not telling me about the two of you," my mother said the moment he disappeared behind the bathroom door.

"Mom, this is not the time to talk about it." I chided her softly so Neil wouldn't overhear. "And there's nothing going on between us. We're just two screwed-up people," I added quickly, and she gave me a skeptical look.

"Screwed up?" she echoed, confused.

"Yeah," I said with a heartbroken sigh. There wasn't any other way to describe us.

Moments later, we were interrupted by the sound of Neil's footsteps, and we both turned to look at him, now standing in the living room wearing a pair of Matt's sweatpants. The sweater, which had an electric blue sports logo in the middle, was too tight on his powerful arms and torso. The pants fit him okay but were a bit too short for him.

"Maybe I should try to find something bigger?" My mother cocked her head to the side and frowned.

"Matt and I don't wear the same size, but it's fine. Don't worry about it," he told her with a hint of irony, almost sounding…nice.

Almost.

"Alas, my husband was not a giant, and he never had all those muscles you've got," my mother said merrily, making me blush. Neil looked unmoved as always and just gave her a smile. I needed to have a talk with her soon; she couldn't be showering him with compliments like a teenage girl with her first crush. "Have a seat on the couch with Selene, dear, and I'll make you some hot tea. Or would you rather have something else?" she asked, heading for the kitchen, but Neil shook his head, declining with a simple "I'm good."

With my mother safely away in the kitchen, we were alone, and I glanced around uncomfortably, unsure about what to do next. Neil wasn't here by accident; he hadn't come to Detroit for small talk over a nice cup of tea.

"So? What did you want to say to me?" I crossed my arms over my chest, and unlike my mother, I wasn't remotely polite. She wasn't the one who'd been hurt, after all. She didn't even know him or what a deceitful bastard he was.

"Cute house you have." Neil changed the subject, looking around the living room off the entryway. My house was completely unlike Matt's. There was no flash or luxury, no crystal chandeliers or giant pools in the backyard. Neil was mocking me, like always.

"Unbelievable. You really have some nerve showing your face here after what happened," I shot back at him while he, utterly calm, looked over my shoulder at the pictures on the wall of me as a child.

"You were funny even when you were little. How old were you there? Five?" he teased, looking at one picture in particular. I was in my mother's arms at the beach wearing a colorful swimsuit and massively oversized snorkeling mask. I should have had her get rid of that picture. Stash it in some drawer or something so I wouldn't feel so embarrassed.

"Don't change the subject." I moved to face him and looked him right in the eye. I only came up to his chest, and his musky smell was so strong it was messing with my head. Neil lowered his gaze to look at me, and I sucked in a breath. His eyes were always speaking in that silent language that I was learning to understand and, just then, they were so obscured that I knew he was irritated by how I was approaching the situation.

"You're trying to piss me off, aren't you?" he whispered menacingly and I glanced warily into the kitchen, afraid my mother was going to see us getting so close to each other.

"I'm the one who should be pissed off, not you," I retorted, and he smiled. I didn't know why, and I didn't even have time to think about it because Neil drew close to me and gently grazed my hip, making me gasp.

I was wearing a normal pair of jeans and a white sweater, nothing particularly sexy, but he was looking at me like he wanted to tear it all off me.

"I like it when you get aggressive, Tigress," he murmured under his breath, moving his face even closer to my lips. After a moment, he took a deep breath and did not kiss me. I knew he wanted to, just like I wanted to, but instead he chose to stand motionless right in front of me, eyes gleaming with lust.

"Now's not the time to be thinking about…" I began to say, but Neil moved closer still until he was right up next to my ear.

"Fucking you?" he finished for me. I could feel his hot breath on my skin, and his chest brushed against my breasts.

His baritone voice hit me like a jolt between my thighs, so I shut my eyes and bit my lip, swallowing hard. A chill ran down my spine and a raging fire ignited in the bottom of my belly.

"My mother is right there. Stop it." I got up the nerve to push him back, but my hands started shaking as soon as I touched him. Neil took a few steps back, still giving me that same amused look, and I realized how hard it was going to be to resist him.

It was hard to resist the urge to undress him and feel his smooth skin against mine; hard not to run my fingers through the thick, wild hair on top of his head. It was hard not being able to kiss and caress his fierce body.

It was hard to resist the flames of desire that enveloped us every time we got near each other.

"I need to be alone with you," he said seriously.

Luckily for me, Neil heard my mother's footsteps and moved away from me immediately. He sat down on the couch, and I could breathe again. He balanced one ankle on the opposite knee and continued evaluating me closely, waiting for my answer.

"Here's your tea." My mother joined us in the living room with two steaming cups, looking at us in increasing confusion as she sensed the heavy atmosphere in the room.

I looked thoughtfully at the clock. It was eight, and I knew my mother was going out with Anton Coleman tonight, but I was absolutely sure that I could not be alone in the house with Neil. I could already picture how it would end: him and me, naked in bed.

I shook my head; I couldn't afford to give in to him. I needed to avoid any compromising situations.

"Selene, I need to leave in half an hour, but…" My mother cleared her throat and looked sternly back and forth between Neil and me. "I am not leaving you here alone with a boy," she said baldly, and my eyes widened in embarrassment.

Did my mother have to treat me like a child right in front of Neil?

I shot her a look, and she recoiled slightly.

"As you know, I've got an…appointment that I can't put off, so…"

"Neil and I will go out," I said hastily to end the conversation. I looked to Neil, chewing on my fingernail, and he frowned.

"Really? Out where?" my mother asked, taking an inquisitive stance with her hands on her hips.

"Not far, just to the diner a couple of blocks over. Neil's never been to Detroit, so…" I gave him a conspiratorial look, and he got up off the couch, looking a little annoyed. I didn't like the stiffness in his face or the tension in his body. But he kept his composure in front of my mother, approaching me with his usual confidence and a phony smile.

"Sure, let's go. If it'll make you more comfortable, Ms. Martin, why not?" He was humoring me but doing so in a blatantly sarcastic way. My mother straightened up warily and scrutinized us both again.

"Okay… I'll go get ready then," she answered, heading up the stairs. The moment she was gone, I rounded on Neil, my eyes narrowed to two burning slits.

"You could have at least tried to sound enthused, you know?" I chided him as his stare, which had become ravenous, fixed on my lips.

"Someone should let your mother know that if I want to fuck her daughter, I will. I can do it up against a wall if I have to. No bedroom required," he said, fully the swaggering blowhard.

"And do you really think I'd let you?" I answered pointedly, and he reached out to touch a lock of my hair. He twisted it around his index finger, fixing his eyes on me, making me see the little flashes of mischief that moved through them.

"Would you have the guts to stop me?" he asked softly, his thumb rubbing my lower lip. He gently traced the edges of it and breathed in deep.

"And would you have the guts to use me again after what you said to my father?" I murmured, and Neil looked from my lips to my eyes.

"I had to say that." He continued touching my lip as he stared sadly at me. The flickers of mischief were gone now, giving way to the more sensitive, more human side of him.

"I don't remember anyone forcing you." I wanted to give myself over to his touch, but I forced myself to remain motionless and simply take it. I could keep doing it, too, for as long as I wanted.

"You don't get it, Selene." Neil rested his forehead against mine and closed his eyes. His warm hand stroked my cheek while his other hand grasped my hip tightly. It occurred to me that he always seemed to need some sort of contact with me, even if it was barely perceptible. It was like it was necessary to give him the strength to talk to me.

"If you were clearer, maybe I would understand better," I managed, and he looked back into my eyes. He pushed aside my bangs and looked at my scar, sighing.

"Well, I—" My mother walked in again on us. Tremendous timing on that woman. Neil immediately jumped back, and I tried to gather myself. I didn't want her noticing how overwhelmed I was by him or the kind of intimacy we shared.

"Uh…Mom…" I smiled stiffly as she sat down on the couch.

"Anton's running late; I'll wait down here. Maybe you should go get ready while I have a little chat with Neil," she suggested and I almost laughed in her face. I knew exactly how that "chat" was going to go. Neil would refuse to utter a single word. He was much less open or talkative than she believed him to be. As expected, I saw him stiffen at the idea of having a conversation with my mother.

I hurried up to my room, though, because I didn't want to leave the two of them alone for too long. My mother didn't think much of guys like Neil, and honestly, what parent would? So I washed up and got changed as fast as I could, pulled on a pair of high boots, and did my hair, leaving it to hang loose over my shoulders.

I hurried down the stairs and immediately spotted Neil, wearing his leather jacket again and intently studying a painting on the wall. My mother, on the other hand, was intently studying him from the sofa, like he was some science experiment.

"I'm ready," I said as I went down the stairs, afraid of getting another lecture from my mother. Fortunately, Matt had only told her about our relationship, not that we slept together. I wanted to get Neil out of there as fast as possible. She'd already told me she didn't trust him, so I was working hard to make sure she didn't ask any more compromising questions. As soon as I hit the bottom step, though, I realized their conversation had taken an unexpected turn.

"You like that one? My daughter is always complaining that I buy too many paintings and we don't have anywhere to put them," my mother was saying to Neil. Neither of them had noticed me.

"Yeah, I actually like Magritte a lot," he answered with a small smile. "This one is called *The Lovers*, right?" He jerked his chin at it. Meanwhile, I crept forward slowly so I could observe the situation, careful not to interrupt them.

"That's right," my mother said, surprised.

"I know it was done in 1928 or thereabouts. It's part of a series; the first one is at MoMA in New York, and the second one is in the National Gallery in Australia. I like the symbolism of it—love interpreted as a feeling that can't be seen, kind of a conflict between our outward appearance and the things we hide even from ourselves," Neil continued with his deep, hoarse voice that made every inch of my skin erupt into goosebumps. Meanwhile, my mother stared at him, thunderstruck, like she wasn't expecting someone like him to be cultured.

I, however, knew how vast, mysterious and rich he was inside. Rich with inner knowledge that he didn't like to brag about. That was his way: He was like a book one could only discover page by page. A book that contained an endlessly variable world, one of infinite depth and unpredictability.

"Yes." My mother blinked, trying not to look too shocked. "*The Lovers* is one of my favorite paintings. Other than teaching literature, art is my great love. I find it completely fascinating," she said as Neil smiled peacefully at her.

"Are you an art lover as well?" she asked him, and he nodded.

"I spent a lot of time with my maternal grandparents when I was a kid. They were very demanding when it came to learning. They wanted all their grandkids to have a classical education. So I had to skip soccer games, having snack time, or riding bikes with friends to go to the museum, visit the library, or take private lessons," he explained, tucking his hands into the pockets of his jacket. That was the point when I cleared my throat and they finally noticed me.

"Oh, Selene, there you are," my mother said, getting up from the sofa.

"We'll probably be home around the same time Anton brings you back," I offered, and she smiled, giving Neil an indecipherable look.

Had her opinion of him changed? I hoped so.

"Neil, are you staying with us tonight?" She spoke to him in a surprisingly fond tone.

"No, I'm fine getting a hotel. I don't want to—" Neil began without any hesitation, but my mother just shook her head and steamrolled over him.

"You'll stay here with us in the guest room," she said cordially, and I wasn't sure if she was pretending to welcome him or not.

What had happened while I was gone?

"Okay, but I think we should get going now," I put in quickly. I grabbed my purse and slipped into my coat while Neil watched me steadily. He was probably wondering about my suddenly solicitous attitude, but I didn't care. I just needed to get us away from the suddenly very dangerous Judith Martin.

I opened the door, and after telling my mother goodbye, I exited, followed by Neil. Shivering from the cold, I tucked myself deeper into my coat and looked up at the sky. There were still some big, dark clouds, and the air was biting cold, but the sleet had subsided, and the sidewalks didn't seem too treacherous if you watched where you were stepping.

For a moment we both just stood there on the porch. We'd never gone out together in New York. But I was the one who had the bright idea of going out. I was very interested to know what Neil and my mother had said to each other while I was upstairs.

"Relax. Your mother just asked me about what school I went to, how old I am, and if I have any dreams I'm chasing."

I turned to Neil as he spoke and saw that he already look prepared for the question I was about to ask him. His ability to always be able to read my mind was uncanny—it never changed.

"Did she ask…" I mumbled awkwardly. "Did she ask about us?" I finished, all in a rush as he reached into his jacket for his packet of Winstons.

"No, and if she had, I would have assured her that her baby girl was still a virgin," he answered cheerfully, sticking a cigarette between his lips.

"You're a dope." I elbowed him gently, and he stared at me, shocked.

It occurred to me almost immediately that we didn't joke like that—or, rather, we only had a few times—so I decided to be serious again and tried to look confident as I decided that I was going to lay down my weapons and try to put him at ease. I would get the chance to hash out everything that happened in New York later.

"Have you ever dated a woman?" I descended the porch steps, turning back to look at him. Neil still stood in the same spot, intent on lighting his cigarette. He tucked the lighter in his pocket and took his first drag as he walked toward me.

"No, and I'm not going to start with you either," he groused, surly as ever. I cocked an eyebrow and smiled slightly as I kept walking. I led us toward the small diner that was kind of locally famous, even though it was totally unassuming.

"I'm guessing you're here in Detroit because you regret all the hurtful things you said to me last time we met and you want to make it up to me," I said archly, while he sped up to walk by my side. Recalling his cruel words didn't bring me any joy, but I was trying to minimize them because I didn't want to get into a fight. I had promised myself before that I would never judge him and try to understand him instead, even if it meant tolerating a disrespectful attitude.

"I don't regret a damn thing," he retorted. There were times when he sounded nothing short of puffed-up and pigheaded, and it was downright irritating.

"Oh no? So what are you doing here then?" I pressed. Despite the fact that I had just decided not to needle him too much, I wanted to understand what had prompted him to set aside his pride and come visit me.

I pushed my hands into my pockets, and we continued walking. Neil glanced around, avoiding my eyes, and I knew he was trying to hide his thoughts from me.

But I knew him now.

"What am I…" he said softly before cutting himself off. At the sound of his voice, I moved in front of him and stopped, preventing him from walking forward. Instead of going around me, he took one last drag, leaned down to stub out his mostly unsmoked cigarette, and stashed the butt in his Winston pack. "I'm here because I wanted to see you," he said abruptly, staring at some random spot over my shoulder.

My heart did a ridiculous little flip at his words, and an instinctive smile spread across my face, but it faded immediately when I thought of another reason Neil might have wanted to see me.

"To use me?" I asked, giving the term he'd always used for our relationship. His golden eyes moved immediately to me, and I braced myself for one of his stinging retorts.

"To be with you," he said softly and quite unexpectedly before speeding up to get away from me. He didn't want me to know his motivations; he didn't want me to see what he was thinking in that moment. But this time, I was determined not to give up so easily. In spite of the sidewalk conditions, I walked faster, trying to keep up with his long strides.

"Explain," I told him between pants. Neil was walking too fast with no consideration for me.

"There's nothing to explain," he snapped, and I snorted.

Why did it have to be so hard to talk to Neil?

"No, you owe me an explanation." I managed to get to his arm and grabbed his sleeve to stop him. My fingers dug into the leather of his jacket, and Neil turned around. He looked at my hand, then at my face with the same dark expression. He didn't want me touching him, but I didn't care just then.

"Do you know what I've been through because of you?" I burst out. I could feel anger rising up from the depths of my heart like a river overflowing its banks, and the idea of avoiding a fight with him melted away. "I had a relationship that basically imploded. I got beaten up by Jennifer. I was mocked by the Krew while you had some random woman blow you right in front of me. I almost degraded myself by having a three-way with you and Jennifer on Halloween even though you knew full well how much I hated

349

her, and finally, my life was at risk because some masked psycho who is after you ran me off the road!" I shouted as he stared at me in disbelief.

His brows drew together, and he yanked his arm out of my grasp, leaning forward until he was an inch from my nose.

"Player?" he whispered in a voice I barely recognized. I hadn't actually been planning to tell him the truth like this, and I immediately regretted it, but now that I'd said it, I couldn't take it back.

"Yeah, it was him," I confirmed, looking down. I could feel his sharpened gaze and heard how labored his breathing had gotten.

"And when the fuck were you going to tell me that?" He seized my chin and forced me to look at him. My eyes glittered with tears, and my lips trembled. I didn't want to cry, but my emotions always got the best of me.

Neil must have seen it because his eyes changed, turning from sinister to warm. He slackened his hold and sighed. Then with a shake of his head, he drew me unexpectedly against him. He held me tight against his chest, and for a moment, I was dumbstruck. His scent surrounded me, as did the warmth of his very ordinary yet—coming from him—extremely intimate gesture.

"Do you see now why I don't want you in my life?" he muttered into my hair, and I tilted my head back to look at him. I didn't even have time to answer before Neil was kissing my forehead, right on my scar, and then moving down to the tip of my nose. Finally, he cupped my face in his hands and rubbed my cheeks with his thumbs while I stared spellbound at him.

"And you see that you can't fight what you feel for someone? I know how it feels," I whispered. It was the truth—I had the same feelings he did, and I knew how powerful, how irrational, and how irresistible they were. They were a force of instinct, not intellect, a blind, intense force that drew us together and wouldn't let us stay apart. It was as though our bodies had chosen each other even before we did.

"And what do you feel?" he asked with a hint of mockery in his tone.

"So much. You feel like the object of your affection is always first in your thoughts, like you would do anything for him, and that brings out both the worst and best in you. You think he's out of your league, and he scares you so much because he makes you feel things so intensely it's like being sick,"

I answered, snaking my arms around his waist as he cradled my face in his huge palms. He looked intently at me, as if considering what I'd just said, then gave me a chaste kiss on the lips, too fleeting for real pleasure, and smiled.

"You on this shit again, Tinkerbell? You know I can't stand it when you get mushy," he chided me sarcastically and walked around me, passing a hand through his thick hair. I stayed there, puzzled. Neil didn't seem to understand how sincere my feelings were and apparently thought I was blowing hot air.

"You've confused sexual chemistry with something that doesn't exist, Selene. I'm never going to stop telling you that." He continued walking, putting more distance between us. Again.

"Are you kidding me? If I was merely attracted to you, I never would have tolerated all the unacceptable things you've done and…" I trailed off when Neil turned to face me, glowering, his gaze now shadowed with menace.

"And if I didn't have this body, this face, my skills in the sack, would you be having those same fantastical emotions?" he sneered at me, gesturing to himself with a smug grin.

"Of course," I answered firmly—he didn't even need to ask, but he stepped back from me and shook his head.

"Such a liar," he said, and there it was. He really didn't believe me.

He turned his back on me and kept walking. And it occurred to me that the sensible explanation for his attitude had a name: Kimberly. She was the one who had twisted Neil's mind, implanting lies in a child's head that lingered even when he was grown. She was the one who had made him believe that all women were the same and, just like her, only wanted to use him. She was the reason he was so convinced that I was lying to him.

"Wait," I said, trying and failing to catch up with him. "Neil. Slow down," I pleaded, but he wasn't listening, so I broke into a light jog until I pulled even with him. "Please stop!" I said, my hand grazing his arm, and he rounded on me, terrified. Inexplicably, he appeared to be genuinely frightened of me, and not because of what I'd just said. He was looking at me like I was some enormous monster ready to annihilate him, so I hunted for a way to calm him down. I needed something normal to talk about.

"Have you ever had a Coney dog?" I asked him, apropos of nothing. I felt truly insane for asking such a dumb question. Neil's face scrunched in confusion, and he cocked his head to one side, giving me a look that was both thoughtful and bewildered. Even like that, he was beautiful, and that realization almost made me smile. Then, I chewed my lip awkwardly as I waited for his reaction. As his eyes slowly returned to the familiar color I loved so much, I breathed a sigh of relief.

"What?" he asked, surprised, so I cleared my throat and rephrased my suggestion.

"I'm hungry, so let's get to the diner." There, now that was a much more comprehensible offer.

"A... A...Coney dog?" he repeated while my eyes lingered on his full lips, which I had decided ought to be illegal. I somehow managed to pull myself away and focus on his question.

"Yeah. It's like a hot dog with meat sauce, and they put mustard and onions on top—"

"I know what a fucking Coney dog is!" he burst out, and I flinched at his aggressive tone. I felt suddenly ashamed, and several seconds passed in which neither of us said anything. I tried not to cry while Neil put one hand on his hip and palmed his face with the other. When the silence got too unbearable, I erupted.

"I am trying to get along with you! I am trying to talk to you, to understand you, to reassure you; I'm doing everything I can, for God's sake! But you are unmanageable!" I continued, having reached the limits of my tolerance. Neil watched me, dumbfounded, before heaving a sigh and ruffling up his hair.

"Okay, okay, calm down," he murmured in surrender. "I have a shitty temper; I do realize that," he admitted with his typical ease.

"I'm hungry, so I'm going to get something to eat. You can follow me, or you can go back to New York right now. You choose." I gave him my ultimatum and pushed past him with a shoulder check that didn't move him an inch. Still, I continued to strut briskly away.

Enough.

"Where are you going?" he called out behind me, but I didn't turn around.

"Away from you!" I answered, waving my hand in the air.

We were having a pretty heated argument right there on the sidewalk in the middle of my neighborhood, but I couldn't care about that.

"Selene!" he called, and I heard his footsteps behind me. I ignored him.

"Tinkerbell," he tried again, like that nickname was going to get me to turn around. Another flop. "Babygirl," he pressed, and I raised my middle finger at him.

"Now that I really consider it, it's not so bad being behind you. At least this way I get a nice perspective on your ass," he said, probably just to needle me, but I continued to walk forward determinedly.

"How good a look can you possibly be getting? I'm wearing a coat, genius," I spit back, aware that he couldn't have seen anything at all and that he was just trying to mess with me.

"I know your entire body by heart. How many times have I had you on all fours?" he said with a self-satisfied chuckle, and I stopped mid-step and looked around hastily, fearful that someone had heard him.

"Are you nuts?" I leveled a furious stare at him and adjusted my purse against my shoulder.

"You're taking advantage of my patient nature here, Babygirl. I don't chase after people, you know," he answered, suddenly dead serious. The corner of my mouth quirked, and I narrowed my eyes.

"Apparently you do because you're chasing me right now, aren't you?" I asked sarcastically, and he cocked an eyebrow.

"Only because I want you to get back home safely. I promised your mother, you know." He winked at me, and I felt the confidence drain out of me.

Did my mother seriously still plead with my dates to keep me safe?

But hold on a second…

How had Neil gotten past her thick armor in such a short time, anyway?

"Stop wondering why your mother trusts me. I'll never tell," he said, and my eyes went wide with surprise. Sometimes Neil's ability to understand me actually scared me.

"I can't deal with you anymore!" I continued walking.

For the first time, I missed us having sex without talking about anything.

Absurd when, just a few minutes ago, the idea of only being "used" by Neil had genuinely upset me. Then, I was struck by a detail I had previously overlooked. Recently, Neil had been demonstrating a certain sexual restraint. On several occasions, he'd touched me without ever trying to cut to the chase. Each time, it felt like something was keeping him from letting go. Even in the pool house, when we had engaged in a kind of foreplay I had never even imagined doing with a man, he had stopped before he reached orgasm. The question was, why?

Lost in my thoughts, I failed to navigate around a pool of slush on the sidewalk. I slid across the icy concrete, and the heel of my boot snapped, making my ankle twist slightly.

"Nothing's going right today," I grunted in exasperation as Neil caught up with me. He looked at the shoe I would probably have to throw away and barely managed not to laugh at me. I fumed at him.

"Well, Cinderella, now that your slipper's broken, where do you think you're going?" he mocked me, but I refused to lose heart. On the contrary, I limped my way past him again. Maybe fate was against me, but like a true fighter, I wasn't going to let anything keep me down.

"Come on, stop. You can't walk like that," came Neil's voice from behind me, and moments later, he grabbed my wrist firmly enough to make me turn toward him. I was about to tell him to let me go when Neil moved to stand in front of me with his back facing my way and crouched down.

"I don't know how long I'm going to be here, but I want you with me the whole time," he admitted. "So get on." He turned his face back slightly and pointed at his strong back, tucked under his tight leather jacket.

What?

"So I'm supposed to just mount you?" I leaned my head to one side and blinked several times.

"Yeah. I'd prefer to be the one doing the mounting, but I'll settle for this," he answered slyly. I should have been expecting that.

"Why do you always have to be such a perv?" I muttered, wrapping my arms around his neck. My fingers brushed against his hard pecs, and just then, his hands slipped down to the backs of my thighs so he could hitch me up. My coat briefly presented an obstacle, but he reached under it, and finally Neil straightened up like I was no heavier than a feather. On instinct, I hugged his hips with my knees.

"You don't mind my perverseness in bed," he shot back wryly. "Hold on to me," he added immediately, and I obeyed him. I also rested my cheek against his ear and let myself get drunk on his scent.

"People who see us are going to think we're crazy," I noted apprehensively as he walked on confidently, making me flinch a little with each step.

"So? How many times have I told you? Fuck what other people think," he answered, and I huffed. Often, his replies left me at a loss for words, but instead of trying to think of something to say back, I just clung more tightly to him and enjoyed the warmth of his body. I could feel my heart throbbing in my belly.

"Keep going straight; I'm taking you to the best Coneys in Detroit," I said, and he shot me a furtive glance over his shoulder. I studied his finely-drawn profile, his upturned eyes, and the long brown lashes from under which two beams of sunlight watched me.

Neil was indeed perfection, but I was moved not just by the handsomeness of his face; I was also drawn to his innumerable expressions. I didn't just appreciate his physical appearance, but also how he carried himself. He had charisma; his every move was masculine, dominating, and damned.

I never would have forgotten Neil; it would have been impossible. That was why I so often got afraid of what I felt for him.

"Is it far?" he asked, following my directions.

"Keep walking down this street and don't be impatient," I chided.

"So the best Coneys in Detroit come from a tiny local place? Do I have that right?" he asked in a superior tone.

"Yup, you can forgo your beloved pistachios for once," I answered drily. "Besides, I like simple stuff," I added, and I felt his guttural laughter.

"I've known that for a while, Babygirl." He gave me an unreadable look, and we kept walking until we reached the corner.

"Is this it?" Neil smiled as he brought us to the door of the quaint restaurant.

"Yup," I confirmed.

We went inside, ignoring the curious glances from the other customers who had turned around to look at us. Neil was still carrying me piggyback until he set me down at a small table for two in the corner. "Trust me— you are about to taste the best Coney dogs in Detroit," I promised him enthusiastically.

"You just can't suppress your craving for wieners, can you, Tinkerbell? If you're in need of a big one, you know who to ask, right?" he answered cheekily, making himself comfortable in the chair across from me.

"This sudden sense of humor you've developed is annoying," I informed him.

"You like it better when I'm sullen?" He turned in profile, and I stared at his full lips, curved into a sensual smile. I liked him all the time, even when he was being a dick, but I wasn't about to tell him that.

"What about when I'm passionate or bossy?" he added provocatively, and fire erupted in my chest. My heartbeat throbbed in the bottom of my stomach, and my cheeks flushed.

"Knock it off." I cleared my throat, and fortunately Neil just chuckled, fully aware of the reaction he was producing in me.

Then we perused the giant menu; I looked for my beloved sriracha Coney with kimchi relish, and Neil cocked his head strangely.

"Let me order," I said and raised my arm as Billy, a fortysomething with a full beard and a ponytail as long as my hair, came over to take our order. "Hey, Billy!" I smiled when I caught his eye. He frowned slightly, looking first at me and then at Neil, who was still carrying me on his back.

"Selene, honey. Nice to see you!" Billy smiled back.

"Two spicy Coney with mustard," I ordered, and Billy wrote it down.

"Two Coney coming up for you and your boyfriend. Hey, what happened to Jared?" he asked curiously, not realizing he was touching a sore spot.

"Hey, Willy, can we get a fucking move on?" Neil cut in with his usual lack of tact. Billy gave him a hard look, then turned back to the kitchen.

"What's your deal? You could have been a bit more polite to Billy," I admonished him. Neil didn't say anything. He just lifted one ankle to balance on the opposite knee and leaned back in his chair.

"Did you take me to a place you used to go to with Jareth?" he asked a few moments later, pointing his golden eyes right at me. What was I supposed

356

to tell him? I considered lying for a moment, but in the end, I opted to tell the truth.

"Yes, I came here a few times with him," I admitted, and he shook his head with a derisive smile. He didn't say anything else.

"Are you planning to go back to school?" he asked abruptly. Changing the subject on a dime was another one of his special skills.

"Yeah. I'm trying to rearrange my schedule to get all my required courses in. Fortunately, Ivan's in my major, and he's been helpful," I answered, deciding to continue on this topic he had brought up.

"Who is this Ivan?" he asked softly.

"Janel's twin brother. She's a good friend of mine," I answered with a nonchalant shrug, but I noticed the stormy way he was looking at me.

"And? Who is he? Your classmate? Your friend?"

Why did he want to know all this detail about Ivan? Did he think that Ivan and I were in a relationship or something? I had never imagined that Neil could be jealous over me. In fact, I'd occasionally tried to elicit a little reaction like that from him in the past, but there had been nothing.

"My friend, yeah. He's a basketball player. His body is insane, and he has these incredible green eyes," I said, laying it on a little thick just to tease him. Ivan wasn't as hot as Neil, but I wanted Neil to think he was.

"Is that right? So why not fuck him?" He looked right at me.

"I might just do that, you know," I answered scornfully.

"Take him to bed then, and confirm for yourself that there's no better lover out there than me," he said softly leaning toward me across the table. Was he trying yet again to push me into the arms of another man? He'd done the same thing the night we went out with Logan and Alyssa, putting on this whole show about some lucky guy who was going to take me home.

"But it makes no difference to you, right? You still have all your blonds at your disposal." I pretended to be perfectly calm, though the jealousy that I always felt cut me up inside worse than any knife.

"What do you want me to say?" he whispered roughly. "That the last person I fucked was you?" Yes, I would have liked to hear him say that I was the only one for him, that I was the only person who had taken pleasure in his body since we'd met, and that I was the only one he'd given his heart. I would have liked to hear that I was special and the right woman for him, but I knew that was never going to happen.

"Okay folks, here are your Coney dogs." Billy came over with a Coney in each hand, fortunately interrupting our ridiculous conversation.

"Thanks, Billy," I said, and he placed the food down in front of us.

"Enjoy your meal." Despite Mr. Disaster's rudeness, the older man smiled at us before turning to take the order at another table.

"Am I seriously supposed to eat this?" Neil examined the loaded dog in front of him with obvious distaste. Reluctantly, he took it, and after the first bite, he demolished it in less than five minutes.

"Just terrible, isn't it?" I said mockingly as he wiped his mouth with a paper napkin. I, on the other hand, enjoyed Billy's delicious creation in demure little bites.

"Let's just call it not bad." He shrugged and leaned back, watching my lips as I awkwardly chewed.

"You dating this Ivan dude?" His honey-colored eyes skewered me, and I gulped down a bite of Coney dog with difficulty.

"No. Not yet, at least," I said, not wanting to rule out the possibility that it might happen in the future. Neil's body tensed.

"So you like him," he observed, watching my mouth lasciviously.

"I didn't say that." I took another bite and turned my gaze away to avoid eye contact with him.

"Look at me," he demanded, and I could feel the desire in his voice, all mixed up with the anger he so often failed to control. Though I didn't quite understand why he was using that tone to speak to me, I obeyed on instinct. I quit eating and lowered the Coney dog to my plate.

"There's nothing between Ivan and me." I ran my tongue along the corner of my mouth to gather up a smear of mustard, and his eyes tracked the movements, turning into two luminous slits. Why was I explaining myself to him? More importantly, where did he get off thinking he could question me about who I was seeing?

"'Nothing' is how it always starts," he answered severely with a hint of suspicion.

"I'm not like you. I can't share my body with just anyone," I told him clearly because I couldn't bear having him think that kind of thing about me. I would only ever be with another man if I fell in love with him, and for the time being, my heart beat exclusively for this walking disaster from New York.

"That's why you could never be with someone like me," he said in a troubled murmur.

I finished my Coney dog, Neil stood up, and said, "Let's go." I stood up as well, lifting up my damaged boot so the broken heel could dangle. Neil walked over and crouched in front of me again.

"Take advantage of my kind mood today, Tinkerbell," he said wryly, and I again clutched his powerful body as he carried me over to the diner's cash register to pay for our meal.

"You two get out of here; it's on the house!" Billy said from behind the register, and Neil gave me a blank look.

"Are you sure?" I asked Billy, who just smiled in response and stretched out a hand with two plastic-wrapped fortune cookies inside.

"Of course. Take these too." He paused and then turned to me before adding, "I hope they bring plenty of good fortune, Selene." He handed the fortune cookies to Neil, who grabbed them with typical indifference. I thanked Billy for everything, and we headed out into the night.

"Let me down over there," I said softly to Neil, pointing to a large tree on the corner. We reached my suggested spot a few moments later, and Neil lowered me to the ground. I watched him straighten back up to his full height, no expression on his beautiful face. It didn't seem remotely difficult for him to walk with me on his back. Neil really was incredibly strong.

"Why are we here?" he asked, glancing around. There was nothing but a single dim lamppost.

The freezing wind whipped against our bodies while his golden eyes put to shame any light from the stars that made it through the cloudy sky.

I'd always thought of Neil as mysterious and unknowable, distant and inscrutable, just like a sky full of stars.

"Why don't we open our cookies?" I gestured to them, still closed in the palm of his hand. He smiled slightly and opened his hand to show me.

"So immature. Do you seriously believe this crap?" He handed me one.

While ignoring him, I broke it in two and extracted the slip of paper from inside.

"You don't have to be a buzzkill all the time." I snorted as he drew closer to me.

"What does it say?" he asked, sounding bored.

"'May I be reborn in your eyes each time you look at me,'" I read aloud. I looked up, letting his golden gaze merge with mine like the sun's rays at dawn becoming one with the sea, taking the waves in hand and leading them into the most beautiful of dreams.

Neil was that too: every bit as intense as the sunrise over the sea.

"You should read yours too," I said, clearing my throat awkwardly. He blinked slowly, then broke his cookie apart with a loud snap, pulling out the paper inside.

"What does it say?" I leaned over his shoulder curiously and smelled him on the tiniest breath of air, barely ruffling my hair.

"'Kiss me like you love me,'" he read slowly, a confused frown on his face. "'Read aloud the request written on your fortune and address it to the person to your right,'" he continued reading, his head cocked to one side. He raised his eyebrows at me. "Why did you get an aphorism, and I got a demand?" he grumbled with an amused grimace.

"Because you're a hot mess and the cookie thought you needed a hand?" I joked, pulling a face. He approached me slowly, all at once growing serious again. I stopped breathing when his hands came to rest around my waist, applying gentle pressure until I was pulled into him.

"So, Tinkerbell…" he said in a sensual whisper while my eyes were fixed on him, spellbound. "Kiss me like you love me…" he added, sounding both amused and seductive. Then he waited to see what I would do.

Oh, God.

"I…don't… I mean…" I blinked dazedly, looking back and forth between his eyes and his lips, twisted into a lascivious grin.

"Kiss me like…" He drew closer still, lightly ghosting the tip of my nose with his and tilted his face. His disheveled hair tickled my forehead. "…you love me," he finished, under his breath.

So, with all the boldness I could muster, I grabbed him by the nape of his neck and yanked him closer to me. I kissed him and let my hands get lost in his hair. I let my lips brush his, slowly, delicately.

He felt soft and hot and—for just a moment—sweet and yearning. Then I gently caught his lower lip between my teeth, and he let out a groan of desire that sent a shiver down my spine.

"Something like that, you mean?" I pulled away slightly and rested my forehead against his. Neil licked his lips and looked at me thoughtfully.

"Did that feel like a kiss to you?" he asked, sounding unsatisfied and sliding one hand up my spine until it was firmly holding the nape of my neck. Without giving me a chance to say anything else, he fisted my hair and pressed his lips to mine urgently, demanding that I open and yield to his tongue.

And in that moment, everything exploded into color.

I felt the earth tremble.

I chased him like a high from some potent drug.

I felt him everywhere and thought no more.

My mind emptied, thoughts draining out only to be replaced with him.

He who was so beautiful and didn't even know it; he who was the most extreme need I'd ever felt; he who I wanted to clasp close to my heart to keep him from running away again.

It felt like an eclipse, our kiss suspended there in the penumbra created by sun and moon.

His hand clutched the back of my neck more tightly while the other one traveled down to my hip, his pelvis pressing involuntarily against my lower stomach.

Neil carved his desires into me, enveloped my soul in his skillful tongue, and stole my breath.

He gasped, and I gasped with him.

We moaned shamelessly in that shadowy spot under a moody sky that seemed to be enjoying the show just as much as we were, with hungry mouths and greedy tongues.

And hell and heaven alike ceased to exist.

Along with all our chaos, his past, my accident, and Player.

None of it existed.

It was just us, if there even was an us.

We were incomprehensible magic.

An unsolvable mystery.

An inexplicable chaos.

"Neil…" I couldn't breathe. Like always, I couldn't keep up with him. But he gave me no respite. He took possession of my lips and continued devouring me like he'd been waiting too long for this moment. His hand moved under my coat, up over my abdomen, and palmed one of my breasts roughly. I groaned, and his fingers tightened even more around my hair. He bit my lower lip and then ran his moist tongue along it.

The dominance in him brought the angel in me to her knees.

We kept going like that. We devoured each other's emotions and desires as though we had been starved.

Neither of us wanted to let go of the other. We paused briefly to catch our breaths and dove back in again.

He took me.

He touched me.

He intoxicated me.

He tasted me unceasingly.

He surrounded me, freeing me while at the same time making me a slave to his desires.

And we continued to make love to one another with our lips.

Our ragged breaths melting together, our hearts fluttering, and lips swollen and shining with the taste of us.

We moaned.

Wanted.

More and more.

So much more.

And I had no further thoughts when his tongue descended upon my neck, leaving me stunned while he moved back up to torment my lips like the demon he was.

Eyes closed, foreheads together, hands shaking, broken breaths.

And…

"What if I did?" I whispered, breathless, and turned completely upside down from his assault.

"What?" Neil opened his eyes and touched my cheek, looking more handsome than ever.

"What if I…" *loved you*, I wanted to say, but the sight of his blown pupils stopped the words on the very tip of my tongue. Neil stepped back from me, alarmed, as though I'd just transformed into a monster right in front of him.

Some of the stars seemed to drip from the sky, as though it were weeping while the rest just faded away, one by one.

My heart snapped in two like a fortune cookie, the fortune fluttering away. Neil always let his eyes do the talking, and I spoke that silent language. Right then, his stare told me everything I needed to know…

15

I knew I'd already contaminated her.

NEIL

What if I…"

Was she seriously about to confess herself to me?

Fortunately, Selene hadn't finished that sentence. The darkness of my pupils had immediately sucked in the crystalline ocean of her gaze. The same ocean where I'd seen myself reflected, lost and drowned, only to surface once again to return to my twisted world.

The only right place for me.

I was the one who was wrong.

I was the one who didn't even know what I actually wanted.

On one hand, I wanted to be alone; I didn't want to be tied to anyone. I couldn't give them anything, and I couldn't honestly expect anything in return. On the other hand, I couldn't get Selene out of my head. The feel of her skin drove me wild, as did her lips, her coconut smell, her legs, and all the lines of her body that God had combined to perfection when he'd made her. Her body was like a road I'd been down before, knowing every bend and curve by heart. But for fuck's sake, I couldn't become dependent on her. I didn't want to have a relationship with her because I would break all the rules just like I always did, and I'd break her heart in the process.

I had hurt her so many times, but it only would have been worse—more painful—if we were in a relationship where she was expecting respect, fidelity, care, and all the other bullshit that comes along with that. I wasn't the right guy for that. I wasn't the kind of car that could stay parked in one garage.

I was a race car, made for competition, for danger, for leaps into the unknown. I was a vehicle that was heading for a crash—to destroy or be destroyed. I was a free car heading straight toward a single goal: nothingness.

Did I want to drag her along with me? No, I would never have done that.

She deserved her happily ever after, the perfect story, and the bright future. She was a princess who needed to meet her Prince Charming. She deserved to build a family for herself with a loving husband at her side and some kids with her pure soul and ocean eyes.

Despite this, I knew I'd already contaminated her to some degree. I'd let her into my twisted world the night I took her virginity and again when I continued to fuck her and fuck her up completely until she ended up in the crosshairs of a maniac. Which was something she herself had confirmed earlier when she'd screamed at me that Player caused her accident.

If I had realized that Selene was falling in love with me, I would have stopped sooner. I would never have believed that stubborn, awkward, lovely little girl could give her heart to me, but destiny had seen fit to give me yet another problem.

I could still hardly fucking believe it. How had this happened?

Selene was looking for someone to lose her head over while I was looking for someone to help me find mine.

We were opposites, too different, two worlds too far apart.

Lost in my thoughts—which were mostly just chaos—I marched quickly back to her house while Tinkerbell followed behind me, limping on her broken heel. The urge to hop on the first plane out of the city and flee like a bank robber with a bag of loot was overpowering. Yet, I still wanted to at least try not to make the same mistake I always did—running away.

I didn't know what to do. Neither of us had said a word after our delirious kiss. A kiss that had reawakened my need to touch her, to make her scream, sweat, shake, and lie beneath me satiated, consumed by most potent pleasure.

I still had overworked muscles and an erection to hide due to the anorgasmia that I couldn't tell anyone about, least of all her.

As I walked, I tasted her sweetness on my lips, recalled the shy little moans that I'd heard from her, even when she tried to stifle them. Her desires bent to my will, like I was a king—a god—who had managed to worm my way inside her. I still could smell coconut; it got me higher than weed, drunker than whiskey, and more blissed out than any experienced whore ever could.

It was just coconut, yet I wanted to absorb the scent through my skin and let it enter my bloodstream where it would flow through me like a panacea, cleansing me of the poison, the memories, and that monster Kimberly's hands on me.

When we got to her front door, I sighed and turned to her but stared into the middle distance and kept completely silent. She was probably embarrassed or upset at my reaction, and I wanted to reach for her but resisted the urge.

"*What if I…*"

No. That wasn't how it was supposed to go. Selene was not supposed to love me.

"Are you staying or…" she said in a barely-there whisper, letting the words trail off. Her voice shook as she wrung her slim hands in an anxiety she couldn't help but show. She was avoiding looking me in the eye, probably because she knew I was pissed and that everything was going wrong.

Any other man in my position would have cheered and celebrated to learn that the one girl he thought was true perfection was essentially offering her heart to him. But not me. I did not cheer because I hated beautiful things. Fate was mocking me, giving me a taste of something beautiful then yanking it away again. I knew because it had happened to me too many times before. I wouldn't fall for it again.

I had lived a life of misery, so I could not appreciate this fairy with the crystalline eyes who'd been dropped into my path.

I belong somewhere else, in a world much different from hers.

"Well?" she managed, her gentle voice twisting around my neck like a rope. In that moment, everything about her irritated me: her pale face, her full mouth, and her very presence.

The fault was not hers, though; it was mine.

I was the one who was flawed, chaotic. The only thing I was certain about was that I had too many uncertainties.

"Shut up, Selene. Don't say a word," I snapped abruptly, dragging out the other part of me. The cruel part that I struggled to control and I myself despised.

It was the part that made me lose control, when the world before me looked like nothing so much as psychedelic art—clashing colors, silhouettes, and fluorescent outlines—like I was under the influence of some drug, but it was really just my own anger.

I was my own worst enemy.

I was breathing too fast. All it took was one word to spring the trap of madness in my head.

"I don't understand why you're so angry." Selene got the keys out of her bag with trembling hands and struggled to put them in the lock. Her first attempt failed, and the key ring fell to the floor. She picked it up and tried again.

"Stop quivering like a coward and open the door," I demanded irritably, and her eyes went wide with fear.

When she finally got the door opened, I followed her into a completely darkened house. Fortunately, her mother hadn't gotten back yet. Selene flicked on the light switch and then abruptly walked upstairs, not deigning to give me even a glance. So, like the pushy dick that I was, I followed her. I watched her ass as she climbed the stairs, longing to give it a slap.

I was a walking contradiction: I resented her but also wanted to fuck her. Goddammit.

"No one said you had to follow me," she scolded, peeling off her coat before she entered her room. I crossed the threshold and immediately appreciated the decor—it was classy and understated. Then I turned my eyes to Selene, who was focused on getting her boots off, revealing oddly colored socks beneath.

"We need to talk," I told her honestly, scrubbing a hand over my face. I was feeling nervy and restless, like I was about to explode. Something was going to burst out of me and wreck everything. I also knew that I was going to hurt her again. After all, it was what I did best.

I'd become so complicated that I myself didn't know the first fucking thing about me.

I felt this bitter tiredness inside me.

I felt dejected, defeated by life.

But mostly, I felt alone.

Like I had been since I was a child, when I would hide in my room to lick my wounds like a whipped dog, wandering confused through the empty streets of an inhumane world.

Like when I wiped away the tears that ran down my face. Like when I shut myself up in my shell, where I could protect myself from everyone. Where I felt safe and at no risk of being tied to anyone. I didn't trust anyone and I couldn't let myself get caught because that was how you died.

I put up my impenetrable wall to keep out the pain but also the love.

And that was what Selene really didn't want to understand.

"This isn't how it's supposed to go!" I raised my voice, making her gasp. Babygirl bit her lip and held her breath, unsure about what to do next—and even more unsure about how to confront me.

"I didn't want..." she started to say, but I cut her off. That was my thing, my signature move: I steamrolled over everyone, hearing no explanations.

"You didn't want what? What the fuck did you not want, Selene?" I snarled manically, and I noticed she was trembling. "You shouldn't have gotten mixed up with someone like me. That word you were about to say isn't something that should exist between you and me; you shouldn't even associate that word with me. What do you not get about this, huh?" I stabbed a finger at her, fully aware that I was overreacting and that she didn't deserve this kind of treatment, but traumatic memories had overwhelmed me at that point and pushed me over the edge.

I was in free fall, and now I was going to land, crushing the terrified girl in front of me.

"I didn't mean to say a damned thing! It was the spur of the moment, the whole situation. I didn't think it through," she said, clumsily coming to her own defense. And she was lying. I knew her very well by then, and she was an open book to me. I knew she was just trying to shield herself from me, to make up for the serious error she'd made.

"So you weren't about to tell me that you've fallen in love with me?" I asked with a sadistic smile. "Except you clearly would have said just that if I hadn't stopped you. And you're not the kind of person who'd say that to just anyone, Selene. You've got your own sickness, you know. Lovesickness. But I'm not your cure, and I am not your medicine!" I explained, my words knife-sharp as I cut carelessly into her heart. "I was not born for love, Selene. I make simple things complicated and complicated things impossible. That's just how I am. It is not my purpose in this life to love anyone. I don't even understand this fucking love thing. Am I making this clear to you or not?" I twisted the tip of my invisible knife deep in the wound I'd already inflicted, feeding off her pain.

There was so much anger in me that I had become a slave to it. I was so disillusioned with life that I'd grown numb.

I was the fruit of this cruel world. I didn't have a heart because it had been ripped out of me when I was just a kid.

I had nothing to give Selene, whom I both wanted and did not want—so passionately.

Sure, I didn't want a relationship with her, but I did want to throw her down on that bed and fuck her, to stop up her mouth with my tongue.

I was the king of chaos, or maybe chaos was the king of me. I didn't know anything anymore.

"It's very clear to me, but this is not my fault. And you are a lunatic! Up until half an hour ago, you were kissing me, and now you're yelling at me for no reason!" Her voice dropped lower with each word, and she pressed a hand over her eyes. She was crying but trying to hide it from me.

Selene couldn't understand me because she didn't know the truth about me. She didn't know what Kim told me—what she was always telling me. That she only used me because she loved me and that our relationship was the special kind of love that no one else would understand.

"But there is a reason!" I snapped at her. "I hate that word 'love.' I don't

369

want to hear it, especially not from you," I said. I knew that Selene wasn't like Kimberly; I knew that my Babygirl would never violate me like I had been violated in that sick relationship with my babysitter.

If only I had the guts to tell her everything.

"You are nuts!" Selene fought back, finally, staring at me with anger and disappointment. I felt relieved. Maybe if she yelled that I was a bastard who didn't deserve her—that I was fucked in the head—it would have made everything feel more right again.

"Yeah, that's right, I am." I sagged against her desk, defeated by my own admission and rubbed my forehead, which had begun to throb.

Selene sighed heavily, and her shoulders slumped. I looked at her, taking note of how her sweater adhered perfectly to her firm breasts, and I considered just shoving her back on the bed and making her submit to me. We could work this all out without ever "talking."

"You should stop being so afraid; stop running away from me and closing in on yourself. I might be the only person who—" Again, I refused to let her finish. Selene simply refused to face facts: I was too remote and too troubled to even think about making a life with any woman.

"Enough, goddammit!" I burst out, then put my head in my hands, an intense burst of pain in my head forcing my eyes shut.

Please stop, I thought. *Don't tell me that I need to open myself up to you. Don't tell me that you might be the one for me or that you could accept me the way I am because I might actually believe you. And then I'd end up believing in the other beautiful things too. You are a beautiful thing, Tinkerbell, much too beautiful. If I opened my heart to you and you decided to leave or someone took you away from me, I would break. If I don't want to crumble to dust, I need to not depend on anyone, least of all you. You can hurt me; you can break me, and I can't allow that.*

I can't let you consume me.

I'm already wounded. But if Kimberly was able to demolish me, you would be able to annihilate me.

And I can't let you do that.

Instead of revealing any of those thoughts to her, however, I kept silent.

"What do you plan to do now?" she asked, and I did not answer. "Was this evening we spent together worthless to you?" Another question I ignored. "Was that kiss meaningless?" Although she clearly hoped I'd answer, I said nothing. "Neil…"

I slowly rubbed my forehead with my thumb and forefinger, trying for a relief that did not come.

"I need to go." That was all I could give her.

"Again? You're going to run away again?" she asked, sounding both incredulous and resigned.

I looked up at her then and saw that her eyes were glittering and her lip quivering. I wanted nothing more than to kiss her and end all this heartache, but she kept talking. "Neil, you have to stop hurting me. Is that why you came here to see me? So you could hurt me again?"

No, that wasn't the reason I'd come. In fact, I had told Logan that I was never going to Detroit and had been firmly convinced it was the truth until my brother said, "If you let someone like Selene go, she won't come back to you so easily." And so I got on the first plane to Detroit to be with my Tinkerbell, which turned out to be an enormous fuck-up.

"You should have been expecting this," I answered cynically as she sat down on the bed, shoulders drawn in around her. Her hands sat limp on her thighs, and her auburn hair tumbled over her breasts. I shook my head, shaking off the idea of consoling her, and headed for the bedroom door. But then, sudden sobbing made me stop in my tracks.

How many times had I disrespected her? How many times had I let her down?

How long could she last, my fairy, before her wings snapped?

I turned around to see her curled up on the bed. I sighed and walked over to her, sitting down on the edge of the bed without bothering to ask for permission. She ignored me while I stared at her little nose with its upward curve. I liked to put a kiss right there now and again, especially when she wrinkled it up, making one of her faces.

"I don't want…" I cleared my throat and stroked her hair. "I don't want you to cry," I managed finally, but she just shook my hand off and wiped away a tear.

"Leave me alone," she whispered, staring out into nothingness.

Meanwhile, I examined her long hair, the color of bronze with reddish high-lights, falling all around her drawn face. Yes, God had really done a good job with her, and her beauty had been my downfall.

"Haven't you ever wondered what it would be like?" Her blue eyes penetrated mine as she sighed gently. Those ocean eyes were making love to me, but my golden ones were fucking her, giving her a clue about how much I wanted her. I touched her hip, and she flinched, tucking her knees in tighter against her chest.

"You should get some rest," I said, deflecting the question. Or trying to at least. She turned sulky.

"I asked you a question, and I want an answer." She sat up and brushed her bangs to one side, revealing her noticeable scar. Despite all the certainty she tried to demonstrate, she couldn't win against my arrogant disregard.

"What was the question?" I taunted her, and she flushed with anger. She leaned back against her headboard and stretched her legs out in front of her. Her lips pursed in an involuntary pout, and I stared hungrily at her. I could have bitten her all over.

"You're such a dick," she said sharply.

"Fairies aren't supposed to say bad words." I smirked, looking at her thighs. It was a tremendous effort not to simply tear those jeans off her.

"That's your problem—you think I'm some kind of magical being, some princess out of a fairy tale, but you're wrong. I'm not living in a castle in the air. I also have shitty things in my past; I've got a messed-up family, a father I don't get along with, and this guy who spits in my face and tells me I don't mean anything to him whenever I try to show him how much he means to me." She said it all in one bitter breath. Then she inhaled furiously and kept going. "If that's what being a princess means, then I have seriously misunderstood all those fairy tales!" She shook her head, disillusioned, and clenched her fists.

I couldn't understand why Selene didn't just spread those fairy wings and soar away from a no-good devil like me or why she kept impressing me, stunning me. When she was so strong and tenacious, intelligent and gentle, attractive and...

Fucking beautiful.

"I've thought many times about what it would be like."

We'd bounce off each other every moment of the day. I would be on you and in you every minute. You would be my angelic adversary, who I'd battle for all my days. I would bite your sharp tongue, kiss your little pout, stroke your sweet-smelling hair, and lick my way around your every curve. I would have you open countless fortune cookies in ordinary Detroit restaurants, and we would chase our fortunes together. I would ask you to kiss me like you loved me a thousand more times but never to say the words "I love you." Then, I would make you get on your knees before me and make you my soulmate. I'd push you away a million times and go get you back a million and one.

Yeah, I had the occasional thought about you and me together.

I looked gravely at her after confessing my partial truth and instinctively touched her cheek. I felt a shiver down my spine as my fingers made contact with the softness of her skin, and she sucked in a breath at the gesture. I stared into her blue eyes, still shiny with suffering, and at her dry lips and clenched teeth.

"Lie down," I whispered, and she obeyed. Then, still wearing her father's sweatpants and my leather jacket, I arranged myself beside her. On my side, touching her hair.

Selene lay before me, and she was staring so intensely at me that I felt naked.

"Will you tell me someday what makes you so angry?" she murmured, delighting in the feeling of my fingers gently gliding through her long hair.

"Sleep now," I answered, studying her rosy cheeks and eyelids puffy from crying. She sighed as I soaked up her coconut smell, trying to capture it in my lungs so I could take it back with me.

"So, will you stay tonight or—" she continued, fighting her exhaustion because she still wanted to talk to me.

"Shh…" I whispered before planting a kiss on her forehead.

Her eyes closed completely then, and after a few minutes, her breathing deepened. She was asleep. I stopped stroking her hair and carefully got off the bed, making sure not to let the springs squeak so she wouldn't wake up.

I trod silently to her desk and rummaged around in her pink pen holder that had a kitten pattern printed on it. I smiled at that childish detail and then wrote a note for her on a Post-it, scrawling the first thing that came to mind. I put the pen back where it went and stuck the meager little message on the top book in a nearby pile.

Then, I prepared myself to do what I did best—run away and leave her disappointed.

I opened the door, which did let out a slight creak, and I took one last brief look at her. The bedside lamp was still on, and soft light illuminated the shape of Selene stretched out on the bed, one hand in a fist beside her lips, the other by her side.

She was my Babygirl, and she would always be my Babygirl.

I crept out of the room, shutting the door behind me, and breathed a sigh of relief as I headed down the stairs and made it to the living room undisturbed.

"Are you leaving?"

I sucked in a breath when I heard Judith's calm, confident voice. I turned to look at her and saw that she was right behind me. She was still wearing her elegant clothes and high heels, suggesting she'd just gotten home.

"Yes. I'll wash the clothes you lent me and—" She shook her head and gestured for me to hold on a minute. She left and returned shortly thereafter with a paper bag in which she'd put my now-dry clothing and handed it politely to me.

"You can keep Matt's clothes. Here are your own."

"Thank you. For the clothes and the hospitality, but I really do have to go back now," I said, taking the bag with a forced smile. I'd sleep in an airport motel or, hell, in the airport if necessary, but I needed to get out of this house.

"Dark…" Judith answered, and I froze just as I'd started checking my jacket pocket for my Winstons. I hadn't had a smoke in too long because whenever I was with Selene, I forgot about nicotine.

She became my addiction instead.

"What?" I asked, furrowing my brow.

"Your name, it's an old, old name that has passed through a lot of cultures. It likely derives from the Gaelic *Niall*, which can mean, among other things, cloud. The Normans wrote it N-E-E-L, the same as the Old French word for *niello*, a pitch-black mixture of alloys used in metalworking. Niello came from the Latin *nigellus*, meaning darkness. And so, as far as those Latin scribes were concerned, that's what your name meant: darkness." She folded her arms over her chest and leaned against the wall with one shoulder while I looked at her in surprise, not expecting the etymology lesson.

"That sounds right," I murmured, putting my hand on the doorknob.

"You were born a Niall—a white cloud—and then some things happened and you became Neel, the darkness. But it's your choice whether you continue being that way or try to return to your original form." She held my gaze, studying me like I was a book of Greek mythology or a student struggling with a difficult test question.

I gave her a cheeky smile.

"Destiny's funny, huh? My name, like me, has undergone a transformation, Ms. Martin. But unfortunately, there's nothing I can do to become Niall again," I said drily before opening the door to feel the bitter night air on my face.

Dark was my name; dark was my nature.

Should I have thanked fate for making me into a thing of darkness? For giving me such a pitiful existence? For making me a slave to sex, a lover of vice, a willing victim to every carnal sin, and allergic to all sentiment?

Did I need to thank fate for dropping this angel with the ocean eyes right in front of me at the wrong time, in the wrong place, and in the wrong way?

Did I say thanks for the nightmares that tortured me constantly?

For a sick whore using me as a child?

For forcing me to flee the one beautiful thing that had ever happened to me because I knew that if I connected to Tinkerbell, I would lose myself?

My life was a game of chess.

And this had been one more point to the fairy and another blow to me, the devil defeated...

16

....

The more I demanded that Selene get out of my head,
the more firmly entrenched she became.

NEIL

I stood outside the library smoking, fully intending to go inside after one
last drag. I put my cigarette out in the ashtray.

I'd been back in New York for a week at that point. I hadn't heard from
Babygirl since then. Since I fled Detroit in the middle of the night, leaving
her with nothing but a crappy little note on her desk.

Even though some time had passed, our kiss was still engraved in my
mind.

Her tongue had tried to communicate with mine in a language I didn't
understand that night.

When Selene kissed me, she plunged into the deep parts of me, the ones
scarred by hatred, anger, and memories.

When she touched me, she tried to touch my soul. She tried to get under
my skin and embed herself into me. She wanted to plant flowers in the arid,
wasted, and frozen tundra of my heart. But that wouldn't be as easy as she
thought.

I immersed myself in my schoolwork to beat back the melancholy and
drive it out of my head. I'd had my last exams a couple of weeks ago, but I
was still on campus working on some independent projects.

"I knew I'd find you here. How's it going?" Logan rested a hand on my shoulder, making me flinch.

"What the fuck! You trying to give me a heart attack or what?" I burst out irritably, and he rolled his eyes at me.

"Come on, I'm on pins and needles here," he prompted, adjusting the shoulder strap of his messenger bag, which was packed with books.

"Passed." I shrugged indifferently, and he gave me a proud smile.

"And that's how you tell me? You're almost there—just one more exam result and then you'll graduate!" Logan shouted joyfully while I shifted to look, bored, at the students going in and out of the library.

"Yeah, it's not a big deal," I answered, annoyed. In reality, I had minimal hopes for my future, especially after I'd handed in a very important architecture project to Professor Robinson and gotten nothing more than a dismissive "I'll take a look at it" in response. I'd been working on it for more than a year, and it was the kind of thing that professors used to assess a student's fitness for grad school and how likely they were to actually go on to become an architect. Professor Robinson hadn't said a thing to me since I gave it to him, and whenever I saw him in the halls, he gave me nothing but the briefest greeting, so I was convinced he wasn't happy with it. Failing something like that was the kind of thing that could put my whole intended future in jeopardy, and with my nature and temperament, I would have a hard time finding some other passion.

"Neil." Logan moved in front of me, scrutinizing me closely. "Are you okay?" He cocked his head to one side for a better look, and I sighed.

"Yes, why wouldn't I be?" I held his stare with my icy one, trying to keep him from looking deeper because I knew that he could read me, and if I let him, I had no chance. A moment later, he took me by the arm and pulled me along with him into a more private corner.

"Bullshit," he blurted out angrily, his hand still tight on my bicep. "You're running from someone who could actually care about you and make you happy. Do you understand that? Selene scares you because you know everything would be different with her. She scares you because she's the only one you've ever really wanted," he told me, not for the first time, and I regretted telling him everything as soon as I got back from Detroit. I was so messed up; I'd told him all about our night out, the fortune cookies, the kiss, the *"What if I…,"* and our fight.

"Enough, Logan." I yanked myself sharply out of his grasp and straightened my leather jacket. "I'm not like you. Selene isn't like Alyssa. We don't have the kind of relationship built on love that you have with all the canoodling and kissing and shit. Get it through your head!" I rapped his temple with my index finger, and he flinched at my touch.

"I'm just saying, you have to stop running from the things you feel. The things you want," he insisted, trying to wear down my armor but to no avail. It had taken me years to build it up; I had been living with it my entire life, and it was a part of me by now.

"Logan, I don't want anybody. I don't want a fucking relationship. I'm never giving up my freedom. I'm not going to compromise myself for the same pussy that half the population has between their legs. Are you clear on that?" The words rushed out of me like a flooding river, a sandstorm, an earthquake whose epicenter was located right there in the small space between us.

"You don't have sex with anyone anymore. How do you explain that?" he threw back at me with a knowing expression that I didn't like at all.

"Because I have a problem. Did you forget? Dr. Lively told me not to have sex for the time being," I explained, lowering my voice. I had always been a private person and did not want any prying ears to overhear such sensitive information.

"So you've gone back to therapy then?" He cocked an eyebrow.

"No," I answered shortly.

"But you're taking his instructions, right?" he asked, and I looked at him, momentarily confused. "Why haven't you tried having sex with Selene? Are you afraid you'd orgasm with her?" he said insinuatingly, and I almost laughed in his face.

"Trust me, I did one of my favorite things with her, and it still didn't work." I gave him a wink and thought back on what had happened in the pool house when I'd climbed on top of her to thrust between her breasts.

Logan snorted. "Sex with her would be different and you know it. You'd feel emotionally involved, and that's why you're trying not to give in, isn't it?" He adopted a know-it-all expression, and I grew angry.

"I need to get back in. I have to finish up some stuff for my portfolio." It was a transparent excuse to end the conversation, and my brother shook his head, refusing to let me leave.

"Have some faith in Selene. If you're worried about her accepting you for who you are, it's already happened. How many times have you gone off the rails in front of her? How many times have you fucked up with her and she's let you right back in?" He paused for effect, but I refused to answer his questions. "Despite all that, she's never judged you," he added, looking into my eyes. For a second, I wondered if Logan had told her anything about my history, but I shook off the suspicion. My brother knew how reluctant I was to talk about that with anyone; he'd never do something like that behind my back.

"She'd be disgusted by me," I answered, my voice melancholy but filled with conviction. No woman would ever truly accept a man like me— someone with such profound wounds—by her side.

"No, she would understand you," Logan said confidently. But I just shook my head and walked back toward the library. I had no desire to continue that conversation; thinking about Babygirl upset me, and I didn't want my mood to be dependent upon her.

And yet, the more I demanded that Selene get out of my head, the more firmly entrenched she became. She was there every hour of the day, constantly making herself known. Sighing, I went back to my table and sat down in front of my book. I grabbed my pencil and began to chew on it, the way I always did when I was focused on something. All around me was peaceful silence, interrupted only by the occasional rustling of some pages. Someone cleared their throat to get my attention, and I looked up automatically. Standing before me was Professor Robinson in a nice suit, a pile of papers clutched to his chest.

"Neil—may I interrupt you?" he asked me politely.

"Hello." That was all I managed before I spotted the smile curving his thin lips.

"I've looked at your thesis project, and I need to tell you that, despite how long I've made you wait, your work has impressed me. It's excellent," he said approvingly. I could hardly believe it. I furrowed my brow and glanced around, noticing two girls at the next table giving me curious looks. I was

Neil Miller, after all. I ran with the Krew and was well known for reasons that had little to do with academic excellence. I stood up abruptly, towering over my professor, and shut my book with a snap.

"Would you like to discuss this somewhere quieter?" he guessed, probably assuming I didn't want to disturb the other students. In reality, I just didn't want them knowing I loved architecture and that I had one of the highest GPAs in the entire major.

"Yeah, let's get out of here," I said, and he gave me a cautious look, but I didn't care. I grabbed the book with one hand and slipped the pencil into my jacket pocket, and then we exited the library.

"So..." Professor Robinson began as we strolled down the campus walkways, occasionally pausing to greet a student. I stayed by his side, eager to hear what he had to say. "As you probably know, Neil, I've always thought you were one of my most promising students, but I was waiting to evaluate your final project to really be sure." He smiled and continued walking along slowly. I slowed to match his pace.

"I'm glad," I managed finally, because this dick had completely ignored me for weeks, making me think that my project had been a total disaster, when in fact...

"I want to make you an offer." He stopped abruptly, and I did the same.

"What is this about?" I asked him, looking him in the eye. Professor Robinson paused a moment before answering.

"I've selected two local architecture students—the two most deserving students—to put forth for an architectural internship in Chicago. You're one of them." I stayed silent while he finished. "It's a highly valuable experience. The duration varies, but the main purpose is to help you learn all the skills a good architect needs. You and the other selected student will be able to make connections with a working microcosm of an architectural studio. You'll get to see everything that goes into the design process. You'll meet people who share your passion and live for free in a shared apartment provided by the program. Travel fees are also covered; all you have to do is pack your bags and chase your dreams," he finished, and I was so shaken up—not to mention shocked—by his offer that I hadn't even noticed when we'd been joined by a third person.

"Professor Robinson, hi." Megan's whiskey voice cut into our conversation. She stopped right next to us, and I gave her a quick look up and down. She was wearing a tight shirt that showed off her ample breasts to perfection and a pair of curve-hugging jeans. Her black hair was up in a high ponytail, and her green eyes seemed brighter than I remembered.

When she walked briefly in front of me, I glanced at her ass, and, catching me, she gave me a self-satisfied grin.

"Megan, I'm glad to see you. I was just talking to Neil about the Chicago internship," he informed her before turning back to me. "Megan is the other program participant. She's a star in the architectural program at Sarah Lawrence and worked as a research assistant for me last summer. All I need now is your answer," he said, sounding excited. My mood shifted abruptly, and in an instant, I decided that it was going to be a hard no.

"Oh great! Don't worry, professor. I'll get Miller on board," she said with an impish look on her face.

"There's no way I'm going to Chicago with you," I snapped, unconcerned with the professor's presence.

"What's the matter, Miller? Afraid to share an apartment with a girl?" Megan taunted, one corner of her mouth curving up into a sarcastic smile, which only infuriated me.

"I like women under me or on top of me, not just generally around. Especially when it's some head case," I said, giving her an insolent wink. Professor Robinson just stared awkwardly at us.

"Um, I don't think this sort of personal information is relevant to the internship I was talking about." He adjusted his glasses with his index finger and continued to watch us, looking bewildered.

"You're right, Professor Robinson. Miller has a little trouble controlling his impulses; you'll have to forgive him." Megan smirked faintly, and I raised an eyebrow, staring hard at her.

"I'd advise the two of you to work out your differences because, should Neil also accept my offer, you will be spending a lot of time together. I would highly recommend you figure this out because your futures are at stake," the professor said, smiling. Then, after saying his goodbyes and recommending yet again that I think about the Chicago offer, he headed off for an upcoming appointment and left the two of us alone.

Immediately, I grabbed Megan by the arm and dragged her somewhere quieter before she had the chance to vanish on me.

"What the fuck were you thinking, huh?" I demanded, inches from her face. But she didn't flinch and just stared levelly back at me.

"I just like to screw with you," she explained.

"Is that so?" I sneered at her. "Well, learn to address me respectfully from now on," I ordered, scowling at her. Unlike Megan, who was looking at me with a barely concealed smile, I was not joking.

"I don't like men who get overbearing with me," she answered.

"I don't like women who keep making the same mistakes over and over," I warned her. Her eyes, with their slim bronze streaks, dug insistently into mine. I released her because I couldn't stand the way she looked at me, the confidence she showed off, and most of all, the way she didn't fear me at all.

It occurred to me that I'd met so many women in my life, and all of them had expressed some degree of fear about me. All of them except Megan.

"You should actually think about the Chicago internship, Miller, and don't drag your feet." She stepped back.

"I'll never share an apartment with you. I can't stand you," I said, looking at her full lips. Specifically, I looked at the dark mole that punctuated her Cupid's bow and gave her a little extra sensual charm. I moved my gaze upward to her eyes.

All at once, I remembered one of the first times I met her.

She was a shy little girl then with the weird habit of always wearing this white ribbon in her long black hair.

I had liked the contrast…

We sat in the garden outside my house in the shade of a tree that protected us from the sun's burning rays. She was wearing a knee-length, dusty pink dress with a scoop neck and a pink ribbon around the waist. It made her look like one of those pretty porcelain dolls my mother liked to collect.

Kimberly had brought Megan to me, like she'd been doing for several afternoons at that point, because she wanted to prepare us for a game we were going to play soon. She said we were going to be the stars of a movie. I was going to play Peter Pan, and Megan would be Wendy. She also said we were going to wear costumes, but something in her eyes didn't feel right when she talked about it.

"So, hello is hola?" I asked, wrinkling my forehead in concentration. I didn't know any Spanish. At my age, I was doing well to speak my own language.

"Yes, hola." Megan pushed a strand of hair away from her face, her full, defined lips curving upward.

"And little girl? How would you say that?" I asked curiously, tucking my knees up to my chest and holding them in my skinny arms.

"Niña," she answered, avoiding my gaze but giving me a gentle smile.

"So you're a...niña?" I cocked my head skeptically and ran a hand over the back of my head. I wasn't good with languages or with memorizing stuff.

"Neen-ya," she explained, sounding amused. Her laughter was youthful and innocent, but it stopped and was immediately replaced with a pained look.

"Ryan says I'm not a niña anymore, though." She pressed a hand to her lower stomach, and her legs tensed up as though his very name caused her this deep-down pain that started in her soul and branched out to every part of her body.

Every place where Ryan Von Doom ruthlessly exercised his power...

I had no idea how much time had passed or why my mind had dredged that little moment up from the depths of my memory.

"You used to like giving me Spanish lessons back in the day," I told her wryly, and after a moment of confusion, she understood what I was talking about.

"You just couldn't figure out how to say niña," she murmured in a gentle tone.

"I wasn't good at memorizing words." I shrugged, watching her. Though we were pretty far apart, I could smell her orange blossom smell mixed with cigarette smoke, and it irritated me.

"You were such a nice boy, and now you've become *maligno*," she tutted, and I raised my eyebrows at her.

"Life has made me what I am," I answered.

"You get to decide whether you're influenced by the past," she answered back firmly, and in that moment, I truly admired her tenacity and how she faced everything head-on. Megan had always been stronger than me. Maybe she'd managed to overcome what Ryan had done to her while I was still powerfully entangled with Kim.

"My babysitter was much better at teaching me words than you were. Do you think I can forget what she did just like that?" My low, harsh voice made her wince.

"And my music teacher taught me a whole lot more than just the guitar," she answered, talking about Ryan Von Doom, the piece of shit. Once upon a time, he and Kimberly worked together. She was a babysitter, which gave her access to children under ten, and he posed as a private music teacher giving guitar lessons. He was professional and precise; his work was impeccable. But only for little girls, each one chosen meticulously. The two of them were well organized and calculated everything down to the smallest detail, and they deliberately targeted the wealthiest families. They were able to gain the parents' trust in no time, and then they could do whatever they wanted, undisturbed.

"I… I've got to go," I said in a confused mutter because going backward in my mind like that untethered me from reality. Sometimes it even made me nauseous. So if I didn't want to vomit right there in the middle of campus, I needed to stop our conversation immediately.

"See you around, Head Case," I told her before spinning around and getting as far away from her as possible.

....

I got home about an hour later.

I had twenty missed calls from Jennifer, but I hadn't returned any of them because I didn't want to hang out with the Krew. My mind was still stuck on the interaction I had with Megan; either way, I had more important things to do, like going to see Dr. Lively.

I hurried to my room and stripped to get in the shower. When I was finished, I got out and wrapped a towel around my hips, walking barefoot through the room and dripping everywhere while I searched for clean boxers and a dark pair of jeans.

As I dressed, I noticed to my displeasure that one of my favorite hoodies was gone.

"Where the fuck did she put it?" I grumbled to myself. I was about to call for Anna and complain because she knew perfectly well that she was supposed to just leave my clean stuff folded on the bed and then...

"Chloe," I realized, barreling through the open door of her room in full tank mode.

"Neil! Do you even know how to knock?" My sister bleated in irritation as soon as she spotted me. She was lying on the bed and, alarmed, pulled out her earbuds. I scrutinized her and saw that she was wearing a pair of black leggings and, naturally, my blue sweatshirt.

"And do you know how to ask permission before you touch my stuff?" I put my hands on my hips and tried to adopt a stern posture. Chloe's gray eyes moved from my naked torso to my tight jeans, and she cocked an eyebrow at me.

"It's January, Neil. Shirtless season is over," she noted sarcastically and shook her head, making her blond ponytail swing from one shoulder to the other. Then she put her earbuds back in and went back to ignoring me.

"I'm shirtless because you stole my fucking sweatshirt!" I shouted, yanking the earbuds out of her ears impetuously. My sister winced and puffed out her cheeks like an outraged child.

"You're so moody! You have a giant wardrobe, and you're getting on my ass about one damn sweatshirt?" she said defensively, jumping off the bed. She faced me boldly, poking an index finger into my chest. It was nothing new for us: Chloe and I argued frequently. Usually because she would sneak into my room and steal my things without asking.

"That's the one I want! It's my favorite!" I groused again, and then, with a taunting smile, I tucked her earbuds into my back pocket.

"Neil..." she wheedled, stepping closer. "You know I love you. Let's not fight." She hugged me. I knew exactly what she was doing. She was trying to sweet-talk me. I was weak against our sibling bond, and both Chloe and Logan knew it.

"Would you please let me keep your sweatshirt? On an unrelated note— you look great; those muscles are popping. Have you changed your workout? Because you look crazy ripped, for real!" Chloe gave me a sneaky smile and batted her eyelashes as she balanced the point of her chin on my chest, still hugging me.

"Don't pander to me; it won't work. I have your earbuds, and you're not going to get them back until—" I trailed off when Chloe stepped back from our embrace, the exact same earbuds cupped in one hand.

What the fuck?

She'd weaseled them out of my pocket after distracting me with a hug.

"What an asshole," I chuckled, shaking my head. She laughed triumphantly and sat back down on the bed.

"I learned from the master." She gave a superior shrug, but I immediately stopped paying attention to her when I noticed what looked like a party invitation tossed haphazardly next to her.

I frowned and, in a catlike leap, grabbed it out from under her.

"Neil!" She hopped off the bed and tried to grab the paper from me, but I raised it up high to read it.

"A masquerade party." My rigid, stern voice was enough to quell her as I brushed aside all her attempts to get the invitation back. Chloe shook the hair out of her face and gave me a nervous look.

"I can explain..." she backpedaled with a gulp.

"What's to explain? You're not going!" I crushed the paper in one hand and tossed it to the ground, giving her a hard stare. She wasn't going to a college party, one where drugs were floating around everywhere and there were veritable rivers of alcohol. It was completely inappropriate for a young girl like her.

"Correct," she confirmed, making me frown.

What?

"I'm not going to go," she explained, letting herself flop down on the bed. "Madison was here, and she left the invitation, but I've already said I'm not going." She sighed and fiddled with the hem of the sweatshirt like she was trying to vent some of the tension she felt.

"You sure?" I asked her, hoping she wasn't lying to me.

"Positive." She nodded and leaned back, putting her earbuds back in and effectively ending our conversation. I decided that, for once, I would just trust her. I wasn't even going to ask who'd given that invitation to Madison, even though Chloe surely knew.

I didn't want to ban my sister from having fun, but my caution was justified. I couldn't have her just walking around freely with some maniac on my tail. Player could attack anyone at any time, and I had to prevent any more harm from coming to my family.

My mind was stuffed full of worries as I went back to my room and pulled on a different hoodie before retrieving my car keys and heading downstairs, ready to go to Dr. Lively's office.

I hadn't actually made the decision to resume therapy, but I did feel the need to talk to my therapist and have him listen to me. Yes, I could expect that most of what I said would make it back to my mother, but he was still the one who had successfully communicated with my demons, the only one who understood my problems and maybe could even suggest a good solution.

But when I got to the clinic twenty minutes later…

"What do you mean he isn't here today?" I said again to Mrs. Kate, the dumpy woman who sat behind the desk in the waiting room. She peered at me over her round glasses and sighed.

"It means you will need to come back another day. Or possibly make an appointment for once," she said impatiently. I headed for the exit, letting out a stream of profanities under my breath.

It had taken me so long to get up the nerve to go there, and just as I finally managed it, my own terrible luck got in my way. I probably wasn't going to go back. The urge to have a conversation with my therapist probably wouldn't reappear so readily…

"Neil."

I halted when someone called out to me. I frowned and noticed Dr. Keller in one of his typical suits, staring at me in a curious, focused manner.

"Good to see you, son. How are you doing?" He smiled, and I cocked an eyebrow in my typical sardonic fashion.

What the hell did he want now? I hadn't talked to him since the time I ran into him at the bar.

"Hi," I said simply, tucking my hands into my jacket pockets.

"Were you hoping to see Krug? He had an event today so he had to postpone his appointments and—"

I didn't let him finish. "No, I was just passing through. I thought I'd talk to him really quick, but don't worry about it. It wasn't important." I shrugged, and he took another step toward me.

"Would you like to go for a walk in the garden with me?" He offered abruptly, and I regarded him skeptically. Why was this guy always trying to get in my business? We barely knew each other, and yet every time we met, he tried to have a conversation with me. He wasn't my therapist, though, and I was reluctant to trust him with anything.

"I've got things to do," I answered bluntly, and he walked around me, heading for the door.

"Great. Let's get going then," he said, like I'd accepted his invitation.

What, did he want to screw with my head the way he usually did in his office?

Still, I followed him outside, curious to see what he was thinking. As soon as I stepped outside, cold air caressed my face. I spotted Dr. Keller not far away and walked over to him, trampling the ornamental plants along the enormous avenue that ran through the garden outside the clinic.

The shrink stood perfectly still, facing an impressive fountain that I'd seen every time I came to the clinic but hadn't really dwelled on. This time, however, I examined it more carefully. I looked at the dolphin in the middle of the water feature, made from cement mixed with marble dust. It perched proudly, as free as the real thing, with a pearl caught in its mouth. Just looking at it, my lips curled into a faint but genuine smile.

Then I focused on the drops of water, disrupting the pool below. They shimmered in the sun like countless blue crystals, just like Babygirl's eyes. All of a sudden, I imagined some invisible hand crafting a surreal painting, tracing the outlines of Selene's pale face and waves of auburn hair against the background of a cloudless blue sky.

Something as inexplicable as she was. Something as immense.

A work of art.

That's what Selene was, but I would never say it.

"Do you know the legend of the dolphin and the pearl?" Dr. Keller noted my presence and spoke again, not looking at me.

"Again with this shit, Dr. Keller?" I burst out before lighting a cigarette and sucking in as much of the smoke as my lungs would allow.

"Call me John," he responded quietly while I continued to smoke, looking indifferent.

"Okay, John. Let me be clear: I don't want to listen to your shit," I retorted, just to irritate the little doctor who seemed to have such enviable self-control.

"In myths and legends from around the world, the dolphin is a friend to man, a symbol of good against occult or evil powers," Keller began, completely ignoring what I'd said. "They represent the link between the earthly world and that of the spirit. They embody the cycle of life, death, and rebirth."

"Why do you have this stupid fucking habit of talking even when I don't want to listen?" I asked him, truly annoyed as I sucked the smoke from my Winston, but John just gave me a sideways look and continued staring at the dolphin, ignoring my attitude.

"I love this fountain because the dolphin symbolizes inner strength, the search for one's destiny, and freedom, which is a value innate to all humans." He just kept going, and I rolled my eyes, becoming resigned to the knowledge that he was going to talk regardless of my total lack of interest.

"The pearl he carries in his mouth symbolizes purification from evil. There's an ancient legend that says when a dolphin finds a pearl and swims away, clutching it like that, it means good luck. It means he had found the right path. He has a lodestar to follow so he will no longer get lost in the vastness of the ocean," he explained, a soft smile on his lined face.

"Listen, John, I think you have a real problem here. You are fixated on folktales, pearls, the ocean, and all this other bullshit..." I let out a plume of smoke and walked over to the ashtray to put out my cigarette. "Also, you need to get off my back." There, I'd made myself perfectly clear. Now the doctor would have to get the message and leave me alone.

"You know, Neil, you're a nice guy deep down," he answered instead, and I gave him a surprised look because I had expected him to tell me to piss off or to complain about how rude and annoying I was.

"Me? Nice?" I repeated with a frown.

Why did it always feel like he was fucking with me?

"That's right. Despite how you refuse to show people anything but your rough edges, I think you're a good young man," he said, taking a seat on a nearby wooden bench. He sat elegantly, one leg crossed over the other, and looked carefully at me. I remained standing, looking down at him from above. "Have you found a girlfriend who can appreciate this tremendous goodness of yours, Neil?" he asked, apropos of nothing, and I almost burst out laughing.

"Why the fuck are you asking?" I raised both eyebrows because I had no idea where John was going with that, and I didn't appreciate him trying to pry into my personal life.

"I'm just curious. You're young and good-looking; you must have some fair maiden chasing after you, no?" He smiled, and I gave him a flat look. *Fair maiden?* What the hell was he talking about?

"I'm not involved with anyone, if that's what you're trying to ask," I told him, irritated.

"So that glass cube with the pearl inside, the one I gave to you a while ago, it didn't bring you any luck?" he asked unhappily.

"Sure it did. The girl I gave it to got into a near-fatal car crash the same day," I informed him. I didn't soften any of that information and watched it hit him like a flurry of blows.

"And why did you choose to give it to her, specifically?"

"She got in an accident. Did you hear that part?" I pointed out obnoxiously, and he looked at me like I was the one who didn't understand what he was saying.

"You said 'near' fatal. I take it she's fine now?" He folded his hands in his lap and tilted his head to one side, squinting one eye slightly against the sun.

"Yes, she's okay." Physically, at least. Emotionally, Babygirl was weathering another disappointment caused by me.

"There—the cube brought you luck, then." John gave me a pleased smile, and I grimaced. This conversation was bugging the hell out of me. "What's the girl's name?"

"Why the fuck do you care?" By that point, my harsh language and tone were completely out of line, but John didn't seem surprised or intimidated by how I was reacting.

"Do you love her?" he volleyed back, and I thought seriously about just walking away. Immediately. But then I looked up and considered. If the sky were a sheet of paper, it would have been easy to just take a pencil and scrawl my thoughts across it. I could even use my index finger to trace the words right there in the clouds, and Selene could read them, and I wouldn't have to explain to her why I'd run away after the night we'd spent together.

Why couldn't life be that easy? I had to talk instead.

Bullshit.

Words were just insignificant sounds. Just yap and babble.

They could hurt, though, and could even destroy.

"Quit it, John," I said menacingly, letting him know that he was overstepping and pushing my limits. Loving Selene? That was blasphemy for me. Sure, I cared about her. I wanted her very much; I felt affection for her and a kind of tenderness, but nothing more.

"I want her. I think." I surprised myself with my answer, which I offered to the doctor with an uncharacteristic lack of confidence.

Fuck.

John just watched me, waiting for me to do or say something else. Then, without really knowing why, I slipped my hand into my pocket and pulled out the paper fortune that said, "*Kiss me like you love me.*"

I'd kept and read it over and over again. The more I thought about it, the more mixed up I became.

"Her name's Selene," I admitted finally. "The last time I saw her, I ran away and left her with a crappy little Post-it note on her desk. It was after I got this," I confessed, handing the incriminating slip of paper to the doctor so he could see exactly what the hell I'd gotten myself into.

"'Kiss me like you love me,'" he read thoughtfully, holding the paper tight between his fingers. He looked up at me, visibly confused. An uncomfortable silence descended upon us. Feeling awkward, I wondered why I was even talking to him about Selene. There were a lot of potential reasons. Maybe I needed to tell someone. Maybe I couldn't keep all my fears inside anymore. Maybe I wanted to learn how to deal with it all? I didn't have a father to talk to about that kind of thing. I never had. I had always lacked a male presence I could actually look up to, so I'd always come to Dr. Lively when I felt like I needed someone who could understand me as a man.

"I asked her to kiss me like she loved me, but I was joking. I certainly don't believe in that bullshit." My voice was low and flat, and I felt suddenly keyed up, so I lit another cigarette. "But I wasn't expecting her to actually do it or, even worse, that she'd try to tell me that she…" I sighed. John's eyes, bright as sand illuminated by the sun, watched me thoughtfully. He wore a small smile that I couldn't read.

"I see. Well, that is indeed a problem," he said drily. "But, Neil, you know that there are a lot of possible feelings, and it's not always easy to identify them precisely." He turned the little paper over in his hands and looked ponderously at it.

"Hmm… Nice, John," I said, looking impassively at him, a shadow moving over my face. "Too bad it slides off me like dirty water." My voice was so cutting that his lips turned down in a crestfallen grimace.

"You know, doctor…" I leaned back against the bench and put out another cigarette butt. "A person's outlook on life changes when they've seen too much harm firsthand. When they've seen it in their own home, the place where they're supposed to be cared for, protected, comfortable, and…" I gave him a bitter smile. "…loved," I finished emphatically.

"Love becomes something different when it's whispered in your ear by a grown woman when you're a child. A woman who touches you without your permission, takes off your clothes, and forces you to engage in sex acts all the while telling you, 'No, Neil, this isn't wrong. This is love.'" I clenched the pack of Winstons in my fist and looked away from John's face, which would undoubtedly be dumbstruck. "This is the first time I've told anyone other than Dr. Lively about that, but that is the reason I hate that fucking word." I turned to John and saw him staring into the middle distance.

"That woman would whisper it to me when I came. She hid the immorality of what was happening, the filthy sex we were having, behind those four little letters. She told me it was a form of love, what she was doing to me, to mislead and cajole me. I still remember how I would run for the shower, soaked in sweat, and I'd scrub my skin raw trying to get her smell off me until I had these little rashy spots all over me. Then my mom would come home and smell something weird in my room, and I certainly couldn't tell her what had happened in my bed…" I observed John's eyes and his clenched-tight jaw. His breathing had gotten labored and his nostrils kept flaring like he was trying to hold back some angry outburst.

"And how long did that situation go on? When did your parents find out?" He cleared his throat and sat up stiffly. For the first time since I'd met him, Dr. Keller seemed vulnerable.

"My parents were always away working. My father ran his huge company, and my mother, well, she was building her fashion house. She only noticed something was wrong when I started having behavior problems— aggression at school, excessive anger, hating to be touched, and insomnia most nights. Typical symptoms of abuse," I explained, chewing nervously on my lower lip. "The whole thing went on for about a year. It was the most hellish time in my life," I continued coldly. John closed his eyes and rubbed his face with his hand.

"And she… Is she…in prison now?" he asked cautiously, trying to catch his breath after being shocked by my revelations. How many similar stories had he heard over the years in his practice? Why was he so shaken up by mine?

"No, she was transferred to a psychiatric facility," I answered vaguely. My head was throbbing, and there was a stabbing pain in my chest that felt like it was crushing my lungs. I felt like I was tumbling into the same abyss I always entered when I remembered.

"I still feel soiled and ashamed of what happened to me. I cannot give love because I got it in the wrong way. I can only connect it to something vile, and I certainly can't get with a girl like Selene. She couldn't even imagine how dark my past really is. If she looked deep inside me, she'd see nothing but emptiness. My family are the only people who know about my issues because I've never wanted people to think I'm crazy. It's still a struggle not to hurt myself or to give in to the wrong temptations, even if they would ease some of my pain. Most of the time, I transfer the pain from my mind into my body and vent it as anger. Hatred. It makes me feel alive, free if only for brief moments. And I don't care about hurting anyone. I don't know who I am, John, and I don't know what I want. I think I've been lost for so long that I no longer even know which direction I'm heading. I'm just wandering through Hell, alone, trying to understand where I belong." I stood up, feeling the need to put some physical distance between us. John also got to his feet with a sigh.

"You need to look inside yourself, son, and think about everything you've dealt with, everything you've managed to overcome. You have to be proud of yourself for going on in the face of challenges that are almost insurmountable to a child. Other people have no clue about the powerful emotions you're juggling."

The doctor tried to put a hand on my shoulder, but I stepped back to avoid being touched. Sensing my discomfort, he tucked his hand into his pants pocket instead. "But you're here right now, and that in itself is a victory. You got back up, tried to move forward like a true warrior. And that's what you are." He gave me a reassuring smile, but my face remained grave as I listened to him. "Thank you for putting your trust in me and sharing that part of yourself." His voice was kind and quiet, and I gave him a small smile in response. Then, I watched as he walked back over to the entrance of the clinic.

After our talk, it was clearer than ever that I could never reciprocate Selene's feelings.

I'd rather keep her at arm's length than slowly lose her over time because of my issues.

I had protected her and tried to be there for her because I knew that I cared for her.

My eyes had known it when they first fell on her, wearing that childish Tinkerbell sweater, and then my body knew it the moment my fingers brushed her velvet-soft skin.

As the story said: Love is not a selfish need to hold someone close, but rather it is letting them go so they can be happy.

She'd be my pearl that I'd try to protect until the end of my days.

And her happiness would be my only goal.

17

It had been wrong to confess my feelings to him.
I should have loved him wordlessly.

SELENE

A week had gone by since I'd last seen or heard from Neil.
Too many times, I had found myself wondering why he'd run away and what was so wrong about the declaration that I hadn't even been able to finish. And to think that, for that moment, everything had been magical. I remembered exactly how he'd kissed me in the park, his tongue tangling with mine and stealing my breath, his hips grinding against me, pressing into whatever gas pedal made my heart race unstoppably. Then I had ruined everything by speaking without thinking, by telling him what was in my heart.

I huffed and tossed my silverware down on my plate, my stomach completely shattered. Thoughts of Neil haunted me; I even thought I caught a whiff of his musky scent in the air like he was right next to me in the campus cafeteria where I'd met my friends for lunch.

"Okay, what's going on with you? You haven't said a word," asked Bailey, who had just finished her salad. Next to her, Janel said nothing; she just looked at me, curious to hear what I'd say.

"I guess I…" I gave a heartbroken sigh. "I just can't keep up with him," I said, suddenly resigned to the notion that I would never be able to manage someone like Neil.

"Are we talking about Neil?" Bailey asked, and I nodded. I'd told my friends everything that happened because I needed to talk it out with someone. While Bailey thought Neil might deserve another chance, Janel argued that he was too much of an asshole with too many problems.

"You should just forget about him," she said just then, waving a hand dismissively before pausing to peel a banana. I pushed my soup aside, sick to my stomach at the thought of eating anything, and looked down at my legs. The entire situation was screwed up. I should have been talking to Neil himself. We should have been facing the obstacles in our path together, hand in hand, going up against everything and everyone. Instead, we weren't communicating at all.

I couldn't understand him and I, in turn, did not feel understood.

It was a constant struggle between us, and I was afraid that I didn't have the strength to keep chasing him. But I was also afraid of resigning myself to the reality that he and I could never be an "us."

"Selene…" Janel laid her hand over mine and looked sadly at me. "That guy only seeks you out to fuck. You should put an end to this toxic relationship," she said, sounding concerned. What she didn't know was that Neil no longer even sought me out for sex. He'd had opportunities, but he always either settled for fooling around or stopped before undressing me and getting down to it. That approach wasn't at all normal for him. Usually he was assertive and domineering, always demanding my attention and particularly physical attention because it was the way he communicated. Now, though, he seemed almost trapped, stuck trying to cope with impulses that he couldn't indulge. I had registered this new behavior, but I still hadn't figured out why he was doing it.

"Yeah, maybe I should." I glanced down again and thought about the note he'd written me on that dumb little Post-it that night: *I'll always be there for you, but not the way you want. I'm sorry I can't stay.*

I smiled bitterly at myself. Why did he come if he didn't know how to stay?

Like always, Neil contradicted himself. His tortured logic was the result of his conflicted personality.

"H-he's too out of control," I blurted out in a sob that made both of my friends jump. "What did he come to Detroit for? Just to hurt me again? All he does is run away, then come back—over and over again. He's completely unstable, has no idea what he wants, and I'm tired of it!" I said in a long rush while the two of them exchanged bewildered looks. I was having a genuine freak-out. "I gave him everything. All of me…" I took my head in my hands in exasperation, and I just barely kept from crying. I had already shed more than enough tears over him.

"Feelings don't always show up in the ways we're accustomed to, you know. Love doesn't always require an explicit declaration. I mean, how many times is 'I love you' said and taken back every day?" Bailey, ever the optimist, put in. "So many. Too many. I don't think Neil will ever be the kind of guy who loves in a conventional way. He'll love the way he thinks is right, the way that conforms to his beliefs." She shrugged, and I tilted my head to one side, confused.

"What do you mean?" Janel asked.

"Just that Neil could very well love Selene while still being just as complicated as he's always been. I mean, he's never going to be someone who makes big declarations with flowers or whatever. From the way you described it, Selene, it sounds like he thinks those kinds of gestures don't really matter. But, believe me, bestie—it's the hidden feelings that usually turn out to be the truest. You don't have to shout at the stars to get their attention, you know? I think Neil's like that. He'll be able to love you someday, but he'll do it in his own way. Maybe that will make it even more special." Bailey smiled at me, and for a moment, a flicker of hope ignited in my chest. Maybe she was right. Maybe Neil attributed some other meaning to the word "love," but that didn't mean he didn't care about me.

"Huh, so when you're not talking about Tyler, you are capable of saying smart stuff. I'm shocked," Janel teased, hand over her heart, and Bailey rolled her eyes.

"Look, I'm an extremely intuitive person," she answered, puffing out her chest with pride.

"Oh yeah, you deserve a standing ovation from the rest of the student body in here," Janel said, and we all started laughing. After that light moment, however, thoughts crept relentlessly back into my mind, turning me glum again.

"So what should I do now?" I was pathetic. I should have just said it was over for me, that I was going to move on and find someone else to date. Instead, here I was brainstorming ways to fix things with Neil.

What a dummy.

"Forget about words of love, Selene. What Neil needs is substance, not style," Bailey jumped in again, like she knew the man better than I did. To be fair, my friend seemed to be better at interpreting my Disaster's thought process than I was. "He doesn't believe in love, right? Then you need to love him without explicitly telling him you love him. Love him when you look at him, when you hold him, when you talk to him, when you joke together, and when you have sex. He clearly doesn't want to hear the words, and he won't accept them," she concluded.

Neil believed in silence; that was true. It had been wrong to confess my feelings to him. I should have loved him wordlessly. Maybe he'd only be able to believe in my love when he felt it inside himself without me needing to say anything at all.

I felt more peaceful by the time I got home; talking to my friends had been really helpful. I joined my mother in the kitchen with a smile on my face, which only got wider when I caught the smell of cherry pie—my favorite—in the air. Content, I flopped down in a chair.

"You're a fantastic mom," I complimented, looking fondly at her colorful apron and matching oven mitt.

"Don't think you're going to flatter your way out of talking to me about... *the thing*," she murmured, stooping to pull the fully baked pie from the oven. I knew perfectly well that "*the thing*" meant Neil and me. My mother still didn't like knowing that I hadn't confided in her, but she couldn't understand how embarrassing it would have been to tell her about my pseudo-relationship. "I'm not jumping with joy at the knowledge that you and Mia's son were—or are—in a relationship, just to be clear," she said in a firm, authoritative voice. "But it's done now. You're an adult, and I want you to make your own choices and take responsibility for them." She sighed as she began cutting the pie into slices, depositing them on our plates.

"And, for the record, I sincerely hope you used protection every time. I don't want a grandchild before you graduate from college! Remember that!"

My eyes bugged slightly as I coughed at the unexpected direction this conversation had taken.

Ever since Neil left, my mother had done nothing but ask me intrusive questions and make all sorts of insinuations. She was perpetually on edge and it was really annoying me.

"Mom!" I raised my voice, my face flushed with obvious embarrassment, but she just turned to look at me with one eyebrow arched. "Can we please not talk about this?" I mumbled, my cheeks fully aflame, and, mercifully, she didn't keep going. "Hey, aren't you going to that spa tomorrow with Betty and your other friends for her birthday?" I asked, changing the subject entirely.

"Yes, though I'm not quite sure about leaving you here on your own for two days," she said uncertainly, untying the apron strings to pull it off.

"Oh my God, I am not a child! I can survive forty-eight hours without you." I made a sassy face at her, and she looked back at me sternly. "Plus, Betty is your best friend. She wants to spend time with you and the other ladies. You've all known each other for years, and it means a lot to her that you're there," I added, balancing my chin on my palm and waiting for my mother to sit down so we could have our favorite dessert together.

"Yes, but—" she began, and I shook my head, cutting her off.

"No buts. You're going," I told her seriously, and she smiled but did not, I noted, give me confirmation. She was definitely still too worried about me, and I didn't want her to neglect her personal life because of it.

....

As I lounged quietly on the sofa the next day, I watched my mother come down the stairs with a small overnight bag. After much back-and-forth, she had apparently decided that she was going to celebrate Betty's birthday with her at the spa, and I wanted to make sure she enjoyed her trip to the fullest.

"I'm still not sure about this," she said huffily as she approached me.

"Mom, you'll be right back here tomorrow night. It's one night." I rolled my shoulders and leaned back against the armrest, stretching my legs out in front of me.

"I know, but I still don't like it. I've already told Mrs. Kamper next door, and she says you can come to her if you need anything. I'm probably going to call you once every half hour, so you'd better answer," she ordered firmly, making me grin.

"Have fun. I'll go to school tomorrow, and I won't even notice you're gone." I rolled my eyes at her, and she made a face.

"You're almost too affectionate, sweetheart," she teased.

"You know I adore you." I got up off the couch and walked over to hug her.

Yet even her love couldn't fill the emptiness I had inside me caused by Neil and his incomprehensible behavior. I tried not to let my misery show, though, until after my mother had left.

Once I was alone, I noticed my stomach was growling, so I went into the kitchen and poked around in the refrigerator. I saw that it was almost empty and realized I should have gone shopping, but I didn't feel like going out. So I shut the door with a huff and went up to my room to take a shower. When I was done, I sighed at the bathroom mirror and wandered around the house wrapped in a towel, my messy hair pulled up into a loose bun. I was dripping all over the floor, but I didn't care. Then I rifled through my dresser and got out a pair of white panties and some black leggings. I preferred to go without a bra because they were so damned uncomfortable, and I selected a plain cropped T-shirt that ended around my belly button. It had an odd little illustration of a monkey in the center of it.

"You look horrible." I babbled at the jungle animal like he was going to respond to me, but I decided to wear it anyway.

I completed the look with a pair of fluffy slippers and went down to the living room, ready to enjoy my alone time. I winced when, almost immediately, the shrill sound of the doorbell interrupted the peace. I pricked up my ears because I knew I was alone in the house. So before I opened the door, I pulled aside the curtain in the window next to the door and peered outside. I couldn't see anybody.

I waffled for a few moments about whether or not I should open the door, but curiosity got the better of me and I gave in.

My eyes opened wide as I spotted Neil in front of me. I went still—so still that I couldn't even blink.

"How long does it take you to open a door?" His warm voice alone was enough to make a shiver pass through my lower belly. My eyes got stuck on his, just as bright and intense as they always were.

"Are you by yourself?" His question broke my temporary trance. I'd forgotten that he was still just standing there on the porch, because I was too busy checking him out. I was about to answer him when I saw his honey-colored eyes doing a similar slow inspection of my clothing. Neil paused to ogle my breasts, the stiffened nipples like hard pebbles underneath the thin material of my T-shirt.

"Well?" he prompted, sounding annoyed, and then advanced vigorously on me, filling all the air around me with the smell of him.

"What are you doing here? My mom isn't home and—" But I didn't get to finish because Neil slammed the door closed behind him, and I immediately found myself pressed up against the wall, enclosed by his much more powerful frame. His lips fell on mine and devoured me in the most over-powering way. He thrust his tongue into my mouth and lashed it like a whip, demanding I reciprocate. The tobacco taste of him mingled with the mint already on my tongue, but there was no care and no emotion. This kiss of ours was all desire, want, and hunger.

"You're not wearing a bra; you know what that does to me," he murmured into my mouth, ignoring my question. He continued to kiss me and snuck a hand under my shirt to fondle me. I gasped, and his powerful, aroused body was plastered entirely against mine, letting me feel the hardness between his thighs. My heart pounded furiously in my chest, goosebumps rippling over my skin, but I felt tense. Too tense.

Did he think he could just come and go whenever he wanted? Did he think that a domineering attitude and good looks were enough to make me forget what had happened?

"No, wait…" I groaned in pain when his hand moved too roughly on my breast, squeezing it in his hot palm until it felt like a balloon ready to burst. "Neil," I said brokenly, managing to drag my lips away from his, which immediately slid down to my neck. Then Mr. Disaster wrapped my hair around his fist and pulled back, forcing me to expose my throat for his pleasure. He licked and sucked greedily at the skin, dragging another moan out of me. After a moment of pleasure, however, I came to my senses.

"Neil, I said no!" I pushed him hard and watched him stagger back. A puzzled look came over his face as I watched him, breathless. Instinctively, I touched a finger to my swollen lips.

"What's your problem? Are you rejecting me? Seriously?" He ran his hand through the unruly hair on top of his head and looked earnestly at me, waiting for an answer.

"What's *my* problem?" I echoed, still gasping for air. "You didn't even say hello! I'm not a blow-up doll, Neil!" I raised my voice, and he frowned like he couldn't tell if I was serious or not.

"It was just a fucking kiss; I wasn't going to rail you up against the wall. Chill out." He looked me top to bottom, his expression condescending.

"You disappeared and left me with nothing but a crappy Post-it note on my desk. How dare you just barge into my home and demand my attention like nothing happened? Huh?" I straightened my T-shirt furiously when I noticed that he was staring at my breasts again. "And look at my face when I'm talking to you!" I ordered, enraged. I was so incredibly disappointed by his behavior and even more so by his incredible arrogance about it.

"First of all, chill out," he repeated scornfully, looking me in the eye. "I don't take orders from anyone, least of all you. Also, you shouldn't get so worked up over a kiss. The last few times we were together, you practically served it up on a platter, and I was the one who didn't give in." He gave me a thin, mocking smile, and I stared at him in bewilderment.

I was going to kick him; I knew it.

"You are such a dick!" I spat at him.

"Because I kissed you just now or because I haven't fucked you in so long?" He cocked an eyebrow and dug his teeth into his lower lip, extremely entertained by the entire situation.

"Enough with this shit, Neil. Since you're here, we need to get a few things straight. Sit down." I gestured toward the couch, and his gaze followed my hand, though his face remained just as smirky.

"Hmm. Feeling aggressive today, huh, Tinkerbell? I have to say, I wasn't expecting this welcome." He winked at me and didn't move an inch. That's when I completely lost my cool.

"Goddammit, stop being an asshole for five minutes! And if you can't do that, then you better get your ass out that door before I kick you out. And I won't be gentle about it. Is that clear?" I shouted, gesturing at the door behind him and watching his smile fade, replaced by the familiar shadow that moved across his eyes. He gave me that bleak stare of his, black pupils catching the light.

"Watch it, Selene," he warned me in a low, serious tone. I shuddered and gulped like I was trying to swallow a handful of nails.

"You need to listen to me for once," I said, more calmly and, unfortunately, less decisively. Neil sat reluctantly on the sofa's armrest, crossing his own arms over his chest.

"All right, hit me with your bullshit…" He sighed and I tried to ignore his inexplicably obnoxious attitude. He was acting jumpy, bored, and even annoyed with me.

"My bullshit?" I shot back, offended. I made sure to keep some physical distance between us. "You're the one who ghosted me with a Post-it note. You do get that, right?" My shoulders slumped, and I sighed heavily. I needed to calm down, or we'd never find a solution to our myriad problems.

"Yes and I think the reason why I did that is pretty clear…"

"Do you think I'm in love with you?" I folded my arms over my chest and adopted a confident stance. "I'm not. So you can rest assured—I just misspoke that night," I lied, although I didn't know whether or not Neil would believe me. He was too smart not to at least suspect I was feeding him a flimsy explanation.

"Okay. In that case, I accept your apology," he said with a shrug.

"I didn't apologize," I said, bemused.

"You should, though. The word 'love' is offensive to me," he answered, staring back at me with his usual stern glower.

"But I didn't say that to you," I said impatiently, and he gave a slow, amused head shake. "And, besides, you are the one who should be apologizing," I went on, and Neil stood up and began walking toward me. I took a step back. Each time he advanced on me like a big cat, it made me feel like small and helpless prey.

"I'll never do that. You knew from the start the kind of guy I was." He stopped just a few inches from me and looked probingly into my face.

"You need to stop playing with me," I told him firmly, and his forehead wrinkled in confusion. I didn't know how else one could possibly interpret our situation, however.

"Do you seriously think I'm playing with you?" he asked, puzzled, and I just nodded in conviction. "Your father thinks I'm a criminal, a delinquent, or worse, some psychopath. I haven't spoken to him since he found out about us, and now I'm standing here with the knowledge that he may very well kill me if he finds out I'm seeing you, and you think I'm playing a game with you? To what end?" He stood rigid and gave me a stormy look, annoyed by my question.

"I don't know!" I burst out. "You won't open up to me, and I can't figure you out!" I flung my arms wide in exasperation, and he grinned. I didn't see anything particularly funny in the situation, but Neil obviously did.

"I'm not playing with you. Whatever I'm doing with you is so real that it's got me completely turned around..." He cupped my face in his hands, and I sucked in a breath. It was incredible how one burning touch was enough to completely shake me. Neil pressed his forehead to mine and closed his eyes, maybe trying to soothe whatever was torturing him deep inside. But I shook my head and pulled his hands away from me. I knew how screwed up he was; I also knew that I should try to understand him. But understanding didn't mean allowing him to walk all over me whenever he felt like it.

"I guess I can't forgive every act of disrespect. Everyone has a limit, Neil," I explained apologetically. As I stared into his golden eyes, I was surprised to see shame there, but he had brought this on himself.

"What are you talking about?" He smiled, underestimating me like he always did. "Shut up and kiss me." He leaned in with clear intention, and when I felt his soft, warm lips against mine, I went rigid. He didn't kiss me in his usual headlong way but limited himself to mostly chaste contact. Even that I didn't want to encourage, however, so I rested my hands against his hips and pushed him away from me.

"This isn't the way to make things up to me," I told him seriously, and he just looked at me. He frowned at first, gradually growing more troubled by my refusal.

"Are we going to keep having this argument much longer?" he volleyed back.

"Yeah, probably until you figure out just how shitty your behavior has been." I stepped back, and Neil looked at me, surprised by my cantankerous attitude.

"I'm not going to apologize," he clarified, still totally certain he'd done nothing wrong.

"I wouldn't know what to do with it if you did," I retorted, just to get another hit in. I knew how disciplined he was and how indifferent to my words he often seemed, but I needed to fight back in some way.

"Are you going to tell me why you're here? I asked once already, but as usual, you ignored me." I folded my arms over my chest and waited for an answer—a real one this time.

Neil backed up a little bit, looking like he finally realized he shouldn't mouth off to me just then.

"I just wanted to see you," he answered shortly.

"For any reason in particular?" I insisted skeptically, and a small, enigmatic smile appeared on his face, capturing my attention. So I cleared my throat and did my best to pretend that I was immune to him.

"Do I need a particular reason to see you?" He shrugged, retreating into his cocky pose.

"Well, you've clearly gone to some trouble to visit me all the way out here in Detroit, and I'm assuming you had some justification for doing that, right?" I asked, and Neil couldn't miss the bitter sarcasm in my voice.

"I'm getting really close to losing my cool, you know," he warned, his body tensing.

"Oh, mine's been lost for a while. Imagine how I feel," I answered immediately. Suddenly, he smiled, and then he burst into laughter, even reaching out to touch my face.

What the hell had gotten into him?

"You really are adorable when you get pissed off, Tigress," he said between gales of laughter while I looked seriously at him so he understood I wasn't going to reciprocate any of this irritating levity.

"Will I still be adorable when I'm booting your ass out of my house?" I cocked my head to one side, pretending to be genuinely curious about his answer. Neil just kept laughing, totally unbothered.

"That sounds familiar. Feels like I've heard it somewhere before." He smirked at me, and I gave him a fake smile.

"You sure have. This asshole in a pool house in New York said it to me," I told him.

"An asshole who nevertheless let you sleep with him," he said, his voice turning seductive as he gave me a sly wink.

"Am I supposed to feel honored?" I had actually appreciated that act of trust from him, but I wasn't going to tell him that. He didn't deserve to know.

"You should feel lucky. It's a privilege I don't grant to anyone else," he answered, his tone so sincere that I was struck dumb. I had guessed that, of course, but hearing him say it out loud was unexpected.

"I'd like to kiss you now, by the way," he added, breaking the silence. I sucked in a breath at the blunt statement and took a step back from him.

"And I don't want you to," I lied. I couldn't allow him to use me and then toss me aside whenever he wanted. I had my pride, after all, and understanding his problems or where his attitude came from didn't mean losing myself completely.

"Liar." He advanced in a predatory way, ready to impose himself on me the way he loved to. He deftly slid a hand into my hair, using it to pull my head to him while the other encircled my waist. He tilted his head and brushed my lips, staring into my eyes. He bit my lower lip and tugged on it as he looked fixedly at me with those golden eyes. Those eyes, where I saw things that were too remote, too impossible.

And it was in that moment that I decided: Even if Neil didn't love me, I was still going to give him everything I could because love did not demand reciprocity.

"Do I have to teach you everything, Babygirl?" he murmured, and I examined his long eyelashes, unable to utter a single word. "I don't ask for kisses. Never." He licked the edges of my mouth, and shivers of desire made my entire body tremble. My most intimate place pulsed, and it got difficult to breathe. I tried to pull back, but Neil insinuated a knee between my thighs, and I jumped. Gasping for breath, I clutched his hips as he began to move his leg slowly, grinding it against my clitoris. I shut my eyes and tried not to moan, fighting the almost overwhelming desire to see him naked. Then, Neil stopped abruptly, and I looked at him in shock. All at once, I was relieved that he hadn't gone further. I was still mad, and I also knew that I wouldn't have been able to resist him.

"Not today, Babygirl," he said in a sensual whisper and gave me that shit-eating grin. Then he backed up a few steps, leaving me bewildered.

"I can't give in. If I did, I'd wreck you, and I don't think you could handle it." He looked thoughtfully at me, and once again, I didn't understand what he was trying to tell me. Neil could never just be straightforward; he always demanded, I guess, everything. "So you can rest easy for the moment, Tigress," he concluded teasingly.

He looked lazily down at my breasts, inhaled shakily, and ruffled his hair in his anxious way. Once again, it was clear to me that he was holding himself back from jumping me the way he wanted to do, and for once, I was grateful. I wanted to ask him what was making him hold back because I knew that, in addition to being beautiful, my Disaster was also deeply perverse and shameless. For a moment, my insecurities rose up, and I worried that I wasn't attractive to him, especially given the way I was dressed. But then I looked down at his pants and saw that he was visibly aroused, so I could safely put aside the idea that he wasn't physically attracted to me anymore.

"Okay," I sighed, looking down at my fluffy slippers. The same ones that Neil then also started staring at. My cheeks erupted, and I braced myself for an insult or something downright offensive, and...

"Fuck, those are somehow worse than the pajamas," he grumbled, and my eyes widened with embarrassment.

"Idiot!" I shot back, and Neil just gave another belly laugh. "Okay, well now as punishment you have to go grocery shopping with me. You can carry my bags so that your trip here has at least one purpose," I said, my voice dripping with sarcasm, and he immediately turned serious again, like I'd told him the end of the world was imminent. To be perfectly honest, I still had no desire to go out for groceries, but as soon as I saw his alarmed face, I knew I had to do it.

"No, no, wait. What? Shopping? Together? That's couples shit." He grimaced and shook his head. He crossed his arms over his chest and looked down his nose at me while I tried not to be distracted by the way his muscles twitched with every movement.

"Do you know how often people go shopping together just to help out a friend? They're mature, considerate, and—"

"And I'm not like them," he said, interrupting with his usual arrogance. He lowered his head to make sure I saw how serious he was.

"If you go with me…I'll give you a reward when we come back." I said archly. I moved closer to him and traced down his chest with my index finger, moving slowly to his abs. I looked up at him through my eyelashes, but I must not have been very convincing because he bit his lip to hide an amused smile.

"What?" I stepped back and put my hands on my hips, one foot tapping against the floor. If Neil was trying to get on my nerves, he was succeeding wildly.

"You can't dangle sex in front of me to get what you want, Tigress." He advanced on me slowly, and I backed up until I hit the wall behind me. I hated—absolutely hated—how confident he was in his mastery of me. "I'm not going to fuck you. Not today…" he said again, propping his elbow up on the wall and checking me out from top to bottom. "Though I must admit, the urge to tear these leggings off you and bury my tongue between your legs is…considerable." He used his index finger to delicately stroke my throat, devouring me with his eyes like a starving beast. Then he grabbed a lock of my hair and began to play with it. "It's gotten so bad, I'd probably have to keep you trapped in that pretty little room all day long and…" he moved closer to my ear and breathed in my smell, his muscular chest pressing against my breasts. "Just dive into you." He took my earlobe between his teeth, and I pressed my thighs together. I probably stopped breathing entirely, but then Neil pulled away abruptly, leaving me off balance and staring at him.

"To the grocery store, then?" he asked. He gave me a mischievous look, fully aware of the power he wielded over my body. Meanwhile, I tried to get a grip on myself. My legs were trembling, and my heart was beating at a gallop, but I tried not to show my vulnerability to him. I went upstairs to change, and as soon as I was ready, I strutted past him like a woman who was completely sure of herself.

Half an hour later we stood outside the grocery store and paused in front of the automatic doors. "Ready for a thrilling experience?" I teased, adjusting my coat as Neil took one last drag from his Winston.

"The shit I have to do…" he grumbled, rolling his eyes. "At least no one in this town is going to recognize me out here acting like some whipped boyfriend." He strolled inside with his usual swagger, and I followed him.

"It'll be so much fun; you'll see," I told him sarcastically.

As soon as we entered, I grabbed a cart and pushed it along in front of me. I glanced back at Neil, who did nothing but huff continuously as we walked along.

"You plan to snort and puff the whole time?" I asked him as I moved around the various shelves, stopping periodically to look at the products on display.

"Are you going to stop every other second?" He pushed his hand into the pocket of his sweatpants, which pulled the fabric taut over the bulge between his legs. My eyes moved there and lingered for a few moments.

"And what product are you perusing now, Selene?" Of course Neil noticed, and my eyes darted back up to his face. His eyebrow was raised, and he had a sexy little smirk that I would have loved to kiss right off him. So, naturally, I turned beet red and awkwardly resumed pushing the cart along.

"Nothing. Don't get any ideas," I sighed.

Ignoring Neil, who was giving me a sideways look, I bent to grab a bag of chips and tossed it into the cart.

"Okay, you have to try Better Made chips while you're—" I stopped when I noticed Neil looking sharply at a graying man right behind us. The guy, who appeared to be in his midfifties, was obviously intimidated and turned away hastily. Neil turned back to look first at me and then at the leggings I was still wearing and frowned at me.

"Don't bend over like that," he scolded sternly before walking a few steps away, looking irritable and unsettled. I stayed rooted to the spot, though, trying to work out what had just happened. "Are you coming?" he prompted.

"Is something wrong?" I asked cautiously as he walked along beside me with his hands still in his pockets and his gaze icy.

"Nope," he answered, sounding annoyed. He didn't even look at me, so I decided not to push the issue. I stopped again, this time to get some pop and other munchies, while Neil looked blankly at the shelves, a bored expression on his face and his mind a million miles away.

"Hey, pistachios!" Out of nowhere, he darted away from the cart like an overexcited toddler, making me whirl around in surprise.

"Are you insane?" I pressed a hand to my chest in fright, but he ignored me as he grabbed three packages of shelled pistachios.

"These are just for me," he said, grinning as he tossed them in the cart.

"Don't worry, I'd never let a package of pistachios drive a wedge between us. We've got enough of those already," I complained, steering the cart toward the candy aisle. "Do you like chocolate? My mother and I go through a lot of it. Honestly, we're kind of fiends for it and…" I glanced back at Neil and saw that he looked especially distracted. I looked around to see what had caught his eye, and then, not far from us, I spotted an older blond woman absolutely devouring him with her eyes. Neil was definitely reciprocating. He stood there motionless, staring fixedly at her, and she was under his spell.

I wasn't sure what to do. Watching him slip back into who he had been— who he always would be—hurt. I kept calm and reminded myself over and over that love meant total acceptance and that it wasn't my job to judge Neil, but to understand him.

I abandoned the cart then and walked over to him, touching his arm. When I was confident that he wasn't about to snap at me, I shifted my attention to the woman in question, who turned away the moment she noticed my presence. Neil then looked at me in irritation, and I braced myself for an outburst, but he surprised me instead.

"Just the dark kind," he said calmly, looking straight into my eyes.

"What?" I asked stupidly.

"Chocolate. I only like it dark."

He was letting me know that he'd heard while at the same time making it clear that he didn't want me asking any questions about why he'd been staring at that woman so entranced.

"Okay, then. We'll also get something with dark chocolate," I said with a small, tight smile, trying to hide how disappointed I was by his behavior. I crouched down to get a candy bar from one of the lower shelves, but as I got back to my feet, I felt a sudden dizziness that made me stumble. Neil's arms caught me in midair.

"Selene, are you okay?" He held me by the waist, staring down at me in concern, and his smell wrapped around me, making me forget about everything else.

"Yes, it's just…a little vertigo," I answered, rubbing my forehead. "Ever since the accident, it happens occasionally. I'm fine, though." I tried to regain my balance while I deposited the candy bars in the cart, but his golden eyes refused to move away from me for even a second.

"Maybe you're overtired. Do you want to go home?" he asked kindly, and I shook my head.

"No, it's gone now. They never last long, and I'm fine." We stared intensely into each other's eyes, and I could tell that Neil was probing for some hesitation in me. When he found none, I let go of him, and we continued our journey. Except now Neil insisted on pushing the cart, his elbows resting on the green metal bar. His bulging biceps did not escape the sly eyes of the various women in the store.

"You doing okay back there?" I glared over my shoulder as I walked ahead of him, focused on getting the rest of our necessities.

"Only because I've got such a great view of your lovely ass. You know how partial I am to it," he answered, openly leering at my butt.

"Okay, we're in a grocery store, so—"

"Here, this is the aisle you need," Neil teased as we turned down the feminine hygiene section. The shelves, packed with intimate cleansers, pads, and tampons, made me remember an outlandish question I'd been meaning to ask him.

"Why didn't you ever use a condom with me?" I turned to find him already watching me. This wasn't exactly how I wanted to have this conversation, but as usual, I'd moved too fast. Immediately, I felt embarrassed.

"Because you told me you were on the pill," Neil answered flatly, still frozen in that cocky stance with his forehead wrinkled in thought.

"That could have been a lie, though. But you trusted me," I said.

"You wouldn't have the balls to lie to me about something like that," he said confidently.

"So that's your decision-making process? A woman tells you she's on the pill, and you just take her word for it?" I lowered my voice, burrowing my hands into my coat pockets. And yes, I probably did look like a little kid just then, but I didn't care. Neil just gave me a mocking smile.

"No. You're the only one I went bareback with. I already told you that; you don't have to keep asking me the same questions to verify that I'm telling the truth," he answered quietly and honestly, and knowing that aspect of our relationship was in fact unique did make me happy.

"Why...only me?" I walked slowly back toward him, looking him in the eye and hoping for an actual explanation. A grocery store wasn't the best venue for this conversation, but with Neil, I had to take advantage of the rare moments when he seemed open to answering my questions.

"Because I know you. I know your sex life and your history. I was your first and only, thus far. Besides, I like feeling you skin on skin. It's different when I sleep with the others," he said, shrugging a shoulder. "I also usually have strict rules about oral. I like to receive, but I don't give."

"But you...uh...to me..." I paused, too embarrassed to continue. Neil just sighed.

"No more questions," he said in a weary mutter.

"I've already got it figured out: I'm special," I said in tones of satisfaction as I watched his eyebrows fly upward. Neil's face grew severe—more severe than usual.

"No, you're being an annoying girl, and that's it," he shot back and walked away from me, but I decided I wasn't going to give up.

"I saw how you stared at that blond woman before." Neil halted the cart at my words and then let go of it to look at me.

"Jealous?" He shot me a born seducer's grin, but I ignored him to grab a few more items and tossed them into the cart.

"No, not at all," I answered, taking the metal cart handle in my hands and pushing it forward. Almost immediately, though, I felt Neil's chest plastered against my back, his huge palms resting over my hands, and his chin balanced on the top of my head. I stopped abruptly, an uncontainable fire spreading throughout my body until it came to rest deep in my heart.

"One day, you're going to have two incredible children. A boy and a girl. You'll have a dog, a beautiful home, and a husband who loves you..." I tilted my face to one side, focused on his deep voice.

"You'll be an independent woman, elegant and attractive. Your husband will be crazy about you. Your daughter is going to have your blue eyes, and her brother will have your strength and tenacity. You'll go on family trips together every weekend. You'll host garden parties and barbecues with music and dancing for all your friends. You'll be an exemplary mother, a dream wife—the perfect woman. Your husband will be a lucky man. One day, Selene, you are going to find out that you're pregnant, and you will be so happy, but when that day comes, I will not be the man at your side," he concluded seriously, looking completely unaffected by that little speech.

I turned fully so I could stare into his luminous eyes. He kept his arms stretched out to hold the cart, and my slim frame was enclosed by his more powerful one. Just then, though, it wasn't his body that was crushing me but his words.

"And what about you? Where will you be?" I tried to match his cold detachment but failed miserably when my lips began to tremble and my eyes started to sting.

"Somewhere out there in the world. I've always dreamed of traveling. Of getting away from everything and everyone. I mean, a person like me obviously can't aim for a family, a wife, and kids, right? What would I be able to give them? My constant chaos? My famously terrible temperament?" He shook his head sardonically, and there was no hint of doubt or second-guessing in his face. "But you, Selene—you were born to live that fairy-tale future." He smiled at me, lifting a hand to gently caress my cheek. Except I flinched away from him.

"Stop it," I whispered, looking away.

"Why? I'll send you postcards. You can tell me all about how your kids are doing or keep me up-to-date on your husband," he continued earnestly, despite the fact that it all sounded to me like the most absurd thing I'd ever heard.

"Stop," I said again, my hands clenching into fists.

"Maybe you're right. Your husband could be jealous of me. I'll send the postcards to your mother, then, and she can give them to you," he said reflectively. It occurred to me that Neil actually believed everything he was saying, and I stared at him in shock.

"Enough!" I shoved him abruptly away from my chest, forgetting entirely that we were in a public place, and I saw his expression turn surprised. "Why are you saying these things to me? Do you take pleasure in hurting me? Is this some kink of yours I'm not aware of?" I raised my voice, ignoring the stares of our fellow shoppers who continued to maneuver their carts around us.

"Hurt you?" he repeated, like I was the one talking crazy. "I just told you how I imagine your future. What's so wrong about that? I want the best for you..." he said calmly, but I didn't respond at all. I straightened my shoulders and tried to project strength the way I always had to when it came to Neil and the twisted inner workings of his mind.

"Selene..." He drew closer to me and tilted up my chin. "You have to accept reality as it is," he said with a wistful smile before brushing past me, leaving a void that was filled only with the smell of him.

I knew that because of what happened with Kim, he believed he didn't deserve a happy future.

He believed that he was tainted. Wrong.

But he was not the problem.

The problem was a past that he couldn't overcome.

Neil was incredible and deserved all the love in the world.

He deserved a joyful future.

And I would have done anything if only it would pull him out of his darkness.

18

He trapped me with his body and stared down at me
with those lovely, glowing, sensual eyes while
I tried to catch my breath.

SELENE

Neil was still in Detroit with me.

When we got back from the grocery store, he helped me carry in the bags, and then we had lunch together at my house. I had no idea how long he would stay, and I was afraid to ask him, but I was happy I got to spend time with him. It felt like we were actually getting to know each other for the first time.

He seemed to get more comfortable with talking as the hours passed, though he would still frequently close in on himself. When he got particularly broody, he would light up a cigarette and scowl, staring off into nothingness.

In those moments, I would just watch him admiringly as he inhaled long drags of smoke. He was beautiful even while doing the most mundane things.

"Why are you staring at me?" He blew smoke out his nose and gave me a serious look. His eyes looked even brighter in the light from the fire I'd lit in the living room's fireplace to keep us warm.

"You're smoking in Judith Martin's house. She's going to kill me when she gets back," I said unhappily. I hated that he smoked. I wanted to get him to quit, but I knew he was too stubborn to listen to me about it.

"Relax, it'll be okay." He took another drag and got more comfortable on the couch while I crouched down by the TV, trying to choose what to watch on Netflix. "Find an action movie, not some ball-shriveling romance," he clarified while I inched across the carpet to sit down on the floor next to the couch.

"What are you doing down there?" He frowned, and I cleared my throat awkwardly.

"Because I'm not going to be able to watch a movie with you right next to me, Neil," I told him, and he laughed lightly.

"I won't bite, Tinkerbell." He winked at me and nestled more deeply into the sofa, his cigarette dangling from his lips.

"Yeah, you've probably taken plenty of bites out of your blonds recently." I continued to scroll through the offerings, hoping some thumbnail would catch my eye.

"What makes you think that?" he asked from behind me, but I didn't pull my eyes away from the screen.

"You haven't touched me since we got back from the store. Just from that I can surmise what's been going on in New York," I said placidly. Although I had slowly gotten more comfortable with him and could have a calm conversation, I still knew that I needed to measure every word with Neil. Even more crucially, I had to figure out what kind of mood he was in before I said certain things to him.

"Is there any cherry pie left?" He changed the subject, and I looked over my shoulder at him. He'd already eaten half the pie, and I was glad to see him enjoying it so much.

"My mom is a real magician when it comes to desserts, isn't she? Wait here." I got up from the carpet and went into the kitchen. I walked immediately over to the remains of the pie on the counter, but just as I was about to pick it up, I was surprised by the ringing of my phone. I tugged it out of my pocket and frowned when I saw Ivan's name flashing across the display.

"Hello?" I answered uncertainly.

"Hey, Selene. Are you at home? Janel wants to know if you want to come with us to this party," he offered, though it was hard to hear him over the weird sounds in the background.

"Not true, Selene! It was his idea to invite you!" I recognized Janel's voice immediately and grinned.

"Well, I actually—" I began to answer, but Ivan was bickering with his sister.

"What the hell are you telling her? Selene, you there? Get ready. We'll come get you in half an hour," Ivan said rapidly, and I was instantly alarmed.

"No, no! Ivan, we'll have to rain check. I have guests over right now, and I can't go out." I tucked a strand of hair behind my ear and sighed heavily.

"Oh, okay. But you'll come out next time?" he asked, and just as I was about to agree, Neil's hands came to rest on my hips, making me flinch.

"Y-yeah, for sure."

My heart fluttered in my throat, and I ended the call and turned off the display before setting the phone down on the counter and pushing it away with my fingers. Neil stood motionless behind me. His chest was plastered against my back, and his erection insinuated itself between my butt cheeks.

"Who was that?" he whispered in my ear, quiet but commanding, as his fingers crawled along the elastic of my pants, heading for the front.

"Ivan. He wanted me to go to a party with him and his sister." I tried not to fumble with my words, though it was difficult to keep a cool head with Neil so close to me.

"Hmm, Ivan again." His breath felt like a light breeze on my neck. "Anyway, I changed my mind. No pie; I want something else instead." He slipped his index finger beneath my waistband, grazing the outside of my panties.

"You need to tell me something about yourself whenever you want something from me. Remember our deal?" My voice was barely audible. I clutched the countertop when his big hand cupped my pubis, grasping me possessively until I sucked in a breath.

"I haven't fucked anyone in a while." He ground his hips against my ass, and I arched back against him with a moan that surprised even me. I drifted into ecstasy as he began to work slowly against me. "And I can't come. That's why I haven't been touching you." He pressed his lips to my neck and slid his hand into my panties, making me flinch. "Should I keep going?" He sighed against my ear, and it occurred to me how difficult it must be for him to admit something like that to me. Although it felt like my head was spinning, I finally understood why Neil had been holding back all this time.

"Why not?" I said in a small voice, swallowing hard because my throat was suddenly unbearably dry. I turned to him, blinking in confusion, and saw his gaze lingering on my eyes. I caressed his jaw, bristly with the beginnings of a beard, and he accepted my touch without pulling away.

"That's none of your business. But if you want to use me, I'll let you," he answered. I hated it when he talked like that with me.

"I don't want to use you." I felt a stab of pain in my chest, and for a moment, it was hard to breathe. It felt like I was going to cry, but I didn't want to do it. "Why are you having this problem?" I asked again, hoping not to set him off with such a personal question. I wasn't stupid; him being unable to orgasm suggested a serious issue and Neil probably knew what the source was even if he didn't want to tell me.

"There's nothing wrong with me physically. That's all you need to know." He smiled, kissing his way down my neck to the place underneath my ear. He breathed in my smell and gave an appreciative groan.

"Are you in pain?" Maybe it was wrong to keep asking him about it, but I needed more information. Specifically, I needed to know if he felt compelled to have sex.

"No." Neil rested his hands on the counter, caging me in as he stared lustfully into my eyes. As soon as I realized what his perverse intentions were, I shoved him, breaking his grasp and fleeing the kitchen in one catlike motion.

"Where do you think you're going, little Tigress?" I heard him call out from behind me as I continued to flee, my hair fanning out into the air behind me, a thrilled—and frightened—look on my face. I wanted him, but at the same time, learning what he was dealing with had unnerved me.

I raced through the living room and up the stairs, my heart beating wildly in my chest. All I could hear was my own panting and his determined footfalls behind me. I knew he could have caught me by then if he really wanted to, but instead he was playing with me.

"I'm going to get you…" He chuckled behind me. At the same time, I threw open the door to my room and darted inside. But before I could close it, Neil leaped forward and blocked it with his shoulder, even forcing in his foot to assist in his efforts.

"No! You can't come in!" I pushed against the door in an attempt to hold him back, but he just laughed heartily from the other side. Then he gave the door a shove, and it flew open. I staggered back, trying not to fall over.

"Where are you gonna run to now? Hmm?" Neil kicked the door closed and looked me up and down, licking his lips lustfully.

"I'll figure something out," I answered, backing away at a measured pace. I navigated around the bed and put more distance between us, never breaking with his carnal gaze.

"I want you, and I'll get you, rest assured." He quirked the corner of his mouth and advanced on me again, a hunter locked in on his prey.

"I don't think so." I gave him a mocking smile, and before he could grab me, I jumped up and over the bed to get to the other side of the room and made a run for the door. But Neil, quick as a gazelle, hooked his arms around my waist and flattened my back against the closed door.

"Got you." He trapped me with his body and stared down at me with those lovely, glowing, sensual eyes while I tried to catch my breath. "Cat got your tongue, Tigress?" he taunted when I didn't answer him.

"You only won because I let you," I said challengingly.

"I was going to get you either way. I'll always get you…" He leaned down to reach my neck and peppered it with moist kisses, coaxing forth my desire.

"I'd say we've done enough playing, and I've given you something of myself…" He grazed his lips over my collarbone and used both hands to grab the hem of my T-shirt, slowly pulling it up and over my head before discarding it on the floor.

"And what should I give you?" I asked breathlessly, honoring our deal. Neil pulled back slightly to look at my bare breasts and smiled in a satisfied way.

"You. All of you…" He made a rough noise in his throat and grabbed my breasts with both hands. He bent his head to envelop one nipple with his full lips.

Instinctively, I touched his soft hair and arched my back away from the door as my legs went weak and my head began to spin.

"Okay, I'll give you all of me, then," I whispered, trying not to think about my soaked panties and all the feelings Neil was reawakening in me.

"Everything you can…" he answered, putting his palms on either side of my head. His biceps twitched with the motion while my eyes eagerly glided down his entire torso.

Then, with the last bit of bravery I possessed, I took the zipper of his white hoodie between my thumb and forefinger and drew it down, letting the fabric slowly draw aside like a curtain to reveal the erotic spectacle of his bulging pectorals and defined abs.

"Do you approve, Tinkerbell?" His white teeth sank into his bottom lip while I traced the ventral line of his abdomen with an index finger and dragged it lower in an exploratory fashion, like I was seeing him for the very first time.

"Very much." I lifted my gaze to lock in on his luminous eyes and slipped my fingers beneath the elastic of his pants, stroking the downy hair on his pubic area.

"I want you, and I can't wait anymore." He grinned lewdly and used both hands to take my pants and pull them down my legs. I helped him get them off, lifting my foot out of one leg and then the other. Not wasting a single minute more, Neil began to kiss my neck while I stroked his half-naked torso. His skin felt as hot and silken as the lips that slid down my body. To my collarbone. To my shoulder. To my breast. But just before they reached the place I wanted them most, Neil paused and shot me an amused glance.

"Sit down on the edge of the bed," he ordered, taking me by the hips and slowly pushing me backward. I obeyed him, trying not to trip over my own feet as I sat down in just my panties. I tilted my face up to stare at him as he stroked my cheek with his coarse knuckles.

"Now spread your legs," he added as he kneeled before me. He looked like a dark angel, his feathered wings long since torn away. Though my body yearned for him, I blushed, and from his amused look, I knew that he'd seen me. I opened my thighs a little wider, albeit hesitantly, and flexed my toes against the floor. His lips started at my knee and traveled slowly up my inner thigh. His wild hair tickled my sensitive skin, and his trim beard rasped against me, but it all felt so good that I felt chills moving rapidly over every part of me. With my palms pressing deep into the bed and my legs spread wide, I felt his fingers hook around my panties. His golden eyes peered into mine.

"Do you mind if I rip these?" He just smiled, and without waiting for me to answer, tore them completely off me and threw them to the floor. The movement took my breath away, and I also felt confused as something twisted in the depths of my stomach, making every muscle down there tighten as the place between my legs throbbed even harder.

"You've done it now..." I answered deliriously, but Neil was no longer looking at my face. Instead, he was staring into the delicate place between my thighs. It felt like he was devouring me with his eyes, and I began to quiver from nerves and arousal.

"I said spread your legs," he said again, more harshly this time. After he'd stripped me naked, I'd involuntarily closed them again, obeying the shy, ashamed part of me. I still wasn't used to sex—for me, it still felt like the first time every time. Meanwhile, Neil was completely comfortable. I obeyed him with a heavy sigh and I spread my legs wider, feeling the tissues of my sex unfurl like a blooming rose. I was laid bare for his ravenous eyes. He bit his full lower lip and then, with a cheeky smile, he seized my legs without an ounce of delicacy.

"Neil," I cried to him, fisting the sheets in my hands, but his honey-colored eyes stayed fixed on me there, seeming to truly adore the sight—to worship it like a deity. He was prepared to light me aflame, to make me his in any way he could.

"Fuck, do I want to lick you." He leaned into my pussy and began showering it with warm, wet kisses. He looked up at me through his brown eyelashes, and wicked fireworks seem to explode in the dim room, lighting up my cheeks.

"Oh God," I murmured as the tip of his tongue drew, hot and voluptuous, over my clit. Neil teased it, sucked slowly on it, and my groan of pleasure was unstoppable. I shut my eyes and ran my hands through his disheveled hair, pressing his head more firmly against me. As promised, I gave him all of me, everything I could. Everything he wanted. I ground myself shamelessly against his mouth, seeking relief from the fire that burned me from the inside out. He kept me pinned with his strong hands, his grip possessive and unyielding.

"I like it when you get into it." Neil grinned wickedly and continued to lap at me with his expert tongue. He moved down, lower and lower, his eyes still locked on my flushed face. "And I love the way you taste." He slid his tongue inside me and moved it like he was kissing me.

"Yes…" I moaned, my back bowing upward. I could feel my nipples growing hard at his slow torture. He licked, and I moaned again. Suddenly, his tongue was replaced with his pinched fingers, and I screamed. He rotated them back and forth as he began to stroke me. His fingers moved in and out, fast and certain.

"Yeah, just like that. Show me how good it feels, Babygirl…" His masculine voice only made me tremble harder and gasp for air. I couldn't hold out any longer; the tension had become unbearable.

I let my head fall back and clutched the sheets in my hands as Neil continued to dominate me. All at once, my brain short-circuited and it got hard to breathe. I rocked my pelvis and took his fingers inside me, all the way down to the base of them. As I did, I felt a wave of heat rising up from deep within me. I felt, as always, the irresistible urge to fill the void I had inside with him.

Only with him.

"Be a good girl. I'm not going to let you come like this…" Neil whispered perversely before slipping his fingers out of me and bringing them up to his lips to suck them clean. "Now, lie back," he demanded, and I obeyed.

I gazed up at him, dizzy and gasping with my heart in my throat and a weird ringing sensation in my ears. I lay down on the bed and bared myself just like he wanted. Neil smiled delightedly and pulled off his hoodie altogether, exposing his muscular chest that my eyes roamed lewdly over. Then he undid his pants and let them fall down his hard legs. He watched me, looking self-assured and hot as hell, and, still watching me, pulled down his black boxers.

I tried to meet his eyes, but Neil knew full well that there was somewhere else on his body I really wanted to look; I wasn't simply lowering my eyes out of embarrassment. With a perfect arrogant asshole grin, he stuck one knee in the mattress and climbed into the bed like a big cat, slow and relaxed, until he positioned himself between my splayed legs.

He sat back on his heels and stared again between my thighs. With his abs tensed, the line down the middle of them made a path leading right to the most powerful—and most frightening—part of his body.

It was then that I gave in to temptation: I looked at his hard cock, which he'd immediately taken in hand so he could pleasure himself in front of me. His gaze changed then. His desire burned higher, roasting the honey of his eyes as he stroked himself unhesitatingly. He was so aroused that he couldn't get his hand around it completely. The veins protruded more than usual and the glans was exposed. For just a second, I thought about getting up and fleeing in fear of what was about to happen to me, but the sight of Neil, nude with his lithe, well-formed body made all my hesitations evaporate. At the same time, a single curl fell over his forehead, covering part of his right eyebrow, and he looked somehow even sexier than before.

I focused my attention on the hand sliding up and down his length. I stared in awe, stunned and a little bit wary. I'd never seen him look so tense, loaded like a machine gun and ready to destroy me.

"Surprised, Selene?" He gave me a goading smile and moved up to grind himself between my legs. Pleasure rose up in me until I was being consumed by flames of my own. "Prepare yourself…" he said, sounding highly entertained even as his voice also grew rougher and more intense. But I didn't care about his warnings or any of his words. I wanted *it* too much.

"Make it quick." I lifted my pelvis up in challenge, and he looked into my core again. Hungry. Hungry like I had never seen him before. Then, with a self-satisfied little smile, he grasped his erection at the base and made a home for it inside my body with one rough thrust. I gasped as my body conformed around him, gritting my teeth.

"Fuck, I missed being inside you…" Neil moved over me and thrust his pelvis against me even harder, making my back bend. His swollen biceps flexed with effort as he began to move, not giving my body any time to adjust to him. I felt like a tiny port struggling to admit a great sailing ship. Neil pulled out and sank back into me, pulling a gasp from me. I clutched his back and tried to move with his thrusts. He continued penetrating me more and more aggressively, driving in deep like I wasn't even a person underneath him. Like he was all alone, lost in the extremity of his pleasure.

"Gentle," I said as I felt his mouth all over: licking, sucking, and biting my neck. He palmed my breast with one hand and pinched the nipple between his fingers, which produced a burning feeling of pleasure-pain. Almost immediately, our conjoined bodies grew slick with sweat. I traced the half-moons on his back made by his tensed muscles. My legs wrapped tight around his hips as they slammed furiously into me, making the bedsprings creak underneath us. I felt it all. All the way. He was sliding in and out of me with unreal speed and force, mixing pleasure with slight pain. My head spun. It felt like I was trapped on some terrifyingly out-of-control merry-go-round. I could hear his panting in my ear, his mouth branding me.

"G-gentle," I managed, barely able to get the word out, but Neil didn't seem to hear me anyway. He was completely enclosed in his own bubble of pleasure as he thrust deep into me. Completely at the mercy of that overwhelming sensation, my vision blurred, and all I could hear were muffled sounds.

I tilted my face down to look between our bodies and watched the inverted triangle of his pubic area colliding with my own sex. I examined the pikorua that ended just above his groin on his left side and watched his abs contract with effort as the sheets tangled around both of us.

"Gentle… Neil…" His name came out breathy, more like a plea than anything else. I moved my hands up to the headboard and wrapped my fingers around the bars there, trying to find something I could use to stabilize my body, which was jerking and sliding with each thrust. Instead, I got the exact opposite: The wrought-iron headboard banged against the wall like it was trying to get through to the other side as Neil continued to pound into me with all his might. "Neil," I cried out, alarmed and thrilled in equal measure. I squeezed my eyes shut and brought my hands back down to his sweat-slicked back.

"Shh…" He silenced me with a kiss. Passionate. Lewd. Rough. He forced his tongue into my mouth and worked it there furiously as he continued to crash his groin into mine. My breath caught in my chest, and I panted like a dog. I couldn't keep pace with him, couldn't match his rhythm. That had never happened before. I began to panic because I had no idea what to do. I couldn't break through his bubble.

"Neil...slow down..." I tried to say, but he ignored me once again. He seemed completely untethered. Untamable. A lion savaging his prey in a fit of blind fury. At the same time, my own body was sending me mixed signals. Even as I grew more aroused and slicker, I also began to ache and feel dizzy. Abruptly, he mouthed my neck, giving me at least a small chance to catch my breath, but his muscular chest was still crushing mine, pressing down on my lungs. My heart had gone crazy, throbbing not just in my temples but in my throat, my wrists, my stomach, and against my ribs. Everything about the moment was insane, twisted, and animalistic, but also...damnably hot. I was experiencing something so erotic, so indescribably intense.

"Keep up with me, Selene, because I'm not going to slow down..." he rasped into my ear, urging me to match his headlong pace. So I committed myself. All the way. I clung to his back, dug my heels into the mattress, and thrust my hips up to meet each of his strokes. "Good, like that... Just like that..." I bit down on his shoulder and began to rock as well, really taking every bit of him, pushing past my limits. All at once, my back arched, and I let out an uncontrolled scream. Then I began to shake all over as I abandoned myself to an orgasm that was as powerful as it was surprising.

But Neil just kept moving. He didn't stop even for a second.

In then out.

Out then in.

Out of his mind.

Honestly, if someone had asked me to describe what was happening in that moment, I wouldn't have known what to say. It was something grand, savage, painful, but unique—so damned unique. And, to my surprise, I discovered that I enjoyed it. It was ecstasy. Pleasure. Life.

I dug a hand into his damp hair and gritted my teeth in both pleasure and pain.

"You're hurting me, you prick," I hissed into his ear, feeling him grin against the crook of my neck as though he'd been waiting for me to say those exact words. He sat back abruptly on his heels and gathered me into his arms. I found myself straddling him like that, our faces level with each other and my thighs open over his groin.

"I may not be able to come, but I can still try…" He held me down against him and rubbed my ass before slamming my back against the mattress, and then I was underneath him again. Finally, I realized what he was trying to do: He wanted to break through the mental block that was keeping him from climaxing. He was fighting himself, and it was a war indeed.

"You're going to feel me everywhere. Today, tomorrow, the whole week," he blurted out, slowly extracting himself from me. With each inch that pulled free from my exhausted, burning channel, I grew stiffer. I didn't have time to catch my breath, though, because he pushed into me again, deeper this time and with even more force and speed. He felt like a hot blade slicing through my flesh, no trace of gentleness in him. His hands fisted the sheets. I scraped my nails down his back, repaying him in kind but nothing could stop him.

"Give me all of you. Your pain, your fear, your frustration. I can take it. I can take you," I whispered into his ear and closed my eyes as he thrust savagely into me again. I emitted a cry of pleasure from so deep within me that it scraped my throat on the way out. I mumbled his name, and when I tried to sit up slightly to change position, Neil pushed me back down with one hand. I was breathless, sweaty, and drained.

"Shut up, Selene. That's exactly what I'm doing," he growled irritably as he delved in and out of me like a beast, though he let out a moan so unmistakably manly that I shuddered.

It occurred to me then that I had been totally conquered by him. Neil had full control, power, and command over me, and nothing was going to stop him. He pressed in again, and my breath caught, my back bowed, and I screamed again, orgasming around him.

"Keep going." I licked his throat and stroked his skin. I wanted him to feel free. I wanted him to face down his demons. I wanted him to know that I would do anything for him. Neil muttered something before biting my lower lip and sucking it into his mouth. Beads of sweat covered his forehead, his eyes were glowing, and his amber skin shone like it had been polished. To me, he was as radiant as the sun, and I trembled beneath him.

"You don't have to feel wrong. I'll never judge you," I said again into his ear, just a whisper amid our panting breaths and the sounds of our bodies meeting, the groaning springs, the sweat, the commingled scents, and the deep, vibrant odor of sex.

"You'd just think I was a monster." He licked my throat in response and moved down to my breasts. He bent over a nipple and sucked it greedily, working it painfully between his teeth before soothing it with his tongue again.

"No. I wouldn't think that," I answered with some difficulty, feeling his guttural groan against my ear. My hands continued to roam over his body. I worshipped all of him: those broad shoulders, that strong back, his slim hips, and butt like marble.

He was a peerless Adonis. A sex machine.

A mass of muscle and sin.

And I did love to sin. With him.

Neil was flawed and unmanageable.

But in that moment, he was also mine.

I touched his soul with my words and whispered all my thoughts into his ear as I waited for him to come.

I was waiting for this savage coupling to end so I could cuddle close to him and hold him. But Neil still seemed to be far from the finish line. He kept drilling into me, more wound up than ever. I, on the other hand, had stopped feeling my body rebounding like a spring with each impact. Instead, I felt like I had liquefied into the mattress—melted and run like wax when the fire gets too close. My hair was a mess, my cheeks were burning, my legs ached, and my body had been beaten to a pulp by the multiple orgasms he'd given me.

"I don't know if…" he managed between gasps, and I lifted my head up to kiss his collarbone with the last of the strength I possessed. Neil looked at me, aroused, ecstatic, and lost.

His nose grazed mine, a drop of sweat dribbling down from his forehead onto my cheek while his lips hovered just over mine, suspended in the midst of our labored breathing. For just a moment, he ceased his assault, but then he picked it back up again, fast and frenzied, punching into me with rapid, deep strokes.

"You'll do it; keep going," I said, my worn-out voice almost inaudible. I put my hands on his hips in an attempt to moderate his thrusts.

But Neil was in the race to orgasm now.

He bolted like a spooked horse, unable to stop himself. I wavered between moments of intense pleasure and moments of true fear that he was going to hurt me, albeit unintentionally. And even though this way of taking me and claiming me was patently insane, I only continued to get more aroused.

"Fuck, you're still so tight…" he noted in a rough, sensual tone. Involuntarily, I contracted all my pelvic muscles to increase the friction between us as Neil moved unstoppably inside me.

"Almost there…" he growled, his breathing labored as he rested his forehead against mine. I let myself get lost in his lush, shining lips; his sweaty face was twisted in pleasure. A pleasure that I felt sure only I could give him. I didn't say that to him, though, and just enjoyed the guttural, masculine sounds of his moans as I gave him all of me, just like he'd asked. I stared into his eyes and tried to hold out against his power, his lusty body crashing vigorously into me, his stamina seemingly inexhaustible. Then, finally, after what felt like an endless number of powerful thrusts, I felt him go stiff and motionless inside me. He squeezed the sheets in his fists and his biceps twitched. The lines of the Māori-style tattoo there seemed to move around his gleaming, sweaty arm. The bed stopped squealing. I stopped breathing. My heartbeat slowed as his honey-colored eyes looked into mine and stayed there. He was coming out of his bubble—coming to me. Neil watched me, his eyes heavy-lidded for a moment before collapsing on top of me, burying his face in the crook of my neck. Involuntary muscle contractions swept over his body, and I stroked his hair as I went along with him through that unstoppable rush that ended in a veritable explosion of pleasure. The long-awaited orgasm had arrived, and it was so intense and went on for so long that Neil shook as he marked me, not just inside my body but also in my soul.

I rubbed his back, feeling his stiff muscles under my fingertips. He gave himself over to ecstasy with a deep sigh and then lay motionless on top of me. His breathing was uneven, and I could feel his heart beating way too fast in his chest. Meanwhile, I was feeling sorer than I ever had before, so I relaxed my legs, and Neil immediately looked up at me. He looked at me with flames of desire still burning in his eyes. Then, all at once, he rose up off me, making me feel suddenly cold. He lay down on his back beside me and stared up at the ceiling wordlessly. His amber skin was dewy, and his muscles were still tensed up. I realized he had to be just as exhausted as I was because what we had just done had not been sex.

It had been heart-pounding.

Pure adrenaline.

In those moments of pleasure, Neil had been able to destroy the enchanted palace.

And he had built instead an enchanting madness all around us.

I watched as he looked up at the ceiling, lost in thought.

"Well, good thing I'm already at home because I don't think I can walk anymore." I broke the silence with a wry comment. Neil didn't say anything for a long moment while my eyes moved from the edges of his profile to his lips, now a darker pink. He was so undone in the afterglow that it somehow made him look even more wildly beautiful.

"Are you okay?" he asked, not looking at me. But his voice sounded confused and annoyed.

"All things considered, yeah," I answered, pulling the sheet up to cover me. My head was still spinning, and my sex was swollen both from arousal and from the constant impacts. My lower stomach was also sore from absorbing his thrusts, and my skin burned in the places where he'd kissed, bitten, and touched me. It had never before been so intense between us.

Neil heaved a sigh and sat up in the bed, passing a hand through his wild hair. I didn't know what he was thinking, but he looked nervous and tense. Was he getting ready to run again?

Where would he go with his wings torn away?

With his face all filthy from ash?

With the past still painted on his body in blood?

"I have to…" He got out of the bed, exposing his toned ass for me as he bent over to grab his boxers. He pulled them on quickly, and I tracked his every motion in silence, stunned and frozen.

"You have to...?" I prompted him, sitting up slightly. When I sat forward, I winced a bit at the uncomfortable feeling between my legs but tried not to think about it.

"Go for a smoke," he answered flatly. Then he grabbed the pack of Winstons and stalked over to the big window that looked out over the garden. He cracked it open and leaned against the sill, lighting up a cigarette.

I considered his behavior, but once again, I didn't know what was wrong with him. I felt let down, hollowed, and used. And not because of what we had done together but because of his arrogant disregard and the way he completely closed himself off in his own world whenever we weren't in bed. I wasn't like Jennifer or his other lovers. Though I'd just worked hard to break him out of the impermeable prison he was trapped inside, I hadn't gotten a single kind touch in response. Not so much as a hug or word of comfort.

Outraged, I got out of bed. My head was still spinning, and I stood unsteadily on watery legs. I made my way to the bathroom after fishing clean panties out from my underwear drawer and examined my reflection in the mirror. My auburn hair was a rat's nest. My eyes shone a vivid blue. My cheeks were stained pink. My lips were puffy from his kisses. I rubbed my neck and brushed an index finger over the marks that Neil always left behind. Always so greedy. Always so hungry. I studied myself more carefully and frowned when I noticed a bit of bruising around my nipple. I looked down, tucking my chin, and touched it with my finger, which only made it throb, and a grimace of pain twisted my face.

Up until a few months ago, I believed sex was the complete union of body and soul.

I had always dreamed of giving myself to someone who would lavish care upon me.

I wanted to feel safe.

Embraced.

Loved.

But nothing had gone the way I'd dreamed.

And now there I was, standing in my bathroom looking at a girl I couldn't recognize.

A woman in love who did not regret her choices.

Despite it all.

"You're such an idiot," I told myself. It was no one's fault but mine. I shook my head bitterly, pulled on my clean panties, and splashed water on my face, trying to get myself back in order. But I sucked in a breath when I heard the window close.

I tried to remain unruffled and stall for time again, but as I heard his footsteps come closer and closer and closer, I couldn't think of anything. I couldn't do anything. I just glanced surreptitiously at his powerful figure leaning against the doorframe, proud and remote as ever. I pretended to stare into the mirror while my thoughts veered uncontrollably toward him.

"If you need to get back to New York, go ahead." I turned to him, breaking the uncomfortable tension between the two of us. I forced myself not to look at him as I walked out of the bathroom, but Neil's warm hand on my hip stopped me in front of him. I stared at an unremarkable spot on his chest while my heart sped up to a ridiculous speed and I gulped.

His hand slid to my back, and he pulled me to him. My breasts pressed against his torso, and a cold chill of excitement ran through me. I had no idea what he intended to do. He brushed my hair back over my shoulder and inspected my neck, then my breasts and hips.

The smell of sex, recently smoked cigarettes, and musk washed over me, and my breath caught in my throat.

"I'm not leaving," he told me after a long silence, his low, deep voice making me vibrate like a plucked guitar string. I stared at him; he was as serious, as inflexible, as always.

"Why... Why are you acting like this?" I shivered slightly. I was, after all, naked and freezing cold. "You succeeded," I muttered scornfully. "If your goal was to make me feel used, you've succeeded and—" Neil pressed his lips over mine on impulse, silencing me. He snaked one arm around my waist and pressed a hand to the nape of my neck, sliding the other one into my hair. It was a chaste kiss, eyes open. The kind of kiss meant to halt my words with a silent rebuke. After a moment, he pulled away and took my hand.

"You're freezing, and yes, I used you, though not in the way that you think," he said, pulling me along with him out of the bathroom. Never letting go of my hand, he scooped up his white hoodie and offered it to me.

"Oh no? So not like you use Jennifer and the rest of them?" I shot back at him, profoundly disappointed as he arranged the sweatshirt over my shoulders.

"Put it on. It'll warm you up fast," he ordered, and I slipped my arms into the oversized sleeves. Neil helped me zip it up, then looked me up and down, his face dazed.

"I asked you a question," I said acidly, and his golden eyes moved from my bare legs to my face.

I smelled musk all around me as I snuggled into his hoodie.

"I didn't come with Jennifer and the rest of them," he answered seriously, rubbing a hand over his face. "Can we go to sleep now, or do you need to keep busting my balls?" he asked shortly.

"Busting your balls?" I echoed indignantly.

"Yeah, that's right. All you do is bitch." He was starting to go off the rails; I could tell from the stormy look on his face, his tight muscles, and the way his voice changed. And all of it scared me. "You are so wrapped up in your own fucking technicolor world, Selene. You're always thinking about what I'm doing with other people, and you still can't see that you are not like any of them. Okay, so I'm not perfect. I don't snuggle. I don't cuddle. I don't whisper sweet nothings into your ear, but so the fuck what? Is there some postcoital rulebook you have to follow? Maybe you need candy and roses or something like that? You're so convinced I use you like I use them because you're incapable of understanding nuance. Several times now you've brought up other women because you're insecure, and maybe that's my fault too because I can't give you the attention you want, but that doesn't give you the right to constantly question me or make me feel crushed about this fucking situation that I can't handle any better than you!" He advanced on me, fuming, and I staggered backward.

"But…" I started to reply, but I trailed off when Neil approached, menacing me into silence.

"You really don't see it, do you? I came to Detroit again for you, to make sure that you were okay, because I knew perfectly well that I was wrong to leave the way I did last time. Because of you, I'm skipping out on my entire life," he ranted furiously, making me tremble with fear. "But you have to understand I am fucked up. I always have been, and you need to stop believing in this nonexistent 'us' you've created. What do you see when you look at me right now? A man or a monster? Tell me!" he snapped, inches from my face, as I stayed plastered against the wall in fear. Neil took me by the hair and yanked me forward, forcing me to look into his eyes. "Tell me. What do you see right now?"

"I see a man who has met a monster on his path," I said softly, and his eyes widened in surprise. He stood motionless for a few moments, then loosened his grip on my hair and took a step back.

"What do you know about it?" he asked me warily. There was no way I could tell him that Logan had told me part of the truth about Kimberly Bennett, so I pretended I didn't know any specifics.

"I figured it out." I squeezed the sweatshirt in my fists and tossed my bangs to one side. I was exhausted and fuzzy-headed. Keeping a conversation going with Neil in that condition was harder than I'd thought. After a moment, he started prowling around my room, unsure of what to do next. Maybe he did want to leave, to run away from me again. But I wasn't going to let him.

"Why don't we try to make all that anguish slip away?" I asked him, and he turned to look warily at me, stopping in the middle of the room. "Why don't we wash away some of that dirt you feel on you? Why don't we give in to the mad urge we both have and you can get a little bit of me and I'll get a little bit of you and we'll both try to understand what we're feeling?" I drew closer to him, fearlessly this time, and Neil just stood there motionless and listened to me.

"Why don't you let me touch you and hold you, because you know that I would never hurt you? Let's chase away your fears and face the world together. Let's beat back your past, erase all the bad memories, and live here in the present. Even if your reality is one no one would want. Stand with me, shoulders back, chest out, eyes wary, and your hand in mine. Because it's there in those hands, linked in fire-forged chains, that we will find our real strength," I finished. Neil seemed moved by my words. His shoulders slumped, and he rubbed his eyebrows, squeezing his eyes shut. Then he strode toward me with a grave, austere frown on his face. I shivered at the idea of him yelling at me again, but instead he took me by the nape of the neck and rubbed our noses together, staring into my eyes.

"Why don't you shut up and kiss me?" he said. I licked my lips, and he immediately seized them. The kiss was merciless, carnal, and seductive. Neil was staking his claim on me, and I no longer even knew where we were. Just like always, I felt completely sublimated and transported to another world. His world.

I clung to him, and only when he stopped to press his forehead against mine was I able to get a breath. He took notice and grinned, fully aware of the effect he had on me.

"I don't want to fight with you, Selene." He touched my cheek and stared thoughtfully into my eyes. "I'm not going anywhere. I'm staying here tonight," he added, and my anger vanished the moment I saw the tenderness woven into his words, a tenderness he rarely ever showed to anyone.

"I don't want to fight either," I said, smiling faintly as I reveled in his touch.

"Then let's just go to sleep." He turned from me and went to the bed. I still didn't know exactly why he'd decided to stay, but I was thrilled to be sleeping next to him again. It had only happened once before, and he had told me clearly the next morning that it hadn't meant anything, but to me, everything shared was incredibly meaningful.

Neil stretched out on my bed, beautiful as any god, and shamelessly ogled my bare thighs, barely skimmed by his sweatshirt. I walked unsteadily over to him and settled myself beside him. A moment later, he pulled me against him with one arm, slotting our bodies together like two pieces of an unfinished puzzle. I let my back rest against his chest and felt him sigh. I felt even smaller like that with his powerful arm clutching me under my breasts. I also felt protected and doted upon when Neil began to rub his nose along my throat.

"How many women have worn your shirts like this?" I asked, biting my lip too late to stop the inappropriate question. I really didn't want to fight again, and I hoped he wouldn't get mad.

"Two," he admitted, and jealousy clenched like a fist in my stomach. I hated having those feelings, but I couldn't stop them. I forced myself not to push him away, but Neil could feel my discomfort and squeezed me harder. "First my sister, and now another fucking girl who is constantly pissing me off," he said softly, nibbling my earlobe and rubbing himself against my ass until I could feel how much he wanted me still. I rolled over on my other side then and looked him in the eye, miffed.

"Why do you always have to be such a grouch?" I sulked, and he gave my back long, slow strokes.

"Don't you like me that way?" He kissed the tip of my nose and looked at me.

"No," I lied. His deep, rough voice sent little spikes of electricity through my chest, and he smelled so good that I forgot any reasonable thing I wanted to tell him.

"Such a liar..." He quit stroking my back and brushed against my hip before tracing the edges of my panties with an index finger. He slipped a hand underneath the fabric, and I shivered.

"You don't like me, but you're wet for me again," he whispered, stroking me between my thighs. Meanwhile, his erection was still pressing against me, a sure sign of his raging desire. Neil never ran out of energy for sex. It was his true medium, the realm where he was able to unleash all his power.

"And you're hard for me again," I teased, and Neil kissed my neck, slowly dragging his hand out of my panties.

"Aaaand it's time for sleep now," he said firmly. "And I'd prefer to have your cute little ass rubbing up on me all night." He rolled me back over into spooning position. Sometimes I felt like my body was just a marionette for him to manipulate with his hands.

I stopped worrying, though, when he put his arms around me and rested his chin on the top of my head, breathing in the scent of my hair. Several silent minutes passed while I looked into the darkness in front of me and imagined I was a tiny butterfly watching us from above. I fluttered over our bodies, wings beating languidly and elegantly, and I admired us as we lay next to each other. The perfect pair on a big bed that smelled of sex, of chaos, of feeling, of fighting, of laughter, of hugs, of our skin and breath, and of kisses.

What a pity that, in reality, almost nothing about us was perfect…
Nothing.

With a strange feeling of anguish inside me, I turned to him again, perhaps hoping to dismantle some of my insecurities.

"Neil?" I said, hoping he hadn't fallen asleep already.

"What?" he answered immediately, sounding bored.

"Do you care about me?" I asked him.

"Go to sleep, Selene." He repositioned himself and snorted.

"A little bit, at least?" I insisted through a sleepy yawn.

"Good night," he shut me down with typical coolness.

"But…"

"Babygirl, stop fucking with me and go to sleep," he ordered grimly, and I rolled my eyes.

"You're an idiot," I shot back at him.

"And you're a fairy. My Tinkerbell. That enough for you?" I felt his breath disturb my hair and squirmed against him.

"No, I want to be exclusive." I turned to give him a sideways glance. I could tell that Neil was considering my request.

"Meaning?"

"No other women. I'm the only one who gets to touch you," I explained, and he didn't say anything in return; instead, he went back to dragging the tip of his nose along my skin. The long silence quickly became unbearable.

"I'll think about it," he promised. It wasn't a yes, but it wasn't a flat-out refusal either. Maybe even Neil had realized that this thing of ours could be improved if he would commit to giving me more than just the same thing he offered to everyone else.

"Thank you," I murmured.

"Selene?" For the first time, he was the one who sought my attention, and I turned again to him. "I might have some nightmares…" he explained in a worried tone, but I rubbed the back of his hand, which was splayed over my stomach.

"Don't worry about it. We'll banish them together. Just close your eyes." I rolled over fully to face him, and after a few moments of hesitation, he obeyed me. Then I deposited a sweet little kiss on his right eyelid and then another one on his left. Neil slowly opened his eyes again, his golden gaze even brighter somehow.

"It's called the angel's kiss. My grandma used to do it to me when I was little and couldn't sleep because I was too afraid of the dark. She said it had the power to chase away any nightmare."

Neil watched me gravely, one corner of his mouth creeping up in a lazy, sensual fashion. He pulled my head down against his chest.

"You are sickly sweet, Tigress. Be aware—I'm going to want these kisses all the time," he said softly. Was that his way of paying me a compliment? I didn't have time to ponder it, however, because Neil pulled me against him, and my heart began to flutter in my chest like the wings of a hummingbird.

"You can have all the angel kisses you want if you just keep telling me about yourself, okay?" I nestled into him as I reminded him of our deal.

"Okay," he answered, and then I closed my eyes, falling asleep.

Neil was circulating inside me by that point.

My love for him was undying.

And who knew? Maybe one day his heart would also transform into a hummingbird?

And would his skin also erupt into goosebumps when he heard my voice?

And would his legs shake when he looked at me?

Who could say?

After all, everyone knows that love is a risk.

And a pleasure.

And an act of bravery.

And a wound.

Of course his inner chaos had gotten into my own head and changed me.

But I was not afraid.

He would always find comfort in my arms, like the arms of an angel.

Because he was a part of me now.

And he always would be.

19

The more time passed, the more of her I consumed.
But what, in the end, would be left of her?

NEIL

I kept staring at the photo of my mother and father.

Mom wore her wedding dress and wasn't smiling.

It looked like she was watching me.

It looked like she was sad.

Dad had an arm wrapped around her waist, and he pressed a kiss to her cheek.

He looked happy.

And, fortunately, he wasn't watching me. I would have been even more ashamed.

Kim said it was more exciting to touch each other in my parents' room.

My heart was pounding hard inside my chest.

"Neil, where are you?" I heard Logan's small voice calling from the other side of the closed door, and I wanted to answer him, but my babysitter wouldn't let me.

"Shh... keep quiet." Kim licked her lower lip and grinned at me. I nodded in surrender and let her continue torturing me. She loomed over me as she told me that she still had so much more to teach me.

I squeezed my eyes shut and tried to keep myself from crying.

I never cried while Kim was hurting me.

All I could feel was my stomach twisting with the urge to vomit.

I focused on the photo of Mom and Dad.

I felt consumed.

Dazed.

Filthy.

Stripped of a soul.

Stripped of dignity.

I'm sorry, Mom, that I wasn't brave enough to tell you, *I thought.*

....

I smoked a cigarette in the dim light of Selene's room, sitting awkwardly at her desk in a chair that was way too fucking small for someone my size. It was late at night, and another one of my nightmares had gotten me out of bed, nervy and sweating.

Kim woke me up once again.

She couldn't handle not being the whore in my head for one single night.

I blew smoke into the air, turning my attention back to Babygirl. I watched her as she lay there snoozing in the bed. Sheets covered her bare legs, and her torso was swathed in my white sweatshirt.

I fiddled with the Winston between my index and middle fingers. I closed one eye and squinted into the burning cherry, which was slowly burning through the entire thing.

And maybe that was me for Selene.

Her combustion point.

The more time passed, the more of her I consumed.

But what, in the end, would be left of her?

I took another drag as the smell of smoke mixed with coconut wafted around between the walls and stared at my Babygirl.

I studied her disheveled hair spread out across the pillow in auburn ribbons, her flexed arm, and her hand closed into a fist next to her plush lips, still swollen and pink from my kisses.

Then I turned my attention to her alabaster skin; there were reddish marks around her throat from my bullying hands. All of my desires were written on her body, a record of the sex we'd just had together.

She was brain-meltingly beautiful, naive, and sweet, and she looked at me like I was the kind of man who was worthy of her purity.

I heaved a sigh and rubbed a hand over my face and up through my hair. I jostled my leg anxiously and stared at Selene again as the darkness welled up inside me.

Sometimes, I had to run.

I had to go and then come back to her.

We had an unhealthy relationship.

We both knew it.

So why was she wasting her time with someone like me?

She needed to give her dreams to someone who could actually make them come true.

She had to save her tears for someone who deserved them.

And her embraces for an angel like her.

Not for me.

I sucked in more nicotine, poisoning my lungs a little bit more as I thought.

Whenever things finally felt good with Selene, my past would grab me by the hair to remind me that I needed to stick to my shadow world. The one with the blonds, my father's punches and slaps, with my own unseen tears and defiled body, with my anxiety, fear, loneliness, and dysfunction.

Every time I tried to step foot out of that chaos, the monsters would drag me back in.

I was trying to stand in her light.

I was trying to follow it.

But how could I do that?

How could I do that when I was still a prisoner?

I walked slowly over to Tinkerbell's bed and sat down, the springs creaking just a little. I held the cigarette between my lips, squinting through the thick smoke, and raised a hand to touch her cheek. I stroked her hair and neck while she slept peacefully on.

"I feel less empty when I'm with you," I told her, knowing that she couldn't hear me. "The room isn't so cold when I sleep with you. But I'm afraid of getting swallowed up. By you. By what you give me. By the things you want from me. Besides, who is going to put me back together when you shatter me?" I asked her, taking another drag. Selene twitched slightly under my hand, but she didn't wake, so I continued. "You have this power...so much of it. You *can* shatter me, but I can't let you. It's been so hard patching myself back up; I can't let you tear me apart again." I had finally copped to the greatest truth of all: I was afraid of her.

I, Neil Miller, was afraid of the seemingly magical power of this girl with the ocean eyes. Fairies were dangerous; I'd known that even as a child. They would encircle you, enslave you, and then abandon you, leaving you nothing but a shambles of misery and desolation. Babygirl groaned in her sleep, slightly parting her plump, rounded lips with their shape like a heart. I scrutinized her long eyelashes and continued to slowly stroke her silken skin.

I'd taken her furiously, full of anger and lust. I wanted her to see that she couldn't keep searching for some good in me, that she couldn't keep pushing up against my limits. I myself was very aware of how abnormal my behavior was and how hard I was to manage. For a moment, I had gotten lost in her body as I sought the oblivion of pure pleasure, but I'd immediately come back to reality, where my life was nothing but shit. "You're not mine, and I'm not yours," I told her, still smoking. "Because we belong to the world, not to each other. We're souls, not things. And there will be someone else for you someday." It was draining to sit there and admit that I wasn't good enough for Selene, to confess that I couldn't give her the things she needed. I understood that she liked me, and I knew that she desired me, but the question always remained: Would she "love" me if I didn't look the way I did?

Kimberly had loved me too but only because I was "a beautiful boy." She told me so plenty of times.

Recalling that caused a wave of misery to move through me, so I got out of the bed and padded barefoot over to Selene's desk. I tossed my cigarette butt in the trash and then poked through the kitten-patterned pen holder, searching for a *black* marker.

When I found it, I popped off the cap and walked over to the mirror, where I could just see my reflection in the dim light. I stared at my body, covered only in my boxers. Long legs, slim hips, defined abdominals, swollen pecs, and broad shoulders. I examined the two tattoos, the swollen veins that branched out into meandering tributaries, dark underneath my skin. I looked like a grown man now, but inside, I was still ten-year-old Neil with all the marks of Kim's abuse visible on me.

All at once, my face shifted. The beard vanished. The eyes softened, the hair grew longer and messier, and the features became more delicate, more youthful. I now wore an Oklahoma City basketball jersey and a pair of blue shorts—the ones I always wore to play basketball out in the backyard. Suddenly, I wasn't in Selene's house anymore but back in my childhood home in New York. My conscience was guilty, my soul was stained, my innocence was decimated, and my babysitter's voice was constantly in my head.

With my eyes locked on my reflection and the memories spinning around in my head, I gripped the marker and began moving its soft tip around on me, like my skin was a canvas to be spoiled, a wall to be graffitied, a paper to be scrawled upon, or a shitty story waiting to be written. I pressed the marker into my skin wrathfully, drawing all kinds of shapes all over myself. Slowly, the rising sun began to illuminate me. Another day when I'd managed to wake up before destiny, but it wouldn't change anything.

After an endless minute, I let the marker fall to the floor and, with the back of my hand, smeared the black ink over every patch of skin I could reach on my chest, throat, and arms. I spit out the cap I'd been clenching in my teeth and stared into my reflection in the mirror again, longing now to smash it.

"Neil." I heard Selene's voice, but I remained motionless.

"Do you see that, Babygirl? There's something broken and twisted inside my head," I said, gazing into the glass.

"What are you doing?" I heard the bedsprings protest and the sound of faint footsteps approaching me slowly.

Was my Tigress afraid?

"It's their fault, too, you know. The people who get raped." I looked out through the glass, talking to her the way she was always begging me to do.

"Wh-what are you talking about?" she stammered. Obviously Selene didn't understand me—she couldn't.

"The Boy liked Kim's attention. He was willing to be touched. He should

442

have told her no, but instead, he let it go on for a year." I smiled sardonically, shaking my head. "I'm filthy because of *me*," I concluded, turning to face her. I immediately locked on to her ocean eyes as they roamed over my body in horror before returning to my blank, lost eyes.

"No, Neil. It's never a child's fault. Never." She paused. "What did you do to yourself?" she asked, quickly wiping a tear away from her cheek. Did she just not want to cry in front of me or had she understood what I was talking about?

"Are you okay?" she asked again, in shock. But she inched closer to me, and I glanced down at her naked legs. My too-big sweatshirt concealed all those head-turning curves. Her hair was a mess, her lips swollen and chapped, and her cornflower-blue eyes, barely open, outshone the sun. She reached out to touch me, but I stepped back from her. I didn't want it then.

"Is this marker?" She grimaced, looking at my chest.

"I've got a stain on me," I confessed, hoping she'd be able to intuit what had happened to me when I was a kid. I wasn't brave enough to tell her frankly about it, but I wanted her to know the truth.

"Then I want one too." She chewed thoughtfully on the inside of her cheek and looked around until she spotted the marker on the floor.

"Watch…" She pulled the zipper of my hoodie down slowly, exposing her round, firm breasts. My eyes fixed on her rosy nipples, especially on the bruise around her areola, as she let the sweatshirt slide to the floor. She stood in front of me in nothing but her panties, and I longed to fuck her again, but I tried not to let myself be distracted.

Selene brought the marker up to her neck and started drawing nothing in particular on the skin there. She did the same on her chest, her stomach, and her arms. Then she rubbed her hands over it, making big smears of ink. Finally, she looked back up at me, delighted and self-assured.

"Now we're both stained. See?" She smiled and let the marker fall to the floor. She drew closer to me until her high, soft breasts pressed against my chest. Her scent made me close my eyes momentarily as I was, for just an instant, transported somewhere far away. To my Neverland. My blood began to pound in my veins. I opened my eyes and stared into hers before moving to her lush lips, her breasts, her slim legs…

"You're cute…" I had told her once.

You are a work of art… I had thought.

I gathered her abruptly in my arms, without any consideration or warning. My hands came to rest on her ass, and I lifted it up with a squeeze, making her wrap her legs around my hips. Babygirl clung to my shoulders as I kissed her with all the desire that burned within me. I kissed her like a starving beast, a rabid animal, and I knew that she liked me that way as well.

"Good morning" was all I said as I carried her into the bathroom. I kicked the door open, and she grinned in my arms. She was so light, small, and sweet-smelling. I didn't even make it to the shower, instead pressing her against the cold tile beside the sink and devouring her, swallowing her moans and giving her mine in return.

"Good morning to you too," she said breathlessly, her face all red, but I didn't stop. I fondled one of her breasts roughly and pinched the nipple in my fingers. I could feel arousal pounding through every part of me, and my cock throbbed beneath my boxers. I had to rub myself against her thighs for some momentary relief.

"Neil, wait…" Selene said in a small voice, and I immediately turned into an ice sculpture.

"What?" I stared into her eyes, steady but eager, and I refused to put her back down.

"It's just that, well, after last night. I'm still a little…sore. Down there," she said awkwardly, and I realized how ridiculous I was being.

"You're right. I'm sorry, Babygirl." I leaned my forehead against hers, and our labored breathing commingled. I lowered her to the floor but still allowed myself a lingering touch on her back and ass.

"I want to…but…" she tried to explain, but I pressed my finger to her lips.

"You should take a warm bath," I said simply. Her eyes lingered on my lascivious grin. "The heat will make it feel better," I added earnestly. I dragged myself away from her then to lean over and turn on the bathtub faucet.

"A bath?" she repeated, sounding confused. I perched on the cold edge of the bathtub as it began to fill with hot water.

"Yeah, come over here." I dipped a hand in the water to check the temperature and Selene approached, blushing, and her boring little panties made her look sexier than she ever could have imagined. The white fabric was darker—saturated—in the center, and I stared at that wet place like an animal that hadn't eaten in months.

"Get naked." I smiled and looked her slowly from top to bottom just to watch her get uncomfortable.

Adorable.

"Quit it," she chided me, but to my surprise, she did exactly as I'd told her. She undressed and exposed her naked body to me with obvious pride. So I accepted the invitation and ate her up with my eyes. The goosebumps that erupted all over her skin confirmed the devastating effect I had on her. All at once, I recalled her sweet taste and licked my lower lip. The urge to taste her again was constant and overwhelming. It was never enough for me—never.

"You're watching me like some pervert," she said shakily, approaching the edge of the tub. Before she could step in, though, I grabbed her around the waist and pulled her to me. My face was level with her stomach, and so I pressed a kiss there.

"Maybe because I am some pervert…" I smiled insolently at her and stroked the back of her thighs as I kissed her soft stomach. The muscles there contracted when my burning lips touched them. "A big one…" I moved slowly downward to her pubic mound and kissed her there as well, taking note of the fact that her goosebumps went all over. Her hands rested on my shoulders, and her back arched. "I'm way past all that decency…" I rubbed my nose against her vulva and licked her stiffened little clit. Then I looked back up at her, sinking into her bright eyes with a wicked grin. "Now, get in the water." I stood up slowly, making sure to rub myself against her and pulling a gasp out of her.

"Such an asshole," she huffed. She smelled of coconut and sex. She was covered in ink and more beautiful than ever.

"Get a move on, Tigress." I slapped her ass, and she jumped before stepping gracefully into the tub like a goddess. She moaned appreciatively, and I stared at her stiff, wet nipples as the clear water lapped against them.

"Aren't you going to get in? You need to get clean too." She gestured at my stained chest, and I gave her a tiny smile, slipping my hand into the water until I brushed against her smooth ankle.

"Do you want me to come in?" I cocked an eyebrow, and she rolled her eyes at me.

"Take a bath with me," she demanded, her voice sensual. She began to toy with her breasts with one hand, looking archly at me because she knew I couldn't resist her.

"Are you teasing me?" I stood up from the tub and grabbed the waistband of my boxers, which I immediately slid down my legs. Her taunting smile faded as her eyes settled on the part of me that she loved and feared the most. I gave her a wry smile and lifted my leg to step into the tub, right behind her.

"It would be better if you got in front of me... I mean...look..." She bleated, but I ignored her and made myself comfortable behind her. I caged her between my legs and let her lean back against my chest.

"No, I need to be back here. Right next to this cute little ass," I whispered slyly into her ear as I minutely adjusted my hips to get more comfortable. She sucked in a breath when she felt my hard-on pressing against the base of her spine.

"Of course, obviously," she said sarcastically before stretching out an arm to grab a blue bath puff and some coconut bath gel.

"Leave it. I'll do that." I plucked them out of her hands in my usual abrupt manner and tried to ignore her protests. I drizzled a copious amount of soap into the water and then threw the puff away on the tile floor.

"What are you doing? That's..." She fell silent as I began to rub her shoulders.

"I prefer to use my hands. I'm a romantic, you know," I murmured seductively, slowly moving my hand down to her breasts and giving them firm strokes. Selene let her head fall back against my chest.

"You never fail to exploit an opportunity, do you?" she groused with a little smile. Then I moved down to her stomach and rubbed her there as well with an uncharacteristic gentleness.

"If I was exploiting an opportunity, I'd be fucking you again. But look at me, pampering you..." I kissed her neck, and my hands moved lower and lower until they were between her thighs. I fondled her slowly, and Selene tensed up. "Relax." I didn't want her so stiff; I wanted the opposite. So I delicately rubbed her clit until she sighed.

"You had a nightmare, didn't you?" she asked in a sad murmur, her hand stroking up and down my arm.

"Yes," I admitted freely, rubbing her stomach again.

"I'm sorry. I thought sleeping with me might help," she said in dismay, turning to look at me. I took the opportunity to push the wet hair off her forehead.

"It's good, sleeping with you…" *But nothing is going to scrub Kim from my head.*

"I want it to be great, not just good." She huffed and scooped up some soap foam in both hands, blowing it away.

"You are such a child. Would you like a few rubber duckies as well?" I sneered, which earned me an elbow to the gut. "Or will you settle for a dragon?" I whispered again, thrusting my hips forward.

"Neil!" She jumped and sent the water splashing out of the tub. I burst into laughter, and she pouted at me. "Not funny!" she scolded, blowing more soap foam into my face in revenge, and I abruptly arranged my face into a grave expression. Selene bit her lip, and then the real battle began. God forbid we take a normal bath.

I pinned her with my legs and began lightly pinching her. Babygirl struggled to break free, laughing. She laughed like a wild thing. It was a beautiful sound.

"Neil, come on. Knock it off!" Breathless, Selene found herself straddling me, wet hair plastered against her breasts as they heaved with her labored breathing. Drops of water hung like crystal ornamentation from her stiffened nipples.

She was fucking magnificent.

"Tinkerbell, you have two choices: You can either get out of this position, or you can let me fuck you for real. You decide." I rested my head on the lip of the tub and slid lower until our bodies were perfectly aligned. But Babygirl seemed to be distracted by my chest. She stared at it, looking like her thoughts were far away.

"You can't feel stained. Not ever," she said softly, running her hands over my pectorals and then up to my neck, scrubbing at the ink stains that were slowly washing away into the water. "Understand? Never again," she said, baldly on the edge of tears. I didn't want her suffering over me and what I was.

I grabbed her wrist and looked deep into her eyes, those pure eyes that fixed on mine, letting me feel every bit of her sorrow.

"Promise me you won't cry for me again." It was more a command than a request.

"What?" Her face took on a look of bewilderment, and I glanced at her full lips.

"Promise me, Selene," I repeated only a little less abruptly.

"I can't... I...don't..." She shook her head, and I grabbed her around the waist.

"I said, promise me." I sat up and glared sternly at her. Her shoulders slumped and she gave in.

"Okay, I promise," she surrendered.

"Good..." I gave her a chaste little kiss on the tip of her nose and made myself comfortable again, my head resting on the cool rim of the tub, my hands firm on her hips. "Now, what's your plan here? You going to ride me?" I teased her, hoping to dispel some of the tension, and her eyes bugged slightly.

"Oh my God, no!" She gulped, and I glanced down at the pink marks dappling her body.

"I know, Babygirl. I was just joking," I told her, and Selene sighed in relief before frowning as something occurred to her.

"What time is it? I'm supposed to go to the university today." She stood up immediately and climbed out of the tub, giving me a very nice view of her wet, gleaming body. My little Tigress had an incredible ass, and one day I was going to take that too.

As she rifled around for a towel, I sank into the coconut-scented water and watched her easily, openly devouring every inch of exposed flesh.

Once she found the towel, she wrapped it around herself, putting an end to my lewd daydreams, and I snorted.

"Chill out. It's not quite eight o'clock, and you don't have to be anywhere until nine. I saw it on your calendar," I muttered as I got out of the tub, although less elegantly than she had done. I got water everywhere.

"No, you don't understand. I have to get my schedule approved, talk to my professors, and get my list of books to buy..." She stopped the moment her eyes caught on my body, hypnotized by each drop of water that ran down my skin. Her gaze wandered down and lingered on my hard-on, the head gleaming and pulled taut.

"But I get it; I won't waste any more of your time." I gave her a goading wink and grabbed a towel to wrap around my own hips.

"Neil..." she called out to me, watching me stand before the mirror. I finger-combed my wet hair one-handed and looked at her in the mirror, giving her my full attention. "I want to know you. All of you," she continued, and her cheeks were stained with red.

I looked thoughtfully at her, not immediately realizing what she'd meant. Then, it occurred to me—the only part of me she didn't know: my *taste*.

"What are you saying?" I furrowed my brow as I turned to her.

"What, you think I can't do it?" She put her hands on her hips in a challenging fashion, like she always did. A little girl getting into big trouble.

"You don't know what you're talking about." I shook my head, looking down at her. I advanced slowly on her slim body, watching her confidence crumble as I did so. I stopped just short of touching her face and stared her down arrogantly.

"You'd regret it," I told her honestly, and she smiled at me.

"I wouldn't," she answered, touching my hips gently, and a little shiver of arousal ran down my spine. I stepped back to escape her touch.

"You know what I'm like." She knew it very well, and I didn't want her to feel used by me.

"I don't care. I want to try it," she said without hesitation. Then, she lowered her eyes and wrung her hands awkwardly. Maybe she was already regretting her offer, or maybe she was just waiting to see if I'd accept? I grimaced in disappointment. I didn't want to give in to her, but I also couldn't help but think about how it would feel to get my favorite kind of foreplay from her. Eventually, my damned instincts won out, and I leaned down to whisper in her ear.

"So you want to suck my cock?" I teased her wickedly, and Selene staggered back a few steps, bumping into the wall behind her. She looked automatically at my naked chest and swallowed awkwardly. But she'd provoked me; she'd let the lion out of his cage, and my little gazelle wasn't going to escape now.

"Right now?" I could tell how afraid she was from the way her face drained of color. I thought too much of her to push her into anything she didn't want to do. But I was a giant asshole, so I wasn't going to pass up a chance to mess with her a little.

"What, are you afraid?" I licked my lower lip and inched closer to her. I dug a hand into her damp hair and pressed my pelvis against her hip to show her that my cock really was ready for her.

"No, not at all," she said softly, looking up at me through her thick black lashes, her ocean stare even more sparklingly clear than usual.

"You sure?" I asked, watching as her cheeks got even redder. "Don't feel like you have to. I'm fine." I touched her chin, and that seemed to embolden her. She reached out and grabbed the edge of the towel I was wearing. It was then that I realized that Logan had been right: I had not only had an orgasm with Selene, but I also wanted to have another one and another one and a thousand more after that.

"I'm sure." She drew close to me and kissed my neck. All I could smell then was her coconut smell. Drunkenly, I moved a hand through her hair while Selene began to slowly kiss every inch of my skin. I exhaled slowly, enjoying the delicate pressure of her lips.

I knew that Babygirl had never done this before, that her lovely mouth was still untainted, and this would be her first time. For just a moment, I had second thoughts.

The innocent yet provocative air that surrounded her, however, shut down every single neuron in my brain. I felt my heart throbbing everywhere as the blood rushed to one specific part of my body.

"You can stop anytime," I told her, reining in my excitement because this was about her. If I had been faced with anyone else, I would have said fuck it and stuffed her mouth full by that point. But not with her.

I would go easy on her.

"No. I want all of you," she answered, kissing my chest. I clenched my fist in her hair and tugged until her face was only a short distance from my own. Selene's eyes widened when she saw the fiery lust lighting up my own eyes.

"This is your last warning. You won't be able to back out after this point." I gave her an insolent smile and leaned against the rim of the sink. A challenge. Babygirl approached me, still half-naked and dripping water. She studied my abs and lower stomach. She looked aroused yet thoughtful.

I gave her a faint, lewd smile, and she looked directly at my swollen cock, still concealed behind the towel.

"I won't back out," she answered, sounding determined.

"Get on your knees," I commanded, touching her soft cheek. Selene moved closer and carried out my instruction, kneeling in front of me. Then I undid the towel's knot and stood in front of her, completely naked.

Babygirl looked shocked by the large, imposing organ jutting upward right in front of her face, and she blinked rapidly at it. Almost immediately, she began to panic, clutching her towel like that was going to help her figure out how to make it all fit. I pressed my lips together to keep from bursting into uproarious laughter.

"Take it easy. Start slow..." I reassured her immediately and caressed her face as she swallowed with visible tension in her muscles. She just kept staring at me like it was something monstrous to run away from me. Maybe she was changing her mind?

"How... What do I... It's too much... I mean... I... Oh, God," she babbled confusedly, turning her big eyes up at me. I gave her the barest hint of a smile. I hated to admit it, but I loved that innocent part of her. For the first time in my life, I was enjoying a girl's naivete.

I liked that funny, sometimes irritating but one-of-a-kind part of her. Fucking one of a kind.

"Touch me." I took one of her wrists and positioned her hand at the base of my cock. Selene wrapped her fingers around me and began stroking it from top to bottom. "That's it." I continued to lean confidently against the sink and watched proudly as my erection swelled more and more against her hand. She stared into my eyes like she was trying to crawl inside me.

What was she after now?

"Now lick it," I said in a hoarse whisper as I slid my hand into her hair and gently pulled her against me. Selene let out an embarrassed gasp, not expecting that move. She swallowed and stuck out her tongue, resting it delicately on the tip of my penis and flicking it impishly. "Yeah, gentle…" I let my head fall back and let out a little groan of pleasure. Which was strange because I was usually pretty silent during sex, but I was becoming so unpredictable when I was with Babygirl.

"You're doing so well, Selene. Keep going."

And she obeyed. Her tongue slowly trailed down to the base of me before returning to the tip and swirling inquisitively around it. All the while, her hand continued to move clumsily over my shaft, and I realized that her fumbling was nothing short of mind-blowing. She was discovering, experimenting, and exploring.

"Now wrap your lips around your teeth and take just the tip in your mouth. Carefully." I wanted so badly to fuck her mouth, but it was Selene kneeling before me, not some random blond.

She is my Tinkerbell, I thought, forcing myself to maintain control.

She nodded and opened her mouth, allowing me to slide right in. Her warmth welcomed me immediately, and my stomach instinctively tensed up from the feeling of pleasure that radiated up through my chest, squeezing me as if in a fiery fist.

"Breathe through your nose." I pulled out slowly and then reentered her mouth. I set a pace and began to dictate the rhythm. It was deeply satisfying to know that I was the first person to do this with her. I held her gently by the hair, my hand at the nape of her neck, and she kept up the rhythm. She seemed to be concentrating so intensely, and occasionally she would look up at me for reassurance, so I'd smile down at her.

How did she look so beautiful even on her knees?

"Good, take a little bit more, but don't push it. I don't want you to gag." My breathing sped up as she worked hard to fulfill my every demand. The more time passed, the more comfortable my Tigress got playing with me, exploring me, and discovering what I enjoyed. Her body was still tense, but she was more confident now. Just how I wanted her. Everything about that moment felt so right, so natural, so genuine, like our bodies were made just for that. Like they were two incomplete halves that complemented each other perfectly.

I watched, enthralled, as Selene continued to pleasure me.

"Yes, just like that," I said in a hoarse whisper while she adjusted herself to the new invasion of her body. "Now suck on it." My voice was heavy with the desire that I was trying to keep under control. I gripped the lip of the sink as Selene took more and more of me into her mouth. I eased in and out of her, rocking cautiously back and forth. She was pleasuring me so slowly it was driving me out of my mind. "Yes, Babygirl, that's good…" I stroked her silken hair and licked my lower lip before pulling her head against me. I felt her hands clutch my thighs for support. "More," I whispered breathlessly, and she squeezed her eyes shut, turning red. "You like it?" She looked up at me and nodded, and I couldn't help but thrust a little harder into her mouth.

I was a devil, but, fuck it, she was divine.

All at once, her azure eyes became glassy, and I continued to hold her by her soft hair, maneuvering her more vigorously.

"Look at me," I ordered. Her eyes flew open again and locked on mine. She was inexperienced but perfect, my Tinkerbell. Then, her hand moved to cup my testicles, and her soft, fleshy mouth indulged me again. But I was insatiable, and I wanted more. So I tensed my stomach muscles and continued to thrust into her.

Minutes passed, I had no idea how many, and Selene began to look tired. Though she should have realized by now that I never came right away. I stroked her hair encouragingly, and she continued moving against me like a goddess. She looked elegant and angelic even in the middle of that act. Even as I, being so massively selfish, took what I wanted from her.

"I'm almost there… Don't stop…" The fire was beginning to rise. It started at the base of my spine and spread. Slowly, it consumed every muscle, every inch of skin. I bit my lower lip and looked down at her. She was so beautiful. Fragile. Like an angel from heaven satisfying the every dark desire of some demon. All at once my balls began to tingle, the veins in my lower abdomen plumped, and blood rushed down to my groin with every stroke.

My erection filled the confined space of her mouth to the brim, making her gag, and I felt her fingers digging into my legs in a silent plea for me to slow down. But I couldn't, not then.

"I'm going to come." Her lips rubbing against my glistening skin felt like something twisted and romantic, all at the same time. I looked down at her, diving deep into her ocean stare.

And did she know it?

That, in that moment, it was her eyes that were sucking me?

That they were annihilating me?

I felt hot and even closer to the edge. I had warned Selene about me, but she refused to listen. So I muttered something unintelligible through my teeth and hung on to her hair, ready to stain her, to make her taste me just the way she wanted. A tremor ran through me from my spine up to my brain. It felt deep and powerful. My vision went blurry, my throat tightened, every muscle in my body contracted, and I erupted inside her.

Boom.

The orgasm was an incredible, uncontrollable explosion. Babygirl forged a real connection between us. We were joined, united, simpatico.

After a moment that seemed to last forever, Selene clutched my legs more tightly and then began to cough, her body trembling. Meanwhile, I was overcome by sudden weakness and had to lean heavily on the sink to catch my breath as I reeled from the aftermath of the outstanding orgasm I had just experienced.

I stared fixedly at her as I tried to clear my thoughts, and it occurred to me that she was likely going to remember me forever. Even if one day there was some other man in my place, she was going to think about me because the residue of my lips, my hands, my tongue, and even my cum was carved into her.

I was taking everything from her, but at the same time, Selene was also taking everything from me.

"You drained me dry, Babygirl," I whispered with a smile. She kissed my stomach and chest as she got to her feet, standing a little unsteadily. Her pale face was completely flushed, and the evidence of my arousal was all over her lips. She looked shell-shocked, but she wasn't remotely used to satisfying that kind of craving. Without thinking too much about it, I pulled her into me and licked her lips, tasting myself there.

"You suck cock marvelously, Tigress. You did so well," I whispered into her ear before swatting her ass and making her jump. That broke Selene out of her spell, and she heaved a sigh.

"That is not true." She ran her fingers over her swollen lips, looking logy and confused.

How was she always so beautiful?

After a moment, she jerked away and turned on the faucet, intending to rinse her face and pat it dry. But I grabbed her hips and pulled her roughly back to me. Selene turned her aroused gaze on me and, yes, she was as innocent as she was indecent, my Tinkerbell.

"It is true. You're still learning, but you did very well." I gave her a fond little smile, and she gave me a disgruntled look.

"You have to stop messing with me, you ass—" She didn't get to finish her sentence because I was kissing her urgently. My tongue met hers, hot and decadent, and our flavors blended together. Just then, my phone rang, but I didn't give a shit and just kept kissing her.

"Neil, you should get that…" Her hand rested on my tensed abs, lighting even that small bit of skin on fire. But I continued to savor her like a sweet treat. I moved down her neck and licked it, finding the hollow of her throat and sucking it decisively and pulling a gasp from her. I didn't care about my phone or whoever might be calling me, I had no desire to move away from her at all.

The phone stopped ringing but started up again almost immediately.

"Are you fucking kidding me?" I huffed noisily and muttered a few curses under my breath. "Give me a minute." I moved around her and walked naked back into the bedroom. I looked around a bit for my phone before remembering I'd left it in my pants. I dug through my pockets until it fell out, and when I saw the name flashing across the screen, my breath caught in my lungs. I glanced back at the bathroom where Selene was focused on drying her hair, and I moved over to the window to take the call.

"What the hell do you want?" I raged at Megan on the other end of the line.

"Hey, Miller. Have you decided what you're going to do about the Chicago internship?" she asked, laughter in her voice, and I rolled my eyes.

"Your timing is for shit. Why are you calling me? How did you even get my number?" I passed a hand through my hair as I looked around for my boxers.

"Well, it's not like it's difficult to get. Pretty much every blond chick at Pace has it," she chuckled, and I began to pace the room.

"I did not give you permission to contact me like this," I snapped, irritated.

"I wanted to know if you'd decided yet. Clock's ticking, Miller," she said, completely ignoring my complaint, and I snorted.

A sudden noise made me turn, and I saw Selene with her back to me, focused on getting a sweater and jeans out from her dresser. She'd put her underwear on at some point; who knew how long she'd been moving around behind me?

"I haven't made a decision yet, Megan, but it's going to be no," I muttered, glancing down at Babygirl's ass while I still could before she pulled up her pants and deprived me of the view.

"How can it be a no if you haven't decided yet?" Head Case volleyed back immediately, and I rolled my eyes skyward.

"Look, I have to go. Try to get off my ass," I chided her and hung up the phone before she could get off another response.

"What's up?" Babygirl asked, gathering her slightly damp hair up into a ponytail on top of her head. I looked her up and down: She was sedately dressed, with no makeup on and her scar visible on her forehead, and I still thought her as lovely as a priceless pearl.

But I needed to banish those thoughts as well as the more perverse ones about her body because I was being an idiot, and the sound of Megan's voice had brought me back to reality, reminding me of who—and what—I was. I'd fucked up again: I'd had sex with Selene, slept next to her all night, and if that wasn't bad enough, then I'd demanded she blow me. This situation was getting seriously out of hand.

"Nothing…" I walked around her brusquely and scooped my boxers up off the floor, pulling them on right away. I didn't even have a real change of clothes, but I needed to get out of there. Immediately.

"What kind of nothing? You were talking to Alyssa's sister, right?" Selene knew who Megan was because she'd met her in a club. She'd actually thought that I was attracted to her that night.

Attracted to *Megan*, for Christ's sake. Nothing could be worse.

I also grabbed my track pants and my white hoodie, which I discovered to my great annoyance now smelled like coconut.

"Yeah, that's right." I dressed myself in a series of rapid, mechanical movements before grabbing my cell phone and sticking it back in my pocket.

"And why has your mood changed so dramatically since talking to *Megan*?" Selene put special emphasis on her name, and I didn't miss the hint of jealousy in her voice.

"Now's not the time for twenty questions, Selene." I flipped on her too rapidly, and Selene flinched.

"Now finish getting ready; I'll drive you to school before I head back to New York." I dismissed her so casually, not even meeting her eyes, because I knew that if I looked into her ocean, I was going to drown there.

"I can get there by myself!" She snapped before pulling a bag out of her closet and filling it with whatever crap girls carried around all day. She grumbled something unintelligible as she worked.

"I'm taking you." It was an order. End of discussion.

"You're being a bully again. I hate when you do that," she railed, not looking at me.

"And you're being fucking immature again. Why don't you just quit whining and do what you're told for once?" I said, going on the attack, and she shook her head at me, disappointed.

"You're unreal. You don't give a damn about me or how our whole situation has impacted my life!" She turned and pointed a finger at me, little but so brave.

"Oh, really? Is that what you think?" I grinned sardonically at her and moved closer until I towered over her.

"Yes. You won't tell me what's going on. You won't tell me anything at all. How am I supposed to understand you? How am I supposed to support you or help you in any way?" She heaved a weary sigh and dragged both hands through her long ponytail, which she had slung over one shoulder.

"These things don't concern you. It's that simple," I answered her with the first dumb thing that popped into my head just so I wouldn't blurt out how mad I was at myself for all the feelings I had been wrestling with for so long.

"Sure, of course. I just need to shut up and take it all. Let you fuck me and wake up sore and covered with marks. Give you a—" She cut herself off, embarrassed, when I gave her a hard look. The kind that could make anyone shut up.

"Don't put that on me. That's the part I hate the most!" My voice grew louder as I became angrier, and my hands clenched into fists. My body was preparing to crush something. She lowered her eyes, seeing the tension in me, and stepped back.

"Look at yourself right now. You treat me like your personal punching bag. I have to just suffer your rages, your demands, and your mood swings. What do you want, Neil? A sex slave?" She gestured wildly, and I watched her full lips, the ones I wanted to kiss and bite again, like she really was mine and no one else's.

"Yeah. If you were my sex slave, that wouldn't be so bad," I answered sharply, and she sucked in a deep breath before exploding.

"I hate you. In fact, you know what? I can't stand to be around you. You are…infuriating, arrogant, controlling, deranged, rude, and disrespectful. Go back to—" But before she could finish her sentence, my phone rang again. Selene stared at my pocket, so with a sigh of resignation, I took my phone out and answered it. If it had been Megan again, I would have told her where she could put her questions in the nastiest way possible. Instead, I saw Logan's name on the screen. I frowned, answering it immediately.

"What?" I snapped.

"Neil," he answered breathlessly, and my mood shifted on a dime.

"Are you okay, Logan?"

"You have to come back home. I'm not sure what's going to happen, but I can tell you it's urgent…" My heart began to pound wildly in my chest. I immediately hung up the phone and, consumed with worry, brushed past Selene without giving her another look. She took my arm to stop me, and I looked at her.

She looked terrified.

"I have to go. Something happened, but Logan didn't say what," was all I said, shaking off her hand.

"Okay, but…will you call me?" she asked uncertainly. I shook my head as I stepped away from her. I was going to hurt her again because I needed to do whatever was necessary to shatter her illusions.

"I never call a woman after I spend the night with her." I looked at her lips one last time and breathed in the coconut smell that lingered in the air. And then I walked out of the room without a second thought.

The most important thing just then was getting back home and figuring out what was going on. When it came to my siblings, nothing else mattered.

20

....

I had a strong suspicion that this was Player's work and,
if that was the case, we wouldn't have much time to lose.

NEIL

'm here!"

Hours later, I walked into the house to find Logan standing in the living room. "I hope you're about to tell me something important because I had to get on the first flight out to get back here this fast," I said flatly, closing the door with a motion of my heel and peeling off my jacket. Then I spotted my mother pacing anxiously on the other side of the living room while Matt tried to comfort her and Miss Anna offered them cups of tea.

"Neil! Where were you?" As soon as my mother registered my presence, she headed for me with arms outstretched. I stepped back, keeping her from making contact, and Matt glowered at me.

Ever since he found out about the decidedly unhealthy relationship I had with his daughter, he'd despised me. He barely said a word to me.

"Darling, calm down," he told my mother. I turned to look him up and down. He was in one of his usual perfectly tailored suits, his beard neat and his black hair slicked back with gel.

"Is someone going to tell me what the fuck happened?" I snapped, reaching the limits of my patience. Just then, Alyssa came down the stairs. Despite his girlfriend's arrival, Logan didn't move a muscle. I could tell from the look on his face that something serious was going on.

"Neil, listen… Okay…this all happened just last night. While you were gone, Chloe snuck out to go somewhere. I have no idea where, and she hasn't come back yet!" Logan blurted out, the words, hitting me like a blast of cold water. Suddenly I found myself in the middle of an earthquake, at the epicenter of a devastating explosion, and my head spun from the sudden rush of blood.

"What?" I'd heard him just fine, but I needed to process the situation; I needed to make it real in my head. The sound of my mother's sobs and Matt's soothing words brought me back to the present before I was ready.

"How the fuck did she sneak out? You were in the house, weren't you? Where the fuck were you when she just walked right out the door? Huh?" With a sudden catlike move, I leaped on my brother and grabbed him by the collar. Everyone winced at the motion.

"I was in my room. I had just seen her. She was lying on her bed reading. She told me she was tired and she wasn't going anywhere and…" he explained, and my grip slackened. After all, I knew it wasn't really Logan's fault. Not even if she'd…

A lightbulb went on in my brain.

The invitation to the masquerade party…

"Fuck!" I shouted, running up the stairs to Chloe's room. Once inside, I started tearing through everything in my path, searching for that paper with the address of the party on it. A few minutes later, I found it discarded under the bed. With the invite clutched in one hand, I raced over to my own room and grabbed the keys to my Maserati.

"Where are you going?" Logan asked when I got back to the living room, but I couldn't waste my time answering him. Instead, I ran outside and strode toward my car. Logan followed me, Alyssa trailing along behind him. I didn't object and let both of them come along with me. I had a strong suspicion that this was Player's work, and if that was the case, we wouldn't have much time to lose.

"I told her not to go! Goddammit!" I shouted, enraged.

Then I settled into the driver's seat and started the engine.

"Stay calm, Neil. We're going to find her." My brother put his hand on my arm, but I immediately shook it off. I drove away from the house, accelerating hard. The tires squealed against the asphalt, and in the back, Alyssa let out a scream, but I didn't give a shit. The speedometer showed a dizzying speed as Logan entered the party's address into the GPS.

About ten minutes later, we pulled up in front of a grand two-story house where the party had been held. I parked quickly and leaped out of the car, stalking furiously up the driveway toward the door.

"If I don't find her here, someone's going to die today," I gritted out when I heard Logan and Alyssa's footsteps behind me. "And our sister is going to be punished," I went on furiously.

I rang the doorbell incessantly until a sleepy-eyed dude with long hair appeared in the doorway. The skin under his eyes was puffy, and his eyes were red and glassy. Whatever he took the night before was probably still swimming around in his veins.

"Who are yo—" I didn't let him finish but shoved him aside and went into the house. I went through the scene before me like a hunting dog, examining everything. The living room was big, with two sectional sofas, a plasma TV, and a coffee table covered in snack bags, assorted paraphernalia, and a bunch of other crap. I moved determinedly into the room, anger boiling my blood as I scanned the inert bodies on the floor, either still asleep or so drunk they looked like corpses. Almost all of them wore masks. Red Solo cups were strewn all over the room along with cigarette butts and roaches. A naked couple was all tangled up on the sofa, and someone else was sitting with their back against the wall.

The air reeked of weed, cigarette smoke, alcohol, and sex. The same mélange that characterized every rager I'd ever attended.

Where in this place is my little koala?

I examined everyone, looking for her golden hair and big gray eyes. I didn't even know what kind of mask she might have worn or how she was dressed, but I knew that I'd recognize her no matter what.

"Miller? What are you doing here?" A short, beefy blond dude stood in front of me, blocking my progress and, consequently, that of Logan and Alyssa.

"I'm looking for Chloe; has anyone seen her?" Everyone knew that she was my sister, and they also knew what would happen if they laid a finger on her.

"Uh, the little blond? Umm… Don't know. I might have seen her… Maybe." He chuckled. He was probably still drunk, and my anger took control: I grabbed the unfortunate man by the back of his head and slammed his face into the wall.

"Neil!" Logan tried to intervene, but I wasn't listening to him. I had skills that I could use to get what I wanted, and this was the ideal situation to put them into practice.

"Where the hell is Chloe, asshole? Try really hard to remember where you saw her last!" I yelled into his ear as I ground his cheek against the wall.

"I… I…don't know… I don't remember…" he babbled, terrified, but I was so angry, so afraid of what could happen to her, and so desperate that I couldn't control myself. Furiously, I dragged the guy into the closest bathroom. Then I used my body weight to force his head into the sink, turning on the cold water.

"Here you go, a little refresher to get your brain working again," I said as the boy squirmed against me, but he was no match for my strength. When I was satisfied, I turned off the faucet and pulled his face up so he could look at himself in the mirror with me looming behind him. I was almost a head taller than him, and he was shaking. "Now, shit for brains, you better remember where you saw her last, or I swear I'll beat your ass." He lifted his hands in surrender, but I refused to let go of his neck. I held him tight, giving him a stormy glare.

"I… I…" he stammered.

"You piss me off and I'm going to get mean. Talk. Now," I said in a threatening growl. No one touched what belonged to me. I'd lose my shit if someone did.

"She was with…with this girl dressed as a devil and…the Krew…" he mumbled fearfully, and I let him go, disturbed.

"The Krew?" I echoed, in shock. Images of Xavier, Luke, Alexia, and Jennifer surrounding Chloe popped into my head, leaving me even more alarmed than I had been.

"What the hell was she doing with your friends?" Logan put in, sounding afraid. He was probably thinking about what dangerous sons of bitches they all were. I raced away from that unfortunate asshole and the nasty bathroom, digging both hands into my hair. I needed to stay calm and think clearly.

I looked up at the second floor, where the bedrooms were.

"Neil, wait!"

I ignored my brother's cry and climbed the stairs. I kicked in every door I found, hoping to reveal Chloe curled up alone in someone's bed. Maybe she'd be a little hungover, but I wouldn't have given her too much shit. What really mattered was finding her safe and sound. But all I found were couples snoozing under the sheets or people who were too stoned to register anything that was happening.

"Damn it," I swore as I stalked down the hall until my eyes alighted on three figures coming our way. I recognized them immediately—it was the Krew, minus Xavier.

"Where the fuck is Chloe?" I vented my anger first at Luke, grabbing him by the collar and slamming his back against the wall. He just laughed and made a face at me, not at all disturbed. Asshole.

"Hello to you too. And it looks like you're pissed off. How unusual." He grinned, but the enraged look on his face made him grow immediately serious again.

"That little ho is probably just cuddled up in someone's bed, relax," Jennifer put in, and I whirled around to look at her. She was in a sexy little nurse outfit with her tits crammed into a fully exposed red lace bra. I let go of Luke and automatically grabbed her by the neck and squeezed one-handed. Blondie gasped, clutching my arm.

"The only ho around here is you," I hissed through gritted teeth. A grin of amusement spread slowly across Jennifer's crimson lips. With her free hand, she reached between my legs and shot me a teasing look.

"You always like it, though." She winked at me, and I released her roughly in a single angry motion.

"Go fuck yourself!" I shouted, disgusted. Sometimes even I wondered how I'd sunk so low as to screw some of the women I'd screwed. "Tell me where Chloe is, or I swear on my life I will make you pay!" I raged, stabbing a finger at each of them in turn. But then Logan put a hand on my shoulder and drew my attention to a petite, brown-haired girl I hadn't even noticed before.

"Madison, you're Chloe's friend, right? Can you tell us where she is? Please…" Logan directed this exclusively to her; his voice was measured, but one could hear the suffering in it. Meanwhile, I rubbed my face and instinctively kicked an empty glass bottle that had been rolling around on the floor. It shattered against the wall with a crash.

"We don't need to beg." I shoved Logan aside harshly, and Madison backed away from me. "Tell me where my sister is!" I demanded, grabbing her by the arm. The girl's eyes went wide, and she stared at me in terror. "Tell me, goddammit! Tell me!" I shook her angrily. "Talk!" I shouted right up close to her face, but she just stared at me in shock.

But I had completely lost my mind by that point. I couldn't do anything rationally. I was trapped on the roller coaster of my madness, and I wasn't going to get off so easily.

"Neil, you're scaring her." Logan put a hand on my shoulder and pulled me back. "She's seventeen years old. You can't talk to her like that," he said disapprovingly, and I gave him a frantic look.

I could feel the rage pulsing through every inch of me; it coiled around me like a snake.

"The only thing we can do is keep looking for Chloe," Alyssa put in.

"Oh great, baby bro's girlfriend is here too," Luke muttered to Alexia, making her laugh.

"Don't be an asshole," I snapped at him, knowing Logan wouldn't tolerate anyone mocking his girl.

"Ignore him; listen to me." Logan grabbed my head and forced me to look at him. "We need to focus on Chloe."

Right. We were just wasting time here with the Krew, and I needed to find my sister.

"You're right," I murmured, and he smiled at me. I turned to the others and eyed them all with a grim air. I brushed past them without another word, hitting Luke with a shoulder check and continuing my search. There were still three bedrooms to go; maybe Chloe was in one of them.

I threw open another door, but there was, of course, no sign of Chloe. When I kicked open the last door, I saw a guy lying prone on the bed with two women on either side of him. One was a petite blond.

My eyes went wide with shock when I recognized one of Xavier's tattoos on the guy's arm. I yanked the sheet off all of them, and he woke with a gasp.

"What the fuck!" he spit bitterly, still half-awake as he turned to look at me. I took a good look at the faces of the two naked women. Fortunately for Xavier, the little blond wasn't Chloe.

"Put some clothes on!" Logan demanded, putting a hand over Alyssa's eyes so she couldn't see Xavier's nude body.

"What the fuck are you doing here?" he raged at me before getting out of the bed and hunting around for his underwear.

"Where is Chloe?" I asked him immediately, but he didn't so much as glance in my direction.

"And why exactly do you think I'd know?" He strode calmly past me and snatched up his boxers, pulling them back on. Logan just stared at him in horror, and once he was dressed, Xavier looked back at him threateningly. "What's wrong, princess? Are you not familiar with the phrase 'hung like a horse'?" Xavier said derisively.

"My girl is right here. Get dressed!" Logan ordered, still with his hand clapped over Alyssa's eyes.

"Logan, I'm not going to look; you can trust me," she reassured him in tones of innocence, but Logan, who had a jealous streak, immediately shushed her.

"You're pretty insecure, huh? Red flag…a big one," Xavier smirked at him before bursting out in a hearty laugh. Logan's face remained deathly serious, and he breathed in deeply.

"You are unbearable. Literally the worst person I know," my brother shot back at him, looking meaningfully at the two women still passed out in the bed. Xavier slipped into his black jeans and gave Logan a wry look.

"Don't get on your high horse with me, princess. Your brother has the same bad habits I do." He winked at him, the son of a bitch, and I decided to break it up.

"Stop talking, dick," I said menacingly, giving him a hard stare, and he held my gaze steadily.

"Talk to me, boss. What is it that I can do for you?" He gave me a lopsided smile and slipped his sweater on over his head.

"What the fuck was Chloe doing with all of you? And I've already been told she was with you, so don't try to lie about it. She didn't come home last night; do you know where she is? Did she leave with someone? Was she drinking?" I asked him all the questions that were swirling around in my head and identified nothing but bewilderment in his eyes. He tilted his head thoughtfully for a moment before speaking.

"No, she was with the little brunette that Luke's seeing. Yeah, your sister was also with us, but only for a few minutes," he explained coolly with no hint of hesitation or holding anything back.

"And then what? What did she do? Where did she go?" I scrubbed a hand over my face, trying to piece together Chloe's night, but all I had was a pounding headache and the horrifying fear of what might have happened to her.

"I have no idea. She said she wanted to take a walk, get some air, or something. I was busy trying to pull those bitches." He jerked a thumb over his shoulder at the women on the bed, and I swore under my breath. Xavier almost certainly didn't know any more than he'd already told me, but I tried one more time.

"Do you know if she took anything?" I was trying to be subtle, though my brother could probably guess that I was talking about drugs. His curious ears hadn't missed a moment of the exchange between me and Xavier.

"Man, what do you think? That I spent my night stalking some jailbait? Besides, I know she's your sister, and I have no desire to end up like Carter Nelson." He lifted his hands in the air as though surrendering to emphasize his point. "I prefer my women a bit more...*mature*." He grinned mischievously, leering at Alyssa, who looked at him with a mixture of curiosity and uncertainty. Logan wrapped his arm around her shoulders, marking his territory.

We were just wasting more precious time.

"Let's get out of here, Logan," I told my brother, walking past Xavier.

"Do you want help looking for her?" Xavier asked, drawing our attention back to him.

"And why exactly would you help me look for her?" I narrowed my eyes at him, examining him intently.

"You know that the two of us are good at dealing with shit." He shrugged, and my brother immediately began shaking his head in agitation.

"Neil, no! He can't come with us. No way! Fuck's sake!" Logan exclaimed, staring indignantly at Xavier.

"Afraid I'm gonna cop a feel of your little baby doll?" Xavier answered provokingly, and Logan moved toward him, but I stopped him with a hand to his chest.

"Give it a rest, Xavier, or I am going to lose my cool," I warned him sternly, and he grew serious as he realized I wasn't kidding around.

"Neil, I don't trust him," Logan whispered into my ear, and I thought about it.

"Unclench, princess. All I'm going to do is lend a hand." He walked past us, unruffled, and I followed him out of the room.

"Quit looking at him," Logan snapped at his girlfriend as we all followed Xavier down the stairs, out the door, and into my car. I had no idea where we were going to go, but then my phone rang.

I pulled it out of my pants pocket and saw an unknown number. Logan leaned over my shoulder giving me a concerned look. We were both thinking the same thing. I answered the call and…

"Neil." The person on the other end spoke through some sort of voice changer so I couldn't tell whether it was a man or a woman. I nodded to Logan, confirming our shared suspicions, and he went white.

It really was Player 2511.

"I knew you had something to do with this, you son of a bitch. Where's Chloe?"

"Ah, kids. They are a magnificent enigma," Player answered delightedly, and my right hand began to shake. I clenched it into a fist so I wouldn't lose control.

"Tell me where she is."

"But that would be too easy, don't you think?"

I snorted and shot another look at Logan, Alyssa now clinging to his arm.

"Shape, color, magic, GYR9391. Solve the riddle inside an hour if you

468

want little Chloe to survive." I was surprised to hear him spit out another puzzle, and I hastened to memorize it, repeating it over and over in my mind as the psycho on the other end of the phone hung up without another word.

"It was Player," I confirmed to Logan when he looked inquiringly at me. "What did he say?"

"He gave me another riddle to solve," I told him, recounting Player's exact words.

"What the hell does that mean?" He frowned in confusion.

"I have no idea. And we only have an hour to find her." The thought of something happening to my sister made me shake with rage.

Alyssa quickly jotted down the puzzle while I apprised her and Xavier of the whole Player situation.

"So you're telling me that some asshole in a mask is sending you these nutty riddles and threatening your family?" The most unhinged member of the Krew asked incredulously as he smoked in the passenger seat.

"That is more or less correct," I answered, starting the engine, although I had even less of an idea where to go now. One hour. Our time was running out.

Player and his fucking games…

But I'd known he was going to strike again, hadn't I? I'd been suspecting that my sister or mother would be the next target, which was why I banned Chloe from going out alone or attending any parties. Especially the kind thrown by older boys she didn't know who could have posed a threat to her. But I hadn't anticipated that her best friend would catch Luke's eye. The Krew went to any party we wanted and brought whoever we wanted along, with or without an invitation. As Luke's girl, Madison had an all-access pass to any party she wanted, and she'd talked Chloe into going along with her.

"Shape probably means geometric shape, right?" Alyssa noted from the back seat, where she sat next to Logan, and I surfaced from the maelstrom of my thoughts. Xavier took another drag off his cigarette and grunted thoughtfully.

"What about the color part? And magic?" I muttered anxiously, trying not to lose my cool or my clear head.

"Well, color…could maybe mean a colored object?" Alyssa answered doubtfully, provoking a scornful laugh from Xavier.

"Ah, beauty and brains. How interesting," he cut in, making her uncomfortable. Obviously he didn't give a shit about the gravity of the situation. I'd decided to bring him along with us because I knew I might need someone as fast and strong as I was. Xavier had grown up on the streets and was used to dealing with all sorts of shit. All you had to do was push him a little and he turned into the worst kind of beast, which was exactly why we got along so well. Fundamentally, we were similar people, though it was difficult for me to admit it. Still, I hadn't considered just how much my friend loved to fuck with Logan and how that might create serious problems for us.

"Neil, either shut him up or throw him out of the car!" Logan said loudly, but Xavier just laughed. I shot a look at my brother through the rearview window.

"Give it a rest," I told both of them and sighed as I went back to thinking over the puzzle.

Shape. Color. Magic.

What did all these things have in common?

And then, all of a sudden, it hit me: a Rubik's cube. I used to play with them all the time when I was a kid and eventually I got to where I could solve it in no time, turning each side to a uniform color.

"A Rubik's cube," I said loudly, interrupting Xavier and Logan's pissing match.

"Okay, so…a toy store?" Xavier suggested.

"A game shop?" Logan countered.

"Wait… There's this skeezy motel outside of town that's, like, eighties themed, and their big thing is that they have this giant Rubik's cube at the front desk, and if you can solve it before they check you in, your room is free," Alyssa said breathlessly, and I smiled. Maybe we were finally getting the hang of this.

"That covers all the clues," said Logan. "Shape for the cube, color for how you solve it, and magic because its original name was The Magic Cube… But what about the GYR9391?" Logan wondered.

"Sounds like a license plate number. Alyssa, do you know the address of that motel?" I asked, and she relayed it to me. I flipped a U and raced toward the dive motel. I drove like a maniac, consumed with thoughts of what might be happening to Chloe in a place like that, and I only got more and more on edge.

"Watch out, tight curve coming up," Xavier warned me, but I kept my foot flat on the accelerator, ignoring the speedometer bouncing around crazily.

"Neil, slow down," Logan cautioned me as well, but instead of listening to him, I clenched my hands around the wheel even tighter and breathed deep so I could concentrate and wouldn't crash. The dangerously tight curve did force me to decelerate and downshift rapidly, though.

"Neil!" Logan yelled, but I managed not to go into a skid. The back wheels squealed noisily against the asphalt as the car slid sideways into a drift. But I was in control the entire time, and at the end of the turn, I spun the steering wheel back the other way, and with a flutter of the gas pedal, I accelerated again. I heaved a sigh of relief.

"You almost just killed us!" Alyssa exclaimed with a hand on her chest. Xavier just cackled and kept smoking with a casual air.

"The princesses back there aren't used to the way you drive," he told me drily.

I slammed on the brakes, making everyone jolt. I pulled into the motel's isolated parking lot and took note of the sign, which barely had enough juice to light up the pavement and peeling walls of the buildings, which looked old and worn down. I turned off the engine.

The more I looked at the place, the more it looked like a front for a prostitution ring.

And, indeed, the minute I stepped out of the car, I spotted a scantily clad woman swaying toward the entrance, accompanied by a much older man. He had a long beard, a belly that stuck out under his white T-shirt, and a generally creepy aura.

"Ugh, it's worse than I thought," Alyssa said, horrified, and just the thought of my sister being there was making me crazy.

I tried to keep a clear head. I remembered that the riddle had also included what was probably a license plate number—GYR9391—and

I began to look around for a car that might have such a plate. The only vehicles I spotted, though, were an old truck and a black motorcycle. My attention was drawn back to Xavier, however, when he opened my trunk (without permission, of course) and took out a baseball bat.

"What are you doing?" I asked, watching him turn it over in his hands before he sauntered over to me.

"I knew you had one of these back there. Luke and I carry them, too, remember?" He flashed me an evil grin, tapping the end of the bat against the palm of his other hand.

"That's insane! What are you going to do with that?" Logan demanded, sounding disturbed, but Xavier didn't deign to answer him. We'd used bats or metal bars plenty of times before when necessary, so it was pretty much business as usual for us.

"We have to find a car with the license plate GYR9391," I ordered, and we all moved across the parking lot like a pack of wolves sniffing out prey. Alyssa clutched Logan's hand while Xavier stood near me, watchful and menacing.

"What if Chloe is in one of the rooms?" he asked, gesturing subtly at the entrance. We didn't have enough time to check all the individual rooms in that disgusting place. And Player had given me a very specific set of clues, so I needed to follow them to the letter.

"I don't think she is," I answered. It was a gut feeling, but those were usually correct for me.

"There! A car with the license plate!" Logan shouted, pointing at a car parked underneath a tree around the back side of the motel. I didn't hesitate; I just pulled the bat out of Xavier's hands and ran for the vehicle, bending down to look in the windows.

Empty.

I looked down at my wrist, confused, and saw we only had fifteen minutes left to solve the puzzle. In a blind rage, I began whaling on the car with the bat, and with each blow I released a little more anger, frustration, and disappointment. Time was going by too fast; Chloe's gray eyes were already more like a distant memory in my mind. It seemed like I could smell her fruity perfume on the air, and I felt a stabbing pain in my heart.

She was a part of me and the fucking psychopath Player wanted to tear her away.

After what felt like forever, I stopped destroying the car. I bent over, my breathing labored, my forehead dripping with sweat, all my muscles contracted, and my pulse jumping around wildly. All the windows were smashed now. The chassis was dented all over.

I threw the bat down on the ground and rested my hands on the roof, surrendering to failure.

"Neil…" Logan approached the trunk, trembling, and jerked his head at it meaningfully. Xavier arrived a moment later, and seeing what Logan meant, tried to force the trunk open, but without a screwdriver or some similar tool, it was hopeless.

"We need to try to—" I began, but my phone rang again. I picked it up immediately and saw another unknown number on the display.

I breathed in deep and accepted the call, saying nothing.

"So, Neil, you tried to solve my puzzle but didn't quite make it," he said, making my jaw tighten. I looked around to see if I could spot anyone watching me, but I didn't see anything. Still, I suspected that Player had some way of monitoring my every move.

"You like to hide, don't you? Whether it's behind a phone or a fucking mask, you're too afraid to be seen for whoever you really are," I taunted him.

"Try to show me some respect," he chided me, sighing deeply.

"Why don't you just come for me directly and stop this whole charade?"

"Because…" He paused for effect. "I have something far crueler in mind for you…" The threat was delivered with a chilling laugh that only made me angrier.

"You're nothing but a coward," I said pointedly, and I could tell from his silence that I'd struck a nerve.

"Don't play with me, Neil," he answered a few moments later, like that was going to intimidate me.

"You don't scare me," I spit, running an unsteady hand through my hair.

"You are my puppet, and I am your master. I pull your strings, Neil, and there's nothing you can do to save yourself or the people you love. Now, I have a new riddle for you: Your sister is locked in the trunk of that car."

He laughed victoriously, and I felt rage coursing through my entire body. Logan's suspicion was right: Chloe was trapped in there.

"Now, bend down. There's one more clue still missing."

I frowned and looked at Xavier and Logan, who were both watching me thoughtfully. Slowly, I crouched down and tried to see what the hell Player was talking about. At first, I saw nothing out of the ordinary. "Look closer," he prompted me, so I braced myself on the ground with one hand and flattened myself completely to peer under the car. Which was where I spotted the metal device, complete with a blinking red light and a timer.

A bomb.

"In exactly five minutes and…ten seconds, that's going to explode," the maniac on the end of the phone informed me. I was frozen in shock.

"So, still having fun playing with me, Neil?"

READ ON FOR A SNEAK PEEK AT THE NEXT THRILLING INSTALLMENT OF NEIL AND SELENE'S ANGSTY DARK ROMANCE IN *GAME OVER*.

PROLOGUE

....

Nothing can save you from the monsters.
Not love, not the power of the stars, not even fairy dust.

NEIL

It was the twenty-fifth of November.

Rain pattered on the windows.

Mom still hadn't come back from work, and she'd called to let Kimberly know she'd be late.

My babysitter had then decided to take a shower and left me alone for a few moments. As soon as she left, I thought: *It's all up to me.* I had to save myself and stop the woman who had been hurting me for a year at that point. So, naked and covered in sweat, I got up off the couch. The irritation around my genitals made me grimace in pain. But I tried not to dwell on it because I had a concrete goal: get to the phone. The sound of running water from the bathroom meant I still had some time left in which to act. I screwed up all my courage and grabbed the phone to call 911.

Trembling in fear, I felt tears building up in the corners of my eyes. I swiped them rapidly with the backs of my hands and waited for the operator to pick up.

"911, what is your emergency?"

I sucked in a breath at the sound of the man's stern voice and spoke, despite my fear.

"I'm at home alone. My parents aren't here. There's a woman here with me. She's hurting me… She does things to me that she's not supposed to do. I… I… Please help me…" It all came out in one terrified breath, and then I heard Kimberly calling for me. My eyes bulged, and I immediately hung up, running back to the couch so she wouldn't get suspicious.

She wanted to play with me again. This time, though, would be the last time.

"Neil." Kim strode toward me, wrapped in a white bathrobe. "Go wait for me down in the basement with Megan," she ordered, and I hesitated. For a moment, I'd forgotten entirely about the little girl downstairs. "What are you waiting for? Get a move on!" I flinched when she yelled at me but got up from the couch and crouched down to pick up my underwear. She came closer to me, though, and I froze. "No, don't get your clothes back on." She gave me an impish grin and stepped aside, gesturing for me to go past her. I just nodded and, shaking, went down to the basement.

It was cold down there, and the cold seemed to sink inside my skin. The light was dim, and there wasn't a lot of furniture down here. Immediately, my attention was caught by Megan's sobs. She was naked as well, standing in front of a camera.

"Neil…" Megan moved cautiously toward me, one arm clasped over her chest, though I wasn't looking at her naked body. "What is she going to make us do?" She wiped away a tear with the back of her hand and stroked her long black hair compulsively.

"I don't know." I lied so as not to scare her. "But I called the police. All we have to do is pretend for a little while," I whispered to her as I cast a furtive glance back up the stairs to see if Kim was coming down.

"The police?" Megan managed. "Do you think they'll…come here?"

"Of course." But I wasn't sure, actually. I hadn't even had time to tell them my address. I prayed, though, that somehow the man on the phone would be able to get here and rescue us.

"I think they're ready, but I'll try it and see." I heard Kimberly's voice and then the sound of the door shutting. She was on the phone. Megan hid behind me, and I tried to be strong for her. "I understand that the buyers are getting impatient, Ryan, but Neil is still too unruly…"

Kim began to walk down the stairs. Her shadow crept ominously along the dimly lit wall. "Yeah, okay. I'll remember. I have to go now. I'll call you back later," she said testily before hanging up the phone.

When she got down to the last steps, I could see she'd gotten dressed in a basic pair of jeans and a sweater. She tucked her phone into her back pocket and approached us before sitting down in a wooden chair. Never once did she take her eyes off our bodies.

"Christ, look how pathetic you are. Why are you shaking?" Kim crossed one leg over the other and sighed in irritation. "Megan, stand over there next to Neil and stop blubbering. Ryan's coming to pick you up in an hour, and he'll be very angry if he finds out you weren't minding me," she snapped.

The little girl came over by my side, her eyes downcast and her legs clenched tightly together. Kimberly was silent for a few moments before bursting into laughter, flinging her blond hair over one shoulder. I could never predict her mood swings, and I suspected that she was crazy as well as evil.

"I don't know what to do with you two. Each of you is worse than the other one." She shook her head, pinching the bridge of her nose. "Ryan and I taught you all of this for one specific purpose," she continued. "And today is the day you're going to put it all into practice. So quit wasting my time," she barked irritably before stretching out an arm to turn on the camcorder. The bright light blinded me immediately. I covered my eye with one hand, the other still between my legs. Megan hid herself behind me and started crying again, which annoyed Kimberly. She got up with a huff.

"All we're doing is making a movie," she explained, putting her hands on her hips. "And you two are going to be the main characters. You'll play Peter and Wendy. It's nothing to be afraid of." She waved a lazy hand through the air before sitting back down.

"Now, Neil," she called out again, her voice so hard that it made me flinch. "Show Megan how you love a woman," she ordered.

I turned to look at the little girl then, and she shied away from me, afraid.

I knew what my babysitter wanted me to do to Megan, but I couldn't bring myself to act like Kimberly.

"Do it or I go to Logan's room. Your choice," she added severely. I swallowed hard. Just the idea of her abusing my brother the way she had done to me was horrifying. But I turned to look into her glacial eyes and shook my head slowly.

"What the fuck is your problem, you little shit? Give her a kiss! Now!" Kim leaped to her feet but then frowned when she heard rapid footsteps on the floor above us. It sounded like someone was running through the kitchen. "Be quiet!" She whispered to me, freezing in place as I approached the stairs, my eyes locked on the closed door at the top of them. My heart began to pound in my chest. I staggered back a few steps when someone kicked the door down. Kimberly gasped as two police officers came barreling down the stairs, weapons pointed right at her.

"Hands up!" The first one yelled while the other looked uncomprehendingly at the camcorder and then Megan and me.

I felt an instinctive shame and a need to hide, so I backed into the corner and tucked my knees up against my chest to cover my body. Megan took refuge behind an old sofa, bursting into full-on sobs.

"Christ…" one of the officers muttered, running a hand over his shocked face.

"You have the right to remain silent. Whatever you say may be used against you in a court of law. You have the right to have an attorney present during questioning. If you cannot afford an attorney, one can be provided for you," one officer recited, handcuffing an unresisting Kimberly, who just smiled mockingly in return.

Then she turned to look at me and appeared to realize in that moment that I had been the one who called the police. Her bright eyes went stormy, her lips curled into a sly plastic grin, and her blond hair tumbled back over her shoulders as the officer forced her to walk.

All at once, her expression shifted, and her face became such a twisted mask of rage that I froze, staring at her, unable to react.

I felt nothing. I didn't cry.

I couldn't understand that it was truly over.

The child-eating witch was walking away from me wearing handcuffs.

She was going to pay for the things she'd done, and I would never see her again.

The memory of her, however, would stay on me, indelible as a tattoo.

No one was going to be able to give my destroyed childhood back to me.

I'd ended the war that Kimberly started, but nothing would ever be like it had been before.

I wasn't a child anymore.

I was a monster, made by Kimberly Bennett's wrongs.

1

....

I felt a wave of heaviness, like my body had been
transformed into lead.

NEIL

In exactly five minutes and…ten seconds, that's going to explode," the
maniac on the end of the phone informed me. I was frozen in shock.

"So, still having fun playing with me, Neil?"

I considered the question.

My sister's life hung in the balance, so I knew I had to be smart if I wanted
to avoid the worst possible outcome.

"Clock's ticking. Good luck." Player ended the call.

I stood back up, staring vacantly in front of me in shock. For a second,
I hoped this was just another nightmare. Anguish and fear that I wouldn't
be able to save Chloe swept over me, rendering me speechless. I had no
idea what to do.

"Neil," Logan called, moving toward me. I didn't look at him.

"Hey, man. What's happening? What'd he say to you?" Xavier clapped
a hand on my shoulder and gave me the mildest shake, but it did nothing.

"Five minutes. We only have five minutes before the bomb goes off."
I spoke like a robot and moved my eyes slowly over to Logan, whose face
drained of color.

"The *bomb*?" Xavier echoed, looked bewildered for a few moments longer. "Then we need to move our asses, now!" He brushed past me and picked up the baseball bat I'd thrown to the ground. "He doesn't get to win," he said, looking determinedly back at me. In one blow, he smashed through what was left of the car's window and stuck his arm in to unlock the doors.

Meanwhile, I just kept standing there silently, still in shock. I felt a wave of heaviness, like my body had been transformed into lead.

"I'll check if there's a trunk release up here. Cars are always supposed to fucking have them. The rest of you look under the floor mats, see if there's anything that might pop the trunk," Xavier ordered. He sat down in the driver's seat and bent over, searching for the lever in question. I continued to watch all of it, listen to all of it and do nothing.

I could feel the sweat running down my forehead, the powerful beats of my heart, the tremor in my right hand...

"I..." I tried to speak, but I couldn't get out an intelligible sentence.

"Neil, time's running out!" Logan grabbed me by the shoulders and shook me, trying to get me to move and my breathing got heavier. "Come back to me. Please. We'll get her in time, you'll see," he said shakily. I didn't even blink, so my brother took my face in his hands and forced me to look at him. "I'm going to go into the motel and ask for help. I know that you're thinking this is your fault, but it's not. We're going to save Chloe. We just have to stay calm and keep a clear head." He clapped my back twice before rushing away with Alyssa in tow.

"Neil, get over here!" I was prodded to alertness only when I heard Xavier's shout.

I hurried over to my friend and looked at him, still not speaking.

I must have looked like a total asshole, incapable of making myself useful in an emergency. It wasn't at all like me to be so passive.

"I found a trunk release cable under the floor mat," Xavier said, showing it to me. "Except it's stuck or something. You're going to have to give me a hand," he told me. I just nodded and knelt down.

He called out to me again, and I turned to look at him, terror in my eyes.

"Listen, man, I've never seen you shell-shocked like this and you need to get your shit together and quick, okay?" He said urgently. He was right.

I stared into his dark eyes, and I could see how worried he was. I wasn't going to fix shit by just standing there and letting the dark thoughts over-whelm me, so I forced myself to act instead of just thinking out worst-case scenarios.

"Yeah…I know," I mumbled, trying to cut the exchange short as I focused on the trunk release, pulling it hard.

"What we need is a pair of pliers," Xavier murmured, wiping his forehead with the back of his hand.

"We don't have the time, Xavier," I said shortly.

"Okay, so let's try this: I'll see if I can fold the back seats up and shift them forward and check underneath for another lever or something. You stay here and keep putting pressure on the release," he said, quickly moving to the back of the car. I stayed in the driver's seat and bent over, trying des-perately to get the damned lever to move. Periodically, I cast quick glances at the motel entrance, hoping I might see what the hell was going on with Logan, but I couldn't spot him there.

"There's no fucking lever back here!" Xavier raged suddenly, and I turned to look at him. He drove a hand through his black hair, sweating.

"Kick it in," I suggested, and his eyes lit up. Xavier had a violent streak a mile wide, and, more than that, he was completely unable to moderate his strength. "Pretend it's your father," I continued, well aware of the kind of sick rage Xavier felt whenever he thought of the man. Xavier didn't say anything but just breathed heavily in response. Then he positioned himself against the back seats, albeit with some difficulty. The car was too small for two people of our size, but we weren't letting that small detail stop us.

Moments later, he started pummeling the back of the car with one leg while I returned to the stuck cable.

"How much time do we have left?" He asked quickly, pausing to catch his breath.

"Not much." I had been keeping track of every minute that passed. Three more were gone by then.

"Guys!" My brother raced over to us and leaned in the open door to reveal an iron crowbar.

"Well, that's fucking handy," Xavier commented, and we both crawled out of the car.

We had to go fast.

I snatched the bar out of Logan's hand and walked around to the back of the car. Then, with all the strength I could muster, I began to force the trunk open.

After three failed attempts, I succeeded.

With one more sharp strike, the trunk sprang open, and my eyes went wide when I saw Chloe's huddled form.

Her wrists and ankles were bound with ropes, a strip of duct tape covered her mouth, her blond hair was disheveled, and her eyes were closed. I didn't waste any more time, hurrying to scoop her up and pull her out of the trunk. I crouched down, clutching her body to me and pulled the tape from her lips.

"Kiddo, can you hear me?" I touched her cold cheek while Logan, on the verge of tears, got down next to me and stroked her hair.

"It's us, Chloe," he said in a pleading whisper while Alyssa and. Xavier stood and watched us silently.

"Come on, sis. Come back to us," Logan added, tortured. Chloe's breathing was so shallow that it was nearly imperceptible.

She had to come back and smile again, to look at me with those impish gray eyes.

She had to come back to my room to get into my closet and take all the sweatshirts she wanted.

She had to come back and tell me what an asshole I was with girls.

She had to come back to make her sassy faces and sulk when we fought and flip me the bird when I said something insulting.

She had to come back because, if my siblings weren't there, I wouldn't be there either.

Because if they were done, I'd be done too.

"I'm right here, kiddo," I whispered, hugging her tightly. I didn't cry. I never did, in fact. I felt so drained, so exhausted that I didn't have any tears left to express my internal state. I just held her tight to me and squeezed my eyes shut, hoping that when I opened them again, I would wake from my nightmare.

But, unfortunately, that wasn't what happened. As soon as I opened my eyes, reality stared me in the face again.

Just this fucked reality.

"Neil…" Chloe's weak voice moved across my skin, raising goosebumps. She clutched my leather jacket with one hand and looked up at me, her gray eyes hitting me like a blow.

"Good morning, kiddo." I smiled, feeling my heart soften and melt like ice in the sun's heat.

"Thank God, Chloe." Logan kissed all over her head the way he used to when she was little: her head, her cheeks, her forehead, her nose.

It was these two, the only good things that came from my childhood.

"We need to run, now!" Xavier shouted, urging us to move. I scooped up Chloe in my arms, and we all began to run with all the energy we had left, lungs burning as we sucked in air.

It was a matter of a moment.

A moment in which we managed to get as far as we could from that doomed car.

A moment in which our lives hung in the balance.

We quickly made it to my Maserati, and I deposited Chloe in the back seat with Logan and Alyssa. Xavier threw himself into the passenger seat, and I got behind the wheel.

And, just then, the other car exploded.

It was blown sky-high, causing a thick cloud of smoke to rise into the air. The shock wave from the blast was so intense that the windows of my car vibrated. I started the car and hit the gas. The tires screeched noisily as we peeled out of the parking lot. In the rearview mirror, I watched as the flames climbed higher into the sky.

"I win, you son of a bitch," I murmured in satisfaction.

ABOUT THE AUTHOR

Kira Shell is a bestselling Italian author with over 600,000 copies of her dark romances sold. She began writing the Kiss Me Like You Love Me series in 2017. The series has over six million Wattpad reads. Kira is a law graduate and lives in Italy.

Instagram: @kira_shell_
TikTok: @kirashell